Praise for *Cold Ligh*

"Goddard weaves a gripping mystery."

Publishers Weekly

"The first book in Goddard's Missing in Alaska series will keep readers glued to their seats as the tension escalates."

Booklist

"A must-read for every romantic suspense reader. Goddard's novels keep getting better and better."

DiAnn Mills, author of *Concrete Evidence*

"Elizabeth Goddard's *Cold Light of Day* is an exhilarating, page-turning race to the finish! Highly recommended."

Carrie Stuart Parks, bestselling author of *Relative Silence*

"Gripping and hard-hitting. Grab a cup of cocoa to keep you warm, because the cold and danger on these pages are as real as it gets."

James R. Hannibal, award-winning author of *Elysium Tide*

Praise for Rocky Mountain Courage Series

"Ever-escalating tension, well-developed characters, and some clever misdirection will keep readers glued to their seats. This skillfully crafted tale of faith and redemption hits its mark."

Publishers Weekly on *Critical Alliance*

"Elizabeth Goddard utilizes her pen like a weaver designs a tapestry. A totally 'unputdownable' book that kept me up late into the night."

Interviews and Reviews on *Critical Alliance*

"A whirlwind adventure from the first chapter to the conclusion . . . *Deadly Target* hit the bull's-eye for me."

Life is Story on *Deadly Target*

"Another great romantic suspense novel with characters readers will fall in love with and a storyline that never slows down!"

Write-Read-Life on *Deadly Target*

"This nonstop thrilling, romantic suspense kept up the pace until the very last page."

Relz Reviews on *Present Danger*

SHADOWS AT DUSK

Books by Elizabeth Goddard

UNCOMMON JUSTICE SERIES

Never Let Go

Always Look Twice

Don't Keep Silent

ROCKY MOUNTAIN COURAGE SERIES

Present Danger

Deadly Target

Critical Alliance

MISSING IN ALASKA

Cold Light of Day

Shadows at Dusk

MISSING IN ALASKA • 2

SHADOWS AT DUSK

ELIZABETH GODDARD

a division of Baker Publishing Group
Grand Rapids, Michigan

Published by Revell
a division of Baker Publishing Group
Grand Rapids, Michigan
www.revellbooks.com

Printed in the United States of America

Library of Congress Cataloging-in-Publication Data
Names: Goddard, Elizabeth, author.
Title: Shadows at dusk / Elizabeth Goddard.
Description: Grand Rapids, Michigan : Revell, [2023] | Series: Missing in Alaska ; 2
Identifiers: LCCN 2023009804 | ISBN 9780800742058 (paperback) | ISBN 9780800745073 (casebound) | ISBN 9781493443505 (ebook)
Subjects: LCGFT: Detective and mystery fiction. | Novels.
Classification: LCC PS3607.O324 S53 2023 | DDC 813.6—dc23/eng/20230306
LC record available at https://lccn.loc.gov/2023009804

Baker Publishing Group publications use paper produced from sustainable forestry practices and post-consumer waste whenever possible.

23 24 25 26 27 28 29 7 6 5 4 3 2 1

To Tina,
you're filled with so much wisdom, faith, and strength,
and you have always been an incredible inspiration to me.
I thank God for you!

I couldn't write a story about a bush pilot in Alaska
without taking my readers on a wild and crazy ride,
so I invite you to strap in and hold on tight.

—Elizabeth

When you pass through the waters,
  I will be with you;
and when you pass through the rivers,
  they will not sweep over you.
When you walk through the fire,
  you will not be burned;
  the flames will not set you ablaze.

Isaiah 43:2

PROLOGUE

Airspace over Zhugandia, East Africa

The old cargo plane vibrated as the pilot descended into the airdrop zone, the turbulence shuddering through Carrie James. She braced herself on a bench a few feet from the secured freight—emergency supplies that could mean the difference between life and death in a food-starved, war-torn country.

Battle-scarred was exactly how her heart felt, especially with Darius Aster sitting so close. She struggled to comprehend his betrayal.

My heart is splitting in two.

Good thing Bongani and his brother Tariq piloted today instead of her.

Darius released the safety harness and stood over her, his dark eyes flashing as he steadied himself against the fuselage. Plowing his free hand through black hair, he worked his stubbled jaw.

How would he explain himself?

"Choose me." Desperation flooded his voice. "Choose us."

Carrie didn't miss the warning that surfaced behind the anguish in his eyes.

"You're the one who's throwing everything away!" Her voice shook. How had he snuck the contraband worth millions onto the plane without her noticing? "You're a good man. I don't believe . . . I can't believe you would do this."

"Believe it." His expression shifted. She'd never seen that look in his eyes before.

Who are you?

Unshed tears burned her eyes. She stared at this man who had been her world.

Her everything.

"This isn't what we do. What we're about." She loved this job. Loved flying in the much-needed supplies to isolated African villages. Aiding people in a way she never could in her military career. Reminding them they were important too and weren't forgotten. "We're supposed to help people, not steal from them."

"Don't you see?" Darius huffed. "This is our ticket to freedom."

Nausea churned in her stomach. She stood up so that he couldn't hover over and intimidate her. And Darius moved to manually open the door specifically designed to eject supplies.

God, help me to make him understand, please. She had to shout her next words to be heard over the wind.

"Stealing precious resources won't give you freedom. It means living a lie, always looking over your shoulder."

He took an unsteady step closer. "Nobody knows. Nobody cares what we do in this war-torn country."

The tears surged forward now, and no manner of trying to close herself off to this outrage could hold them back.

I wish I had a way off.

A way out.

Did Darius assume she would go along with his theft? He'd already committed the crime, only admitting his actions after she spotted the uncut gems nestled inside the crate and questioned him.

God, help me. What do I do? What do I do?

Her breaths came too hard. Too fast.

His gaze softened, and he took a step back. "Just relax, will you? I'll handle everything."

He was probably hoping he could persuade her, but he was wrong. "Why didn't you ask me before you made this decision for us? You should've known I would never agree."

"That's exactly why I didn't ask. I figured I'd tell you, eventually. You shouldn't have been nosing around."

"Well, I was. So, now what?" She glared, trying to challenge him, threaten him, and will him to choose the path of love all in one look.

Raw pain flickered in his eyes and pinged through her heart. *There—he's still there. Please come back to me.*

Pulling her against his chest, he crushed her lips with a desperate kiss that bruised body and soul. Did he think this was love? She shoved him off, freeing herself.

"Get away from me." She loved him, but he'd ripped her heart from her chest. "I can't be part of this. Please, choose us. Choose me."

"I have a buyer, and I've already been paid. Now I must deliver. And for the record, I am choosing us. I'm choosing to *save* us."

How could she have been so wrong about him? Such a fool?

"Count me out. I can't be part of it."

He stared at her, long and hard, then his gaze turned dark.

Cold.

Empty.

A chill shivered through her. Before she could dart out of his reach, he seized her arm and dragged her to the open door of the cargo plane.

Wind rushed at her from behind. Roared in her ears. Fear paralyzed her.

He wouldn't. He couldn't.

Heart in her throat, she took in the man before her, now a stranger. "Please! Don't do this. You don't have to do this."

But his eyes held a cruelty she'd never seen before. She couldn't have dreamed or imagined he could harbor so much darkness.

Evil.

"I'm sorry. We could have been good together. But I can't . . . I can't trust you now!"

The man she loved shoved her chest, punching the breath from her, knocking her out of the airplane.

ONE

Ten Years Later
Alaska Panhandle

Detective Trevor West wrestled with the foregone truth. When someone went missing, the first forty-eight hours were vital.

For loved ones, those excruciating hours turned into prayerful days, then agonizing weeks and hopeless months.

And now it was July, over a year later.

Am I a fool to hold on to hope?

But even the state of Montana would only declare a missing person presumed dead if they had not been seen or heard from for at least five years. Who was Trevor to argue with that?

Early this morning, he took an Alaska Airlines flight from Bozeman, Montana, to the Alaska Panhandle, connecting through both Seattle and Ketchikan. He'd never been a fan of flying, and in one day he'd seen more than enough from thirty thousand feet to last him a lifetime. With travel time and layovers, getting here took eleven hours. He tried to shake off the grogginess as he stepped off the boat that had brought him from the state capital of Juneau via the Alaska Marine Highway to Shadow Gap. This place was endless snowcapped mountains surrounded by a temperate rainforest, and miles of ocean waterways flowing around a thousand islands, coves, and bays. Literally. He knew because he read the pamphlet on his way here.

Standing on the dock, he inhaled the crispest, cleanest mountain air he'd ever breathed, and that was saying something since he lived in Montana. But he wouldn't expect anything less in Shadow Gap, the small town hidden in a pristine fjord.

Tugging his jacket tighter, he disembarked with a few other adventurous souls who'd been on the ferry with him, and clomped along the planks toward the end of the dock in search of one familiar face in particular.

Chief Autumn Long waited for him at the end of the pier, a tenuous smile cracking a face framed by curly dark hair. He couldn't see her oddly colored eyes until he closed the distance.

She shook his hand with a good, strong grip. "Detective West. It's good to see you again."

Trevor had taken leave and traveled to Southeast Alaska last fall after the Alaska Bureau of Investigation's failure to locate Jennifer. So, given the circumstances, he couldn't really say the same, although the information she gave him two days ago had ignited hope.

And *that* scared him to death.

His gaze snagged on the engagement ring on her left hand. A lot could happen in a year. "You're engaged. Congratulations."

With a big smile, she held up her hand and flashed the ring. "Yes. Thank you."

"Who's the lucky man?"

"His name is Grier Young."

"When's the wedding?" *Why am I asking so many personal questions?* Probably procrastinating.

"We're looking at October." Her smile slowly faded.

Right. Time to get to the business at hand. He walked with her to her Ford Interceptor.

"I got here as fast as I could," he said.

Which was not fast at all when it came to traveling from the lower forty-eight to Alaska. He fisted his hands in his pockets. Stopping at her vehicle, he opened the passenger door. Before he stepped inside, he glanced up at the impossibly blue skies.

Thank God it's summer.

Chief Long had agreed to meet him and give him a ride, but if he ended up staying for more than a day, he would need to secure his own transportation.

Inside the vehicle, Chief Long got settled, buckling in. "Is there anything you want to go over first?"

"Not before. Probably after."

"Fair enough." She steered the vehicle onto the street.

Trevor peered out the window, getting once again familiar with the small town as she drove slowly down the main strip, passing between the quaint old structures on both sides, including on the left, the Lively Moose and the Rabid Raccoon, and to the right, the smallest police department he'd ever seen, squeezed in between a thrift store and a pharmacy.

"They live up in the mountains about four miles," she said. "But it'll take fifteen minutes, give or take, to get there."

His gut churned at the reminder of their destination and the purpose for his trip. "Do they know I'm coming?"

"When they made the discovery, they were informed that I might have more questions. I told them I would be coming by today to talk."

"But they don't know *I'm* joining you." He wanted to clarify so he understood what he was walking into.

"You know how it is—it's better to see their reaction than to have them mentally prepared. I think seeing you in person might trigger more."

"Agreed."

He stared out the window and took in the lofty snowcapped mountains that disappeared from view when she took a turn and steered deep into a lush rainforest, which stunned him with even more beauty.

If only he'd come to bask in the scenery.

Why, God? Why couldn't we have found this lead sooner?

Because Trevor was lost in his thoughts, the drive went by faster than expected, and he squeezed the handgrip as Chief Long steered up a steep and narrow path to a cabin. He ignored the queasiness. Even though he lived in Montana now, he hadn't gotten used to heights. But he always enjoyed the view. A person could see so much more when standing above it all. *Lord, I need a big-picture view to know where to go and what to do next.*

He needed a new perspective if he was going to find answers.

As he climbed out of the vehicle, his body protested the long flight from Montana. He hiked up the incline, following Chief Long to the front door, the movement setting off a wind chime that hung from the porch awning.

The door opened promptly and a fiftyish couple met the chief with somber smiles. The two noticed Trevor standing behind her. While Mr. Nobel's eyes widened, his wife's narrowed.

Chief Long shifted toward Trevor. "This is Detective West from Montana. Detective West, this is Joyce and Walter Nobel, Monica's parents."

"Good to meet you." Under the circumstances, he realized *good* was the wrong word.

Mr. Nobel stood two heads taller than his wife and wore silver-rimmed glasses. His hair was graying, and his brown eyes crinkled at the corners with a smile he didn't mean. "Come on in. I don't know what more we can tell you, but we'll do our best."

Trevor followed Chief Long into the sizable log cabin with rustic furnishings. He had noticed a shop and log chipper near the cabin. He'd bet that Nobel had made his own furniture, after he built the cabin.

"Make yourself comfortable." Mrs. Nobel's gray-streaked

black hair was frizzy and barely contained, her face etched with lines of grief. She gestured toward a floral sofa with a log frame and similar-style taupe chairs near large windows that opened to a stunning view of the fjord and inlet.

Trevor remained standing. But Chief Long gestured subtly that he should sit too. She knew her people, so he'd comply. She eased onto the edge of the sofa opposite them, and he slid wholly into an old, well-worn chair.

"Mr. and Mrs. Nobel, Chief Long tells me that your daughter knew Jennifer Warner."

They both nodded. Mrs. Nobel sat forward. "Monica went missing in May of last year." Tears prevented her from continuing.

Mr. Nobel cleared his throat. "Her body wasn't discovered until that August." He paused, frowning, pushing past his own grief. "The things she had on her person were returned to us. They've been in her room in a box. It wasn't until this week that we . . . " He took his wife's hand and squeezed. "We just couldn't bring ourselves to look at her stuff. Not yet. It's hard to accept that she's gone."

The process of learning the details could be painfully slow, and Trevor's jaw clenched tighter even as he tried to remain patient. Inside he was screaming. Shouting.

He put on a compassionate expression. "Go on."

Mrs. Nobel's chin quivered. "A ziplock bag contained her watch and a few items that were found in her pockets."

Elbows on thighs, Trevor leaned forward and clasped his hands. "Tell me about what more you found." The reason Chief Long had called him.

Mrs. Nobel shared another look with her husband. "We found the message Jennifer left with Monica. She was supposed to pass it on to Jennifer's brother."

He'd already been informed of the message.

"If something happens to me, give this to my brother."

"Do you have the message?"

"I do." Chief Long stood to retrieve a small manila envelope from her jacket pocket.

He took the envelope and, inside, found a small key and a folded slip of paper. A pang sliced through him afresh. "When was the last time Monica saw Jennifer?"

"We think Monica met with her a few days before she disappeared."

"Before *who* disappeared?"

"Monica. Our daughter. Sorry, Chief Long told us that Jennifer has disappeared too."

Chief Long cleared her throat and looked at Trevor. "A connection was never made between the two women during the ABI's previous investigation, as you now know. When the Nobels contacted me with the news that they'd discovered the envelope, I learned about Monica and Jennifer's connection and then informed them of Jennifer's disappearance."

Trevor thought she might include an apology, but it hadn't been her investigation. The ABI had missed key information. Trevor had missed it too.

"You came all the way from Montana to investigate. You must think this is a lead. We're sorry we didn't find it sooner. We assume you can find her brother to pass it on to."

"Yes. We'll pass it on." Chief Long apparently wouldn't give out information Trevor wasn't willing to share. Or maybe she didn't want the Nobels to know the truth yet.

"Did Monica tell you anything about Jennifer?" Trevor asked. "Where she was going? What she was involved in?"

"We know she was a photographer, but that's all. So many photographers—amateur and professional—flock to Alaska. Monica said she had a geoscience degree."

"Yes." Geology. Interesting she would have shared that much. "How long was Monica friends with Jennifer?"

"We don't know, exactly. Monica told us they met through

an online photography group. They talked about going on a photo trek together."

That all tracked with what he already knew.

"What else can you tell me? Did Monica say anything else about Jennifer?"

Slow down. One question at a time. His personal stakes in this boiled over and would overwhelm them.

"I'm assuming since you came here from Montana, that you know her brother. That's why you're here. I'm surprised he didn't come too."

Oh, he came. He lifted his head and held the woman's gaze. "Jennifer is my sister."

Is . . . He couldn't bring himself to even think "was."

Because, yes, he admitted that he was a fool to hold on to hope.

TWO

Taku River Valley, Southeast Alaska

Sometimes the only way out of the fire is to walk through it.

She could chalk it up to the life of a bush pilot.

"All in a day's work," Carrie James mumbled as she hiked up the steep incline toward the mountain cabin.

She never had to leave her Helio Courier floatplane sitting on the water to make deliveries. Clients understood they had better be waiting for her arrival. Most of the time, they were anxious to get their supplies.

Elias Hall was no exception. Although this was her last delivery for the day, she'd expected to see him standing on the rudimentary dock he'd built, waiting with a big grin behind his thick reddish beard. He would take his packages and pay her in cash or with a check.

Like many of her clients, off-grid meant off. Grid.

But Elias hadn't shown up for the delivery, and Carrie had no choice but to investigate.

Some people lived so far away from civilization, no one would know if anything happened to them. No one was around to request a welfare check. So in more than one way, Carrie's job delivering supplies to isolated people was vital to their survival.

Elias had cleared the trees along the path from the water to build his cabin. The place was serene, and she wanted to take a deep breath of fresh peace, but she had a bad feeling about his no-show.

Especially when she heard his dog, Koda, barking from inside the cabin.

Finally, she approached the log structure that managed to blend in with nature. Almost breathless after her hike from the river, she clomped up the porch and knocked on the door. "Elias, it's Carrie. You in there?"

Koda's barking grew loud and frantic.

Hands in her jacket pocket, she waited for Elias—*God, please let him answer*—and glanced around at the thick forest, the river below, and the mountain peaks in the distance.

Please, let him be home and not hurt out there in that unforgiving wilderness.

Without his dog. Yeah. He wouldn't leave his dog. Would he?

Elias didn't answer. From the way the dog barked, Carrie knew Koda would open the door if he could. Elias wouldn't normally be without Koda. He must be inside.

She tried the door.

Shoot. I'm gonna have to kick it in.

That is, if she could. The door was heavy and thick to keep out the cold winters.

She kicked several times to no avail. Pain ignited in her bad leg. Carrie hobbled around the cabin to peer into windows. At the back, she gazed through dirty glass into the bedroom, feeling awkward but sensing Elias was in trouble. Sure enough, he lay on the bed, unmoving.

"Elias!" She knocked on the window.

He barely moved, but it was enough for her to know.

Alive. He's alive.

But just hanging on by the look of him. Koda rushed into the room and barked at her.

"I have to break the window. I'm sorry!" She found a chunk of firewood and smashed the window in. Cleared the glass. Then stacked more wood so she could gain purchase and climb through.

Carrie tumbled ungracefully to the floor. Koda licked her and whined. He was a beautiful Samoyed and looked like a small polar bear. "You're a good boy."

Fortunately, the dog remembered her or else he might have given her a different reception.

Ignoring the pain in her backside, which had taken the brunt of the fall, she hopped to her feet, rushed to the bed, and took in Elias's face. He was pale and sweaty, and his breathing was raspy. He didn't open his eyes. A rotting stench hit her nose.

Dread gripped her as she gently touched his forehead. "Oh, Elias. You're burning up."

She peeled back the blanket and glanced down the length of his body. Blood seeped through a bandage on his lower leg. Her heart sank. Sepsis, if she had to guess—a life-threatening medical emergency made even worse because of his location.

"I hate to leave, but I need to call for help. I'm going to use your radio. I'll be right back."

She hurried out of the room and into a tidy living space, which she didn't have time to appreciate.

Radio, radio, radio . . . There. A satellite phone sat on the table against the wall. She reached for it. It wasn't charged. Great. Neither was the VHF radio. How long had the power been out? Elias shouldn't have issues since the power came from a combination of solar and diesel generators. No wonder it was freezing in here.

She didn't have time to figure out the issues or to build a fire. How had Elias kept warm enough? If she could do something for him here and now, she would, but he would die without help.

She also smelled the evidence that Koda needed to be let out.

"Come on, boy. You need to go outside, and I need to hike down to my plane and radio for help."

She unlocked the front door and opened it wide for him, and he dashed off into the woods. Old injuries screaming at her, Carrie hobbled down the hill toward her plane on the river, then she spotted a fearsome sight.

A moose stood in the grass near the pier at the bottom of the incline, blocking the path to her plane.

Stopping in her tracks, Carrie came up short. But she didn't stop fast enough.

Out from behind the moose stepped a calf.

Not good.

She slowly stepped back.

What am I going to do? I need my radio!

The moose stared at her and snorted. She hadn't meant to make the massive creature feel threatened.

"Nice moose. There's a good moose. Now, please go away. I need my radio."

Carrie took another step back. Slow and easy.

The cow shook her head and grunted, then pushed the ground with her big black muzzle, her huge brown eyes staring at Carrie. Barking, Koda burst from the woods and raced toward the moose.

And the larger-than-life creature charged Carrie.

Run! Pulse racing, she twisted on her heel and ran, her injured leg dragging, aching, throbbing. Heart pumping, she reached deep inside and found the determination to pick up the pace.

But it wasn't enough.

Carrie stumbled to the ground. She rolled and looked into the eyes of the furious mother moose who would crush her. She couldn't have outrun the cow anyway. What had she been thinking?

Koda suddenly appeared—standing between Carrie and the moose—barking, defending.

Saving her life.

Gunfire split the air.

The moose turned and trotted away from Carrie and toward her calf, then together they headed to the cover of the woods.

Carrie collapsed flat and released her pent-up breath. Standing over her, Elias held his rifle toward the sky, then dropped to his knees and fell sideways to the ground.

"Elias!" She rolled over and crawled to him. "How did you—"

"Knew . . . you were in trouble."

"You're the one in trouble." She had no idea how he'd been able to gather his strength and scare that moose away.

"If you made it this far, I can get you to the plane. No sense in waiting on someone to come for you." She scrambled to get him back on his feet. The two of them stumbled forward.

We'll crawl if we have to.

She hoped she could bear the brunt of his weight, because he leaned hard on her, and she joined him in gasping for breath.

"Not much farther. You can do it, Elias. Come on."

It was all Carrie could do to get the door open wide and assist him over the pontoon. Heart pounding, she gave all her strength to heave him forward until he fell into the seat.

Relief washed through her, but it was short-lived. She grabbed a bottle of water and poured it into his mouth. Strapped him in.

"Come on, Koda." The dog wasn't about to be left behind and eagerly hopped into the plane. He licked Elias's face, then jumped into the back seat. "That's a good boy."

She moved to shut the door. "I need to close up the house."

"Leave it. I got nothing worth . . ."

Your life.

She got it.

THREE

Trevor sat in Chief Long's Ford Interceptor outside the Forest State Bank.

"It's got to be a key to a safe deposit box," Chief Long said. "With no routing number or anything to identify which bank, you might as well start here. This is the only bank in town. If it doesn't work, you can go to the Haines National Bank and a couple others."

He stared at the small key that Jennifer had left with Monica to give to him. Maybe it would open a bank box that held the long sought-after answers and end the agony. Or it could be nothing but an empty box. If it held some cryptic clue, that could lead him to more questions. But if it helped him find his sister, he'd take whatever he could get.

"If you want, I can go inside with you. I called ahead and spoke to the bank manager—Daniel Hopper—about the circumstances. Jennifer is missing, not declared deceased, so the bank hasn't sealed the box yet. Still, it could mean we need to go through the legal processes, though he assured me you could open it."

"No, it's okay. I know you have more on your plate than to chauffeur me around."

"I do, in fact. But I want to know what's in the box too, that is, if it's relevant to finding a missing person. The note was meant for you, so I called you, but the wording does raise questions about her disappearance."

Indeed. "I thought safe deposit boxes went away with the dinosaurs. Seems like people can store their important financial documents in a digital vault of some kind."

"Unless they need originals kept safe." She sighed. "Look, I know you're afraid of what you might find."

She seemed to understand more than he would have expected. Trevor had been itching to get here and find out what he could, but now, fear paralyzed him.

"This seems surreal. All I ever wanted was to be there for her, to protect her, especially after everything that happened with her abusive ex-husband." He released an incredulous huff. "I was a Deputy US Marshal in Chicago, and I resigned to become a county detective in Montana so I'd have no travel and a lighter schedule. Jennifer moved with me to the small town of Big Rapids, far away from trouble. It was the best way to keep her safe, short of changing her name and giving her a new identity."

"Like the Marshals do in the WITSEC program," Chief Long said. "It's tragic that not more can be done for women in those kinds of dangerous situations."

"Exactly. And it gets to me. I'm in law enforcement and still, I couldn't protect her. She disappeared anyway, though supposedly not at the hands of her ex-husband."

"You mentioned being a Marshal. Did you work with witnesses?"

"No. My main responsibilities involved tracking fugitives. But that's behind me now. I enjoy my job as a detective. After a few months, Jennifer got a job in Bozeman, about an hour away. When she mentioned going to Alaska, I encouraged her to knock it off her bucket list. But she never came back." He shook his head and stared out the window. Why was he talking about this with the chief? She'd already heard the story.

"I'm sorry."

"It's okay. Believe it or not, I'm a police chief for half the day and a therapist for the other half. You've got this, Detective West. Trevor. If you want your privacy while opening the box, I'll wait here for you."

"Thanks. I'll just be a few minutes."

"I need to make a call anyway." She grabbed her cell.

Trevor exited the Interceptor and made his way to the establishment. His palms slicked as he opened the door and stepped into the bank, which surprised him with the kind of decor one expected in a big-city building rather than one in small-town Alaska. But nope. Marble floors and brass rails and faux mahogany surrounded him.

He approached a teller. "I'm supposed to meet the bank manager, Mr. Hopper."

She looked over his shoulder and smiled. "Mr. Hopper will be right with you."

Trevor turned to see a tall, round, balding man approach. He shook the man's hand. "Detective Trevor West."

"Daniel Hopper." The man eyed Trevor. "Chief Long isn't with you?"

"She's on a phone call."

"I see. Follow me."

Mr. Hopper led him into a room and placed a notebook in front of him. "I'll need to see your identification, please."

Trevor showed Mr. Hopper his Montana driver's license.

"Now, if you'll just sign here."

Trevor signed his name. Mr. Hopper examined his signature, comparing it to another.

"What are you doing?"

"It's our policy to not only look at your identification but also compare your signature to the one we have on file, from when you opened the safe deposit box."

Trevor considered the man's words. "Can I see the signature card?"

Mr. Hopper showed him the card with *his* signature, or rather, a very good forgery of it.

The bank manager studied Trevor. "I thought it was strange that Chief Long called to ask about giving you access when you're clearly on the safe deposit box with Ms. Warner. That's why I didn't bring up all the necessary requirements for you to open the box without her."

Banks had security cameras, but Trevor feared it had been too long and they no longer had the security feed of who was with Jennifer and signed the card to obtain the box. He would let Chief Long look into that.

He pursed his lips so he wouldn't say something to delay things. "I'm ready to open the box."

Mr. Hopper led him into the bank vault and into another room where safe deposit box doors lined the wall. He found the correct numbered door, inserted the bank key and turned it, then Trevor used the key Jennifer had left him to unlock the door.

"I'll give you some privacy." Mr. Hopper left him alone.

Trevor opened the door and slid the long, narrow container out of the compartment. He stared at the box Jennifer had secured—*in case something happened to her.*

His hand shook as he slowly lifted the lid.

FOUR

At the dock in Shadow Gap, Carrie watched a gurney cart Elias toward the waiting ambulance to be taken to the local hospital. Koda whined, showing his aching heart. She ran her fingers through his thick, white fur. "It's gonna be okay. He's gonna live." She held his face and looked into his eyes, and the dog licked her lips. "You're a good boy."

Now, what to do with you.

"Isaac won't mind keeping you a few days." *I hope.*

After the ambulance drove away, Carrie coaxed Koda back into her plane, then she got in.

Her hangar was a mere hop, skip, and a jump across the water around Eagle's Bluff near where glacier-fed Goldrock River flowed out of the mountains. Shadow Gap residents had to cross a bridge to get to the hangar and what was left of the airstrip after a mudslide last fall.

She steered the plane to swoop in and land on the river again, then taxied toward the pier connected to the hangar where she'd ended her day for nearly a decade. She expertly parked her plane next to the dock on the cantilever lift. After scrambling out, she held the door for Koda to escape. He bounded out of the plane and sniffed around. Standing tall, she tried not to hobble on the planks the short distance toward the hangar that opened to the water.

Covered in grease, Isaac worked the manual lift to raise the plane out of the water. His weathered and tanned skin made his gray hair almost look white. "You're later than usual."

Barking, Koda ran up to Isaac and sniffed around his feet.

"And you brought a dog."

"His name's Koda." Carrie explained that she'd transported Elias to the hospital and Koda needed a place to stay.

When she started for the office, she hesitated, uncertain if she could actually put weight on her leg after the day she'd had.

Isaac tossed her a cane, and she caught it. "Thanks."

Isaac stared at Koda as if trying to decide if he liked him or not. They could figure out what to do with the dog later. She leaned on the cane and made her way into the hangar.

"Watch your step, Carrie. Sorry—I've been too busy to be organized today."

"I'll say."

Isaac was a genius mechanic who'd kept their piloting business going for years, and he prided himself on keeping the hangar clean and safe, but today he'd left the floor a veritable minefield of tripping hazards—electrical cords and air hoses. She weaved around several tool chests and a myriad of wrenches, lamps, and parts on the ground.

Did he seem kind of off? Or was that her imagination? Regardless, she knew it would be clean and organized before he left. Always was.

"What happened to your 'safety first' motto?" she teased.

"I'll get it all back in place when I'm done here tonight."

At the door, she turned to see if he was going to follow. "You're working late tonight, I guess."

"I don't go home until the boss goes home."

She half smiled. She'd never been sure who the boss was.

He quickly dropped his grin. "Good thing you were there for Elias. I hate to think what would have happened to him otherwise."

"I radioed his closest neighbor. Red Lankin lives twenty miles downriver. I asked if he could lock up the house. Fix the window. I can't muster enough energy to go back and get it done."

"Carrie. You can't save the world."

Funny. She used to say that same thing to her missionary parents. After they died in a plane crash while in Mozambique, she joined the US Army out of her need to get far away and follow orders. And somehow, she'd found herself back in Africa, wanting to save the world.

Now she was in Alaska, *not* trying to save the world. "No. But I could save Elias." She tossed Isaac a grin.

Koda lapped up a water puddle next to a hose. "And his dog."

"You could have asked the neighbor to keep Koda. I don't know if he'll like it around here with just me, a plane, and the river."

"So take him home." While she lived in an apartment above the hangar, Isaac had made the cabin on the property home, and his place was fifty yards through the woods.

"Like he's gonna stay there all day. And if he comes here, he'll want to chase the critters."

"You know I couldn't leave him there with Elias gone. We'll figure it out tomorrow. I'm not taking him back tonight to see if Red will keep him."

I can't face off with that moose again. She'd left that part out. She made it to the office and dropped into her chair. A fan blew in the corner. She leaned the cane against the wall next to the desk.

I hate that cane.

But she could never tell Isaac her true feelings—he'd carved it out of acacia. That tree grew only in Africa. What would she have done without Isaac all these years? He was by her side during her lengthy hospital stay, then months of rehabilitation, then finally, he settled them both in Alaska on the other side of the world from her previous adventures—in another hemisphere completely. "*Where he can never hurt you again.*"

Isaac was like a father to her when they worked for Global Relief Services, and now he was her business partner at SEA Skies—short for Southeast Alaska Skies. She couldn't fathom what she would do without him, so no, she wasn't going to tell him she hated the cane.

It's not that I hate the cane. It's that I hate needing it.

She leaned over to pet Koda, who'd followed her. "You're probably hungry." She hadn't thought about dog food. "I'm betting Isaac's got some scraps he could feed you until we get you settled somewhere." Elias wasn't going home any time soon.

She closed her eyes and listened to "Only the Good Die Young" by Billy Joel playing on Isaac's radio. And she just might have fallen asleep where she sat, until Isaac strode into the room and disturbed her.

The long hours and his age showed as he eased onto the bench next to the far wall.

"Tomorrow, I deliver medical supplies," she said. "And then I have two days to get my act together before heading off to see Kaya." She missed her African friend and could hardly believe Kaya would be in Texas, traveling with an a cappella group. "You sure you don't want to go too?"

Making arrangements to be gone for ten days was risky. She had to farm off her clients to another local pilot, David Strong. She sometimes worked for David while he took time off as well. Isaac had made all the arrangements for her trip, and she had a feeling he was trying to get David to officially join SEA Skies.

Isaac ran the business and fixed the planes, and what did she do?

Nothing but fly them.

"You need this break from me," he said. "It's good for you to get a change of scenery."

She laughed. "You mean you need this break from *me*."

He joined her, his old laughter filled with wisdom and love. Then his expression grew somber. "I'll be fine. I'm getting too old to travel, and besides, I like my quiet space here. Never thought I'd end up in Alaska, of all places on God's green earth." His eyes flashed, then he looked away.

She suspected he hadn't meant to mention their reasons for landing in Alaska. Feared it would trigger her.

But I'm stronger now.

"I'm going to miss you," she said.

"It's only ten days."

Seemed like a lifetime. "Well, at least I have a day or two to convince you to come with me. Kaya would love to see you too."

But Isaac wouldn't change his mind. She couldn't help but think he *wanted* her away from him for some reason. She knew him well enough to sense it.

He stared at the floor, concern etching his features. "We need to talk."

Finally, he would tell her what was bothering him. "I thought that's what we were doing."

Koda suddenly jumped up, barked, and raced to the open door right as a thirtysomething man appeared and knocked on the frame.

He bent down and made quick friends with Koda. "Hey, boy. It's nice to meet you too." He remained crouched a few moments, giving Koda love and attention, then stood and looked between Carrie and Isaac.

Jeans and boots and a jacket. The most intense blue eyes she'd ever seen. He had a rough-and-tumble look about him, but it was his eyes that drew her attention.

When her attention should never be drawn.

"I'm looking for Carrie James." Those blue eyes locked on her.

"We're closed," she and Isaac said at the same time. Wow, he really did want to talk to her. He never turned away business.

The man walked into the office. "You come highly recommended."

"Who recommended me?"

He stepped forward, a quirk in his grin to go with his dimples. "Chief Long, if that makes a difference."

Carrie stood, and though pain spiked through her leg, she absolutely would not reach for that cane. "I have one last delivery to make tomorrow, then I'm getting ready to leave for ten days. Isaac can set you up with another pilot who is covering my clients while I'm gone."

Isaac stood too, and shook the man's hand. "I'm Isaac. I keep the planes and the business running."

"So you're both mechanic and office manager?" Blue Eyes asked with a warm smile.

She should absolutely not be thinking of him in terms of his amazing eyes.

"That, I am. And you are?" Isaac's smile was kind as always, and probably only Carrie could see the strain behind his expression.

"Detective Trevor West."

Detective.

Interesting.

Isaac studied the detective a few moments, then said, "I can set you up with another pilot. His name is David Strong. What exactly do you need?"

Detective Blue Eyes, er . . . Trevor West pulled out his cell phone and showed Isaac and Carrie an image of a beautiful brunette. She had a smile and dimples just like the detective's.

"Do you recognize her?" he asked.

Unfortunately, yes. "She went missing last year." Carrie took a millisecond to take in the rest of him. No doubt about it. "And you're her brother." *Are you here to find her after so many months?*

He nodded. Pursed his lips as if he struggled to speak.

A knot lodged in *her* throat. Where would she be if Isaac hadn't searched for her and found her broken and dying in the African bush?

I can't do this. I'm leaving, for crying out loud.

But inexplicably, her next words rushed out. "What do you need from me, specifically?"

As if she would take this one instead of handing it over to David.

Detective West pulled a folded legal-size envelope from inside his jacket, then tugged out photograph prints. "Jennifer took these."

Carrie looked at the stunning scenery. "They're beautiful, but it's nearly impossible to take a bad picture in Alaska." *Oh, why did I say that?*

The guy made her nervous for some inexplicable reason. She bit back a flurry of questions. *Just let him talk.*

"She left these in a safe deposit box for me."

Carrie shrugged. "As in a farewell gift? What?"

"I'm a detective. She left these in case something happened to her. What does that sound like to you?"

Carrie stepped closer. "May I?" She reached out.

He handed over the photographs. Each one depicted an area in Southeast Alaska, a recognizable area—at least to Carrie, who'd traveled the region extensively.

Oh no. No, no. I can't do this.

But Blue Eyes had hooked her. "You think these are some sort of a trail of bread crumbs? You know, like Hansel and Gretel?"

He took his time looking at her. Had the Hansel and Gretel reference stumped him? "It's possible," he said. "I have to follow them to find out. I need to know what happened to her once and for all. Now, can you help me or not?"

"Southeast Alaska is over thirty-five thousand square miles of mountains, inlets, and Tongass National Forest, plus thousands of islands. Most of those photographs are of distinct areas, which is fortunate for you. I recognize a couple of places. I'd have to think about the others, but they look familiar."

The idea of following these crumbs with this blue-eyed detective energized her.

What am I doing? I'm leaving. I can't be the pilot he needs.

She glanced over at Isaac, whose judgment had always been far better than hers. He subtly nodded, and she read the affirmation in his eyes.

Seriously? She handed the pictures back. "I can give you a day and a half. I need the rest of the time to pack and tie up loose ends before my trip." She hadn't taken a day off since coming to Alaska, and really, nothing besides Kaya could pull her away.

Detective West looked between her and Isaac, as if second-guessing his request. Then finally, he nodded as if to himself before saying, "Fair enough."

"Tomorrow I make a medical supply delivery. You can ride with me, and we'll fly over where the pictures were taken. Meet me here at five a.m."

"What if I need to land and get a closer look?"

"Right now, I only have time to fly over. Landing and walking around asking questions will take you more than a day. Or you can see if David can help you. But his schedule might be full, and it could take a few days to squeeze you in."

"Flying over could be a good first step." Detective West shook her hand and held it longer than necessary before dropping it. "I appreciate your help more than you know. This is urgent. I know it sounds strange since Jennifer has been missing for over a year. But I now have in my hands what I should have had last year. I won't let this go to waste."

She read in his eyes what he didn't say. He would do anything to find his sister. Her heart lurched at his sincerity.

Detective West exited, and she waited until he climbed into what she suspected was a rental truck and drove away before she turned to face her friend, her mentor, the man who'd been like a father to her. "Why did I let you talk me into this?"

"Talk you into it? I didn't say a word."

"You didn't have to. I heard you loud and clear."

"You make a lot of sense, Carrie." He snorted.

The irony wasn't lost on her. "Seriously, Isaac."

"Well, what do you think you heard me say?"

"And I quote, 'You need to be the one to help this man find his lost and broken and possibly deceased sister in the Alaska bush.'"

Isaac's chuckle was long, deep, and rich, and with it, his mantra flooded her mind as well. *"Focus on what you've always done, Carrie—caring for others—and you'll heal on the inside, just like you have on the outside."*

"I have a good feeling about this," he finally said.

"That makes one of us." *I have a bad feeling about this*. She rubbed her forehead. "This is so messed up. Now, what was it you wanted to talk about?"

FIVE

What am I doing here?

Docked at a short pier next to the hangar, Carrie James's plane rested on a platform on the water. Trevor sat in the cockpit and stared out at the Goldrock River flowing by. The hangar and dock were banked against a gentle portion of the current.

Carrie fiddled with something on her dashboard.

"I'll be right back." Just like that, she hopped out of the plane.

If he was going to change his mind and give up this crazy plan, now was the moment. When he first saw her last night, she wasn't what he'd expected. Truthfully, he didn't know what he'd expected. He only knew that Carrie James wasn't it. He'd pictured a rough exterior that testified of a lot of flight experience.

Chief Long had said as much.

With her big green eyes, peaches-and-cream complexion, and long ash-blond hair pulled into a ponytail, Carrie could have been seventeen. She looked young, and to his way of thinking, didn't look the part or like she could hold her own in what had to be a job that required fortitude. But as soon as she spoke and moved, she had an air about her. A determined, fierce demeanor that let him know she had experience, all right, and not necessarily just flying planes. But it was the guarded look in her eyes that weirdly haunted him last night.

He'd seen that same kind of haunted look in Jennifer's eyes, and it disturbed him for reasons he couldn't understand. Carrie James wasn't his problem, and he needed to stay focused on his mission.

Squeezing his eyes shut, he thought about his beautiful sister. Why did she leave him the pictures? Had her friend Monica Nobel misunderstood Jennifer's message to give the key to Trevor if something happened to her? Then, of course, there was the matter of her getting someone to pretend to be him and forge his signature.

Acid burned his throat.

Chief Long had talked to the bank manager about the security footage, but just like Trevor thought, they only kept footage for six months. Over a year ago, Jennifer had walked into the bank with someone posing as him, presenting identification, Mr. Hopper claimed—maybe to cover their mistake?—and signed the document. So Jennifer had thought what she was putting in the box was important enough to keep in a bank.

Why not email him the digital images? Or email Monica the images to forward to him if something happened to her? Any number of ways she could have done this would have worked better. But without all the facts, his opinion counted for nothing.

So he had these photographs. What did they mean?

Why be so cryptic?

After everything they'd been through together, she could have told him. All he could get out of her behavior was that she hadn't wanted him interfering.

Big brother.

Previous US Marshal.

Current county detective.

They were all good things—except in this case, when she believed she had to keep secrets because he might try to stop her. In early May of last year, she flew to Alaska with a friend from Montana. He never heard from her again after her last text in late May explaining that she was staying a few more days and would check in at the end of the week.

During the ABI's investigation, Trevor learned she'd gone alone. There'd been no friend. And Shadow Gap was the last known location on her cell phone. He was beginning to think she'd shut off her cell so no one could track her.

Since he was a Grayback County detective, he'd been able to get inside information regarding the questioning of her boss at EchoGlobal out of Bozeman and learned she had taken a two-month leave. All their leads were dead ends.

Until today.

God, please don't let this be a dead end.

He'd spent ample time on his knees begging God, and then he got the call from Chief Long. His gut clenched all over again. He wanted to hold on to hope that she was still alive out there somewhere.

Somehow.

Someway.

Carrie's voice carried out to him from the hangar doors, pulling him back to the cockpit, water all around. He glanced up to watch her and Isaac. By the looks of them, they were in a heated discussion. The fluffy white dog, Koda, she'd called him, sat next to Carrie and looked up at Isaac as if he'd sided with her.

Good boy. Trevor chuckled.

Trevor had sensed her hesitation to work with him, even for a day, but she seemed to take her cues from her wise old mechanic partner.

Thank you, Isaac.

Maybe he could go with David Strong, but Chief Long said Carrie was the one. The chief had great things to say about her. But it was what she didn't say when she started a sentence, hesitated, and then stopped talking altogether that left him doubting his decision.

But he was here, and he was doing this.

No turning back now.

He couldn't give this up, this one last shot to try to find out what happened to Jennifer. And God willing, to find her alive. So it looked like he was going to ride shotgun in an old plane with pontoons and a distracted pilot who wasn't invested.

Isaac worked the manual lever to lower the plane into the water. Carrie bounded toward the plane, then climbed up into the cockpit and strapped in.

She handed a headset to Trevor, then put hers on and started flipping switches on the dashboard. The weather forecast squawked from the radio. Carrie had an iPad too, with a weather app. She scribbled something on a small clipboard strapped to her thigh.

Then she glanced at Trevor and smiled. "The weather changes so much that this is almost a wasted effort." She pointed at her windshield. "I rely on what I see out the window."

"I hate puddle jumpers," he mumbled under his breath.

"What's that?" She quirked a grin his way.

Nothing. "I'm not a copilot. Just so we're clear."

"I believe you. Oh, and just so we're clear, bush planes, or puddle jumpers, are one of the only ways to make it around the state of Alaska. I mean, sure, we could take a boat, but we wouldn't make good time." She taxied the plane onto the river.

"Are you going to radio? You know, talk to someone. Say those special words. Alpha Bravo Yankee November." *I sound ridiculous.*

And he was rewarded with an amazing thousand-watt smile. He hadn't expected that or the effect it would have on him.

"One. I'm not trafficking onto a runway with multiple planes. And two, I operate outside of controlled airspace most of the time, not to mention I fly at low altitudes."

Yeah. "I don't know what that means."

"It means there's no ATC—air traffic control tower—for me to communicate with in this location. Not saying that's always the case, but flying in Alaska is a different animal than in the lower forty-eight."

"Yeah, I don't fly much there either. Just ignore me." *Shut up and let her concentrate.*

"Have you ever been on a floatplane?"

"No, actually." He hated admitting that small detail, and she didn't need to know he hated flying. Period. "What if you need to land on, well, land?"

"Southeast Alaska has plenty of lakes and rivers where I can land. Isaac's working on fixing the Cessna, securing the equipment to make it amphibious so I can land on water or land. In the meantime, this Helio Courier might be old, but it's my favorite plane."

Her favorite old plane accelerated. "We had a small airstrip. Did you see it?"

"What was left of it, yeah," he said. "Looked like a landslide took it out."

"We have the rainy season to thank for that."

Nice.

The small plane sped down the river going with the current, then lifted, rattled, and shook. Trevor gripped his seat. "So what's the plan?"

"First stop, I pick up the medical supplies delivered from Seattle to Juneau and then dropped by the bush mail run at Mountain Cove, just north of Juneau. Then I take the supplies to a village near Windfall Lake. Most of your sister's pictures were taken south of Juneau. While I get the supplies, you ask questions in Mountain Cove. You get a half an hour."

"What?"

"An hour at the most, then we head on to the lake to deliver the meds first. These supplies are life and death. Understood?"

"Yes."

"Then I'll fly you south."

"I've never put much thought into how people who live remotely get their supplies. Especially life-and-death medical supplies. I figured if things were that bad, someone might move close to civilization."

"It's not always easy to move just because you want to."

"So how long have you been doing this?"

"Almost ten years. When I first came to Alaska, I worked for Alaska Airlines on 'the milk run.'"

"The milk what?"

"Run. The milk run is what we call flights between the small towns in Southeast Alaska to provide them with needed supplies. Like this medication. The only problem was that there are more small communities and villages that aren't on the milk run route. Underserved communities."

He had to admit, that news was fascinating. *She* was fascinating. "How did you get started in this business?"

"That's a long, convoluted story."

That she wasn't going to share. Fine.

"And you? What's your story, *Detective* West?"

"Just call me Trevor, please."

"Okay, Trevor."

"You want me to share mine, but you're not willing to share yours?"

"Pretty much." She flashed him a grin.

A cute grin that sent a warm spark through him. A deep ache doused the spark. After his marriage to a woman who'd cheated on him with his best friend ended when she died tragically seven years ago, he'd put the thought of romance out of his mind.

For good.

Then Jennifer's issues with her husband had required all his focus. And now certainly wasn't the time or place to suddenly be interested in a woman. But he couldn't help that he found Carrie James intriguing.

"I was a Deputy US Marshal before I settled in Montana to become a county detective." To help Jennifer, but if Carrie wasn't sharing, he wasn't sharing either.

"I'm curious. Chief Long sent you to me, so she knows about the pictures. Is this part of an actual investigation?"

Chief Long had seen the pictures, and like Trevor, she didn't know what to make of them. If Jennifer had meant to send a message, it was entirely too vague. Chief Long would contact the ABI to pass on the information and let them take it from there. Since the photographs covered a region much bigger than the police chief's jurisdiction, it was out of her hands.

Trevor wouldn't wait around for the ABI to decide if the information could help locate Jennifer. They didn't find her before, and he wasn't counting on them now. They'd failed him once already. Besides, as a detective he knew this wasn't enough to go on—at least for someone who wasn't out of their mind like he was. Maybe they would look into her case again and start up the search, but not at the same velocity as Trevor, who was already well on his way to following the proverbial bread crumbs, as Carrie had called the pictures.

Still, Chief Long had offered Trevor any support she could provide, all the same, knowing he was doing the right thing by diving in headlong on his own. He was an experienced investigator, and as a former Deputy US Marshal, he had searched for fugitives. He almost wished that Jennifer was a criminal on the run. He might find her faster that way.

His heart palpitated, and he drew in a few calming breaths.

"Trevor?"

"I guess that depends on who you ask."

"I'm asking you."

"It's still open. But I'm branching out on my own."

"I don't blame you."

The plane angled severely to the right as it swooped out of the mountains and followed the water. Nausea roiled in his gut. His chest tightened, making it hard to breathe.

He couldn't let Carrie see what a wimp he was.

"You okay?" she asked. "You look a little green."

"I'll be okay. Just try to fly steady."

"No such thing. The weather is always changing."

As if proving her point, she banked left and hit turbulence.

"You did that on purpose."

Her musical laugh almost made him smile.

"How long does it take to get to Mountain Cove?"

"Twenty minutes."

Trevor's body was numb from the vibration—or maybe it was all in his head. He focused on the stunning landscape, which was grand enough to take his mind off the flight for half the time.

The other half he thought about his sister. She wouldn't be the first photographer who'd caught something on camera that put lives in danger. If she'd endangered herself with her pictures, she hadn't included the incriminating photographs in this stack.

What are you trying to tell me, Jennifer?

"We're in the Lynn Canal now," Carrie said.

He glanced down at the water. "Glad you know where you're going."

He spotted a cruise ship along the Alaska Marine Highway. People taking time to spend with loved ones, exploring God's creation and the beauty of this part of the world. If only he could be on a cruise ship right now, with his sister by his side taking her pictures that way. Why hadn't he suggested a cruise? He pulled out the images again and discovered he hadn't shown them all to Carrie.

"We're landing soon," Carrie said. "Can you hold your cookies a bit longer?"

She wasn't going to let it go, was she? "I'm good."

The small town along the Inside Passage came into view, and Carrie skillfully landed on the water.

Trevor breathed easier now, but he still held on tight as she steered the plane across the blue depths and then slowed on approach to the seaplane dock. "This is my stop. I'll pick up the medication at the hangar. If you're going in to town to ask questions about your sister, make it quick."

Though they hadn't reached the dock yet, Carrie shut off the engine and let the plane simply float in. Before the plane got to the pier, she removed her headset and unbuckled. At the dock, she quickly opened the door and hopped out to secure the plane.

Perfect timing. Now, *that* took some skill.

Trevor scrambled out too and hopped over the pontoons onto the dock.

He held up one of the pictures—this one mostly treetops—to show her. "Do you know where this is?"

"You didn't show me that before."

"It was stuck in the envelope. I didn't see it. You know the place?"

She took the photograph and studied it. "There's not enough here to distinguish the location. It looks like the rest of the millions of acres of Tongass National Forest."

"But if you look close, you can see some kind of building beneath the canopy."

She slowly shook her head, then thrust the picture back at him. "I can't tell. I'm sorry. Maybe you'll learn something from the other photographs that will lead you to *this* place. Was the picture the last in the stack?"

"Yes. I thought the order might mean something too." *Glad I'm not the only one.*

She started walking toward a large aluminum hangar at the end of the dock.

Trevor kept pace with her. "In that last photograph, the building in the woods, what could it be?"

"How should I know? It could be someone's shop. Or a business or operation of some kind."

"You're right. I'm impatient. If this is the last picture, then I want to start there."

She turned to him, her hands in her jacket, that guarded look in her eyes again. "While we're here, you should ask around about her before we move on. And if I were you, I'd be discreet. I wouldn't show the pictures she took in town."

"Don't worry about me." He already knew there was a danger element, and he would be watching for any reaction to his questions about Jennifer.

They continued walking, and he tucked the pictures away in his jacket.

"The town square is a few hundred yards ahead," Carrie said.

He needed to think like Jennifer. Where would she go if she were here?

Walking beside Carrie, he couldn't help but notice she had a slight limp, favoring her left foot.

Interesting. He would like to know what had caused the injury. Did it have anything to do with how guarded she was behind her warm demeanor?

Get a grip. Her life was none of his business.

He was here in Alaska for one reason. One mission.

To find Jennifer.

SIX

Stay on course.

Easy enough to do while flying, but not so easy with the rugged detective taking up space in her plane. He seemed restrained, holding back his rough-and-tumble side. His desperation nearly broke her heart.

But she no longer had a heart, so how was that possible after only a few hours with him? She didn't have the answer. All she knew was that he stepped into the office last night and a powerful longing surged through her.

And she knew better.

She'd let a dark, handsome alpha male with charisma draw her in once before, and she learned her lesson. One lesson was enough. She hadn't seen through to the deepest part of his heart to the lurking darkness.

The shadows in his soul.

And Detective Trevor West?

What do I know about him?

Nothing.

She met him last night. End of story. But something about his utter devotion and complete determination to find his sister pounded against the fortress of her heart. Okay, so maybe she still had one, but she thought she'd built a solid rock wall fifty feet thick and a hundred feet tall around what was left of her broken, shattered soul.

Her heart still ached, still hurt if she let her thoughts go back.

But I survived.

Carrie let herself breathe.

And God is with me.

That was all that mattered. And her issues of the heart shouldn't interfere with her helping the guy as much as she could. She whirled around to find that he was no longer walking with her. Instead, he'd moved to stand at the water's edge.

What was he doing?

I shouldn't. I really shouldn't.

But she made her way to the water to join him. His back was to her as he looked out over the pristine flowing Lynn Canal. A cruise ship headed north, and a ferry south. She took in his profile. His contemplative, brooding expression concerned her.

"Look. I'm sorry I can't help you more, but I'll think about that picture and see if I can figure out where it was taken. That's all I can do." True enough, but she was probably giving him false hope.

"I'll take what I can get." His voice sounded gruff. Tight. He briefly glanced at her, his blue eyes flashing. "How long have you lived in Alaska?"

Carrie would give him her usual spiel. She glanced at her watch. If this was how he wanted to spend the time she'd given him, that was fine with her. "About a decade."

"What's your story?"

"You already asked me that."

"Don't forget, I'm a detective. I don't give up so easily." Then he gave her a wry grin.

She didn't miss the deep sadness behind his gaze. "Well, then.

Let's just say I hope you never have a reason to investigate me." Asking questions about her "story" was bad enough.

"Why? Got something to hide?"

"Don't we all?" She smiled. *Okay. Am I flirting? Because I better not be flirting.*

"Indeed." His serious expression again. "Where were you before you came here?"

This line of conversation was starting to feel intrusive, but really, his question was the usual conversation starter, if a passenger wanted conversation.

"I'm not great at small talk. I usually deliver stuff and things and a select few passengers." The stuff and things didn't ask questions. *Thanks a lot, Chief Long.*

Where was I before Alaska? Carrie fought the need to close her eyes, as if that would block out the images of baobab and acacia trees, the sunrise on the Indian Ocean. The sheer beauty of it could overwhelm her.

"You okay?"

Of course he'd noticed her brief mental expedition. His words brought her back to the moment—to the here and now—the mountains and deep blues and emerald greens of Alaska.

"I'm fine."

"Were you in the Air Force?"

Wow. He really didn't give up, did he?

Don't make me regret helping you!

"No. How about you? What did you do with the Marshals? Did you work with people in witness protection?"

"WITSEC?" He cleared his throat. "No. I tracked fugitives. I found people."

The hairs on the back of her neck and arms lifted. She didn't know why exactly. An awkward chuckle escaped. She wasn't a fugitive. But neither did she want to be found.

"Um, listen. I need to pick up the supplies. If you're going to ask if anyone has seen Jennifer, you'd better get busy. Come on." She gestured for him to follow as she walked toward the hangar and town.

He joined her, though she could tell something still bothered him.

"Look, can I be honest?" he asked.

What a strange question. "Well, I would hope you're always honest."

"It's a figure of speech. I'm telling you what I haven't told anyone."

Uh-oh. Carrie did not want to get pulled in too deep into his life. His problems.

"I'm not sure I want your honesty." She angled to catch his reaction.

"That's fair." Trevor appeared dejected, his blue eyes darkening.

The very least she could do was listen. "Okay. I'm listening. Be honest with me."

But you're not going to change my mind.

"I mentioned earlier that it's been over a year since Jennifer went missing. Before she did, she trusted a friend to pass information to me in case something happened to her. But her friend died before she could pass it on, and I didn't get this information until this week." He held her gaze, long and hard.

Carrie felt the pain in his voice—he feared he was too late to save her. "I'm so sorry this happened. I don't understand, though. You're a detective. Why didn't your sister give *you* the pictures instead, with that same message? In case something happened."

"She knew I would try to stop her."

"Stop her from what?"

"She was an *amateur* photographer. I thought maybe she'd taken a picture of criminal activity, but if she did, then she didn't include that photograph."

Carrie paused. They were almost to town anyway. He could

walk the rest of the way, and she could check in at the hangar. "People go missing in Alaska for a thousand reasons, but you're thinking that she didn't go for a hike and get lost. That someone might be responsible."

"Yes. It's the worst-case scenario, frankly, but I have to strongly consider that possibility."

Carrie drew in a shuddering breath. She knew who the bad guy was in her life. The monster under the bed. Chances were low that she'd ever run into another one. But Trevor was still trying to discover who harmed his sister.

"So what more, Trevor?"

He shrugged. "I really don't know, except she was a geologist for EchoGlobal in Montana."

"And she came to Alaska to take pictures?"

"I don't know if that's why or if that's the only reason, but that's what she told me. She took leave from her job and never came back to Montana. I have nothing real to go on here but a hunch. I'm searching for something, anything that could help me find her. And I was kind of hoping that—"

"That I would go with you today and agree to see it through? Be honest." After all, he'd brought it up.

Slowly nodding, he maintained eye contact—those blue eyes couldn't pull harder on her heartstrings. And she got it. She also had a gut-wrenching feeling he hoped to find Jennifer alive. Stranger things had happened. After all, Carrie had survived a two-hundred-foot fall from a cargo plane without a parachute.

"It's my turn to be honest. I don't have the time to help you. I told you I could give you a day and a half. I shouldn't have agreed to even that. I'm sorry, Trevor. I need to get these medical supplies, and we need to get going."

She growled inside at Isaac for encouraging her to do this, though he really hadn't said a word. Detective West was trying to pull her in deeper and sway her moral compass, whatever. He should have hired someone else. But what was done was done. Time to cut the heartstrings before she got too invested, too emotionally connected with her already twisted-up heart.

"Meet me back here"—she glanced at her watch and frowned—"in half an hour. You have my cell number if you need me."

Carrie left Trevor to his business in town, and she entered the hangar. Inside she found Jordan Peterson, who always handed off supplies, in the office. Jordan was in his late forties, and silver threaded his thick brown beard and temples. He had big, muscular arms but a paunch too. So just a big guy who maybe didn't work out his core.

"Hey, Jordy." She plodded to the counter. "You got something for me?"

She smiled, expecting him to hand off the box of medical supplies that were kept locked away.

Jordy turned around empty-handed and shook his head. "Not yet."

Carrie blinked a few times, trying to comprehend this new development. "What do you mean? I'm on a schedule."

"We're all on a schedule. The Air Alaska flight was delayed."

"But why?" She shook her head as she went through Flight 63's flight plan in her head—starting in Seattle, stopping in Ketchikan, Wrangell, Petersburg, and Juneau before ending in Anchorage.

"I couldn't tell you," he said.

"This is not good." She turned from the counter and chewed on her lip. She'd need to let the Benallys know she'd be delayed.

"You're not alone, Carrie. Every stop will be late today. People aren't gonna be happy. It's not like this hasn't happened before. We have to be flexible."

"I'm sure Jasper isn't happy either." This would delay his mail delivery. Jasper Reed delivered both the mail *and* packages, and Carrie needed only the medical supplies from him to take to the Benallys.

Carrie bunched up her lips and crossed her arms. She blew out a heavy sigh. This wasn't Jordy's fault. But she'd tacked onto her day taking Trevor south to those regions his sister had photographed.

"What's the ETA?"

He shrugged. "Jasper's hoping he'll be here by eleven o'clock."

"Eleven? That's four hours!"

"I might not look smart, but I can tell time, add and subtract."

"Call me if he gets here early. I'll be back."

"I never doubted it." He sent her off with a grin.

She headed for the exit. Did she have time to fly Trevor around to look at bread crumbs? Flying over was one thing, but he really needed to stop if he was going to learn anything. Chief Long had directed him to her because she'd traveled extensively in this region. Maybe all she needed to do was inform him what she knew about each picture. Why hadn't she thought of that before? Except, there was the matter of that last picture she couldn't place, and he might still need her help for that.

Of course her last run for ten days would have to be delayed.

She was about to call Trevor when she spotted a voice mail *and* a text from him. The text directed her to listen to his voice mail.

"I found another pilot who says he knows where this last picture was taken. I appreciate all you've done for me. I hope there are no hard feelings."

She stared at her cell. How could he have found someone else so fast? She hadn't realized he was even looking. Regardless, there was no way anyone could know where that picture was taken. The guy had to be conning Trevor.

The good news was, just like that, she was off the hook.

She should be relieved. Instead, she stomped her foot. Pursed her lips. Maybe she didn't want to be off the hook.

Way to get me curious about your lost sister and then toss me aside.

She didn't have time to get involved, and she had gone out of her way to make sure he knew her help would be limited. So why did this disturb her so much? She could think on it while she got a cup of coffee at Whale of a Tail Café. She loved Anik's blueberry scones. Maybe Flight 63 would come in early. Jasper would get here sooner. She found a booth by the window and nodded to a man sitting a few tables down, looking at his iPad. He happened to glance up at her at the same time. She'd seen him before.

He had a Vandyke beard, a goatee with a mustache. Basically, he was Tony Stark, only with a shaved head—and he creeped her out. She wasn't sure why. Maybe it was his cold eyes.

With a coffee and scone before her, she looked through emails on her cell, searched the internet for things to do in Dallas, where she planned to meet Kaya, until finally, she grew tired of trying to ignore her instincts.

Something was terribly wrong with Isaac. He was off. He hadn't shared what he wanted to talk to her about last night or this morning before she left. And something was off with Trevor too. That situation also unsettled her, even though he'd moved on to another pilot.

It's none of my business.

What a wasted day. Why did she have to meet Trevor West? He was the first man in forever who had made her stop and look. She could almost be angry at him because he'd made her pause and think about the fact that she hadn't wanted a man in her life. But Trevor made her think that maybe, just maybe, she might. Of course. *Of course* their paths had crossed briefly. Here one minute and gone the next.

Served her right.

When she got the call that Jasper had landed, Carrie exited the coffee shop, noting that Vandyke was long gone. Back at the dock, she made her way to her plane, holding the small box of medical supplies under her arm and feeling a smidge of disappointment that she wouldn't see Mr. Blue Eyes again.

At least not today.

She almost stumbled when she spotted Vandyke walking up the boardwalk toward her, as if coming from a plane. He must be a pilot too. Still, she didn't feel comfortable as she walked past him. She sensed the sudden shift in the air but was too late to react when a hand covered her mouth. A bulky bicep wrapped around her, pinning her arms. She dropped the box and screamed, but the sound was muffled beneath his hand.

She opened her mouth and bit down with every intention of taking a chunk. He loosened his grip enough so that she could escape, then she turned and punched him in the nose. Blood spurted, and he covered his face. She grabbed her package and raced to her plane without looking back.

The boardwalk planks pounded behind her.

He was coming.

She wouldn't be able to release the mooring and get in the air fast enough to get away from him. Heart pounding, she considered her next move.

"Hey, what are you doing, man?" a deep male voice demanded.

"Mind your own business." Vandyke?

She reached for the rope to release the plane and risked a glance behind her. A man was facing off with Vandyke. Someone had intervened on her behalf and was now standing between her and her would-be abductor.

Please, don't get hurt. But I have to get out of here.

Carrie held up her cell and took a picture. Vandyke glared at her, then turned around and hiked up the boardwalk. The guy who'd defended her was now on his cell. Calling the police?

"Thanks for what you did!" she called.

Talking on his cell, he looked at her like he was confused about her actions.

She climbed into her plane. "I have to go. I have to deliver these supplies."

She didn't have time to talk to the police and would tell Chief Long. She'd gotten the guy's picture too. The faster she escaped, the better. She went through the simplest preflight check possible before starting the engine and maneuvering away from the dock.

Heart pounding, she couldn't be happier to be in the air once again. Who was that guy? She hadn't been so shaken since . . .

Don't go there.

But her hands, her whole body, shook as she tried to get her bearings and deliver the supplies. If Trevor had been with her, maybe Vandyke wouldn't have been so bold. No. She'd taken care of herself and gotten free. She didn't need Detective Blue Eyes to protect her—or anyone to protect her. But someone had followed her and grabbed her in broad daylight.

A sour feeling festered inside.

At least she wouldn't have to think about giving Trevor flight time tomorrow since he'd found someone else, although she had a feeling that someone was trying to dupe him. But he was a detective. Let him fend for himself. After making her delivery, she could pack her bags and relax because she was getting out of Dodge and going to Texas.

That is, after she figured out what Isaac was keeping from her and might have been going to tell her before she left this morning. She'd tried to get it out of him, but instead he grew angry and short. Not the Isaac she'd known forever. Were they behind on the bills? What? Maybe that was it. Their business was failing.

After the delivery to the Benallys at Windfall Lake, she flew straight for Shadow Gap. She tried to contact Isaac several times, but he must have had the radio blaring or the fan running—something to prevent him from answering.

It was late in the day, though the dark of night never truly came this time of year, by the time she swooped up the Goldrock River, then skated across the water and slowed next to the dock. Carrie hopped out and secured the plane. The hangar door was open. Normal.

Only Isaac wasn't standing there, waiting. Smiling. Ready with an encouraging word or an apology for snapping at her, or to finally share what he'd been planning to tell her.

Oh. Maybe he was retiring. He was quitting on her. Her stomach dropped to her feet. Then she heard Koda barking from inside somewhere. Koda was locked in the office?

The hangar was completely dark. If Isaac had gone home, he never would have left the door open, though they didn't have anything to worry about out here except wildlife straying inside. That was reason enough to close shop.

Chills crawled over her. She calmed her pounding heart and stepped into the dark hangar.

"Isaac?"

Koda's barking grew more frantic. That sound brought with it the memory of Elias lying in his bed near death and sent her pulse racing.

"Isaac?" His name was a whispered croak on her lips.

Carrie reached over and felt around the wall until she found the switch and turned on the lights. The florescent tubes flickered and buzzed from the ceiling, and she let her eyes adjust to the sudden brightness. At least she could see that monsters weren't lurking in the darkness waiting for her.

The place was pristine again. So Isaac had cleaned up and apparently left for the day. No. That couldn't be right. He always waited here for her.

She stepped into the hangar, but the sense of wrongness made her wary.

Her blood curdled at what she saw.

SEVEN

Trevor slammed the door behind him as he entered his room at the small Shadow Gap motel—Eagle something. Eagle Nest. Eagle's Bluff. That was it.

He ran his hand down his scruffy jaw.

I need a shave.

A shower.

A vacation.

And not necessarily in that order.

But Jennifer came first.

He'd barely slept since arriving in Shadow Gap. But he didn't have to be wide awake to know that the pilot he'd hired, Trapper McAllen, had taken him for the proverbial ride—he'd been conned. He shouldn't have dumped Carrie James so quickly. At least she'd been honest with him. Honesty was a quality in short supply these days, and he'd been a fool to trust someone else, just because Trapper had given him hope. The guy took advantage of Trevor's desperation. However, Trevor shouldn't have been so trusting. So gullible.

He wouldn't have even thought about hiring a bush pilot, except Chief Long recommended Carrie. Now he realized, too late, he should have stuck with her. But he couldn't go back and ask her for help again. She was halfway out the door on a ten-day vacation when he caught her the first time.

This day had cost him several hundred dollars. Money and time wasted. He was no closer to finding Jennifer or learning what happened to her.

He slumped onto the edge of the squeaky mattress. *God, is she still alive out there? Help me find her.*

He closed his eyes, not wanting to say the next words. *No matter what I find. Help me bring her justice.*

He got up and paced the small space, walking around both sides of the bed when what he really wanted was to kick something. Punch something.

Trapper had flown him around all right. Jennifer took the photographs in May—at least he thought she did—and the ground was still frozen in some places, but spring breakup was well in process. Maybe that was all the difference it took, and he couldn't tell what he was looking at. At least Carrie had known the landmarks, or village marks, whatever marks were required to identify a place.

And even if he hadn't blown it, she was leaving and couldn't give him the time to investigate. He at least should have gotten the locations from her, and he could take it from there. Why hadn't either of them thought about that?

With at least that information, he could find his way there and explore, investigate, as long as he wanted. One thing Trapper said was helpful. He mentioned Jennifer's guide. Trevor thought she'd taken a ferry or hired a pilot, but he hadn't considered she might have hired a guide.

I need to focus on this like it's an investigation into someone else's missing sister.

He needed to disengage himself emotionally. Only problem was, Trevor wasn't entirely sure that was possible.

How could it be?

He shrugged off the self-recriminations and focused. Trevor needed to find out who took Jennifer out and about to grab these photographs. In Alaska, that stack of choices had to be a mile high. He couldn't ask Monica because she was also dead, killed by a foreigner and lost under an avalanche until her body was discovered months later. Coincidence? Related? Would the ABI's MCU—major crimes unit—look into that aspect of her death and Jennifer's disappearance once they got the news that Monica and Jennifer were connected?

That aside, short of finding the guide, he was stuck trudging the path his sister had walked, following the trail she left—intentionally?—and he was slowly sinking in the mud. He was no closer to finding out what happened to her, and with his training and experience, this was unacceptable. He had failed himself.

After he'd failed Jennifer.

He moved to the window and stared out at the town below, the mountains in the distance overshadowing the river—Carrie James's hangar was at the river. In the middle of his personal nightmare, he thought of her deep-green haunted eyes. He pictured her trying to hide her limp and remembered her kindness.

She'd reached out to him, connected, there on the water at Mountain Cove. He'd seen in her eyes that she really wanted to assist him, but there wasn't much more she could do. A small part of him wanted to help her too—but he didn't know with what. Nor had she asked.

She wouldn't want that from him anyway. Was he so desperate to redeem the loss of his sister that he wanted to help Carrie, a woman who had the same haunted eyes as Jennifer?

He pulled the manila folder out of his pocket and stared at it. Jennifer had held this same envelope in her hands, thinking of him when she stuck the photographs inside. She'd coerced someone—the unknown guide?—to go with her to secure a safe deposit box.

Opening up the envelope, he reached inside to take another look at the photographs.

Why did you leave me these—

His stomach lurched.

The photographs were gone.

He dug around and looked deep inside, but they weren't there. Did he drop them? He glanced around the floor, the bed, under the bed. The entrance. The photographs falling out of the folded envelope in his jacket didn't make sense anyway.

Trapper McAllen.

Heart pounding, Trevor punched the wall—not hard enough to put a hole in it but enough that he flinched in pain.

The pilot never gave him back the photographs. He'd handed back the envelope and Trevor had assumed, he'd trusted, that the photographs were inside. The walls shifted around him, and he eased into the lone chair.

How could I have lost the clues Jennifer sent me? He had planned to give the photographs to the secretary at the PD to make copies for the ABI before he left the offices, but he'd been too distracted. Too rushed.

As for Trapper McAllen—he'd called the guy at least once. He tried the man's number again and it went to voice mail. Trevor left a message with details and specifics just short of a threat—he needed those photographs. He had to dial down the stress or he would explode. He lay down on the bed, crossing his arms behind his head. Closed his eyes.

Jennifer—why didn't you just call me? Tell me?

That would have saved him so much trouble, and in fact, it could have prevented her disappearance altogether. With everything she'd been through—an abusive husband who sent her running—why did she take the risk here in Alaska?

What if her ex—Drake Warner—was involved? He was questioned when she disappeared and was working in oil down in Texas. Had alibis. If Trevor saw him in Alaska, caught wind that Drake had come here for anything at all, he would track him down. Considering that Drake worked in the oil industry, it wasn't a stretch to believe he could be in Alaska. But the guy had gotten married again. Creep. Too bad no one warned his new wife about his abusive habits.

Enough lying around. He had to do something. He bolted from the bed and moved to the laptop on the desk. After a quick internet search on bush pilots, he found the small group Trapper flew for—McAllen Air. Right. That made sense. Despite the name, the website made it appear that it wasn't a one-man operation. Maybe he couldn't get Trapper on the phone, but he could talk to someone else and get his photographs back. Trevor called the main number. At 9:00 p.m., he expected to get an answering machine, voice mail, something, but a woman answered.

Without taking a breath, he explained what had happened and what he needed, slowly stopping his flow of words when he realized she was sobbing.

Then she screamed at him. "Trapper is dead. He died in a plane crash today, you idiot."

She ended the call.

Trevor stared at his cell.

He died in a plane crash? Trevor's hands shook, and he dropped his cell. It bounced and landed under the bed.

Grief hit him in the chest. He'd had nothing but ill thoughts and anger toward the guy, and this whole time he was already dead? Already facing his Maker?

Trevor had been in that plane today—

Life was fleeting.

Is this even where you want me, God? I don't know anymore. I just don't know.

He needed fresh air, after all. Trevor left his room and exited the motel. A few stores remained open, along with the Rabid Raccoon and the Lively Moose. He kept his head down, ignoring everyone he passed. He couldn't face another human being at this moment.

God, I need peace. To get that, I need to know what happened to Jennifer.

Carrie James had seen the pictures. She could take him.

He would have to get down on his knees and beg. He got in his rental truck and headed out of town toward the airstrip, with no clue if she was already back now and asleep in her bed or if he would find the hangar wide open as he'd found it before.

Fresh relief washed through him, along with a sliver of hope when he saw the lights at the hangar were on.

He drove up. Parked. And took a few breaths to gather his nerve. Hopelessness surged inside—Carrie wasn't going to give up her vacation to help him. Was he an idiot?

Yes. A desperate idiot.

A strange noise drew his attention. The dog whined from somewhere, along with another sound. The hairs on the back of his neck lifted.

Trevor reached for his Beretta, held it ready, and stepped inside the hangar.

Shock rolled through him.

Crimson smudged Carrie's face as she sat on the floor, cradling Isaac, rocking him back and forth. Blood pooled on the floor beneath the man.

A millisecond passed before Trevor could act. Carrie's mournful cries cut through his soul, and instinct took over.

He rushed forward, letting his gaze search the hangar, but he saw no one else inside. Putting his gun away, he dropped to his knees next to her. "Carrie . . . Oh, honey . . ." Grief twisted his insides. "What happened?"

But her mournful cries wouldn't allow an answer.

Trevor pressed his finger against Isaac's carotid artery to confirm what he already knew was true, then he closed the man's unseeing eyes. Now, how did he help Carrie?

He slowly tried to extricate Isaac from her.

"No, no! Get away from me!" She resisted his efforts and pulled the body back to her as if unwilling to accept his death.

"Come on, Carrie, he's gone," Trevor whispered, hating the words. Hating that he had to be the one to say them.

Trying again, he gently shifted her away from Isaac and took her into his arms. Pressed her face into his shoulder and moved them both a few inches from Isaac's body. Against Trevor's chest, she shuddered and sobbed, her cries ripping his soul.

Oh, God, please, please wrap her in peace that only you can give.

He tried to console her, knowing his efforts would fail. "I've got you, Carrie. I've got you."

EIGHT

Carrie slumped in the chair in the office.

Her body numb.

Her soul inconsolable.

Hadn't she cried enough tears in this lifetime? The door was closed, but she knew Autumn's officers were looking around and the body was being prepared to transport to the coroner's office.

Trevor had held her. Comforted her. She hadn't had the presence of mind to refuse his comfort. She got blood all over him, but he didn't care. He just got down on the floor and into her mess with her.

Into Isaac's tragedy.

The detective was out in the hangar with Autumn's other officers. He and Autumn brought Carrie into the office, and then Trevor left and closed the door behind him. She assumed that was so she wouldn't have to look at Isaac's body. The detective's brilliant blue eyes had snagged hers and, in that moment, she saw his pain and sincere concern.

She couldn't process what she saw in Trevor's gaze any more than she could comprehend that Isaac was dead. Absently, she ran her fingers through Koda's fur, slowly realizing that her actions had coated his white fur with smudges of red.

Autumn remained in the small office with her, standing against the wall. Carrie was only a few years older than Chief Long, and they'd become familiar acquaintances like everyone in this town, but their relationship was not personal enough that she would call the woman a close friend. Regardless, in Shadow Gap, people looked out for each other and that's all that mattered.

Carrie swiped at the new flood of tears. "I don't understand."

"Accidents happen, Carrie."

She shook her head. "Not to Isaac. His motto was 'safety first.' Tell me how a guy with that attitude could trip and hit his head on a rolling ladder? He knew better. The ladder wasn't even where it should be."

Autumn studied her, lifted her shoulder. "He could have been putting things away, and that's when he tripped over the compressor hose."

"Stretched across the floor like that? Nowhere near the air tools?" She blinked up at Autumn who'd already taken her statement. "What if this wasn't an accident?"

"Are you suggesting foul play?"

"I mean, maybe he was murdered." She croaked out the words, hating the sound.

The police chief arched a brow, her strange mismatching eyes searing through Carrie. "What would make you think that?"

With the shock of Isaac's death, she had completely forgotten about earlier today, but the memories rushed through her again.

"When I was in Mountain Cove today, a man followed me. He was in the Whale of a Tail Café and then at the seaplane dock. I didn't think a lot about it. But then he grabbed me from behind." Her voice shook.

"It's okay. Just take your time, Carrie. Tell me what happened."

"I bit his hand and then punched him in the nose. He released me, and I ran to the plane. I wouldn't have had time to get away if a stranger hadn't stepped in. Vandyke ran off."

"You know who grabbed you?"

"Not his name. In my head I called him Vandyke because he had one of those beards. And he reminded me of Tony Stark, only he was bald too. Evil, bald, and ripped. I can't believe I escaped, honestly." Wait.

She fished her cell out of her pocket and found the image, then handed it over to Autumn. "That's him. Maybe the stranger got a video of the attack. I don't know."

"Send that to my phone."

Carrie already had Autumn's number and forwarded the image.

Staring at her cell, Autumn nodded when it dinged. "Got it. Okay, what happened next? Did you call the police?"

"I think the stranger who helped me did, but I took off. I was already late delivering medical supplies, and I needed to get back. I guess I was worried about Isaac."

"I'll contact the Mountain Cove PD and see if they apprehended him."

"But now I'm here and Isaac's gone. I don't know, Autumn. I have a bad feeling about this. Isaac was big on safety, so I can't see him being so careless. Something had been bothering him. He said that we needed to talk when I got back, and it sounded important, but I'll never know what he wanted to say. Maybe the man who grabbed me is connected. You have to look into this."

The chief said nothing for a good long while. She probably thought Carrie was simply grasping at straws—anything to make sense of what happened. But even then, it didn't make sense.

"Of course I'll look into it. Angie and Craig are documenting everything now. We'll learn more once the ME informs us," Autumn said. "But do you have any idea who would want to murder him?"

"No. It's . . . I don't know. Everyone loved him."

"But you spent a lot of your day everywhere but here."

"Ask his friends. He was close to Hank, Otis, and Sandford. That group of men. Mostly he minded his own business."

Autumn pursed her lips, understanding in her eyes. "You know bad things happen in life."

The words stung, and Carrie squeezed her eyes shut. When the chief crouched in front of her, she opened her eyes, even though she didn't want to face Autumn right now.

Regret swam in her gaze. "I'm sorry, Carrie. I shouldn't have sounded so insensitive. I'll do what I can to learn what happened, but if we find that it was an accident, you have to accept that, okay?"

Autumn stopped short of the usual platitudes.

Everything happens for a reason. It's not ours to ask why.

None of that worked for Carrie, but still, she sensed that Autumn was only saying what she believed Carrie wanted to hear.

"I don't know." Carrie pressed her hands to her face, her shoulders rocking with grief, but this time no tears.

Autumn stood and gently squeezed Carrie's shoulder. "I don't want you to stay here alone tonight. You can stay with Dad and me, or at the Lively Moose."

Autumn's grandparents' place.

"I want to stay here." Where Isaac's words, his essence, could echo off the hangar walls. "And remember. Because I know when I come back to this empty hull of a place, empty without Isaac, he'll be gone for good."

And that was something she'd have to accept before she was ready.

"If you're right and he was murdered, this isn't a safe place. Plus, it would be a crime scene. You can't stay here."

"You don't believe he was murdered."

"You brought it up. I haven't ruled it out. There's the matter of the man who tried to abduct you. You have my promise that I'll investigate, and if there's a connection, I'll find it. But in the meantime, I want you some place safe."

"I'll grab a few things."

Autumn's fiancé, Grier Young, cracked the door and stuck his head in. "Can we come in?"

After a glance at Carrie for her permission, Autumn waved him in. Grier opened the door all the way and entered the office, followed by Autumn's brother, Nolan Long, an Alaska State Trooper. Last year Nolan was posted in the Shadow Gap region as their official Alaska State Trooper, after the budget was amended to reinstate the post because of the increased criminal activity.

Grier approached the chief. "Hey." His voice was gentle, and he almost reached for her but stopped or caught himself. "Angie told me where to find you."

Nolan looked between Autumn and Carrie. "Anything I can do?"

Autumn practically whispered, but it wasn't like Carrie couldn't hear. "Help me get Carrie situated."

"Carrie situated." The words ricocheted in her mind and heart, reminding her of what seemed like another lifetime when Isaac whispered similar words to the doctor in a Zhugandia hospital.

"Please, save her."

The doctor had merely said, in Swahili, *"I make no promises."*

And now ten years later, Isaac was the one to die. Carrie was the one left behind. What would she do without Isaac? He'd been her anchor. Her refuge.

Dressed in his typical old green Army jacket and a knit cap over his long, greasy hair, Hank Duncan, one of Isaac's favorite people and the local cryptozoologist, stepped inside and crowded the office space. Grief etched deep lines in Hank's already weathered face. He couldn't seem to speak for the tears clogging his throat.

He knelt to love on Koda. "Hank was supposed to bring Koda by the cabin today. He never showed."

"I'd like to talk to you more," Autumn said. "Could you go ahead and take the dog, Hank? I'll be by in the morning."

Hank stood, his lips pressed into a thin line. "I'll see you then." He glanced around the clean, organized office. "Do you have a leash?"

Carrie shrugged. "No."

"That's okay. Come on, boy, I've got a treat for you." Hank tugged a hot dog from his pocket and lured Koda away.

The man had come prepared. The sight could almost make Carrie laugh.

"Could someone also check and see how Elias is doing?" Carrie asked.

"We'll take care of everything," Autumn said. "I spoke with Elias this afternoon. We're praying he'll be back on both feet in no time. I won't sugarcoat it. He's still fighting to keep his leg."

The numbness returned. "Good to know." Carrie felt like she was shrinking into herself, and the walls were closing in and suffocating her. She tried to suck in air, but the oxygen seemed thin in the stuffy and overcrowded room.

"Come on, Carrie," Autumn said, gently urging her to stand.

"I'm okay. I've got this." But she stumbled. Autumn and Nolan caught her, steadied her.

"You don't have to be so strong all the time. Let your friends take care of you," Autumn said. "You've had a big shock today."

No. Isaac was the one who'd had a shock. And she trusted no one like she'd trusted Isaac.

I'm stronger than this. She shrugged free of the helping arms.

"I'll help you gather your things upstairs. We've already

checked your apartment," Autumn said. "Then Nolan will take you to town. Did you decide where you want to stay?"

"Yes."

Half an hour later, she found herself settled in an upstairs guest room at Autumn and Nolan's grandparents' place—the Lively Moose. The room was comfy, and the place was peaceful, and she felt safe. The establishment wasn't a lodge, but space was available under certain circumstances.

Carrie had become one of those "certain circumstances."

NINE

A hand covered her mouth. Strong arms gripped her so she couldn't breathe and dragged her deeper into the darkness. She screamed, but nothing came out. No one could hear her. No one had seen her abduction. She clawed the air, reached for her plane that sat floating in the dock, oblivious to her need to escape.

She was better than this. Stronger than this. After everything she'd been through, some random stranger wasn't going to take her down. She pushed back the panic.

Isaac stood at the end of the pier looking for her. She cried out.

"I'm here, Isaac. I'm here. Help me. Save me." But instead, he climbed into her plane and taxied it across the water, then took off and disappeared on the horizon.

Darkness edged her vision, while bright lights flashed. She was going to die this time.

Carrie reached down inside her—one last time—and found the strength she needed. She kicked the abductor's shin and stomped on his foot. When his grip loosened enough, she butted his head. He cried out in pain, and she escaped his grip. Ran as fast as she could. But Isaac had left her without a way to escape. She didn't turn back to see who had taken her. She had to put distance between her and her abductor. But she heard the ground pounding behind her. He was closing in.

After hopping into a small V-boat, she started the engine and steered away from the dock. She turned to see the man who'd grabbed her as he reached the slip where the boat had been moored.

Darius?

Her heart ricocheted.

Carrie sat up, gulping air until her hammering heart finally calmed. She sat on the edge of the bed and leaned over. Two days ago, Isaac died. She couldn't lie around or stay curled in a ball—at least not forever. And now she was twisting everything up in her dreams. Vandyke had grabbed her. Not Darius.

Isaac had made sure they relocated to the opposite side of the world and would have no interactions with the man. He'd let others believe she'd died that day.

To keep her safe.

She crawled back into bed and tried to push the bad dream out of her thoughts. She drifted in and out of a restless sleep.

When you pass through the waters, I will be with you.

When you pass through the waters, I will be with you.

No matter how many times she repeated the words, she was having trouble believing them tonight. She totally felt separated from God.

She rolled over and spotted an old Bible on the side table. She sat up and turned on the lamp, which offered soft lighting. Perfect. She flipped the Bible open to what had to be a much sought-after verse since it fell right open to that spot.

"When you pass through the waters, I will be with you; and when you pass through the rivers, they will not sweep over you. When you walk through the fire, you will not be burned; the flames will not set you ablaze. Isaiah 43:2."

"Of course," she said under her breath.

I know you're trying to reach me, Lord.

But reading the Bible tonight was an exercise in futility. Instead of falling asleep, she was more energized.

She had a business to run. And sadly, a funeral to plan—but according to Autumn, not until the ME released the body. Isaac had no family, but his funeral would include many friends.

As for the business, Isaac had been the one to manage everything. She flew the planes. At least she had ten days off to figure out why Isaac was dead. Why her world had been turned upside down. She couldn't go see Kaya in Texas now. She'd call her old friend and talk to her about it. She could go later. Worst case—or best case, she wasn't sure—she would go back to Africa and see Kaya when she finished her tour with the a capella group.

She closed the Bible and set it back on the side table.

She knew what she had to do. She had to learn the truth about why he was killed. So she got dressed. The sun would be up soon, so it didn't feel like she was sneaking out in the middle of the night. Even though it was early, she still found Ike Lively downstairs making breakfast sandwiches.

"You're up at the crack of dawn." He slapped slices of ham over opened buns.

She eyed the sandwiches. "Those sure look good."

"People like to grab 'em before they head out. Grab'n Go is what I call 'em."

"Would you have time to take me back to the hangar?"

Tall, with silver hair, he laid the top buns on all the sandwiches, then looked at her, a glimmer of concern in his eyes. "I know my granddaughter wanted you to get some rest before you went back. Maybe stay longer. But I see in your eyes you're determined. I would be too. I'll take you up the road. Give me five minutes to wrap these up, then I'll grab my keys."

Twenty minutes later, Carrie stood next to Ike's truck parked at the hangar.

"I thought there'd at least be crime scene tape." She sagged. Chief Long hadn't taken her seriously.

"There was. It's gone now," he said through the driver's-side window. "She told me late last night that she released the scene. Otherwise, I wouldn't have brought you here." He winked.

Right. Carrie should have known. She glanced through the woods. Did the officers also look at Isaac's cabin?

Ike climbed out of his truck and stood next to her. He scratched his jaw. "I didn't think about the place being isolated like it is, and with a possible crime having been committed, maybe I should take you back."

"No. I'll be fine."

"You got your gun?"

"It's in my bag. I'll be sure to keep it handy."

"Autumn isn't going to be happy I brought you back so soon. But I won't be the one to tell her. I'll leave that up to you."

"I appreciate that, Ike. But I have to come back some time. Might as well be today. Thanks again for letting me stay at the Lively Moose. You're the best."

"I doubt that very much, but I've lived a long time and seen more than my fair share of tragedy. What you do here isn't my business. Do you need any help?"

"Nope. I'll be fine. I just need to think."

"I understand." He walked with her to the door situated next to the wider hangar entrance. "You sure you're okay?"

She wouldn't invite him to go any farther. "I'm good. And if you or Birdy ever need a ride somewhere that requires air travel, it's on me." She looked up at Autumn's grandfather and produced the best smile she could, though she knew her heart wasn't in it.

He pressed his lips into a thin line and nodded. "While that's not necessary, I'll take it. Let me know if you need anything. You have my cell number."

"Yes, thanks."

She waited while he got back in his truck and drove off.

Carrie stood outside and let the sounds of birdsong, insects, and the nearby Goldrock River rush over her. She stepped up to the door and stuck the key into the lock and stopped.

Listened.

Footfalls? Someone hiking through the trees toward the hangar? She marched around the structure and peered at the woods. The trees were much too thick and dark to see if anyone was there.

Get a grip.

She'd need to look at Isaac's cabin too. Maybe she'd find something that would clue her in to what he'd wanted to tell her or who might have had a hand in his death.

Carrie entered the hangar, and the smell of oil, grease, and fuel accosted her. No matter how clean he'd kept the place, those smells remained. After flipping on the fluorescent lights, she opened the office door and turned on the lights in there too. The more light in the place, the better. She passed the Cessna and moved to the hangar doors that opened up to the dock and the river and her old Helio Courier. Isaac had been working on the newer Cessna for her to start flying instead. She released the breath she'd been holding. Seeing her old plane anchored on the water brought relief after her nonsensical dream in which Isaac had flown off in it.

Maybe it hadn't made any sense, but the dream had stayed with her and left her unsettled. She would need time to recover from the trauma.

A chill crawled over her again. She got the sense she was being watched, and she rubbed her arms. She suddenly wished Hank hadn't taken Koda with him. Maybe she'd call and ask him to bring the dog back. Of course, Koda couldn't replace Isaac, but at least she wouldn't feel so alone here.

Time would tell if she ended up staying and running this place herself, but right now, Carrie couldn't come to grips with what had happened. She sat in the quiet office of the business she used to share as the cold summer breeze rushed in.

Isaac's gone.

Isaac's gone.

What am I going to do?

Survive. That's what.

"Anyone who can survive . . ."

Isaac's words again. After her body was shattered, it took a long time to heal, but her heart took even longer.

She began to walk around the hangar, though the kind of clue that would give away Isaac's murderer might not be found around the office or in the hangar or lying on the usually spotless floor.

As she exited the hangar, she tried to avoid looking at the spot where Isaac had been and what was left of the bloodstain. Carrie headed for the trail to Isaac's cabin. The sky was brightening with daylight, but it was probably another fifteen minutes until sunrise. The morning was still cool and the woods were dark as she approached his cabin. A small animal skittered away as she pushed through the thick foliage. Isaac hadn't wanted to disturb the nature and preferred to let the green encroach on his home.

But honestly, right now, the dark woods kind of gave her the creeps.

At the door, she glanced around behind her. She hoped they'd searched his cabin for evidence as well. The local police didn't have all the forensic tech, but they were trained to collect evidence, so she'd have to trust their work.

Carrie pulled out her keychain, which included a key to Isaac's cabin in case of some unexpected emergency. Neither of them could have foreseen his death as the emergency. She started to unlock the door but noticed it was cracked open. Had someone from the Shadow Gap PD forgotten to lock up?

Again, she glanced behind her, then shoved the door open gently with her foot.

Why didn't I bring my Ruger pistol? Or at least a lug wrench?

She slowly walked into the dark cabin and turned on the lights near the entrance, which instantly illuminated the small living area and kitchen off to the right behind a counter. The floor creaked under her steps as she walked to the center of the room and took in the space where Isaac had lived.

Now, to check the two bedrooms to see if she could find something that might help her know what he'd wanted to tell her.

Isaac, why didn't you just say it? Why didn't I just make him?

Carrie crept into the first room. This looked to be where Isaac slept. Guilt surged through her for even being here. He'd been here. Breathing. Humming. Praying.

Tears streamed down her cheeks and blurred her vision.

On the side table next to his bed were a few pieces of paper. An envelope on the floor. Bills and junk mail. Hard candy wrappers. Nothing to tell her anything at all, except that he hadn't been as neat as usual.

What was bothering you, Isaac? Who killed you?

What did she think she would find? She perused the next room—a home office with a computer. A ham radio. A few carpentry tools. Again, cluttered and unusual for Isaac. When he first purchased the property, this place was falling apart, and it still needed a lot of upkeep. As far as Carrie knew, Isaac loved his life here, but maybe he had grown restless. Maybe that's why he'd suggested she take time off and fly to Texas to see Kaya.

On the desk she found a hand-scratched note.

"I'm coming for you."

The paper shook in her hand as she lifted it. Was she reading too much into it, or was this a threat?

Yes. Very definitely a threat. Who would possibly send a warning like this to Isaac? Had he gotten into some kind of trouble and that's what he'd planned to tell her? But how? Where? When?

She stuck the note in her pocket and then practically ran from the cabin, though she stopped long enough to lock the door behind her. Carrie raced down the trail back to the hangar, branches reaching for her, needles and leaves scraping her as she ran. She dashed into the hangar, then went directly into the office.

Carrie plopped into the chair at Isaac's desk and drew the note from her pocket. Autumn would be furious that she'd moved it from the desk. She hadn't been thinking.

Carrie stiffened at the sound of tires crunching along the gravel.

Unless it was Chief Long, she didn't want to talk to anyone. See anyone. She just wanted to close her eyes and sleep for a year and then wake up from this awful, horrid dream.

Trevor stepped into the office, and for some inexplicable reason, her heart jumped at the sight of him. Concern was carved into his rugged face. She couldn't tell him to go away. He'd been there for her in the worst moment of her life. Holding her. Comforting her. And now he was here in her office.

Except for the breeze drifting in and out through the hangar doors, quiet surrounded them.

Maybe she couldn't ask him to leave, but she could ask him something else instead. "Why. Are. You. Here?"

She hadn't meant to be rude. Or had she?

"I'm so, so sorry, Carrie."

Breathe in. Breathe out. "Answer my question."

He averted his gaze. Stared at the floor. "I was wrong to come."

He turned and left. Isaac wouldn't have turned him away.

Wait. Growling, she pushed from the chair and caught up with him. He was almost to his Tacoma pickup rental.

"I'm sorry I was so rude." She held back a sob. "I'm struggling right now. Just tell me why you came." Then she remembered. "You were the one to find me with Isaac. You were here. Why did you come back?"

His shoulders dropped, then he straightened and pulled out the envelope. "The pilot I hired instead of you—I'm sorry, by the way—he didn't give me the pictures back. I spent yesterday trying to figure out if I could do this without you. Without those pictures, I have nothing to go on now. You saw them. You know where she went. Carrie, I need your help, but this is entirely the wrong time to ask you. I don't know what I was thinking coming here this morning. Please, forgive my intrusion."

The concern in his expression deepened. Before he could ask her how she was doing, she redirected. "What made you think I'd be here so early? It's only five a.m."

He shrugged. "I don't know, really. It's what time you had me meet you before. I saw you run into the hangar from the woods. Everything okay?"

"Yeah, sure. I went to Isaac's cabin. Just to look around. Listen, Trevor. I think I know why you're here. You came here because you're desperate," she said. "In your shoes, I would be desperate too."

He stared at her. Trying to read her thoughts? Measure his next words?

While she couldn't be sure what he was thinking, she did know one thing. Detective West was trying to be the best brother he could be. The best man. The best detective. And she could hear Isaac's unspoken words rise up and echo around her heart chambers. "*You need to be the one to help this man find his lost and broken and possibly deceased sister in the Alaska bush.*"

Ten years was a long time, but it seemed like yesterday that Isaac had found her. Unfortunately, the memories remained seared into her mind, scarring her heart. The same could be said of finding his body.

Her legs started to shake. She hoped Trevor didn't see.

"Didn't you track fugitives in your job?"

He slowly nodded.

"Then maybe we can help each other," she said. "You need my piloting and my memory. And I need your help to find Isaac's killer."

TEN

What killer?

Trevor took in Carrie's appearance. Her green eyes were pensive. Her long hair was pulled back, but strands hung down as if she'd fought with her inner demons and lost.

This was the person whose help he desperately needed.

But at what cost? He had to tread carefully. "We need to talk."

Closing her eyes, she angled her head as if this was a hard decision. Finally, she said, "Okay."

He followed her back through the hangar, where he could feel the emptiness without Isaac, though Trevor had met her business partner only briefly. But the man was charismatic and filled the space with his presence. That sense was confirmed with Trevor when they entered the office where he'd met Isaac.

If he'd been murdered, Isaac needed justice.

Carrie crossed her arms and waited.

"Before I was a detective in Montana, I tracked fugitives. I mentioned that. But I'm not aware there's a fugitive to be tracked. What am I missing?"

Again, she closed her eyes for a few breaths, then opened them again. Determination flashed in her gaze, and she explained about Isaac's safety rules. "Don't you see? Someone could have wanted it to look like an accident. Even if he broke his own rules and didn't put things away, Isaac would never have positioned the hose or the compressor where they were found."

He pursed his lips. "Anything else?"

She stared at him long and hard, and he got the feeling she had something to share but was considering whether this was the right moment and he was the person to share it with.

"A man grabbed me in Mountain Cove, but I escaped. He'd been following me. That's enough for me to believe this was more than a simple accident."

That news stunned him. A few heartbeats passed before he could even respond. "I'm so sorry, Carrie. I'm sure the Shadow Gap PD is processing the evidence. They'll hear from the ME regarding the cause of death. If Chief Long needs help, she can get the ABI involved."

"You're not saying anything I don't already know."

He should take her offer if he wanted her help, but he wouldn't mislead her. "I'll help as much as I can, but this isn't my jurisdiction." *Or my investigation.*

"And yet here you are searching for your sister."

Touché.

He knew the look of someone who'd been let down. "If Chief Long decides Isaac's death was an accident, you won't accept her assessment."

"No."

Trevor drew in a long breath. *I can't get in the middle of this.*

"Look, Carrie, why do you think I can help? Chief Long has the tools, and if she doesn't, the state will handle it."

"Detective West, how many crimes go unsolved?"

Unfortunately, at least half. "You already know or you wouldn't have asked. What's your point?" But he thought he had an idea.

"Investigators let you down in the past, but here you are searching for your sister, and I see in your eyes that you won't give up until you know the truth. If I agree to help you find Jennifer, I want you to have that same determination to find Isaac's killer. Chances are neither the locals nor the state will find his murderer, and chances are the killer is long gone from the state of Alaska. You have the ability to travel in your search, and you have the determination. So, what do you say? Do we have a deal?"

"I'll need to talk to Chief Long first."

"Talk to her, but if you want my help, I'll need yours."

She knew how to drive a hard bargain.

"I get the feeling there's a lot going on here that you haven't told me." Or else she wouldn't so quickly ask for his help. He was a stranger. Or maybe, like she said, it was his determination to find out what happened to his sister.

Something flashed behind her eyes. Yeah. He'd hit the mark. She was holding back.

"You're right. There's more. I found this note in his cabin this morning."

She thrust a small piece of paper at him. He read it without taking it from her.

"'I'm coming for you'?" Trevor lifted his gaze to her. "A threat?" Then he lifted his hands. "Whoa, whoa. That's evidence, and we should treat it as such. Do you have a plastic bag we can put it in? Something? Where did you find it, and why didn't the police find it?"

"It was on his desk. I wasn't thinking when I picked it up. I was freaking out, okay?" She dug around in a drawer, where she found an envelope and stuck it inside. "This will have to do."

She handed it to Trevor, and he took it from her as if he was sealing their pact. *What am I doing?*

"I'll do everything I can to help you find Jennifer," she said.

"I'll take you to each place. Stop where possible and give you time to look around."

"What about your trip to Texas? Maybe it would be better if you left for a while."

She shrugged. "I've put it on hold for obvious reasons."

Should he agree to something without all the facts? Common sense warred with his need for answers. But he could see in Carrie's eyes that's all she wanted too—answers.

Carrie closed the distance between them and thrust out her hand. "So do we have a deal or not?"

He shook her hand, feeling the strong grip and watching the certainty in eyes that were emerald like the forest around them. Finally, they sparked with life. She needed the hope he offered, just like he needed that same hope.

Okay. Yeah. They had a deal.

"So, how do we do this?" He was unsure where *she* wanted to start, because *he* wanted to get out there right now and travel to the places Jennifer had gone to find what she wanted him to find.

"I'm going to get my plane ready. It's still early, so we can get going. We'll focus on following Jennifer's bread crumbs. As for you, you can start looking into Isaac's death. I'll give you one hour."

"That's not usually how I work." Considering he couldn't officially work on this just yet, he would need to get creative to keep up with his end of this deal. "I told you I need to talk to Chief Long first."

"And you'll probably find her at the Lively Moose this time of the morning. But if I were you, I'd start with Isaac's friends. Hank Duncan might have been the last person to talk to Isaac. They were supposed to meet the day of his murder, and he never showed up. Chief Long can take you there, and you can tell her what you're doing if you think it's necessary. Oh, and pack lightly."

Carrie walked out of the office and left him standing there watching her go.

"I might need more than an hour," he called as he followed her through the hangar to her plane docked outside on the water. "Did you hear me? I might need more time."

"Just hurry." She waved him off.

She'd put a lot of thought into how to go about starting the investigation. The last thing he wanted was to step on law enforcement's toes. Trevor didn't take Chief Long for a slacker. She was on top of things. She probably wasn't going to like the fact that her evidence collectors had missed this one small important piece.

There was nothing for it but to talk to the chief—he got in the Tacoma and headed to the Lively Moose just before six in the morning. Parking the truck, he spotted Chief Long entering the restaurant with the man he'd met the night Isaac was killed—Grier Young, her fiancé.

They might not like that Trevor was going to interrupt their breakfast. He opened the door and took a right where booths lined the window on one side. At one of the booths, Chief Long sat across from Grier, holding his hand. The next booth over, four older guys guffawed over cups of coffee and what was left of breakfast.

How did he get Chief Long alone to talk about this delicate situation?

I guess I don't.

As Trevor approached, Grier continued talking to the guys in the next booth.

"Sandford, you don't know what you're talking about. Otis told me—"

Oh, man, this was going to be harder than he thought. He was going to have to interrupt the whole gang. Then again, he didn't care. Mission Jennifer was all that mattered.

He cleared his throat. "Chief Long."

She glanced up and released Grier's hand.

"Trevor." She smiled. "I'm surprised to see you here. What can I do for you?"

"Can I have a minute?"

Grier slid over to make space. "Have a seat."

Trevor sat next to Grier as the waitress appeared. He had the envelope tucked inside his jacket pocket and wouldn't reveal it yet.

"What can I get you?" the waitress asked.

"We've already ordered," Autumn said.

"I'm not going to be that long. Coffee, I guess." Given Carrie was prepping her plane and he had limited time, he hoped Chief Long could take him up to see Hank Duncan, but right now that didn't seem like a possibility.

"What's going on?" she asked.

"I'm in a predicament." Where did he start?

A few seconds passed, then she said, "I'm not going to put words in your mouth."

Okay. "I don't want to step on your toes or into an active investigation, but what are your thoughts on Isaac's death?"

Autumn's nod was exaggerated, and she welcomed the mugs of coffee as the waitress set three cups on the table. After the woman left, Autumn took her time doctoring her coffee.

"I'm aware that *Carrie* thinks Isaac might have been murdered. Of course, I'm exploring all possibilities."

"Have you finished gathering evidence?"

"Yes. Grier?" She looked at him and drank from her cup.

"I took pictures. Ross and I dusted for fingerprints. A lot of Shadow Gap residents have been to the hangar."

"So was it a murder or an accident?" Trevor pressed her.

She arched a brow. "Why are you asking?"

"I want to know if this is an active murder investigation."

Autumn toyed with her spoon, dipping it into her coffee. "Don't tell me. She wants you to find Isaac's killer."

"How did you know?"

"Just a hunch."

The police chief shook her head and blew out a long breath. "We have no reason to think it was murder other than Carrie's suspicions. The ME's report will tell us more." Autumn held his gaze a few moments as if considering her next words. "Okay, Detective West. I'm willing to let you join the investigation if you think she'll tell you more than she's told me. I trust you'll keep me informed on both investigations—your sister's and Isaac's."

He angled his head and studied the chief. She didn't run her police department with an iron fist so much as a need for justice and the truth, however she could get it. He admired her even more.

"Don't misunderstand," she added. "The moment I learn something new, I'll take the appropriate action, which could include calling in the state troopers and their investigative branch. Nolan is in town and will loosely follow, as it is. But, Trevor, this is a distraction from finding Jennifer."

"It's part of the deal Carrie made with me to help me find my sister."

The waitress set two plates of eggs and bacon on the table, refilled their cups, then left.

Autumn looked at the plate of food in front of her. "I'm not surprised. Carrie is gutsy."

"There's something else." He pulled the envelope from his pocket and set it on the table between them. "This might change your mind about Isaac's death."

The police chief looked at the envelope, then lifted her gaze, suspicion in her eyes. "What is this?"

"Carrie claims she found it on the desk in Isaac's cabin. Did you search the cabin?"

Chief Long opened the envelope and stared at the note. Her expression remained unreadable.

"Yes, we searched the cabin," Grier said. "Let me see that."

He looked at the note. "She said this was on the desk?"

"I believe so, yes."

Grier pulled out his camera, then brought up images. "I've sent these images over to be logged, but this is the desk two nights ago after Isaac's murder. This note was not on the desk."

"Did you look *through* the desk?"

Grier narrowed his eyes. Didn't like Trevor's questions? "I gave it a cursory look, yes."

"I can't believe Carrie didn't leave it there and call me." The chief leaned in and lowered her voice. "It's looking more like she was right about Isaac."

Fortunately, the men behind them had struck up their own conversation. Trevor guessed this was business as usual around here—the police department discussing investigations in a booth at the local diner.

"It's possible she could have written the note," Grier said. "She wants you to believe it was murder."

"I hope that's not the case, but we'll need to check into that. I'm going to talk to her." Chief Long's tone was tight.

"I'll do it," Grier said. "I'll take a deeper dive for evidence at the cabin. I can ask her to show me where she found it."

"That's a better idea." After taking a long sip of coffee, she finally looked at Trevor. "We'll search for answers on our end—for both Isaac's death and Jennifer's disappearance."

Grier shifted and stared at Trevor with a grin. "Excuse me, I need to get out."

"What about your bacon and eggs?" But Trevor got it—Grier wanted to find out what was going on.

"I wasn't all that hungry to begin with."

Trevor moved to let him escape the booth, then Grier made a beeline for the exit. Chief Long watched him go. Trevor slid in across from the chief again.

"I'll need to question Hank," Trevor said. "You can give me directions to his place or take me there."

"I'll drive you up. I can understand why she asked you to find Isaac's killer."

"And why's that?"

"You're a stranger here for one thing, and she might prefer you looking in places she doesn't want me going. You'll go home at some point and take her secrets with you."

Trevor took a sip of his coffee instead of commenting. That was not even close to the reason that Carrie had given, and yet it still might have merit.

She leveled her gaze on Trevor. "Are you sure you want to take this on?"

Are you sure you want to let me?

"Not at all. But Carrie has something I need. She saw the pictures and knows where they were taken, and I didn't get those copies made for you."

"She could just tell you where you need to go, and you could use a different pilot."

"That's true, but one of the locations she didn't recognize."

The chief pursed her lips. "I think there's more to it. I think you want *her* to be the one."

"*You* recommended her." But yeah, he was on this journey. "And I need a pilot who's invested." And now Carrie was as invested as Trevor was.

ELEVEN

Carrie had finished up her preflight checklist.

Where is that guy?

It was nearing nine o'clock. Carrie never left the hangar this late. Grier had stopped by to talk to her about the note, and after that, she'd done some research, so the time hadn't been a complete waste. Still, she was tired of waiting on the detective and needed to get away from the hangar. Get away from where Isaac was murdered.

Clear her head.

She lowered the platform holding her Helio Courier into the water. Trevor strode through the hangar door.

She couldn't wait to find out what he'd learned from Hank, but she needed to lock up the hangar. Sigh. No leaving it open all day now that Isaac was gone and wasn't here to guard the place.

His expression drawn, Trevor stood on the dock near the plane, appearing handsome and haggard at the same time. As he looked out over the river, she admired his sturdy form—he was tall and rugged in a "wilds of Alaska" sort of way, or in his case, Montana. But she could easily picture him in the African bush, and that set off a flood of chaotic emotions. An unwanted memory of another tall, dark, and handsome stranger suddenly washed away the image of Trevor.

She forced the images out of her mind.

What am I doing asking this man for help? I don't even know him.

But knowing someone didn't always make the difference. She wanted to hear what he'd learned, but she needed to get in the air before she changed her mind about all of it. "Get in. I'll lock the place up."

Carrie headed for the hangar doors. She held back the sudden surge of tears and shut the place down. Isaac was gone, and nothing she did now could bring him back, but learning the truth about his death would help. She understood Trevor's determined pursuit in a visceral way now, which was tragic.

Regardless, she needed to spread her wings and fly. The one thing that gave her peace and clarity. The Goldrock River was rough today. The sky was clear, but a storm could unexpectedly roll in off the Pacific and challenge her. She loved every minute of the adrenaline rush the Alaska skies gave her. Back in the plane, she handed him a headset and they both strapped in.

"You took your time getting here," she said. "I told you we needed to get going."

"Don't you want to know what Hank said?"

"You can tell me on the flight." She taxied down the Goldrock River until the plane lifted off the fast-flowing current.

The splendor of Alaska rushed at her, overwhelmed her, and then soothed her soul. And taking in the snowcapped mountains, emerald forest, and pristine waters from the sky might just wash away the pain—at least for a few moments.

She was taking action. Doing something. That had always been the remedy.

Clearly uncomfortable, Trevor shifted in his seat.

She wanted to chuckle. The detective was brave, strong, and

smart when his feet were planted firmly on the ground. But flying wasn't his thing. What a shame. Maybe this experience would change his mind. Or not.

"You okay there?" *Blue Eyes?*

"I'll survive. Where are we going anyway? You never said."

"Well, if I'm right, the first picture was taken at Kootznoowoo."

"Kooznoo . . . what?"

"It's what the Tlingit call Admiralty Island. It means Fortress of the Bear. It has the highest concentration of brown bears in the world."

"Wonderful," he said with zero enthusiasm.

"We don't have time to look for bears, don't worry. It's just south of Juneau, so it'll take roughly an hour. You good with that?"

He sighed. "I asked for it, so I'll just have to buck up."

"I like your attitude. Now you can tell me what you learned from Hank."

"Not much. Before I met with him, I told Chief Long about the note you found and handed it over."

"I know. Grier came by. I showed him where I found the note, then came back to complete my preflight check."

"I didn't see his vehicle."

"He left pretty quickly. Said he forgot something and would be back. They have Isaac's key, so they can get in and out of the cabin as needed. The hangar too. I'm relieved to get away from it for a few days." *With you.*

The thought startled her.

"Hank said that something had been bothering Isaac. What do you know about Isaac's state of mind?"

So it wasn't just me overanalyzing Isaac. "He definitely seemed off lately, and said he wanted to talk when I got back, but it was too late. He'd already been murdered. At least now they have the note and believe me."

The way Trevor rubbed his chin and looked away—she'd already learned that was a tell. He was holding out on her.

"What?" She glanced at him.

"The note wasn't there when they checked the cabin before."

"Oh. I get it. You think I could have written it. I already talked to Grier about it, and we're good. Just another reason for me to stay gone with you for a few days. He doesn't think it's safe for me to stay at the hangar right now."

"I agree."

"You can't seriously think I would write that note just to make sure they believe me that he was murdered?"

"I didn't want to believe it, but I don't know you that well."

"What? We've known each other a few days now." Maybe it was the wrong time to grin at her sarcasm, but Carrie couldn't help it.

And then you held me through one of the most traumatic events in my life.

"Like I said, not that well. But let's get back to the investigation. Usually we check with friends and family and find out if someone had enemies. Who do you think could have left that note?"

"Like I told Grier, I don't know. How could I? It shocked me. I've known Isaac a long time, and this is out of the blue."

When Trevor had no response, she continued. "Chief Long is good with you helping me?"

"She's about finding justice, whatever it takes, so I'm assisting her in this investigation when it comes to working with you and wherever that might lead us. I just don't have police powers. Can't arrest anyone."

"I hear a *but* in there."

"Either you're keeping something from me, or you know more than you think you do. I need to know everything."

"I've told you everything."

But not really. Isaac knew something.

Everything had gone smoothly for them for a decade. What was happening? She'd had one traumatic incident in her life—besides her parents' death—and she lived on the far side of the world away from that danger.

She wasn't ready to reveal her traumatic past to Trevor yet. At least she had time to think, maybe do some research on the side, while she transported him.

"I promise, if I think of anything, I'll tell you. In the meantime, let's focus on exploring the places your sister photographed. And while you were gone to see Hank, I had a little time on my hands, so I did some research on my own."

"And?"

"Reach into the pocket behind my seat. There's a manila folder." She banked right and blew out of the fjord and straight down the Lynn Canal.

He retrieved the folder. "What's this?"

"I printed the information out for you. I learned that Jennifer hired Amos Fitzgerald to guide her. Maybe you already knew that, but I decided to check into it in case you didn't."

He opened the folder and flipped through the pages. "No, I didn't. But I should have. Nothing was said to me. The investigators looking into her disappearance should have told me—that is, if they had learned this much. Where have you been hiding your skills? You obviously have a knack for detective work."

"It was nothing. I got to thinking about Amos. He died in an accident last year. I called up North Country Outfitters who refer guides that are big on photo treks. I asked if Jennifer had booked with any of their guides and they told me no, so I asked about Amos specifically, but he'd quit working for them. We were acquaintances, and he'd send business my way. I wanted to follow it through, so I called his girlfriend, Naomi Wakefield. She confirmed he'd been the one to guide Jennifer."

"Really. You did this when?"

"I mean, I couldn't just sit around and do nothing after the preflight check." She released a heavy sigh. "Naomi remembered Jennifer because she was his last client before he died. Said he'd been acting strange."

Interesting. "Did you find out where he took her? Was she searching for something?"

"No. But Naomi found the receipt to confirm it was her, said he was paid by EchoGlobal, though, not Jennifer. Didn't you say your sister was a geologist for that company?"

"I don't think you need an investigator's help, Carrie. You've learned more than the officials investigating Jennifer's disappearance."

"Nah. I followed a hunch. It's all about perspective. I can see things you can't, at least regarding Jennifer."

"Apparently you could see things that the ABI couldn't. Too bad they didn't get you involved."

"This information doesn't lead us anywhere, so I'm not sure how much good it is."

"It helps. It's something. Things aren't adding up, though, since I know she was on a leave from the company and now it looks like they paid for a guide."

"As for perspective, I recognize that you can see things I can't about Isaac. Bottom line, we're probably both too close to our personal tragedies to see clearly."

"Maybe you're right. At the very least I need to call EchoGlobal and ask questions."

"I would have thought someone already asked. You, specifically."

"They've already been questioned, and their official response was that she was on leave. Obviously, someone there might know something they haven't told anyone." He was practically growling now.

"So call them, but wait until we reach all the places she wanted you to see—and in order. There's a reason for it. It'll take us two days, maybe three, to see everything."

At least focusing on Jennifer's disappearance and helping Trevor eased Carrie's own pain. Isaac had been right about that, like he'd been right about so many other things.

Trevor was shaking his head. "She might have taken all the pictures to simply confirm the photography angle and throw someone off if needed. But I agree, we don't want to take the chance we'll miss something," he said. "You know, Carrie, you really surprise me. If you ever want to get out of the transport business, you should apply to law enforcement. You're good."

Warmth surged through her at his compliment. She hadn't been fishing for one. And she didn't want to feel warm inside either. "Thanks, but I'm good right where I am."

She left Trevor to his thoughts for a while, then pointed out the sights as they traveled. "Just over those mountains you can see the Juneau Icefield. Sometimes you can even catch a glimpse of Devil's Paw, which is the highest peak in the icefield and serves as the boundary between Alaska and British Columbia, but I'm not flying that high today."

"You sound like a professional guide."

She smiled. "It comes with the territory."

"I recognize Juneau, especially with the cruise ships," he said.

"Admiralty Island is coming up pretty fast."

A few minutes later, they traveled across the island's rainforest coastline, then edged the mountains topped with tundra and ice fields, flying low over millions of acres of old-growth forest.

"I have to admit," he said, "it's breathtaking."

"That, it is." The plane hugged the coast along the west side of the island until she spotted their destination. The mostly Tlingit village of Angoon.

She descended until the plane touched water, then steered toward the floatplane dock, turned off the engine, and let momentum propel the plane toward the dock. Experience helped her judge the current and the wind to bring her plane in safely.

After removing her headset and unstrapping, she opened the door, watching the dock. When they floated up to the dock, she hopped out and grabbed the rope to tie up the seaplane.

Then she met Trevor on the platform.

"I'm impressed," he said. "It takes some skill to get that right."

She shrugged. "A floatplane is basically a flying boat, only with pontoons."

The way he looked at her, she hadn't convinced him. He had entirely too much admiration in his blue eyes.

"Welcome to Angoon," she said. "I mean, when we get there. It's about a quarter of a mile hike to town."

"I saw when we flew over. It doesn't look like much. How did you know this was the place?"

"Follow me." Carrie led him toward the town. "There are eight pictures in total. There are four places to go."

"You're saying the pictures are taken in sets."

"Exactly. In this case, the first one is a general image from the air. Trees and a coastline. I was pretty sure it was Admiralty Island only because I've flown over so many times, but I couldn't be sure. The second picture of the Brown Bear House confirmed that it was Angoon."

They continued toward the town and passed a group of old wood-framed houses with beveled siding. On one of the houses, someone had painted two bears facing each other. "See? That's the Brown Bear House. Keep walking down that road and you'll see the Killer Whale House. It's part of the Tlingit clan houses. Next to it is the Raven House, Needlefish House, Steel House, Dog Salmon House."

"Now I get why Chief Long thought you'd be able to help. I can see how a pilot could know so much about Southeast Alaska. Thanks, Carrie."

"We're here, so now's your chance to ask around about your sister."

"Where's the nearest pub? Restaurant? Coffee shop?"

"Nothing like that in Angoon, but I'd suggest the Island Trading Company—that building in front of us. Since Jennifer was here, chances are good she went there too."

Trevor took the lead toward the building, and she had to pick up the pace to keep in step with him. She got it. Now that he was finally at a place that Jennifer had marked for some inexplicable reason, he intended to find answers.

While she was here, Carrie wished she could take the time to remember Isaac. Like take a nice walk in the woods and soak in the endless quiet of the old-growth forest or sit by the water and listen to the tides lapping the shore. But Trevor was desperate to learn what happened to Jennifer so he could help Carrie find Isaac's killer. And she was good with that too.

TWELVE

Like one would expect of the only grocery store in town, the Island Trading Company was a massive supply warehouse as well as a specialty boutique that sold local wares, Alaska Native and Pacific Northwest art, Angoon sweatshirts, candles, fishing supplies, T-shirts. They stocked everything. He imagined the locals could order through them as well.

His whole body was jittery at the prospect of talking to someone who had actually seen his sister. The photographs confirmed she'd been here—at least if she took them herself—and he was now walking the path she had walked.

God, please let someone remember her. Talk about her. Tell me something. His pulse roared in his ears, and he had to quiet his soul if he was going to hear anything. Learn anything.

He needed the encouragement if he was going to hold on to hope that this endeavor wasn't a colossal waste of time. Even if it felt that way, he had to keep going or else he would never know what happened. His experience in law enforcement reassured him that good old-fashioned canvassing—walking the streets and talking to people—made the biggest difference in solving cases.

Carrie headed down the aisles, giving him space while he

approached the black-haired woman with glasses who stood behind the counter punching numbers into a small calculator.

She glanced at him with a smile but continued working. "Can I help you, sir?"

He flashed Jennifer's picture on his cell. "I'm Detective Trevor West, and I'm looking for this woman. She went missing last year."

She laid down the calculator and adjusted her glasses, then narrowed her eyes. Her lips flattened. "I remember her."

His heart jackhammered. She had seen Jennifer. Remembered her. He didn't care that the woman's tone was less than friendly and her expression had soured. "What can you tell me about her?"

"She was a photographer, but she lied."

"What do you mean?"

She moved from around the counter to stand in front of him and crossed her arms. "We keep our forests pristine. Clean. She lied."

Carrie had approached but hung back at the endcap, looking at pickles. Listening?

Trevor shook his head and refused to glance at her or ask for help. "Look, I don't know what she was doing here. I only know that she is missing. Tell me what she lied about." No point in arguing with the woman.

"She was in the forest and took samples. Then chartered a boat to the north side of the island and sampled from prospects in the mining district."

That still didn't explain what she'd done to get this woman riled. His chest grew tight.

Just be patient.

"What kind of samples?" He might sound like an idiot, but he wouldn't assume anything.

She scowled at him. "Rock chips. Stream sediment." She shrugged. "What do you think?"

"I don't know. That's why I'm asking. How do you know all this?"

"It's a small community. Word travels fast."

He stifled the urge to rub his jaw and pace.

What did you get yourself into, Jennifer? Making the locals angry was never a good idea.

He wanted to ask the woman why taking samples had upset her, but even in Montana many frowned on mines for what they did to the environment. He wouldn't insult her with that question. But he would be honest. "She was my sister, okay? I'm sorry that you're not happy with her actions. Please, what more can you tell me?"

The woman's expression softened, and compassion flickered in her eyes. The tightness in his chest eased just a little. He'd never been this nervous when investigating, but then again he'd never been in this position before. As far as he knew, the investigation into her disappearance never got this far, figuratively or geographically.

"That's all I know. I'm very sorry for your loss."

For his loss? His gut tightened at her words—as if she knew Jennifer was gone. He pushed past the anxiety and kept a straight face.

"Can you tell me if she returned from her charter?"

"Yes. We were glad to see her leave the island."

"Where did she go from here?"

She shrugged. "I don't know."

"Can you tell me who took her north?" Maybe Jennifer had shared information with this person that could help him learn what happened to her.

"It's a small community, but I don't know everything." She grinned.

A couple of burly men approached the counter, their arms loaded with fishing supplies and groceries.

The woman glanced at them and smiled, then spared Trevor

another compassionate glance, but her gaze told him more. She had work to do. "If you'll excuse me, I need to take care of my customers."

He backed away from the counter, and the two men stepped up to set their supplies down.

Maybe Trevor should have bought something. But she'd clearly been upset with his sister, and he doubted anything he bought would change her attitude or glean him more information. Jennifer had offended people.

If he didn't have a bad feeling going into this search, he had one now. His insides coiled. He turned, expecting to see Carrie, but she wasn't looking at pickles anymore. She was gone. He walked up and down the aisles until he confirmed that she wasn't inside the store, so he stepped outside. Salty ocean air met him, along with a cool breeze and a bright summer day. The view was incredible but didn't include Carrie.

Was she frustrated with his line of questioning? What? Where could she have gone? He texted her that he was waiting and would give her a few minutes to respond or return before he went looking for her. At least he had two bars here. He moved away from the store entrance and stepped out into the sunshine.

The beautiful day didn't wash away his unease.

"Pssst."

Trevor lifted his head at the sound. Turned to look when he heard it again. Carrie peeked out from the store entrance, then exited and stopped. She looked over her shoulder. Glanced around.

"I looked for you inside," he said. "I thought you'd gone."

She rushed forward to grab him and tried to usher him away from the store. "Time to go."

But he wasn't so easily herded. "What are you talking about? Why?"

She released him and hiked away, and he followed.

"Where are you going?" he asked.

"To the floatplane dock. Where else?"

He caught up with her. "Mind telling me what's going on? I was trying to figure out who I might talk to next while here." Like the person who took Jennifer north, if he could find out who that was.

"Someone is following us."

"What? Where are they? How do you know?"

She was practically running, and he took long strides to keep up. At the dock, she approached the plane and opened the door.

Trevor turned his back to her, looking at the path to town. "I don't see anyone. What did he look like?"

"Big. A thick brown beard. He wore a beanie with a moose on it."

"What else?"

She glared at him. "We'll talk when we take off. Just get in the plane."

He rubbed his mouth, then slid his hand around the back of his neck as he searched the area around them. "Carrie, no one is following us now."

"He was in the store. As soon as you asked about Jennifer, he walked to another aisle and got on his cell phone. His exact words were 'They're here, asking about *her*.'"

The words made his blood boil. That was it, then. He would find the guy and get some answers. He started walking back toward the town.

Carrie caught up with him. "What are you doing? We have to go."

"I'm not going anywhere until I find this guy."

"Look. You can't face off with anyone right now. This guy—he was big, okay? I followed him, peeked out the door, and saw that he had joined a friend outside. They were *waiting* for us."

Trevor stopped walking and looked at her.

"I guess I didn't think about the possibility that taking you to these locations could get you into trouble, and it could be dangerous," she said. "I didn't want you to get hurt."

"*Me?* What am I? Chopped liver? I'm a detective, remember? I'm a trained law enforcement officer."

Her big green eyes came back to him, pain mingled there. She was thinking of Isaac, and she didn't want Trevor to get hurt. Didn't want to go through that again.

Still, he had to find the men and question them. "Why didn't they approach us, then? You said they were waiting."

"One of the guys got another call, and they walked the other way. I thought it was our chance to leave before they found us." She jammed her hands into her jacket pockets. "I got a picture of them."

She handed over her cell with the image. She wasn't kidding. One of the guys had huge biceps. "Oh yeah, I see what you mean." If the men were trying to get to Trevor, the situation wasn't safe for Carrie. He handed her phone back. "Text me this image."

He waited for the image to appear on his cell. "Wait here. Any signs of trouble at all, anyone walking toward the dock, you get in and take off."

"You can't be serious. You know, people here are friendly, but it doesn't sound like they liked your sister, so you wouldn't get any help if you got into a confrontation with those two. I'm just saying."

"I didn't come this far to walk away when I'm this close."

She flattened her lips. "I understand. But be careful."

Trevor scraped a hand through his hair, frustration boiling to the surface. Should he search for this guy? Bring Carrie into danger? Or just move on to the next site?

He glanced at the pilot. She was strong, but she hadn't signed on for trouble.

"I'll be fine waiting here," she said. "I promise, I'll leave if either of those guys comes toward the dock. I can come back to get you or call for help if you need it."

"I'll be back as soon as I can." Trevor took off at a half jog toward the village, keeping his eyes open for the man in the picture or anyone else who might be watching him a little too closely.

He wanted to know who the guy had called—someone was behind Jennifer's disappearance after all, and Trevor meant to find out.

But an hour later, he had come up empty. Why did the two men who'd supposedly been waiting for him to come out of the store suddenly disappear? He asked around, but no one had seen the men. He texted with Carrie throughout his search, and no one had approached her.

He gave up and headed to the seaplane dock. He had a feeling they would encounter the two men again, and he hoped so.

Once they were in the air, Trevor relaxed. He'd been too wound up. Exhaustion was already weighing on him, and the day was only beginning. His stomach growled. Was it already lunchtime? Maybe on their next stop they could find a restaurant.

He hadn't heard from Chief Long and needed to contact her to see if she had any new information on Isaac's case. "Okay, what's the next stop?"

"Petersburg. I need to refuel, then we'll head to a small Native American village on Clackon Island just north of Wrangell. The next picture was taken there."

"What clued you in this time?"

"Totems."

"Totems? I've seen them around. What's special about these?"

"They're lying down instead of standing up. Don't ask me why. It's a mystery. While I was waiting on you to return, I booked us at the lodge."

"I hope they have a place to eat. I didn't get breakfast." Just a cup of black coffee, which he hadn't gotten the chance to drink because he was focused on Chief Long and her reaction to his news, and then they'd gone to talk to Hank.

She scratched her head and scrunched up her nose. "We'll grab food in Petersburg, because honestly, I can't make any promises about the lodge on Clackon Island. So, tell me what the woman at the trading company said."

"That Jennifer lied about being a photographer and was here to collect samples—minerals, rocks, and dirt. Earthy stuff."

"Geology stuff. She was on a scouting trip for her company."

"It doesn't sound right." He watched the small town disappear as Carrie flew inland over a bay instead of following the shoreline.

"What do you mean?" she asked.

"She had taken leave, for one thing. And if it was for her company, she wouldn't have been sent to do that job alone."

"And yet that woman said she was collecting samples. How do you know she wouldn't have been sent alone? Were you a geologist?"

"You're right. I don't know that much about it." He blew out a breath. "But she wouldn't have had anything to hide if her task was on the up and up, right? Seems to me she was on a clandestine operation."

"You make it sound like she was a spy."

"She was definitely trying to keep things under wraps." But she couldn't be a spy.

Because spies had a short life expectancy.

THIRTEEN

Hands clasped behind his head, Trevor rested on the bed in the small room of the Grin and Bear It Lodge on Clackon Island. His room had a nice sliding glass door to enjoy the view, which he might have appreciated except what he really wanted was the dark of night so he could get some sleep. The blinds over the door didn't darken the room enough for his taste.

His stomach growled even though they'd grabbed some snacks after eating in Petersburg. At least the Grin and Bear It Lodge included a small restaurant appropriately called the Lazy Bear Café, but it had closed before they arrived. He had much bigger problems than food, so with those immediate needs satisfied, he hoped he could sleep.

But his mind was working overtime, and he couldn't shut it down. He thought back to his conversation with Chief Long. He and Carrie had stopped in Petersburg and were eating sandwiches at Glacier Express Café when the chief called him back. He'd sent her the images Carrie had taken of the two men.

"I have Carrie on speaker," he'd said. That way Chief Long would know she was listening in and wouldn't ask if Carrie had told him anything useful. They both hoped Carrie might provide more insight into Isaac's death—something she didn't realize she knew.

"We got nothing on this Vandyke guy," the chief said. "Mountain Cove PD is working to get the security footage. They took a statement from the man who stepped in to help Carrie get away. They have issued the appropriate alerts. I'll see what I can find out on these two characters you texted me."

"Thanks, Chief."

"Between the attack on you in Mountain Cove, Carrie, and the man at the Island Trading Company who called to inform someone that you, Trevor, were there asking about Jennifer, I'm scratching my head. Though it goes without saying, I'll say it anyway, you should both be careful and watch your backs. In fact, it might be best to step away."

A slow drum started at his temples. "It's been over a year, and the ABI found nothing about Jennifer. I'm not stopping, especially now that I'm making progress."

"I had a feeling you'd say that. I'd do the same if it were my sister."

Good. "There's something else. We know Jennifer was on leave from EchoGlobal while in Alaska, but Carrie learned that the *company* paid for her now-deceased guide, Amos Fitzgerald."

"Something worth looking into. Why don't you let me take this? You can't give it the time while you're island hopping. I'll put one of my officers on it."

"*Your* officers. I don't want to deal with ABI right now."

"I understand."

"I could get my fellow Grayback County detectives to follow up, but since you already know the details, if you have time to look into it, I'd appreciate it. Now, what about Isaac's case. Anything?"

"We haven't heard anything from the ME yet. Have you made any progress?"

He kept his focus on the phone and avoided Carrie's eyes. "Not yet. Still working on it."

"All right. I have to go. Keep me informed." Chief Long ended the call.

Carrie stared at him. He knew a question was coming, because although he had tried, he hadn't sounded natural in his response to the chief.

"What progress was she expecting?"

"I told you I would help find Isaac's killer."

"Detective West?"

"Are you using my full title like a mother scolding a child?"

"Maybe. I sense there's more."

Sharp woman. "She wants me to find out if you have anything to add that you haven't told us."

Carrie stared at her plate and swallowed. "I told you what I know. Something had been bothering him."

The waitress had approached, and Carrie had excused herself to the ladies' room.

That was hours ago. Now he lay on the hard bed, wide awake. He might do better if he didn't fight the rising tension, so he got up and pulled on his jeans before opening the sliding glass door. As he stepped onto the small first-floor porch, he saw a wide clearing in the trees that opened up to a view of the water. The brisk night air startled him, and he settled into a rustic hand-hewn log chair to look out into the nautical twilight—the sun was just below the horizon, but the brighter stars could still be seen.

The night sounds and peaceful surroundings could lull him to sleep. Just as drowsiness started to pull on his lids, a twig snapped.

Trevor became instantly awake.

He held his breath and listened. Another crack. Probably an animal.

Something crashed through the woods. Yeah. That was definitely a large animal of some kind. A bear or a moose maybe.

The inn's brochure—a sheet of paper—included warnings about the wildlife while hiking or fishing or simply enjoying the outdoors but mentioned nothing about the danger that might occur while sitting on the lodge room decks. Though the porch included a log railing, he doubted it could truly protect him.

The hair on the back of his neck stood on end as he reached for the door to go back inside. Trevor quietly opened the door and slipped back into his room.

A large animal had crashed through the woods, but a two-legged creature was also out there. He wouldn't get that intense of a feeling from an animal. He secured his shoulder holster, which held his Beretta, and exited his room into the corridor, closing the door behind him. He moved quietly down the hallway to go outside and reconnoiter the place.

Exiting through a door in the back, Trevor pulled his Beretta from its holster and stepped outside into the cool night. He approached the side of the lodge where his and Carrie's rooms were located. In the shadows, he could see a dark silhouette at her door. Tall and bulky, a masked man was trying to break in.

Trevor crept forward, hoping to take the intruder down. Maybe he could get the answers he needed.

The door suddenly opened, and the man disappeared inside.

"Hey!" Trevor shouted and raced forward.

Heart hammering, Trevor jumped across the railing, kicked aside the log chair blocking his path, and entered Carrie's dimly lit room. He pointed his gun at the masked intruder, who backed toward the door and held her hostage with a knife to her throat.

Trevor aimed his gun at the man's head. "Let her go."

The man said nothing at all but continued backing away until he was flat against the door and held Carrie so that Trevor couldn't risk the shot.

Trevor stepped forward. "Let her go and I won't kill you where you stand."

A small gasp escaped Carrie. Trevor could barely see in the

room, but he imagined the man had pressed the knife against her throat and drawn blood. She suddenly tumbled forward, and Trevor caught her as the man opened the door and fled the room.

"Are you okay?" he asked as she stepped out of his arms.

"Go," she said. "Go get him."

Trevor raced out of the room and down the hallway, following the sound of pounding feet. He pushed through the side exit to follow the man outside and into the dark forest.

Somewhere in the distance he could hear the large animal. But no sound from the man who'd slipped into the woods. He wanted to run after him, but there was no way to track him, nor did he want to face off with what was probably a brown bear.

A sound drew his attention and he swung around, leading with his gun, prepared to take the man down.

"It's me," Carrie said softly.

He dropped the pistol to his side, relief rushing through him. Relief and frustration. "What are you doing here? Get back inside."

Carrie huffed. "Is that an order?"

"We're both sitting ducks out here," he said. "Let's go."

They hiked back to the lodge. Inside, he cleared both their rooms and grabbed his things, intending to stay in hers.

She held her Ruger. "I could have stopped him with this, Trevor." She set it on the table next to the bed. "I've never shot anyone before, and I kept seeing Isaac on the floor and all the blood." Frowning, she shook her head.

"Don't beat yourself up. It's not easy to shoot someone, even if you have the training and you're defending yourself." He glanced around the room and sighed. "One problem. I don't know how we can sleep here now."

"Who could have broken into my room and why? It sounds weird, but the way he held me, grabbed me, it felt familiar. Like the same way Vandyke grabbed me. Maybe I'm imagining it. Do you think it was him?"

"No way to know just yet. I'm calling security." He picked up the room phone and dialed the front desk. After ten rings, he hung up. "No answer."

"Call the local police."

He searched the small desk and side table.

"What are you looking for?"

"The information page they gave us."

He found it beneath her bed. "There's a number in case of emergencies."

Trevor finally connected with a woman who he assumed was dispatch and explained the attack. "Can you send an officer out?"

"I'll be there to get your statements."

"Thank you." *I think*. He stared at the phone before he hung up. "Someone is coming."

He paced Carrie's room, holding his gun by his side. "Can we trust the people at the lodge? How would someone know that's your room? Come to think of it, can we trust the officer who's coming? The one-person police department?"

"You're assuming it wasn't a random break-in," she said.

"A random break-in would have gone for *my* room. I'm at the end of the building next to the woods."

Hugging herself, she rubbed her arms. "And he came right for me. Didn't act surprised to see me. Like he was there *for* me." She dropped her arms and gasped. "Oh no. What if someone was after *me* at the hangar and got Isaac instead?"

She sat on the edge of the bed.

He approached her and knelt. "You can't think like that, Carrie. This might have nothing to do with what happened to Isaac. There's no way to be sure how it's all related—Vandyke, two suspicious guys in Angoon, and now tonight's attack. How could anyone follow us here?" He stood and scratched his chin. "What if someone has copies of the pictures Jennifer took or knows exactly where she went, so they also know where *we* are going—island hopping, as it were—following the dots on a road map?"

"I don't know. I guess it's possible," she said. "But why? What do they want with me?"

"Maybe they don't want us to find out what Jennifer was up to and hope to harm or scare you—you're the one who has those pictures in your head." He should have taken a picture of them. They would be on his cell phone right now if he'd been able to think past his grief. "You should just tell me the locations that you know, and I'll get a different pilot and figure the rest out. You could go on the trip you planned."

He studied her, waiting for her answer.

"I could. And the entire time I would be thinking about Isaac. And since I don't know why someone killed him, I can't know if I would even be safe in Texas. I'm probably safer here with you. And I want to be part of this. Because after we find Jennifer, if Chief Long hasn't solved Isaac's murder by then, and chances are good that she won't, I want to be with you when you put all your determination and focus on finding his killer."

He pressed his lips together. What could he say to that? Carrie James had a way of making him want to be better. Try harder. Offering a tenuous grin, he nodded.

Her eyes sparked with admiration, and *he* had something to admit too. He liked that from her. He *liked* Carrie. She held his gaze longer than necessary and then suddenly pushed from the bed and paced the room.

"What are we going to do tonight?" she asked.

"Only a few more hours until dawn. We'll talk to the police officer, then you can get some sleep and I'll stand guard."

A knock came at the door. "It's Coral. You called me?"

The voice sounded familiar, but he didn't recall that she'd actually given her name on the phone. He opened the door to a grandmotherly woman with salt-and-pepper black hair. "I'm the VPSO . . . Village Public Safety Officer."

He gestured for her to come inside.

Breathing hard, she ambled in. No uniform. No gun. And looked them over, then arched a brow. She held up her phone and pressed the record button. "Now, what's your story?"

Trevor glanced at Carrie, who stood behind Coral. She shrugged.

He shared the details.

When he was done, she said, "I can conduct an investigation. These rooms are now a crime scene, so I'd advise you to get other accommodations."

"What?" Carrie huffed. "This is the only place, and we took the last rooms. We have nowhere to go."

"Well, let me make it quick, then." Coral flipped on the lights and then took pictures with her camera. "I can't dust for prints." She rubbed her nose. "There's something else you should know. I can't protect you." She dipped her chin and lowered her voice. "If you get into trouble again, you're on your own. Sounds like you know how to handle yourselves. Just be careful."

"Aren't you going to call the Alaska State Troopers?" Carrie asked.

"Yes. We work closely with them, but our motto is 'First Responders—Last Frontier' for a reason, so it's going to take a while. Won't be tonight, I can tell you that."

Trevor admired the woman for taking on this task with no real backup. He thrust his hand out. "Thank you, Coral. I'm a detective from Montana. I have a weapon, as does Carrie. We'll be fine. We just wanted to let you know about the intruder." He pulled up the image of Jennifer on his cell. "I'm looking for this woman."

A sadness deepened in her wise eyes. "I haven't seen her. But if she stayed here, Bucky would know."

"We asked the guy who checked us in. Skinny. In his late twenties, maybe."

"No, that's Rupert. Bucky's tall and about my age."

Trevor nodded. "We'll ask him in the morning."

"Be careful tonight, then. You plan on staying longer than a day?"

He shared a look with Carrie. "Depends on what we learn from Bucky." And they had two more places to explore—that is, if they could figure out the location of the last place. "Thanks again. If we stay longer, I'll buy you a cup of coffee."

Her smile was infectious. "I'll let you. I'm heading home. Call if you need me again."

Trevor closed the door and heaved a sigh. "I can't see my sister traveling to these places alone."

"She didn't. Remember, she had a guide."

"Who is now dead." The woman at the Island Trading Company hadn't mentioned anyone with Jennifer. "Tonight, let's stay in one room. We can take turns keeping watch."

"My thinking exactly. Wake me up in two hours." She plopped onto the bed.

He arched his brows. "Two hours? I'd prefer the pilot have plenty of rest. I can sleep on the plane." Sort of.

"We take turns. I don't need much sleep." She lay on her back and tucked one of the pillows over her head.

He peeked out the window. Secured both doors. When he finally took a seat, Carrie had curled onto her side, with her back to him. He was glad the chair was uncomfortable, otherwise he might fall asleep and die while dreaming.

FOURTEEN

Wind whipped around her, the sound roaring in her ears, cold slipping beneath her clothing.

Her chest hurt. She might have an imprint of his hands deep in her skin, but even deeper her heart had shattered into a million pieces.

Her body wasn't far behind.

He hung out the door, staring, watching her fall. Did he regret his decision?

Shock rippled through her, but adrenaline spiked, jolting her to the reality of certain death.

The plane disappeared, and she flipped over to face the earth coming at her—alarms blared in her ears.

"Carrie, Carrie, wake up!" Arms gripped her.

Darius? Had it all been a mistake? A bad dream?

She gasped awake, bolted upright. "What? What is it?" She rubbed her bleary eyes.

Not Darius.

Trevor.

And alarms. She'd been dreaming. She moved to the edge of the bed. "Is that—"

"Smoke alarms. I hope the lodge has the required sprinkler systems to put out the fire. We need to get out of here." He tugged her to her feet. "Grab your stuff."

After slipping on her shoes, Carrie grabbed her duffel that she never unpacked, and glanced at the clock. Three in the morning. She'd gotten only a couple of hours of sleep, if that.

With his duffel slung over his shoulder, Trevor brandished his pistol and leaned against the wall near the door.

"What are you doing?"

He held her gaze. "This could be an attempt to flush us out of the lodge."

Her chest constricted. "You can't seriously believe that."

"Can't risk it." He slowly opened the door and peered out. "Let's go so we can get lost in the crowd."

"It has to be a small crowd. The lodge isn't that big."

He exited the room, and she was right on his heels, running toward the exit and the fleeing guests. The smoke grew thick. Her heart rate kicked up to go with the overall panic of everyone trying to escape. The crowd slowed at the door. A bottleneck.

The place was heating up with the crackling fire.

Crackling fire? "I don't think the sprinkler system is working."

Could someone have tampered with it? She was getting paranoid like Trevor.

The exit was a mere ten yards. A man exited.

"Come on, Carrie!"

"I'm right behind you."

The ceiling suddenly crashed in and flames exploded, blocking their way.

Carrie screamed as she ran into Trevor, who'd stopped in his tracks. "Back, back, back," he said.

"How could it have grown so fast?" Carrie froze in place, unable to move.

Trevor grabbed her arm and tugged her away from the collapsed ceiling and quickly spreading flames. They ran in the opposite direction and at the end of the hallway turned right to find the lobby already in flames too.

We're trapped!

Smoke choked her throat, making the lump that had lodged there even more uncomfortable. Trevor led them back around the corner. Flames were consuming the hallway. He kicked open a guest room door and raced into the room.

Carrie followed him inside.

He moved to the sliding glass door. "We're getting out this way."

Carrie followed him, then hesitated. "But if they wanted to flush us out, or kill us, they could just shoot us as we escape."

"They could. But I'll do everything in my power to prevent that from happening. So I need you to trust me."

She nodded. *Like I have a choice.* "What's the plan, then?"

"We head to the plane and get out of here."

Smoke billowed beneath the door to the hallway, quickly filling the room and choking them both. He tore back the blinds. The woods were lit up with the bright light from the burning lodge.

He shook his head. "I don't like this, but there's no other way. Keep down as we get out of here." He gently slid the glass door open.

She crawled out onto the porch, crouching with Trevor. "I'll leap over first, then cover you as you climb over. Stay behind me. Keep close."

Trevor hopped the railing, and she quickly followed, landing on the soft earth.

"Follow me to the trees," he said. "Keep to the shadows."

"It's hard to see deeper into the woods with the fire." Carrie palmed her gun and turned her attention to the villagers who had already started lining up to toss water on the blaze.

"I see Coral. She's in the bucket brigade," he said. "I need to talk to her, so stick close."

They crept through the woods, then made their way up the volunteer line until they found Coral near the front.

"I have information for you."

"Get in line," Coral said.

Carrie got in line with Trevor right behind Coral. Volunteers shifted to accommodate them and passed empty buckets back and full buckets forward. Trevor practically shouted at Coral so she could hear him over the blaze, allowing Carrie to catch every word too.

"Someone set the fire. It was deliberate."

"What makes you say that?" she asked.

"Come on, see how fast it spread?" Trevor passed her a bucket.

"I'll tell the troopers when they get here. The lodge is old and the wood is dry, and maybe not up to code, but I agree with you."

"You do?"

"Yes. If I held a match up to a big tree, it wouldn't catch fire. The same is true here. The lodge is built with huge logs, and it's hard for them to catch fire, so it was fire-resistant to a point. This fire is moving fast, like you said, *and* burning the logs."

Coral suddenly stepped out of the line and drew them with her. She herded them over to her vehicle. "You're telling me this because you're assuming it has to do with the attack on you."

"It's possible," he said.

"I think I'm supposed to tell you to stick around and wait for the troopers, but if this is the reason for the fire, then you brought trouble to my village and I don't want any more. I have your contact information. You should go somewhere safe. Send me the picture of Jennifer, and I'll ask around if someone has seen her. Who is she to you?"

"My sister."

Coral's eyes held understanding and compassion. "I thought so."

"I need you to find out everything you can. Why she was here. Can you do that for me?"

"Do you *trust* me to do it?"

"I have no choice unless I stick around. I think someone was trying to flush us out. Even standing here now—"

"You're putting yourselves and everyone here in danger. If the fire was because of you, then you've already put people in danger. I'm not blaming you, but please go somewhere safe. Do you have another contact for me? Someone else I—"

"Yes," Carrie said. "Chief Autumn Long of Shadow Gap."

Her face lined with concern, Coral nodded. "Do you need anything else from me?"

"No." Trevor swiped his arm across his forehead. "Just keep in touch if you learn anything about Jennifer. You can coordinate with Chief Long if you find out who started the fire."

"Will do." Coral glanced at the bucket brigade, then back to them. "Unless you have your own boat or plane, I'll need to arrange transportation for you at this hour."

"I have my plane," Carrie said. "We'll be fine, thanks."

"Good. I need to get back to helping with the fire." Coral's expression grew determined, then she turned and headed to the lodge, calling over her shoulder, "Take care."

Carrie and Trevor left the chaos behind and hiked down the path that hugged the woods. The sky was beginning to brighten in the early twilight of morning, but it didn't chase away the dread and fear. Nerves on edge, she kept close to Trevor as they put distance between themselves and the destroyed lodge.

He seemed uptight, aware of everything around him. She felt safe with him as they made their way to the floatplane dock erected at the cove off the inlet. If the person out to get them was watching from deeper in the woods, Carrie and Trevor would be easy targets as silhouettes against the flames engulfing the lodge on one side. And against the brightening sky on the other.

Was this really about *her*? If so, why would someone go to this much trouble?

Or was it about Trevor and his search to find Jennifer? They couldn't know, and she wouldn't jump to ill-founded conclusions, except, well, someone did break into *her* room and seemed intent on what—taking her? Or killing her?

What did the intruder want with her?

Finally, they made it to the seaplane dock area, but they didn't step out into view. Trevor hid with her behind a big cedar, the acrid scent of smoke filling the air. He glanced behind them. She followed his gaze, and through the trees, the bright orange flames remained visible along with the desperate community that had mobilized to fight the flames.

She took in the marina down from the floatplane dock and let her gaze skim back up to the planes. "Doesn't look like anyone has disturbed the boats or planes."

"Looks can be deceiving," he said.

"Way to reassure me."

"Let's go." Trevor started forward.

Together they hurried up the boardwalk. The planks protested as they passed two planes docked in slips next to where Carrie had secured hers. Carrie took the lead after Trevor turned, walking backward to make sure no one came after them. She hurried ahead of him to get things moving.

A man stepped out from behind a white Cessna and blocked her path, pointing a handgun at her. The man from Angoon with the moose cap. Moosehead!

She pulled up short, stopping in her tracks, and took a step back. Fear spiked through her as she peered down the muzzle of his gun. Before she could blink, Trevor stood between them and disarmed her would-be shooter. He could have been shot!

But the man headbutted Trevor and landed punches to his gut. The two wrestled, fighting over Trevor's gun until it clattered across the boardwalk.

"Stop it!" Carrie fired her Ruger into the boardwalk, the blast quaking through her.

Trevor and Moosehead separated. Gasping, they glared at each other, ready to pounce again. Moosehead eyed his gun, which rested precariously on the edge of the boardwalk.

"Don't even think about it." Trevor picked it up and aimed it at the man. "What do you want with us? Why are you following us?" To Carrie, he said, "Call Coral. Tell her we need her here."

"She can't do anything. She can't arrest me," Moosehead said. "Doesn't even carry a gun. You're not going to do anything either."

The man suddenly rushed Trevor. Gunfire resounded. The two men went into the water, and the splash doused Carrie too.

Her heart ricocheted. She aimed the Ruger at the water. *What am I thinking? I can't shoot or I might hit Trevor.*

Where were they? She leaned over the edge, willing Trevor to come up for air. A splash drew her attention to the other side of the boardwalk.

Trevor stared up at her from the cold water.

"Where'd he go?" Trevor grabbed the structure and hoisted himself up to sit on the edge.

"I don't know. I didn't see him come out of the water. Are you okay? I thought you'd drowned. You could have been shot when you disarmed him."

"He didn't intend to shoot."

"You could tell that how?"

"He hadn't put his finger on the trigger. I didn't see that intent in his eyes either, but I had to act before he made that decision."

So, basically, he'd put himself in the line of fire to save her.

"That was risky." Dripping wet, he stared at her, his blue eyes flashing wild as he climbed to his feet. More than relief filled her, and she tugged him to her. Pressed her forehead into his sturdy, wet chest. At least the fleece beneath his waterproof jacket would keep him warm. He wrapped his arms around her. "It's okay."

What was she doing, leaning into him? Her emotions had her on a rollercoaster. She didn't even recognize herself.

"He's getting away." Trevor said the words flatly as if he didn't care enough to let her go.

She almost smiled to herself. Finally, she let reality break the moment and lifted her head.

"What?"

"He's getting away." He gestured toward the shoreline. "There."

"Are you going after him?"

"No. Chief Long has a picture. I'll send it to Coral as well and tell her to watch out for him. She can pass that on to the troopers who show up. But I have a feeling he won't be on this island long, and we'll see him again. And next time, we'll be ready."

Next time?

FIFTEEN

Once they were in the air, relief blew through him. At least for the moment, they were out of danger. Never mind that it would probably be waiting for them at their next destination.

Trevor had taken off his soaked jacket and wrapped himself in a blanket that Carrie grabbed from the back seat. She'd cranked up the heat as well. Thanks to the special waterproof phone sleeve in his jacket, his cell would survive.

He tried to relax, but his gut remained tight as the plane increased altitude until he could look down and see the islands, mountains, and waterways. Admittedly, the view was breathtaking, but he struggled to breathe for multiple reasons. Part of him wished he'd chartered a boat, but that would have taken entirely too long.

I made my bed, I have to lie in it.

Maybe after this time flying with Carrie, he would grow accustomed to it and get over his fear. He might never get used to this, but honestly, he *wanted* to. He wanted to love it. For her. The thought startled him as he stared out the window and listened to the whining hum of the engine.

Why would he want to love flying just for Carrie? He'd never had stranger thoughts, not to mention it was the worst timing.

Dude, you don't even know her!

Not that well.

That they had been thrown into a pressure-cooker situation wasn't lost on him. Stuff happened fast. Emotional connections were made. He knew all about it.

He didn't want to think about the fact that every time he looked into her eyes was like looking at the emerald rainforest. He didn't want to think about the graceful way her lithe and athletic body moved. The way she aimed her gun at their attacker like she'd practiced taking down bad guys every day of her life.

Carrie James was a force to be reckoned with. He was taken aback the first moment he met her.

"You're awfully quiet," she said. "Like my mom used to say, 'A penny for your thoughts.'"

Like I could possibly share my thoughts. "Is that what you think they're worth?"

She favored him with a glance and a half smile. She looked energized instead of exhausted. Is that what flying did for her?

"I'm just thinking through everything."

She blew out a long breath. "A lot has happened in a short time. I can't wrap my mind around it."

"We need to find out who this guy is."

"Moosehead?"

"Who?"

"I've taken to calling him Moosehead. You know, he wears a beanie with a moose on it."

Moosehead? Vandyke? Things weren't looking good when you had to start naming the bad guys.

"Don't forget, he's probably the one who set fire to the lodge and endangered a lot of other people, or he's working with Vandyke and they were both there. The village probably won't welcome me there ever again. That is, if it turns out the fire was started by our stalker—because of me. Or because of your search for Jennifer. Which is it?"

"I don't have the answer, but we know that guy was working for someone." Was Carrie attacked because she would lead Trevor to Jennifer's body? If discovering Jennifer's whereabouts was the issue, then Trevor should be the one targeted.

Jennifer's body.

A knot thickened in his throat. Not once had he ever let himself think of it. Why had the thought that she was most likely dead suddenly invaded his mind?

No. She's not. Hold on to hope. I need to be a fool just a little longer.

The plane dipped abruptly. He held his breath.

"Sorry about that."

"I'd like to say it was no problem."

"I don't take you for a liar," she said. "I try to offer as smooth a flight as possible."

"You're doing great." He chuckled.

"Thank you for saving me back there."

"You're welcome." An image filled his mind—Carrie James firing her Ruger. "And thanks for breaking up the fight on the dock."

"All in a day's work."

"I hope that's not the case." If Moosehead was anticipating their stops based on Jennifer's path, they needed a new plan. "Listen, we need time to think about everything before we take this next step, the third location. Do you mind if we stop somewhere that isn't charted in the photographs—on the off chance that they followed Jennifer or knew her stops and that's how they're anticipating where we're going?

"We need to talk about what happened, and I'd like to do that without Moosehead jumping out from somewhere. I only saw one guy this time, so I don't know if he lost his partner."

Or if Vandyke was the one who grabbed her from behind at the lodge. He was masked this time, at least. Moosehead didn't seem to care if they saw him.

"I thought time was wasting," she said.

"I want to hash through everything we know so far, and to do that, I need a big cup of black coffee. I don't want to have to look over my shoulder to drink it. Bacon and eggs, or whatever they've got, would be nice too."

"Come to think of it, we never got to eat at the Lazy Bear Café. I hear you, Trevor. We're only forty miles from our next stop," she said. "Number three, which is Elotin Island. It isn't even populated. Okay, well, a few people live there, ten or fifteen, maybe, but I don't know where that last picture will lead. I've kind of been hoping we could gather a few clues that would help. But so far nothing. But if you want to stop before then, I know just the place where we can catch our breath. Kendall Island is only fifteen miles. There's a small village called Shady Cove, a nice generic name for you."

"Our next stop—Elotin Island, you said? So, in the picture there was a boat. That was it. An old canoe. How do you know that's the island?"

"It's historic and listed on the US National Register of Historic Places. I filled in for the mail delivery briefly, so I know about it."

You're really something. He didn't know why he should be so impressed with her. After all, this was her job.

The lavender sky morphed into bright pink and blood orange. Trevor couldn't tear his gaze from it.

"I know I've already said this," he said, "but another way to say it is that I'm glad I didn't go with David to guide me. You know your way around Southeast Alaska like nobody's business."

"David knows his way around too. But he didn't need you to track a killer for him."

"I haven't done much in that arena, Carrie."

"And I hope you don't have to, but the situation presented itself, and I took advantage. Once we find your sister, I'm going to hold you to our deal."

Carrie said nothing more because . . . sun. Glorious sunrise.

Brilliant molten gold spilled from the sky. It took his breath away.

Carrie donned sunglasses and flew southwest.

If he were a crying man, he might feel some tears right about now as the unspeakable colors left him in awe. Still, emotion clogged his throat. If he wasn't searching for Jennifer, he wouldn't be here at this moment, in the skies over the Alaska Panhandle as the sun made its dramatic appearance.

With Carrie James.

Though he hated flying when he started this journey, these moments with Carrie might just change his mind. As she descended toward the water and yet another island, disappointment rose in his gut at the fact they would soon be landing and leaving behind the breathtaking beauty found only in the skies.

That's something new.

He never could have predicted he would want more time in the air.

Too soon, they docked and climbed out of her plane. She adjusted the duffel slung over her shoulder and covered her yawn, then shook her head. He was still mildly cold from the brief early morning dunk.

"This will give us a chance to catch our breath. But what if we stay here longer?" she asked. "Shady Cove has lodging available. Okay, well, it's just up the proverbial rung from a hostel, you know. More than renting one of the beds in a room shared with several others."

"That could put us behind schedule, but maybe you're right. We could grab a catnap this afternoon, then head to our next destination later in the day."

She scrunched up her face. "I'd rather stay the night. Arrive early tomorrow." She blinked, and her green eyes widened. "Maybe we don't fly at all, but instead charter a boat."

"Carrie. Coffee first. Please."

"Okay. Okay."

Clearly, she didn't have the same caffeine addiction issues he had. He followed her while looking at his cell. "I hope this place has cell coverage. Right now I don't have any bars."

"I think it does near the lodge and main part of the town. The outskirts, probably not. The lodge is just up there." She pointed toward a two-story brown clapboard structure.

Trevor walked next to Carrie down the main strip of yet another small community in Alaska. He'd been to Juneau and Anchorage, so he knew the Last Frontier had cities, but it had far more villages and very small towns.

"There's a lot to explore here." She looked at him as if searching for something. "We're not here to enjoy the sights, but after this is over, if you ever come back . . ." She trailed off, frowned, and turned her attention to the Shady Cove Lodge and the adjoining Shady Cove Eatery just ahead.

How could she think about enjoying sights after everything she'd been through? *They*'d been through. Then again, she might need to focus on the good this world had to offer or risk losing her mind. He knew all about survival techniques.

And focusing on the good gave him perspective.

His cell buzzed, and he stopped to look. "It's Coral," he said and answered the call. "Detective West."

"Detective. I got your text message with the picture. Haven't seen the man before. But I'm asking around about him. If he burned down the lodge, a lot of people are angry with him. That's putting it mildly. But more importantly, I wanted to let you know I had a chance to talk to Bucky. He saw your sister. But she wasn't going by Jennifer. She checked in under Lori Fisher."

"As in, she had an actual fake ID to that effect?" he asked.

"I asked the same thing. Bucky said she paid cash, and he doesn't ask questions."

"When did she check in and out?"

"May of last year. I'll send you the details in a text so you'll have them. I asked him how he remembered her name after so long, and he said she was pretty and memorable."

Trevor pictured Coral shrugging.

"Did she check in alone? What did she do while she was on the island?"

"I'll try to find out more. I had a sibling who went missing once, so I understand the agony."

"I'm so sorry to hear that. Can I ask what happened?" He closed his eyes, regretting the insensitive question.

"We found her at the bottom of a cliff. She loved to hike the outdoors alone."

Sometimes you shouldn't ask a question unless you really want to hear the answer. He sucked in a breath.

"That was long ago," she said. "Sure, I miss her, but time heals all wounds."

"Thank you, Coral. Please send me the information you gather on my sister. And if we can learn what she was doing on the island, that would go a long way in helping me to discover what happened to her." He ended the call. Swallowed hard. Fisted his hands.

Time heals all wounds?

"Everything all right?" Carrie had stepped up and drew his gaze. "You don't look so good."

"I'll explain after—"

"Coffee. I know."

He was glad for the interruption.

At the Shady Cove Lodge, Trevor opened the door for Carrie, then she led him across a small lobby to a rustic-style diner that matched all things Alaska.

After settling into a booth, Carrie and Trevor ordered the Big Alaskan—the biggest breakfast meal on the menu—along with coffee. Trevor begged the brunette twentysomething waitress named Daphne to leave the carafe. He downed two cups before he let his mind shift back to the building dread.

The questions.

And while Carrie stared into her coffee mug, he stared at her. Were the attacks solely related to her? Or did they have to do with the fact that she was assisting Trevor in his search? If they had nothing to do with Trevor and Jennifer, then that meant they were likely connected to Isaac's death.

She was attacked the first time after she flew Trevor to Mountain Cove. He'd been asking around about his sister and then hired a pilot to show him around.

His thoughts were fuzzy and running together.

Could his actions have drawn the wrong attention? Then someone followed Carrie to the airport and back to her plane where the attacker made his move.

And someone else murdered Isaac?

He poured more coffee.

Daphne brought two plates loaded with bacon, eggs, hash browns, and buttered toast. Trevor had also asked for a short stack. He wasn't going to be able to eat all of it. But after blessing the food, he and Carrie dove in. It had been a good long while since they'd had anything substantial to eat, and they'd used a lot of energy running from fires and fighting off bad guys.

He turned his thoughts to Isaac's death—Carrie had asked him for help, after all, and Chief Long welcomed the added assistance.

And, actually, thinking about this took his mind off Jennifer. He had nothing more to add to the puzzle at the moment. His heart needed a break, so when he came back to his investigation into her disappearance, he would have clarity.

After he finished half the food and drank another cup of coffee, he lifted his gaze.

Carrie hadn't touched the food on her plate, unless staring at it counted. As if sensing him watching, she glanced up. "I should have taken a nap before we had breakfast and coffee."

"Oh, so now you're finally getting tired. If you're in the air, you're vibrant. Living the life. But when your feet are on the ground . . ."

"What? What were you going to say? Finish it."

"You're human like the rest of us."

She chuckled and rubbed her eyes. "I usually have a lot more stamina than this, I promise." Grief struck her features as she stared off into the distance. Then she took a stab at her eggs, but she was just playing with her food now, moving it around her plate.

Before Trevor could make heads or tails of what was going on—who had come at her—he needed to know a lot more about Carrie and Isaac.

"All right. Time to talk."

"What? Can't I take a nap first?"

"Just answer a few questions, then we'll get rooms. Why don't you tell me the real story?"

Her head came up fast. "Excuse me?"

"Shadow Gap is a small town. Everyone loved Isaac. He was troubled. We know that from what he said to both you and Hank."

She stared at him. Her shimmering eyes made her look innocent and pure, but shadows that could only come from trauma and the harsh realities of life lurked behind her gaze.

"Come on, Carrie." He sipped his coffee now before he drank too much. It might be too late. Maybe he should have waited until he wasn't too dull headed to ask her. But time was wasting. "I've been around the block a few times."

"What does that even mean?"

"It means I recognize that you know more than you're telling me."

"I wouldn't hold back about this. Isaac needs justice. You know everything."

"You're wrong. I don't know everything. I don't know your past. How you met Isaac. Why you came to Shadow Gap of all places."

"None of that matters." She picked up a piece of bacon and crunched on it.

His questions had stirred her appetite. Good. "I beg to differ."

She stiffened. Her eyes hardened.

He was making her mad. Even better. Maybe anger would make her tell him everything.

"Why does it matter?"

"When I track a fugitive, I know everything about him. His past, where he's been, can tell me everything I need to know about where he's going."

She tried to keep her face expressionless, but pain ignited in her eyes. "Look, can we talk about this later? Remember, you need your pilot to get her rest. I'm going to book our rooms. I'll get one for you too, and you can just pick up the key at the counter."

He slid his credit card across the table. "Use this for both rooms."

"If they'll let me. Your key will be waiting at the front desk."

Carrie grabbed the card, then abruptly stood and left him sitting at the table.

She would talk. No doubt about it. And in the meantime, he would finish breakfast. He texted Chief Long to ask if she had learned anything new. She would get back to him when she could.

He buttered the pancakes and poured syrup over them. He was going to finish this breakfast—he had no idea what the next twelve hours would hold or when he would get to refuel. But his mind couldn't just let things go for a few moments. He brought up the image of Jennifer on his phone and shook his head.

Like he needed to get Carrie to talk, he needed to get his sister to talk.

Dead or alive.

The thought gutted him.

He should sleep too, but he wouldn't be able to. Daphne stopped by the table to switch out the carafe and pour more coffee. "Where's your girlfriend?"

"Oh, she's not my girlfriend. We're just working together. She went to her room." Why did he feel the need to explain his relationship with Carrie?

She swung her long hair around just so and smiled. "I get off in a couple of hours. I could show you around."

Her words surprised him. He was entirely too distracted and had to grasp for an answer.

A slight furrow grew between her brows, then she smiled again. "It's beautiful here. I'm a tour guide when I'm not working as a waitress."

He scraped a hand over his jaw. "Sure. Yeah. Maybe. Give me your number. If I decide I want a tour, I'll give you a call."

Her cheeks reddened, and she smiled again. She wrote her number on a napkin, then flitted away. Maybe Carrie would be up by then and Daphne could show *them* around.

She suddenly turned around and returned to the table. "So, that picture on your phone. Who is she to you?"

His heart jumped, but he kept his face straight. Tried to read hers.

"Someone very important to me. Why do you ask?" He searched her eyes. "Have you seen her before?"

"Yeah. But I can't talk now. In two hours?"

"In two hours, then."

Great. Trevor couldn't be sure she wasn't just working him. Maybe he'd take that nap after all so he'd be ready to face off with Carrie, and now Daphne, and get answers. Shady Cove wasn't in the pictures Jennifer left him. This stop hadn't been part of their plans, so it was strange that Daphne had seen her—if she really had. Then again, if someone was island hopping, this stop was next on the path toward Elotin Island. So Jennifer could have been here, or rather, Lori Fisher, just like if they followed a road map and made a stop along the way.

Then he got a text from his new friend, Hank.

Call me.

After grabbing a key from the front desk, Trevor went to his room and gave Hank a call.

"It's Trevor. Did you remember something?"

"Nope. I *found* something. I listened to my voice mails. It's kind of embarrassing, but I didn't know how to do that. Sandford suggested I learn. He's the one who said Isaac might have left me a message."

"Well, what did it say?"

"He said he wouldn't be able to bring the dog by. But he wanted me to know that Carrie might be in trouble. Someone was after her. He wanted me to protect her if something happened to him."

If something happened to him. Jennifer left a similar message for Trevor.

"Thanks, Hank. You think of anything else, let me know. Go ahead and share that with Chief Long."

"Already did."

Trevor ended the call. Someone was after Carrie, but Isaac was the one who died. And now, since they were together, it fell to Trevor to protect her. Because of the attacks, he'd already shifted into protection mode. Now he better understood the increased threat level.

He stared out the window at the marina and the whitecaps on the water in the inlet as the wind picked up. He sensed danger was building like the storm clouds gathering in the distance.

SIXTEEN

Carrie tossed the pillow she'd pressed over her face. After a short nap, she felt groggy instead of rested like she'd hoped. She lay in bed, staring at the ceiling, and thought back to Trevor's words.

"His past, where he's been, can tell me everything I need to know about where he's going."

She didn't have a ready response to his question, though she should have expected it. Trevor wanted to know about Isaac's and Carrie's pasts to find possible connections to his killer. Any good investigator would ask those same questions. What brought them to Alaska happened so long ago that she couldn't fathom Isaac's death was related.

God, please don't let it be related.

Unwanted images rushed at her.

The look in Darius's dark eyes.

The feel of his hands against her chest as they shoved her. Gulping air, she sat up. Carrie didn't want to think about what happened before, to remember it—even after a decade.

She'd built a new life now. Isaac too. But his death required answering those questions, facing the shadows. Did she need to know those answers before she told Trevor about what happened?

A text pulled her thoughts to the present. Trevor wanted to meet her downstairs. She dragged herself off the lumpy mattress, splashed water on her face, then ran a brush through her hair and put it up in a ponytail. Her nap didn't improve the circles gathering under her sad eyes. She didn't like what she saw in the mirror. The sudden wish to look more attractive for Trevor flitted through her mind.

No. Just no. Don't even go there.

Since Darius, she hadn't sought companionship with anyone else. She couldn't even touch that obliterated part of her heart—it remained radioactive to the rest of her. Deadly. Going there could destroy her.

Enough.

She grabbed her wallet and stuck it in her jacket pocket, then bounded down the steps to search for Trevor. Only a few people lingered in the lobby. A man stood from a chair and turned. Her heart skidded.

Mr. Blue Eyes.

She hated her reaction to him—like she was seeing him for the first time, all over again. A dark-haired beauty also stood and joined him, standing close. What was their waitress from this morning doing here? Carrie almost stumbled but kept forward momentum until she approached and forced a smile.

"Carrie." Trevor gestured to the woman. "You remember Daphne?"

Ah. She hadn't gotten the woman's name. "You were our waitress this morning. Nice to meet you. I'm Carrie James."

"Trevor told me about you."

I can't say that he mentioned you.

"So what are we doing?" Carrie stared at Trevor.

He glanced around the lobby. "Let's talk outside."

He led them out the doors and into the woods near the water.

Carrie got a closer look at Daphne's appearance. Beautiful long, dark hair and big brown eyes. Long, thick lashes. Daphne flashed Trevor a gorgeous smile, obviously flirting.

Weirdly strange and inappropriate jealousy pinged around in Carrie's chest. Really? She had zero reason to be jealous. She ignored it but couldn't overlook that Trevor appeared to enjoy Daphne's flirting a little too much. Trevor hadn't smiled for Carrie like that, revealing he had more dimples in his right cheek than his left.

What is the matter with me?

They finally stopped near the edge of the water and watched a ferry coming in.

"Why are we here? What are we doing?" Carrie's tone was less than friendly, and she didn't care.

Trevor cleared his throat. "Daphne is a local island guide, and it turns out she has information about Jennifer."

That changed everything. Now she understood why Trevor was being overly friendly. Or maybe it was simply wishful thinking on her part. She shook off the errant thoughts.

Trevor looked at Daphne. "I waited until Carrie was here, so now you can tell me about my sister."

He'd waited for *her*?

Daphne nodded and pursed her lips, glancing at Carrie, then back to Trevor. "She chartered a boat, the *Sea Mist*. I know this because it's my brother's boat and charter business. His name's Chad Bateman. I work with him on the weekends, and one Monday morning when I was heading home, I saw her approaching his boat."

"So she was here. On this island when she chartered it."

"Yes."

"Was she with anyone?"

She shook her head. "Not that I could see. But is she okay?"

"Why do you ask?"

"She chartered the *Sea Mist* for a round trip. He took her

to Essack Island and was supposed to bring her back, but she never returned to the boat." Daphne shrugged. "People change their plans, so Chad didn't worry about it."

"Except he mentioned it to you, so he was worried about it. Did he report it to the police?" Trevor asked. "What's the protocol for something like that?"

Daphne frowned, and her gaze flicked around. "Look. I don't know. Like I said, it happens a lot. People don't show up because they make other plans and don't think to tell him."

"What about their money?" Carrie asked.

"They pay in full up front. No refunds."

That didn't sound right, especially in a place like this. If someone didn't show up, they could be hurt and need help. Just like when Elias didn't show up. Carrie investigated. There had to be a protocol for this in the charter boat business too. She could figure that out later.

Trevor pressed his fisted hand to his lips. "Jennifer would have canceled if she made other plans, so something must have happened."

"Chad didn't know that. And for all I know, he reported it to the local PD." She shrugged and glanced away, then bit her lip. "Look. He was scared, okay?"

Her story had changed—and fast. Carrie studied the woman and Trevor's reaction to her last statement.

He narrowed his eyes. "What did he have to be scared of?"

"I'm only telling you because she's your sister." Daphne's frown deepened, and she looked out over the water. Gathering her nerve? Changing her mind or story again?

"Please, Daphne. I'm desperate to find her. Please tell me everything you know."

She nodded. "But you need to be careful. Something is going on at Jacob's Mountain."

"Jacob's Mountain?"

"On Essack Island. It's where he took her. The Tlingit call

it *shaa xeiyí*, meaning 'the mountain casts a shadow,' or *shaa nani*, 'Mountain of Death.'"

Trevor glanced at Carrie as if he expected her to know all things Southeast Alaska. Maybe she'd kind of led him on about that. The mountain, the island. Carrie had never had business there, and maybe that's why she hadn't recognized that last photo, if that's where Jennifer went. But she remembered reading a few things about the island.

"Jacob's Mountain," she said. "Are you talking about the Superfund site?"

"Superfund site." Trevor arched a brow.

Was it a question or a statement?

"I don't know a lot, actually," Daphne said. "There's hazardous waste from a mine that was shut down a long time ago. Someone is supposed to clean it up. Chad could tell you more."

"I'd like to talk to him," Trevor said. "Can you give me his number?"

"Of course. He has a satellite phone because there's not much cell coverage where he travels." Daphne found the number and showed it to Trevor, who entered it into his cell. "You can meet him in person," she added. "If you're looking for Lori, I mean Jennifer, he could take you to the island. That's why it bothered him. Why it scared him. He never takes anyone there, so he was hesitant at first."

Trevor's eyes darkened. Maybe her brother should have refused, and the fact that he didn't report Jennifer missing under the circumstances had to boil Trevor's blood. But he was scared for a reason, and they needed to learn more from her brother.

"I think that sounds like a good idea," Carrie said. "Let's give him a call, charter his boat, and we can talk to him then."

Trevor scowled. "If he's already booked on another charter, we can't wait for him to get back."

"So call him and find out." Carrie thought Trevor should be encouraged by this news because it meant following the picture trail had led them somewhere important. They wouldn't even have to go to Elotin Island now, location number three. Still, the locations were a simple map. A hop, skip, and a jump over islands. And following the pattern, she guessed Essack Island would be next after Elotin. Maybe.

"I think we need to get to the island tonight." Trevor's tone was low and pained.

"And I think we should talk to her brother first," Carrie said. "Before we go. We cannot go traipsing over to a mountain the locals gave a scary name until we know everything."

"I'm guessing you don't want a tour of Kendall Island, then." Daphne sounded like she wanted to defuse the growing tension between Carrie and Trevor.

Carrie looked to Trevor. "Well? What are we doing? Getting a tour of Kendall Island or going to the mountain?"

"She was here. It's not in the pictures she left, but what if she took samples here too?"

Right, looking for whatever geologists look for. "Um . . . Daphne, could I have a few moments alone to speak with Trevor?"

Daphne nodded and moved to the rail near the water's edge.

Carrie stepped closer to Trevor. "Look, we know Jennifer made it back to Shadow Gap. She gave the photos to Monica. She isn't somehow still on that island. You're acting like if we get there, you're going to find your sister. One more day, time to talk to Chad, isn't going to hurt." Carrie held her breath—had she overstepped? Her words sounded harsh.

The pain in his eyes, the deep lines of concern carved in his forehead, made her hurt for him. She didn't want to see him suffering, and maybe she'd just added to that.

"Good point about the timeline. Daphne can possibly help us to know." He held Carrie's gaze as if waiting for her permission.

"Okay. Sure. I didn't have anything more to say." She just didn't want to say so much in front of their new acquaintance.

Trevor walked toward Daphne, and Carrie instead moved close to the water, observing the surface and watching the clouds rolling in. The weather was shifting and could ground them. Not good.

He finally approached Carrie and stood next to her. "We know that she opened the safe deposit box in May and then gave the key to Monica." He sighed—heavily, deeply—and it cut through her heart. "It looks like she left the pictures in that box for me because she was afraid that when she returned to the mountain in June, she wouldn't come back."

She can't still be there, Trevor. She can't still be alive. But Carrie could never say that to him. He held on to hope like it was a lifeline for him personally. Deep inside, she admitted that she couldn't know whether Jennifer was still there or she didn't survive. Or was being held prisoner, but it seemed highly unlikely.

Trevor had to know that too, deep inside. He just wasn't willing to admit it.

"We should wait until early in the morning to go, so we'll have all day to try to find where she went next. We'll have time to connect with Chad before then too."

She glanced behind them. Daphne was gone. What did he say to her? Carrie had the urge to touch his arm. To comfort him somehow. She understood what he was feeling all the way to her marrow. She'd lost someone close to her too.

Just days ago.

What happened to you, Isaac?

Brows furrowed, Trevor turned around and searched the area as if something had set him on high alert.

"What is it? What are you looking for?"

"Just a feeling. I think we've stayed in one place too long. Let's get in the air. We know where she went, and we don't need all day to find it."

Mountain of Death, here we come.

SEVENTEEN

Someone's after her.

He knew that already—after everything that happened. But getting the confirmation set him on edge. Still, the recent attacks on them seemed to be tied to his search for Jennifer since his questions at the Island Trading Company in Angoon had triggered Moosehead to call and report back to someone.

But now he knew that Carrie was in double the trouble. Danger was coming at her from different directions.

The sensation that someone was watching crawled over him. They already knew they were being stalked. They'd expected someone to be waiting for them at Jennifer's next stop, but this place—Shady Cove—wasn't in the photographs. Still, it made sense—someone had known her travel plans and followed her, tracked her somehow.

"All right, Trevor. I can see something has you spooked," Carrie said. "And now you've got me worried. Are you sure you don't want to stay?"

"Yes. I'm sure. We can come back if necessary. But Daphne's

information is the biggest lead we've gotten so far. We need to talk to her brother, but we're not staying here." Quickly, they returned to the lodge to grab their duffels. While still in the lobby, he got out his cell. "Let me just text Daphne that we're leaving and remind her to stay safe."

She'd been the one to warn them about the increasing danger, and now they were walking right into it with their eyes wide open.

"Is she going to be okay?"

"I hope so. I think she wishes she hadn't talked to me in the first place."

"I think she likes you, Trevor. She wanted a date with you and maybe used the fact that she'd seen Jennifer to get your attention, and that resulted in her telling us more than she'd intended."

Carrie's words surprised him, and he searched her eyes.

She arched a brow. "Come on, you can't tell me you didn't notice."

He sagged under her accusing stare. "Maybe a little."

Was she jealous? *Daphne has nothing on you, Carrie James.*

"What did you tell her?"

"I told her to hang out with family or friends tonight. That we're leaving, but she shouldn't go anywhere alone."

"Good advice. I'm a little concerned about the weather, so I need to check a few things to make sure it isn't going to be a problem for us. But as long as I have a five-hundred-foot cloud ceiling and visibility of three miles, we're probably good to go."

I feel much better now. He would keep his sarcasm to himself.

At the seaplane dock, while Carrie did her preflight check, Trevor both texted and called Daphne's brother, leaving a voice mail message that explained their plans and Trevor's need to speak with him. Maybe he was coming on too strong, and

Daphne's brother might decide to avoid Trevor at all costs. But he would track the guy down if he had to.

It wasn't like he had bread crumbs to follow. Still, the charter boat had a path it frequented. He stared at the registration number on Carrie's Helio Courier, N543TS. Why hadn't he thought of it before?

"I've been thinking about this all wrong. I figured those guys knew Jennifer's path or had the pictures and that's how they found us on Clackon Island. Broke into your room and then set the lodge on fire. Could they actually be tracking your plane?"

Carrie bent down and released her plane from the dock, then she stood tall and stared at him. Her eyes widened. "They absolutely could be." She released a heavy sigh. "I'm such an idiot. I didn't think—"

"I should have asked earlier."

"There are a ton of apps available to watch planes. Track them. See where they're going. Even look up at the sky overhead to see what's flying over you." She pressed her hands over her eyes.

"It's okay, Carrie. This is all happening so fast. But now that we know how they could have tracked us, even here, then is there a way to stop them?"

"Absolutely."

"How?"

"I turn off the transponder. No transponder, then the ADS-B—Automatic Dependent Surveillance-Broadcast—won't give away my location."

"The what?"

"It's hard to explain. Pilots are required to have it in Class C or B airspace, but I spend most of my time in Class G, or uncontrolled airspace. But Isaac wanted me to have the tracking system so I could see other planes and they could see me, and there would be less chance of a collision—a huge problem in Alaska. The coverage out here, though, can be spotty if I'm in the mountains. But it can work at the weirdest times. Let me turn off the transponder." She climbed inside the plane.

He got in too and strapped into his seat. "Are you okay with this?"

"It's no problem. I always fly as if I'm out here alone anyway, but when I can, I radio with flight service stations." And just like that, she turned off the transponder.

Whatever it takes. He hoped that was enough.

"The issue now is, they probably already know where we're going," she said. "They must."

"Right. I guess the good news is that we're getting away from Shady Cove without incident."

As they taxied on the water, Carrie listened to the weather report. Clouds and rain had moved in. Trevor's heart rate kicked up.

"I'm taking off directly into the wind, and it'll be a short takeoff. The less time I spend on the rough water, the better. Hold on."

The less I know, the better.

The one-engine plane abruptly lifted, and Trevor watched the water speeding by beneath them. After a few moments in the air, Trevor let himself relax. But he didn't like the way the wind buffeted the small plane.

"I know we left the island because you think we're in danger again, but I think we should stop somewhere before going all the way to Essack Island or anywhere near Jacob's Mountain until we know more and at least talk to Chad."

Trevor had his cell pulled up and the map downloaded. "I know you don't want to go to the island yet, but I'm going today. No point in holding off. Take me to the town on the south side. I won't go to the mountain, though, until I know more. I promise."

She said nothing else. The clouds pressed down on them, but Carrie kept well below them, traveling along the waterways.

Heavy turbulence shook the plane.

"The air seems rougher today." He sensed that had to do with more than just the weather.

"Oh, it is, I assure you."

"Somehow I get the feeling we're not talking about the same thing." He could grouse too.

"I don't get the rush to the scary mountain. This doesn't seem very detective-like to me."

Maybe not. "This is my sister, Carrie. Put yourself in my position."

He hadn't known her long, but he knew her well enough to see her visibly relax.

"Okay. You're right. I'm sorry."

"Look, if I had known this mountain would be our final destination, we could have started there." Trevor stared at the rain coming down in sheets. Tried to ignore the wind buffeting the plane.

She let out a soft chuckle. "You don't *know* it's the final destination."

He let that sink in. "True enough. But the pictures indicate that it is. You were right to insist that we follow the trail left by the pictures in order. And they created a path as it was, so we would have ended up there even without learning about Jennifer's chartering the *Sea Mist* to take her to Jacob's Mountain." The information Daphne shared was leading him closer to getting the answers.

"I still think it's strange. She placed the picture in a safe deposit box in case something happened to her? Why not just tell you the whole story and leave that in the box?"

"Don't you think I've wondered the same thing? She could have saved so much time and trouble. Maybe she wasn't sure about what she would find in that mountain, but she knew she'd find something. She knew it was dangerous. She left me the road she took to get there. I don't know."

"Maybe the truth, laid out plainly, would be too dangerous. She was too afraid for herself. Too afraid for you, or anyone who might find it. If someone else opened that box and somehow got their hands on the information, the photographs wouldn't mean anything to them. But if you found it and opened it—"

"I would know to follow the bread crumbs."

"And she knew you, Trevor. She knew you would dig as deeply as she was digging to find the truth."

"The evidence. And along the way, I've learned to be wary. I needed to know what I was walking into, and I couldn't truly understand until I took the time to find the truth on my own."

Trevor hated every minute of this insane search.

"I think that meeting the store clerk in Angoon," Carrie said, "and learning from her the islanders' feelings about what Jennifer was doing was just as important as the fact that she was taking samples but pretending to be a photographer."

"It's possible, but all this is part of the bigger picture. That's why I need to get to that mountain."

A few moments later, she asked, "Do you believe you'll find her on that island?"

"I honestly don't know." His throat grew tight. "But I can't bear to think of her death."

He regretted the words. Carrie was still suffering from a great loss of her own. If Jennifer had died on that mountain, or because of her search, her death was tragic. Like Isaac's death, Jennifer's death wouldn't come in her sleep at a ripe old age.

"Thinking about it just feels wrong to me," he added.

"In your heart and mind, your sister is still the living, breathing woman you know," she said.

And I'll save her. I have to save her.

"I can't accept such a tragic end to her life. Not when I've done everything I could to protect her from the danger that chased her before."

"Before?"

"Her ex-husband was abusive. But it seems Jennifer got herself into a different kind of danger. Probably more than she could have imagined. So that's why I'm anxious to get to the Mountain of Death. That is, if we make it. Honestly, this morning with that amazing sunrise, I thought I might actually learn to enjoy flying."

She sent him a huge smile. "Really?"

And with that smile, Carrie James was just as captivating as this morning's sunrise.

"Yeah, but today the flight is rough, and I might never want to get on a plane again. No offense."

"Oh, I'm offended. You can't just say 'no offense' and remove that from the context." She laughed.

Nope. Didn't want to fly again. Even with the vibrant and beautiful Carrie James, who was very much alive and breathing. And he needed to focus on keeping her that way.

He rubbed the back of his neck.

The task weighed heavy on him, was more pressing to him than searching for Jennifer. That thought rocked him. Hank's call vibrated around inside of him. Another reason he wanted to leave the island *today* was that he didn't have a handle on who was after Carrie.

She refused to answer questions about her past when he asked over eggs and bacon. He suspected Chief Long was counting on him to pull teeth to get those answers if he had to.

"What's going on, Trevor? I get the feeling there's something you're not telling me. Does it have to do with Jacob's Mountain? What am I missing?"

"It has more to do with what *I'm* missing."

"I'm all ears. What are you missing?" she asked.

Information you weren't willing to share. He needed to give her a reason. And here it was. "I know what was bothering Isaac."

"How could you know? And that doesn't sound like you're missing information if you know something. You're not making sense." Carrie's voice shook.

The plane took a sharp dive, then leveled out. Was that deliberate? On second thought, waiting until they landed to have this conversation would be better.

He'd unsettled her. "We should talk about this after we land."

"We're talking about it now. What was bothering Isaac? You can't withhold that from me. What have you learned?"

"Easy, Carrie. I'll tell you everything you want to know, but if you want my help, then you're going to have to reciprocate."

"What do you mean?"

"You're going to have to tell me everything I want to know. A deal's a deal." Oh, he was playing dirty.

"I'm going to flip this plane over. Do loops. Something. If you don't tell me."

He believed her.

Okay. Okay. "Hank found a message on his voice mail. Isaac said someone was after you. So he was worried and wanted Hank to watch out for you. Nothing more, but we both know what he meant."

"In case something happened to him." She pounded the throttle. Tears gushed down her face. "Blast him!"

"Can you fly this thing while you're upset? I didn't know the right time to tell you. I wanted off the island because I had the feeling that someone was closing in. At the very least, I should have waited until we landed. Please just relax. I'll find who did this. But I'm going to do what Isaac asked of Hank and keep you safe in the meantime. Please, get us there in one piece. In fact, I'm fine if you want to land right now. Anywhere. I don't care. We can talk about it like two rational and *alive*—"

"I can't land just yet. I need to find the smoothest water possible, and below us is anything but smooth."

Trevor opened his mouth to speak—

A loud bang cut him off. His heart ricocheted in his chest. "What was that?"

Carrie said nothing, but her frown spoke volumes.

"Carrie, what's going on? What was that?"

"I think the engine exploded."

Smoke filled the cab.

"Exploded?"

The propeller slowed to a complete stop. But they were still in the air.

"What's happening? What are you doing?"

"I need you to calm down and stop asking me questions. I need to radio the nearest flight service station and let them know we've lost engine power and my plan of action."

"Are we going to crash?"

"Absolutely not. This plane will glide. If I can just find smooth water, I'll bring us in for a safe landing. Let me concentrate."

She radioed, and he wished he didn't have to listen to the words. "Mayday, Mayday, Mayday, we've lost our engine . . ."

Lord, I have to find my sister. Please don't let me die yet. Please help Carrie land this plane! His silent prayer was more of a demand and a shout to the Almighty.

She flipped a few switches. Messed with knobs on her dash. "I'll glide as long as I can, and the plane will slowly descend onto the water. Piece of cake."

"I thought you needed smooth water." It looked rough to him. "Have you done this before?"

"Not without power. But better on water than on the land.

Now, say a prayer. I'm searching for the smoothest spot, and I'll bring her in."

"I haven't stopped praying."

"There are no guarantees in life. So in case I die and you live, I can't think of anyone who might be after me, except the man who killed me."

The man who killed you?

EIGHTEEN

He wouldn't talk to Carrie. She needed 100 percent focus. His breathing quickened and his shoulders and back stiffened, bracing for the next few moments as they continued to glide.

Keep it together, man, if it's the last thing you do.

With islands on both sides of them, the blue water filled his vision and the whitecaps grew larger as Carrie brought her Helio in for a landing without power.

The fuselage shook, and he thought it would break in half.

"Hold . . . on . . ." Carrie's voice vibrated. "I'm going to try to get us closer to the island, because I don't know about you, but I can't swim halfway across the strait. It's going to be a hard landing on the less-than-smooth water, Trevor, so brace yourself."

Ten seconds later, the pontoons hit the water first. The plane shuddered and suddenly flipped upside down.

What happened? Out the window he spotted a pontoon, which had snapped. Water rose, gushing into the cab, and Trevor held his breath. Now it was up to his chin. He worked quickly to unstrap himself. The plane was sinking.

He would drown if he didn't release the straps. The very things that protected him while flying and landing would kill him now. But his fingers felt thick in the dark, icy water, and he struggled.

Come on, come on, come on . . .

His lungs burned, and he would soon breathe in water against his will.

The clasp released, but it was no time for relief. Finally free, he shoved up to the small pocket of air where his feet had once been. Carrie hadn't freed herself yet.

Maybe she was having trouble releasing the straps too. He drew in a breath from the decreasing space, then stuck his head into the water.

Carrie's arms floated.

Oh no. No, no!

Trevor quickly unleashed her and pulled her up for air, but she wasn't breathing.

God, please, no! Help me!

His pulse roared in his ears. His lungs screamed for oxygen.

If he drowned, Carrie would die too. He'd gotten them into this, and he had to get them out. He opened the door and carefully maneuvered her out of the cockpit, then around and over the wings, tugging her up and onto the surface, breaching the water.

Good thing he could swim, or they would both die. The plane hadn't gone down in the middle of the strait, or he'd have a good five miles to swim. Still, he had about two hundred or more yards to make it to the small island that hugged the larger coast of a bigger island. Carrie never lost her head and had thought out the best plan for landing on the water in the worst of circumstances.

The least he could do was get her to safety.

"Stay with me, Carrie. We're going to make it." *I'm going to get you there.*

The water was cold—even in the summer—and chilled him to the bone. Made him numb. But he wouldn't stop.

He would never stop.

She coughed, gagged, and spewed water. The pressure he'd put on her chest while swimming must have triggered the reaction.

Relief propelled him forward. "Hang on. We're almost there. I'll get you there."

Finally, his feet touched the ground, and he freed her. She stumbled forward next to him in the shallow water until she reached the gray sand on the beach and dropped to her knees. Emptied her lungs some more.

He remained standing and eyed the island. At least here they were able to easily get out of the water. The foliage all around looked thick and forbidding. About ten yards in, the tree line started. He made his way inward along a small stream that emptied into the strait.

Trevor glanced behind him to check on Carrie. They had both nearly drowned. Nearly died. But he couldn't take time to process that now, or they could still die. He turned back and approached her. She was dripping wet. They both were. If they didn't get warm soon, they would succumb to hypothermia on this cold, wet day. At least the rain had let up.

He noticed the knot on her forehead, and a few scratches. "You're hurt."

She shrugged out of her dripping jacket. "It's not bad. Really, I'm good. Thanks. You?"

"I'm alive." But for how much longer? He glanced around again, taking in the beautiful scenery and their unfortunate predicament. *What are we going to do? Survive, that's what.* Even though she'd radioed on an emergency frequency, he wanted to confirm someone was coming. He needed to call for help.

After that call, he wanted to ask her just what happened

back there. Was she thinking what he was thinking? He fished for his cell in the special compartment in his coat, then he remembered . . . and looked up at Carrie.

Her green eyes grew wide. "What is it?"

"Bad news. I lost my cell. I had it out to look at the map instead of in my jacket. Even if I could find it, it wasn't waterproof." He gritted his teeth. Could this day get any worse?

"Mine is." She stuck her hands down into her pocket and pulled it out. "But no signal. I need my satellite phone." She stared at her sinking plane. "Someone sabotaged us. In a personal way. Someone is sending a message."

Oh, man. Did Moosehead do this?

"We can talk about it later," he said. "I need to build a fire. But the plane is sinking, and I also need to swim back out there and get our stuff. Your satellite phone. Our money and duffels. Otherwise, we got nothing. How are we going to make it out of this?"

"You build a fire. I'll get the stuff. I carry a state-required survival kit in the plane, and it does us no good at the bottom of the strait." She began removing her shoes. "In the pack I have a week's worth of food—for one person, that is. But I don't plan on staying here a week. It also includes a fire starter, ax, fishing gear, flares, and a sleeping bag."

"You're still shivering."

"So are you. But I'll live. We both will."

"I'll stack the wood, then, and get it ready."

She quickly waded out into the water and dove in. Trevor stood and paced the shore's edge, looking for kindling that wasn't saturated from rain. Plus, pacing helped him work up some warmth.

He shook his head.

Jennifer had wanted him to learn the truth and knew it was dangerous. He never should have gotten Carrie into this, but here they were. He moved to the edge of the woods, hoping he could find something to use, considering everything was soaked through and through. He found some hemlock twigs—the oils inside burned even when wet—and some low-hanging spruce branches. He'd need a lot more kindling than usual to get this fire going. Then he dragged an old, dead cedar branch over to the rudimentary camp he was creating. While he had built a stick fire before—by rubbing sticks together to create the required friction and heat—he didn't want to go through that again. He wasn't even sure he could do it with the wet wood. But Carrie's fire starter would do the trick.

Water splashed, and he looked up to see her dragging their waterproof duffels along with a larger bag that had enough air to float. He waded out and grabbed the gear. She coughed and hacked and shivered. He tossed their things closer to where he'd been stacking the wood for the fire.

She swiped a hand over her face and eyes, then plopped down on the ground and leaned against a driftwood log. "The satellite phone is broken. Cracked."

Trevor let that sink in for a moment, but he couldn't dwell on it. They'd find a way out of this.

"I'll grab the fire starter and get a fire going, and you can change out of your wet clothes."

"The fire will be enough." She hugged herself.

"There's a blanket in here along with the sleeping bag. Which one do you want?"

"The blanket, if it's still dry."

"Everything's dry." He tossed her the blanket.

Then he threw some protein bars at her feet, along with two bottles of water. Crouching near the kindling, he said, "Now, if I've done my job, this should start up quickly."

A small flame started, then burst into bigger flames that spread to the logs. Trevor grabbed another bottle of water and pulled his gun out too.

"What are you doing?"

"I need to wash off the saltwater. I won't use much water, I promise."

When he was done, he set the gun on the log to dry, grateful the rain had stopped, then dropped next to her.

She lifted the blanket for him to join her.

He scooted closer and wrapped an arm around her, hugging her to him. "Just so we're clear, this is so we can share body heat."

She narrowed her gaze, but amusement swam in her eyes too.

"Here, eat a protein bar. Drink your water and hydrate." She ripped the package open and handed it to him.

"No, you eat."

"I'm going to eat mine, but with your arm around me, it's not like you can open your own bar. Now, eat."

Taking the bar, he chuckled. They were going to be okay. They had survived what he assumed was a sabotaged plane, and now they would somehow survive the wilderness on a tiny island long enough to get help on a bigger island. He bit into the crunchy peanut bar that had an overwhelming vitamin aftertaste.

She took a few bites and chewed, then finished off the bar. With the blanket hanging across her shoulders and back, Carrie lifted her knees and pressed her chin against her arms.

"Feeling better?"

"Yeah. Definitely warmer. You?"

"Yes."

She tilted her head toward him. Her blond hair looked dark when wet. Her gaze lit on him. "Thanks for pulling me out of the plane. That was risky. I would add that it was heroic, but you need me to get you out of here."

"Are you saying I'm not a hero?" She was partly right. He shot her a half grin.

And she cracked one to match his. "I'm kidding. Of course you're a hero."

The tightness in his chest eased a little. Was he *flirting* with her?

"Haven't you heard the saying there is truth in jest? You're welcome, by the way. Of course, I would have pulled you out, regardless, but you're right about me needing you to get us out of here. I have no idea where I am."

"I don't know about that," she said. "You look like an adventurous type, kind of like Bear Grylls. You have skills and training, and I'm pretty sure that even without me, you would survive just fine on your own."

"Maybe. But you know the area and the people, so I'm glad I don't have to do this alone. Stinks for you, though." He chuckled. He couldn't deny that it was going to be a lot easier with this capable, beautiful woman by his side.

He stopped his thoughts right there. Still, he snuggled her closer, enjoying the warmth that finally seeped into him from her body and the blazing fire.

She sighed and relaxed against him. Trevor couldn't have anticipated the sudden contentment that filled him. It didn't take a rocket scientist to recognize that it had nothing to do with the fact that he was warming up and everything to do with the fact that Carrie James was next to him.

He reminded himself that she was close to him for practical reasons. Nothing more.

"You built a cozy campsite here," she said, "but we're not staying."

"I know. We had to get warm."

She suddenly shifted away and was on her feet before he could blink. "And I'm as good as new, thanks to you."

Grumbling inside, he joined her to stand. He hated to waste the fire, the moment, to rush off to . . . oh yeah, Mission Jennifer. And they were so close.

He scratched his jaw. Carrie had distracted him. But he'd give himself a break—they'd nearly died.

"Carrie, you have a knot on your head. Scratches. You're still cold. I don't think you're as good as new. So, sit down. You're not warm enough yet."

"One word for you. Bears. Brown bears. Okay, two words. And I might love to *fly* out into the bush and over the wilds of Alaska, but I'm not *really* a wilderness girl."

"Someone is coming to help us, aren't they? You radioed for help, plus what about the ELT?"

"Ah, so you know about that, do you?"

"Yes. Emergency Locator Transmitter."

"Well, once the plane hits the water and submerges, the signal won't transmit. We flipped, so that means it pretty much did nothing, and the transponder is off. But I radioed our emergency, so someone knows we're out here. But maybe it would be better if I hadn't radioed and no one knew where we were. Or they thought we died in the crash. Catastrophic engine failure is a possibility, but with that explosion, I'm convinced our plane was sabotaged."

"How long will it be before help arrives?"

"Out here? The average time from LKP—last known position—to rescue is thirty-one hours. I shortened that time for us with my distress call, but the plane went down miles from that location. They'll see it on the water unless it sinks completely. We've got flares, so we can signal them."

"You could die while you're waiting," he said.

"We're not going to die. Maybe this waterway isn't as traveled as the Alaska Marine Highway, but we could still see a ferry or boat before we spot the Coast Guard. We can use the flares to get their attention. But honestly, since someone sabotaged the plane and followed us, I'm not sure I want to be found."

Isaac had said someone was after her. She said that the sabotaged plane was personal. What did she mean? He needed to hear the story behind Isaac's warning. What did Carrie know that she wasn't sharing?

"So, sit down and talk. We need to finish the conversation we started on the plane."

And he needed to push the trauma of the plane crash out of his thoughts. This was a good way to do it.

Frowning, Carrie eased onto the ground next to the log and crossed her arms. Trevor didn't sit next to her this time, but instead took a spot a few feet from her at the opposite end of the log. He had a feeling she would not welcome his warmth. Maybe he didn't need hers either.

"I want to hear all about what you meant when you said you couldn't think of anyone who would want to kill you except the man who killed you." Those words had clung to him, leaving him unsettled since she'd said them. It seemed surreal. Or had he dreamed it all?

"Do we have to do this now?"

He scrunched his face up. "I don't get you. There's never going to be a better time. No one is around to hear you tell the story. You wanted me to help you find Isaac's killer, and as far as I can tell, you're the only one standing in the way. So, please, I want to hear this story."

Carrie stared into the fire. Her eyes grew big and luminous. He almost wished he hadn't asked. But she had a story to tell, and it could be the key to finding Isaac's killer and stopping the danger she was in.

Finally, she hung her head and sucked in a breath. He heard the pain in her exhale. "That plane. That old Helio Courier was my father's. He was a missionary and flew his own plane in and out of the African bush. When I was eighteen, he and my mother died in a plane crash—different plane. Along with a few belongings, he left that plane to me. Still, I couldn't fly it. Not for a long time. I went into the Army instead. What else was I going to do?"

"Wait. You were in the Army?"

"Yep."

"So you were a pilot?"

"Back then, I had my pilot's license but needed a four-year college degree to pilot in the Army. But like I said, I couldn't fly anymore. I didn't *want* to fly."

"So what did you do?"

"Ironically, I ended up as an aviation operations specialist. I handled flight plans. Anything that had to do with the aircraft and the pilots."

That must have been agonizing, and he didn't know what to say. He didn't want to get sidetracked, so he said nothing and waited for her to share the rest of her story.

"I thought the Army would keep me focused on something besides my loss, but I was wrong. I spent four years in the Army, and during that time I started flying again on the side, getting my hours back up. Then, twelve years ago, after I was discharged, I joined a humanitarian organization, Global Relief Services, as a pilot. The work was similar to what my parents did as missionaries. It was hard but fulfilling work. I felt like I was doing something in this world, ya know?"

She angled her head at him, waiting for his answer.

"Yeah, I do." He wanted to make a positive difference by bringing justice.

"That's where I met Isaac. He was an aviation mechanic. I told him about my father's plane, and it turned out that he'd known my father and worked on the plane for him. Isaac was all about helping missionaries fly their planes, so it made sense that he would know my father. Isaac talked me into flying the Helio Courier, the best African bush plane. My father's plane. We had it transported to the headquarters, and he got it back into working condition once again. We connected and became close. He was like a father to me, or an uncle. I don't know—like family, I guess. I had no one else. And now my plane is gone. It's all gone. My parents. Isaac and, now, the only thing I had left of them."

"I'm so sorry, Carrie."

Her face twisted as the flames danced in her eyes. "I was on a cargo drop when someone I trusted betrayed me." She shook her head. "It was so long ago, but I still have nightmares. I still feel gutted. Betrayed."

He understood all of it, except one thing. "But you said a man killed you. What did you mean? He broke your heart?"

She lifted a shoulder. "Yeah. Sure."

Trevor pursed his lips. He shouldn't have added that last bit. He should have let her talk without making suggestions. "Listen, Carrie, there's more to this story. I get that you have trust issues, but I'm not here to hurt you or betray—"

"Like I would let you." She glared at him.

The anger behind her words startled him, and he hesitated before asking, "Who killed you and why?"

Whatever she meant by that.

"A man I thought I loved. I thought he loved me too. When I discovered he was transporting valuable contraband, he killed me."

"But clearly he didn't."

"He *pushed* me out of a cargo plane. We were coming in for the drop, and I fell two hundred feet. What do you think he intended? I was told that I did, in fact, die."

The words slammed into him. Someone *pushed* her from a plane? He couldn't fathom that. He shoved his hand through his still-damp hair.

Someone had to have found her and revived her. He had a feeling that person was Isaac—and now Isaac was dead, and his last message was that someone was after Carrie. Trevor needed the rest of this story. Who shoved her? Why did she think the sabotaged plane was personal? That alone made him believe this could be connected to what happened before. He needed more information. All of it, but he wouldn't press her just yet.

He was still trying to wrap his mind around the image of

her falling from an airplane. Someone who claimed to love her deliberately pushing her.

She'd personally experienced the worst of humanity. Trevor stared into the fire and tried to absorb her news. He hadn't expected it. How did someone recover from that? They didn't.

As he watched Carrie stare at the fire, he knew . . .

She hadn't.

NINETEEN

Her breathing picked up with his barrage of questions and having to revisit the past. She hadn't talked about it with anyone. Really. Ever. Isaac had been there to pick up the pieces, so he knew. What was there to talk about?

"And you're still injured." He gestured to her leg.

"I don't want to think about the number of broken bones, but my leg was shattered. It took a lot of surgeries before I could walk without assistance. Sometimes I still need my cane."

"I hate that you have to think about it again, but I'm just trying to understand your past. It's possible that it's related to what happened to Isaac."

"I don't know how."

"Revenge."

"After ten years?"

"That's a good point, but it doesn't negate the possibility. Please tell me about the contraband you mentioned. Are we talking drugs? What's the story there?" Trevor stoked the fire.

Carrie sat forward to soak in more heat. "You've heard of blood diamonds. Conflict diamonds."

"Sure. Who hasn't?"

"It's not just diamonds. It's any natural resource in a conflict zone that's sold to fuel the fighting. A new gem was discovered in Zhugandia called merazite. It's considered rare and highly valuable."

"How much is it worth?"

She lifted a shoulder. "Ten years ago, roughly a quarter of a million a carat."

"So it was this merazite you're calling contraband."

"Stolen from the country's resources or purchased and therefore funding the conflict. I wanted no part of it. I was shocked when I saw the uncut gems hidden in with the other supplies." Telling Trevor was like reliving the entire event, and she thought she might lose the protein bar she'd eaten.

"I never could have guessed any of this," he said.

"I didn't expect you would have."

"Nor have I ever heard of that gem."

She scoffed a laugh. "Unless you're caught up in that world, you wouldn't. There's a host of gems you've probably never heard of."

"How do you know so much?"

"I was aware of merazite because of the work I did in that country. It had become a conflict gem after its discovery, and after what happened, I spent some time reading up on gems. That's the extent of my knowledge."

She hugged herself tighter and stared hard at the fire.

Please don't ask me any more questions.

A few minutes passed, and she relaxed. She'd given Trevor a lot to swallow. A lot to think about. Maybe he could figure out who was behind Isaac's death from what happened ten years ago on the other side of the world.

Carrie had spread her jacket across a log so the layer of fleece could dry out. Once it was wet, it was useless. If their rescue didn't arrive soon, she would vote for leaving.

Whether they would walk around the island, following the

shoreline, or cut through the thick rainforest to go across was yet to be decided. Either way would take time. Depending on the underbrush, crossing the island might actually be out of the question.

She dreaded the trek. The questions, on top of having ditched the plane, had left her exhausted.

But the fire was great.

She hadn't wanted him to sit next to her, so she'd deliberately been off-putting to scare him away. But maybe she shouldn't have, because deep down . . .

I want him to sit next to me and warm me up. He'd wrapped his arm around her and pulled her close to share their heat and chase away the cold. Never mind that the warmth she'd soaked up from him comforted her in ways she couldn't explain, or maybe didn't want. Carrie deliberately kept her distance at all times—emotionally and physically, if possible.

But Trevor made her feel safe.

Secure.

She hadn't felt that way in so long, she couldn't even remember. She hadn't expected it. Nor had she expected that she would want to feel it again. But due to her own stubbornness, here she was sitting alone and wishing for the comfort Trevor provided.

She was practical and hardworking. Cared about her fellow humans, but—*God help me*—she didn't need a man in her life.

Ever again.

Leaning against the log, she fought the battle in her mind. But he'd pulled her out of the cold water. Out of a sinking airplane. He'd saved her—like Isaac.

Unfortunately, she kept seeing Isaac lying dead on the floor. Blood everywhere. Anyone who helped her, saved her, would end up dead. She hated that her thoughts had turned morbid, but she couldn't unsee Isaac's body. That would haunt her forever.

And as for the man brooding against the log, she needed to know *his* story, but she fought that need. Because, on one hand, they shouldn't share their sad stories and develop any resemblance of an emotional connection.

Was it too late?

Though she'd resolved it shouldn't happen, somehow that connection with Trevor was forming in the middle of this journey to find answers. How could that be? Despite her best efforts, she was drawn to him. She flicked her gaze from the fire to Mr. Blue Eyes. He stared at the flames with a serious expression that said he still had plenty of questions. He lifted his gaze to take in their surroundings again and frowned, then he glanced her way.

Held her gaze.

Her heart beat double-time. Not good.

Right now, she had no power to stop the way he affected her, even in the middle of this volatile situation that included escalating danger. Carrie pressed her palms against her eyes. The faster they found answers, the quicker they could be done and she could get back to her life.

Wait. No. That wasn't right.

I can never get back to my life.

Once again, her existence had been ripped from her.

Before the emotions clogged her throat, she might as well hear from Trevor—the sad story she shouldn't hear.

"Okay, Trevor, I've told you my story. Now I want to know yours. I want to know something personal. I've shared with you the most traumatic experience of my life, next to Isaac's death. And I feel exposed." Vulnerable.

Trevor stared at her from beneath deeply furrowed brows, and it felt like he was reaching across the space to comfort her.

"I was married," he said.

She hadn't let herself wonder if he had a girlfriend or wife waiting back home, but she'd had the feeling he was alone. "What happened?"

"I found out Lisa was cheating on me with Wade, my best friend." Trevor turned his face to look at the woods instead of the fire, or Carrie.

Pain edged his voice. So he held on to the past too.

"We fought, and she left the house upset. She died in a car accident not a mile from our home." Trevor shook his head. "And Wade moved away. He never faced me."

Carrie regretted asking him to share.

"That was seven years ago. Then Jennifer's husband became dangerous to her, and I focused on keeping her safe." He looked at the fire again, a deep sadness in his eyes.

The emotion rolling off him was palpable. "I'm sorry, Trevor. Please forgive me for asking you to share something that caused you pain. I was wrong. And for the record, I hope you don't blame yourself for what happened to either your wife or your sister. You're one of the good guys in a world where there are so few."

A boat motor drew her attention. She started to scramble to her feet but paused. "A boat. We can get out of here now."

"Unless it's whoever has been following us. Tracking us. The person who sabotaged your plane."

"Good point. But I turned my transponder off before we left." Still, Carrie hesitated, wavering between ducking behind the log and rushing out to wave her hands. "It doesn't look like the Coast Guard."

"Stay here." Trevor slowly stood, gripping his gun.

The small boat drew close to the shore, and a gray-haired woman stood.

"We saw a plane go down. Was that you?" She gestured behind her as she shouted. "My husband and I were over on the far side of the strait."

"Thanks. That was us, all right."

"We're here to help. Are you hurt? Need medical attention?"

Carrie got to her feet and glanced at the woman, then back at Trevor. "No, we're both good."

The woman and her husband didn't appear threatening, though Carrie knew personally that looks could be deceiving.

"We can take you where you need to go."

Smiling, Carrie shouted back, "We'd appreciate it."

Trevor put out the fire. They donned their somewhat dry jackets and gathered their duffels and survival supplies. The boaters steered right up to shore, and Trevor and Carrie climbed into the couple's small V-shaped boat. Carrie was careful not to rock it.

"It's not much, but enough to get out on the water and fish," the man said.

"Thank you for coming to check on us," she said. "I'm Carrie, and this is Trevor."

"Shelly. Tom." She gestured to her husband as he angled them away from shore and started the motor. "Glad we can be of assistance. We called the troopers to let them know about the crash but didn't know how long it would take someone to get here."

"I appreciate you coming to our rescue," Carrie said. "If you have a satellite phone or radio I could use, I'll call to let them know we've been rescued." The troopers could inform the Coast Guard. She also needed to call the National Transportation Safety Board—NTSB—about the crash.

Shelly handed over a satellite phone, and Carrie took it. "Where can we take you on one tank of gas?"

"We don't want to put you out. The nearest town or village will be fine." Any small community. Civilization.

Carrie focused on contacting authorities to let them know that she and Trevor had been rescued, so any ongoing SAR efforts could stop.

"The nearest town is Two Saints Cove. It's around the other side of Scott's Landing, where you made your camp, and across the inlet on Essack Island."

"That's perfect," he said.

After the plane crash, she was even less prepared to stop on Essack Island. She would rather go anywhere else, frankly, but she wouldn't argue with him now and make a scene. The nice couple might dump them in the water and move on.

Still, she should be grateful that someone had found them so soon and they wouldn't have to trek across the island and encounter who knew what—like a bear. Or who knew *who*—someone unfriendly or Moosehead or Vandyke.

Now wasn't the time to let her fears take her down. Focusing on the steady hum of the motor, she let the waves soothe her nerves. The loss of that plane, along with Isaac's death, seemed like the end of an era for her.

Isaac.

She hadn't deserved his kindness. That deep ache squeezed her heart again, and she gulped air. The wind in her face helped her stay focused and get control of her emotions.

Trevor leaned in. "You all right?"

No! I'm not! How could either of them be all right in the middle of these intolerable circumstances?

She simply nodded in response and briefly glanced his way. She saw in his eyes that he didn't believe her. Scraping a hand through her tangled hair, she stared out at the shores of the island. The dense and beautiful Tongass National Forest and wilderness areas filled the entirety of Southeast Alaska all the way from Prince of Wales Island to Skagway. She couldn't imagine a more beautiful place in the world, bursting with both islands and mountains, forests and glaciers, fjords and bays.

Maybe that's why Isaac brought them here, because where else was as beautiful as Africa?

Before she had too much time to think on things she'd prefer to let rest, the small boat dropped them at the edge of the dock. Trevor paid Shelly and Tom enough money to fill their tank, plus some for their assistance, but they refused the extra. Duffels in tow, she and Trevor marched up the dock toward the small community of Two Saints Cove. She noted that *now* the water was smooth and the clouds had blown over.

At least they had survived the crash. She had drowned, but Trevor saved her. She'd been revived twice now in her life. Emotion thickened in her throat as she took in Detective Trevor West.

His whiskers had grown, and he had a rugged appearance. Carrie liked the rough-and-tumble look on him.

"Now that I lost my cell, I can't bring up the picture of Jennifer and show it to anyone. I can't ask if someone has seen her. I need to get my hands on a satellite phone so I can get her picture again. Let's hope we can find a shop here that sells them. Plus, I need to call Chad. Right now, he can't call me back."

"I'll get us a couple of rooms at the local motel, and we can clean up. I need to call the NTSB about the crash."

"You can use my satellite phone, that is, when I get it," Trevor said. "I'm guessing the cost of using the landline in the motel to call long distance from a remote island is probably outrageous."

"Probably less than using your satellite phone," she said. After getting rooms at the Rivercrest Motel, Carrie took a long, hot shower. She tugged her extra clothes from the duffel, grateful that the bag was waterproof, but that hadn't saved her Ruger since she hadn't put it back in there. She examined the knot on her head and was relieved it wasn't that bad. After cleaning up the scratches along her cheek, she didn't bother bandaging them. She sat on the edge of the bed and reached for the phone.

A knock came at her door. "It's me."

She left the call for later, opened the door, and smiled. Without thinking, she reached up and rubbed her finger down his cheek. "You shaved? I kind of liked the scruffy look." Ah. Now. Why had she said that? It was entirely too personal.

His blue eyes held her gaze for longer than necessary and turned her insides to Jell-O. She'd gotten herself into this and would get herself out. Carrie pushed past him, closed the door, and stepped out into the parking lot.

"What now?" She squinted in the sudden brightness.

"According to the motel clerk, there's a shop across the street where I can buy a satellite phone."

After purchasing a combination satellite smartphone that cost over fifteen hundred dollars, Trevor led her along the boardwalk, grumbling the whole way about the price. Then he suddenly stopped and looked at her. His smile unsettled her.

"What?" *Stop looking at me.*

"Come on, let me buy you something to eat," he said. "You look like you've had a harrowing few days."

"Oh, really?" She was not flirting.

She couldn't flirt. She was in mourning over the death of her friend. Trevor lifted his arm as if inviting her to walk with him. She took his arm and strolled next to him as if she'd been doing it for months.

No.

A lifetime.

They entered the next shop on the boardwalk. Kolinski's Koffee.

"Do they have internet access?" she asked.

He pointed at the sign. "Yep. But it's not free."

Trevor would have to pay if he wanted to search the internet, just like he'd paid for the phone. Neither of them was sure the satellite smartphone would do what he needed it to do, but at least they could connect to civilization if they found themselves stranded on an island again. Trevor picked a corner table in the back.

Carrie stared at the menu without seeing.

"You're awfully quiet," he said.

"It's been a long day."

"Protein bars don't take you far. Make sure to go large. Given our track record, we can't be sure when we'll eat again."

That made her smile. "Our track record? Right you are."

He stared at the satellite smartphone.

"Can you get it to work?"

"I hope so. If I can figure out the phone, I can do two things at once. I can feed you and get Jennifer's picture. And . . . bingo. Got her picture and downloaded it to the phone."

Trevor's expression grew sad as he stared at the image. The waitress approached, and Carrie was grateful for the interruption. "I'll have your special," she said.

"Same," Trevor said.

The waitress chuckled. "You don't even know what it is."

"I'm sure it's good," Trevor said.

"Suit yourself. And to drink?"

"Water," they said simultaneously.

"Water and coffee," Trevor added. "Lots of coffee."

The waitress left them. "Now that I have a phone again," he said, "I'd like to call Chief Long and fill her in. She might know something too."

The waitress brought them each a bowl of halibut chowder and crispy slices of sourdough bread. After she left, Trevor snatched up the satellite phone. "Go ahead and eat. After I talk to Chief Long, I'll call the lodge where we stayed and get ahold of Daphne so I can get her brother's number. I need to have a conversation before I get into this situation loaded for bear."

"Nice choice of words, and by the way, all I wanted was for you to be prepared." Carrie focused on eating her soup and munching the bread. She hadn't realized how hungry she was. Like Trevor said, protein bars only went so far.

After he left a message with Chief Long, he called Daphne, then got ahold of Chad. Trevor stood abruptly from the table and walked outside. She watched him through the window as he talked. Maybe he hadn't wanted anyone in the café to hear that conversation, or maybe he needed fresh air.

He finally returned to the table and sat down, then took a bite of his soup.

"Is it cold now?"

"It's still warm."

"Well?"

He grinned. "I hit the jackpot."

"I gathered."

"Chad is dropping off a charter at a nearby remote wilderness area—a fishing guide along with three men. I'm going to pay him double to pick us up here. Daphne warned him, too, that I needed to talk. I think she tried to warn him *away*, but like I said—"

"You're paying him double his going rate."

"Right." Trevor finished off his soup and bread quickly.

"So it all worked out," he said. "Except for your plane. I'm sorry about that, Carrie. When this is all over, I want to help you."

Help me how? She didn't want to ask, because then he would make promises he couldn't keep. Carrie didn't like to count on anyone. The only person she had counted on was gone. "When will he be here?"

"Unfortunately, it won't be until tomorrow morning."

"That's for the best. We could use some rest, and it's getting late."

"While I'm anxious to learn more, I think you're right. In the meantime, I need to do my homework on the internet and learn more about Jacob's Mountain."

Trevor focused on his smartphone and searched the internet, his brows furrowing as he read.

"You going to share?" she asked.

"Sure, it's an old mine that's considered a Superfund site, but there's another mine to extract rare earth minerals that runs alongside it now. Both mines are owned by GenCorp Mining. Lots of articles about environmental hazards. Lots of articles about all the safety measures put in place." He shrugged. "I guess we can't know what's really going on until I get there, which brings me to another point."

He put his phone aside to look at her. "I didn't ask Chad to take me there over the phone because there was a chance he might not agree, and I need to talk to him in person. Then I'll bring it up. But I arranged for him to take you back to the nearest airport so you can get on a plane and go somewhere safe."

His words startled her. "What? No. I'm in this with you until the end."

"Why? There's no need. You got me where I needed to be. We both know it's dangerous."

"Someone is after me, remember? I'm safer with you."

"And me taking you to the Mountain of Death is dangerous. That isn't safer for you."

"Neither is leaving me alone. I mean—" What was she saying? Was she actually telling him that she couldn't take care of herself, because that wasn't true. But he dropped this on her suddenly, and she wasn't prepared for her reaction or response. "Look, Trevor. I'm in this with you. I don't want you to do this alone."

He reached across the table and pressed his hand over hers. Electricity surged up her arm. She snatched her hand back.

No. Just no. "I can't stand the thought of losing one more person." As if Trevor was someone she could lose.

"You almost died back there. I thought I'd lost *you*. So you're not going with me."

"You don't want me hanging around anymore. Fine." She crossed her arms and looked away, trying to hold it together. Since when did she let someone get under her skin like this? Since when did she act like a child? She would blame the sheer exhaustion. When she could finally look him in the eyes again, she said, "I'm the one who got you this far."

Mr. Blue Eyes leaned forward, warmth flooding his gaze,

and she couldn't breathe. "Don't you remember, Carrie? This is all you promised to do."

She stared at him, unable to argue. "Well, that was before."

"Before?"

"We're a team now."

"We are?"

His words hurt, when they shouldn't. She wouldn't let him see.

"You don't have to worry. I'll keep my word to you and follow through with making sure Isaac's killer is caught."

What could she say to any of it? Nothing. She knew better than to let him grow on her. Those blue eyes, that rugged jaw and strong, athletic form. Broad shoulders. And his desperate need to find his sister that touched her soul in the deepest part.

She grudgingly followed Trevor outside, and they walked toward the motel.

Being so close to his destination, he could just toss Carrie away. Walk away from her, just like that. And it hurt. She was an idiot. He wasn't doing anything out of the ordinary, and she should've expected this reaction from him.

And with that, she could do it too. She could toss Trevor and his search for his sister away.

Carrie didn't care one iota.

But that wasn't true.

How had she let herself grow attached to Detective Trevor West so quickly? Why was she so hurt? She'd worked hard to protect herself. Part of her security system included not getting close to anyone—anyone like Trevor, who, yeah, okay, she found attractive in a visceral, heartfelt way. She was drawn to him when she didn't want to be drawn to anyone. She'd let him make her *need* him.

I cannot need anyone. The one person she counted on was gone. Dead. Murdered.

She held back the angry tears. She wouldn't give up.

This wasn't over until it was over.

At least she had some time to convince him to let her go with him. "Tomorrow when Chad arrives, we'll get on that boat. Ask him what he knows, and then hopefully we'll go see what Jennifer came to see. Find out what she was doing. And we'll do this *together*."

She expected him to disagree, but he said nothing and just kept walking along the storefronts. Was he considering her words? If so, she would nudge him a little more. They stood in front of her door at the motel.

"Trevor, please. Don't go alone." It didn't have to be her, did it? He could wait and go in with someone else.

Because I keep seeing that image in my mind of Isaac's body, only now it's you. I can't lose you too.

TWENTY

He looked into those gorgeous eyes, even when he knew better, because yes, this woman had the power to change his mind. Danger had chased them all the way here, and as they got closer to the truth, the danger was increasing incrementally. They might not survive the next attack.

"Chad is going to take you someplace safe," he said. "I texted Chief Long that I wanted you to be protected and asked her to call me. I'm not going to just leave you without protection."

"No."

He studied her, searching for a way to make her understand. He hadn't known her long, but he knew that he *more* than liked her. He was drawn to her strength in adversity, and his heart ached for what she'd been through.

"I can see those wheels in your mind turning," she said. "I get it. But we're here now. Like it or not, we're here on the island with the Mountain of Death. This isn't *your* town or island. Or even your state. This isn't Montana." Hands in an iron-fisted grip of his collar, she tugged him closer. Her face was millimeters from his. Heat and desperation spilled from her. “I can’t deal with another person I care about getting hurt. You are not going to the mountain without me.”

He fought a smile. He liked her spunk. But her words had him searching her eyes, gripping her arms.

“Another person I care about.”

He saw the truth of it in her eyes, but he didn’t know what to do with it. “I guess we’ll just have to see how it plays out.”

She nearly sagged against him in relief. “And we’re talking to Chad *first*. That’s all I’ve ever wanted. I’m sure you’re a great investigator, but this is personal for you, and that changes everything.”

Yes, yes, it does. He couldn’t see straight for his anger. But he had to stop letting that get in the way.

She smiled and stood on her tiptoes to kiss him on the cheek, then turned to unlock her door. He got the feeling she was trying to rush, but she fumbled with the key before finally opening it. “I’ll see you in the morning.”

Carrie shut the door.

He stared at it and smiled. That kiss had suddenly infused him with energy when he really needed to rest. This could definitely be another sleepless night.

The next morning, after Carrie and Trevor had breakfast at Kolinski’s Koffee, they headed for the marina. Trevor maintained situational awareness, making sure they were still here alone and no one had followed them. Though the transponder had been turned off, this small town was located on the island with Jacob’s Mountain. They were closing in on the source of danger. He could feel it in his bones, and that put him on edge. At the end of the block, he peered around the corner. No one suspicious looking drew his attention. They crossed to the next block where he led her to the back of the buildings, stepping around the bear-safe garbage bins and occasional parked vehicle. They made their way to the boats moored at the marina, which was still another fifty yards away.

"Look," she said.

The *Sea Mist*, a fifty-foot older yacht slowly made its way in. "There's our ride."

Once he was on the *Sea Mist,* he'd finally get a chance to talk to someone who had spent time with Jennifer. As they headed toward the slip, Chad impressed Trevor with his ability to single-handedly dock a yacht. After completing the task, the guy hopped off the boat and started heading toward town.

As Trevor and Carrie strolled toward Chad, Trevor lifted his hand, letting him know they were his next charter. Chad stopped as Trevor approached the dark-haired man in his late twenties, early thirties, who he'd recognize anywhere due to his resemblance to his sister.

Trevor thrust out his hand. "You must be Daphne's brother, Chad."

Chad's eyes narrowed despite his tenuous smile. "And you are?"

"Trevor West and Carrie James."

"Okay. Just making sure." He was rightly wary but started toward town again.

Trevor blocked his path. "I'd like to get going now."

Chad's brows furrowed. "I need supplies."

He hoped he didn't scare the guy away before they had a chance to talk, but these were desperate times. "Look, someone's been following us, and I don't like to stay in one place too long. So, please, just take us out into the water. Get us away from here. Maybe drop us off on the other side of the island. You can get supplies there, can't you?"

His forehead creased. "You said you had questions. But I don't want any trouble."

Like it or not, this guy was involved simply because he delivered Jennifer to the island. Although he might not fully understand the danger he was in. He knew too much. Eventually that could catch up to him. It *had* caught up to him.

Trevor measured his next words. "*Nobody* wants trouble. My sister is missing. Can you help me or not?"

"I can answer questions, but I'm not sure I should take you to Yakutan. That town is close to Jacob's Mountain."

Exactly. "I'm paying you double your fee, remember? Can we just go?"

"Make it triple."

Seriously? "You're taking advantage of us."

"Have to make it worth it, man."

"Let's go."

Chad turned back and led them to the *Sea Mist*. "I could use help releasing the dock lines."

"You got it."

Carrie and Trevor released the dock lines from the cleats, while Chad started up the engines.

"We're good to go!" Trevor shouted once they were aboard.

Chad steered out of the slip and away from the dock.

"Can you get the bumpers?" he shouted from the helm.

"Sure thing." Trevor pulled the small hanging buoys that protected the yacht from slamming against the dock.

The boat picked up speed, and Trevor was grateful they were finally on the last leg of this journey. At least he hoped this was the final destination. At the stern, he watched the town disappear, giving way to the Tongass National Forest. He needed to brace himself for what he might learn. The thought opened a rush of images. He'd spent all this time keeping hope alive by imagining himself finding Jennifer, saving her. But now he tried to mentally and emotionally prepare for the possibility that at the end of this long, brutal journey he could find his sister gone from this life.

Acid rose in his throat. Not yet. He wouldn't let hope slip away until he saw for himself. Found the truth. Sucking in a breath of salty ocean air, he headed inside the wheelhouse.

Carrie was already inside, waiting. At the helm, Chad steered with confidence between islands.

"Thanks for agreeing to pick us up. We lost our ride when someone sabotaged the plane."

"What?" Chad's eyes widened. "Are you saying your plane crashed?'

"Carrie does an amazing water crash landing."

Chad grabbed his *Sea Mist Charters* ball cap from the dash and tugged it on. His expression grew pensive. He subtly shook his head as if to himself. Probably regretting agreeing to meet Trevor.

"Look, you're in this whether you want to admit it or not. You were in it before I asked to meet you, because my sister hired you. We need to get justice for her. That's the only way you'll be safe. Now, tell me what you know."

Chad stared straight ahead as he steered. "I make it my business to know nothing about my clients. Daphne should have kept her mouth shut. But"—Chad glanced between Carrie and Trevor—"she was trying to get on your good side. She liked you. She told me she'd made a mistake and said too much—that she'd seen your sister."

Yeah, and getting the information out of her hadn't been easy once they started asking questions. "We're here now, and you better tell me what you know."

"Are you threatening me?"

"That depends."

"I'm going to have to sell this boat and leave the Panhandle. That's what I know."

"So you understand how dangerous this is," Carrie said. "You knew how dangerous it was when you took Jennifer."

"Daphne said Lori's real name was Jennifer. I'm not going to take you to Yakutan now, man. I can't. You can pay me the regular charter. I'll drop you as close as I can."

Trevor could always charter someone else after he got more information from Chad. "We have a deal if you'll tell me every single thing you can remember about your interaction with my sister."

"I can do that. Your sister wanted me to take her all the way to Jacob's Mountain. I ferry people around who don't want to take the public transportation ferries or need to get to special locations not on the ferry route. She wanted the northwest side of the island. Nobody goes there who doesn't belong to that operation."

"Then you've transported others to that location?"

"No. The operation at Jacob's Mountain has its own dedicated transport in place."

"What do you know about the operation?"

"More than I want to know."

"And that is?"

"Years ago, some corporation bought that whole side of the mountain. The purchase included a new claim along with the nearby uranium mine that's now declared a Superfund site. My understanding is that their operations included cleaning up the site as part of the contract. The activity has picked up the last two years, so either they're cleaning up the hazardous materials as agreed or someone made a discovery worth a fortune. It would have to be worth a lot for the trouble it takes to get in and out with heavy equipment."

Trevor scratched his itchy jaw. *Jennifer, what did you get yourself into?*

He eased onto the bench, leaned over his thighs, and pressed his face into his palms.

Carrie sat next to him and squeezed his shoulder. "We're close to finding answers now. What do you want to do? Should we just call the AST in and let them at it?"

He dropped his hands at that. "No one cares about finding her more than me. No one ever got this far in the search for her. I'm not walking away from this. We still don't have evidence that would get them moving anyway."

Her eyes filled with concern. Compassion.

He suddenly noticed Chad wasn't at the helm. "Where'd he go?"

Boots clomped up the steps from belowdecks. Chad carried a box, which he set on the deck in front of Trevor.

"What's this?"

"It belonged to your sister."

And you're just now telling me this? Trevor couldn't breathe. "You didn't hand it over to the authorities? Why do you still have it?"

"She left it here and asked me to keep it. Said she would be back for it. Easier if she didn't have to carry it around. Only she didn't come back."

"Daphne said you weren't worried because people often don't come back. She mentioned that, for all she knew, you'd told the police. She also said you were scared."

"I didn't tell Daphne everything. I didn't want her involved. The truth is, I *did* tell the locals. I'm a licensed captain who charters passengers, and I'm obligated to tell authorities when passengers don't return as scheduled. I don't know what happened after that. But I had a bad feeling about it, so I just told Daphne a little different story so she wouldn't worry."

"But she knew you were scared and figured out some of it."

"You were right when you said I'm already in this. It was just a matter of time before someone showed up looking for her." He lifted his gaze to Trevor's. "I'm sorry."

Trevor felt the pain in his words, but that didn't keep him from wanting to punch the guy. "She needed help, man. You could have told someone else if you believed the locals hadn't done enough. You could have saved her."

Chad shook his head. "I'm just one man."

Carrie pointed at the box. "What's in it?"

Trevor's insides quaked. "Yeah, Chad, what's inside?" He wanted to hear from Chad before he opened it.

Chad pursed his lips as if deciding whether telling the truth would be worth it. "I'd like to say I didn't look, but I did. You'll have to see for yourself."

Carrie hesitated, then glanced at Trevor for permission. He nodded.

She lifted the lid. She pulled out what looked like a hazmat suit and held up a gas mask.

Trevor thought he would lose his lunch. He knelt and touched what remained.

"A Geiger counter?"

TWENTY-ONE

Jennifer was preparing to walk into a radioactive area?

That alone was bad enough, but did she go in without protection? A high enough dose of radiation could kill in minutes, and that death would be the worst kind of pain.

Carrie dropped the hazmat suit and mask back into the box. She couldn't have guessed the contents of that box. Trevor stared at the items, his face pale, his features twisted.

She didn't want to see the items anymore, and squeezed her eyes shut. Did the sight make Trevor sick too? She didn't even know his sister, but the brief time she'd spent with Trevor was enough to make her care about him on a personal level. What they found in the box was enough to unsettle anyone, and Carrie felt disturbed to her core.

Close it. Just close it up.

Trevor stood while she wrestled with getting it closed again. She could do this one simple thing for him.

After shutting it, she stood and risked a glance his way. The severe emotional pain in his features gutted her. Why had she looked? She wanted to go to him. Hold him. Somehow comfort him. But nothing she did would take away the pain. The harsh reality of what Jennifer willingly walked into.

"Trevor." Her voice croaked with her whisper.

His bright blue eyes were shuttered. She suspected he was trying to rein in the fear. Push it down and compartmentalize. They still had a long way to go in finding Jennifer.

No sense in jumping to conclusions. Well, except for one. She stepped closer. As if she had any say in his life. "You're not going in there."

He sighed with a shudder. It broke her heart, what was left of it.

"My sister did, and she went without the hazmat suit." He stepped away from Carrie, then stared out at the water. "Jennifer had a rock hammer and a geologic compass. Hazmat suits are for firefighters, emergency medical techs, and yes, people handling toxic spills. Don't forget the Geiger counter, which tells us this is about radiation. But the suit is here, and she's not. What could it mean?"

Carrie didn't press him. He needed time to process this new information.

Trevor moved closer to the helm, where Chad looked straight ahead and pursed his lips.

"You've told us more than I thought you would," Trevor said. "But what else? Why you? Why did she trust *you*?"

Carrie was surprised he hadn't shouted at Chad. Hadn't paced and fisted his hands in anger like she'd seen before. Instead, he sounded broken.

"Maybe she's a good judge of people." Chad lifted a shoulder. "I have a good reputation in these parts."

The guy wasn't a very good liar. Should she step in? "I know how it works around here too. You aren't listed with the local charter boat websites like a lot of outfits. I know. I looked. So that means someone referred you."

"Who was it?" Trevor asked.

Now Trevor fisted his hands. His patience was running out. She didn't have to know him well to see that.

Neither did Chad. If he knew what was good for him, he would start giving up more information.

He squeezed the helm. "Guy by the name of Fitzgerald."

"Amos Fitzgerald?" Carrie stepped forward and put her hand on Trevor's arm as if he needed her reassurance. She was doing that a lot lately, and she wasn't sure why. "Did you know he's dead?"

Chad adjusted the speed. "Yes. I hadn't heard from him in a while, so I contacted Naomi and she told me."

"When you heard he was dead"—Trevor held back his growl, just barely—"did you think his death was connected to Jennifer?"

"Look, man." Chad sounded desperate. Scared. "I had no idea. I try to do my job and stay out of things. People disappear in this state far too often. This is Alaska. It's a hard place to work and live. Some jobs are more dangerous than others. Being a guide is one of those, depending on where you go and who you guide. So, no, I didn't connect those dots."

"Or maybe you didn't want to connect the dots."

"I'm not sure you *can* connect them." Points for Chad.

And with that same attitude, Trevor had stayed out of Jennifer's business too. Maybe he could have done something to help if he'd been a nosier brother. Then again, he could have gone missing too.

But he was here and grousing like an angry brown bear. Carrie might need to be braver than she felt if she wanted to deescalate the situation.

She grabbed one of Trevor's fisted hands and opened it. Slipped hers into it and gently squeezed. Grabbing his hand was *not* something she'd been doing a lot lately, but it could anchor him before the tension ramped up.

With her hand in his, she said nothing but held his gaze,

willing him to calm down. She understood his outrage. The whole time Jennifer was missing and law enforcement agencies searched for her, no one found Chad—he had deliberately stayed under the radar. She wasn't sure how she felt about him.

Good guy? Or completely irresponsible jerk? Or he knew to be afraid for his life and Daphne's—so *he* was protecting *his* sister by not getting involved. Trevor might understand that, but much later.

"Chad," Carrie said, "is there anything more you can tell us? Anything at all? Even a small thing, even if it seems inconsequential?" Honestly, he could have led with the box. He could still be holding back.

Shaking his head, regret rolled off him. "I wish there was. I wish I could help. She was kind, and I had hoped to see her again."

Trevor walked to the stern, leaving her alone with Chad, and stood on the other side of the pilothouse so she couldn't see him. "What you said before about selling the boat, I think you're right. You and Daphne should at least disappear for a while. Maybe store the boat. Whoever is behind Jennifer's disappearance will know you talked. You helped us. You could be in danger." Was she stepping out of her lane to warn him?

"Yeah, I know what I said, but I can't sell the *Sea Mist*. It belonged to our grandparents. This has been a family business. They're both gone now, so I keep it going. And listen"—Chad gestured over his shoulder—"like he asked me, I can take you somewhere safe. It's the least I can do. I could be the reason his sister didn't get help. I realize that now."

Carrie heard the regret in his voice, but it was too late for Jennifer. "The safest place for me is next to him."

She was in this now, and she wanted to see it through. But more than that, Trevor would protect her even with his life. Her heart pounded at the thought. She was tough on her own, but someone murdered Isaac and had her quaking in her shoes.

Images of being pushed from the plane in Africa rushed through her. She struggled to hold on to the idea that she could trust Trevor that much. He was only one man against some dangerous, nebulous entity.

She wasn't invincible.

Wasn't bulletproof.

She wouldn't do something foolish. But she'd already been killed once, and like Isaac told her, God had a reason for leaving her on this earth. Isaac had wanted her protected. Maybe, just maybe, she needed someone in this with her. Someone like Trevor.

"I'll check on him." Her leg suddenly bothered her again—it happened at the weirdest times—and she tried not to limp on her way to the stern, where Mr. Blue Eyes peered out at the water, watching the wake left by the *Sea Mist*. Now that she thought about it, the amazing skies reminded her of Trevor's eyes.

"We need a different plan," she said. "You can't just waltz in there and demand to see your sister."

"I won't. I'll check it out first, don't worry."

"If I had my plane, I could just fly over."

"We already tried that. Someone took you down, remember?"

How could I forget? "And that's why I'm safer with you." She chewed on her lip. She was putting too much trust in him. Depending on him.

I shouldn't. I really shouldn't.

Isaac would want this. She had a feeling she was right on that point. Isaac had sent her away with Trevor, after all, knowing that he wanted to tell her someone was after her. But he didn't tell her. He waited.

After a few moments at the stern, she left Trevor to his thoughts. He needed more time alone.

"Everything okay?" Chad asked at her approach.

"Sure. I'm just going to stick that box down below, if that's okay. For now. We'll want it at some point, I'm sure."

"You can set it on the table and I'll put it away."

She picked it up and made her way belowdecks to see the nostalgic-styled galley. Family business, huh? She and Isaac had kind of run their cargo and transport business like a family. Above deck again, she found Trevor approaching.

Before she could say anything, he started right in.

"Do you know how Jennifer got into the place? The mine, the claim, whatever it is?" he asked.

Good question. Chad hadn't offered anything up without pliers, except the box.

"She walked right through the front. She'd been there before with a group of scientists. Consulting geologists, she called them."

"How do you know that?" Carrie asked. "Why didn't you tell us before?"

"I can't think of everything, okay? I don't know what you don't know. I didn't see the group, but she told me."

Jennifer had trusted Chad. Told him things. And left her brother simple photographs. Oh boy.

Trevor paced. "Consulting geologists."

"You said she wouldn't have taken samples alone, Trevor. So she wasn't."

"At first."

Carrie's head was starting to hurt. "She didn't like something she saw, so she came back."

Trevor rubbed his forehead. "To try to gather some kind of evidence. So she could be a whistleblower." He sighed heavily and eased onto the bench. "I encouraged her to go to Alaska. She said it was on her bucket list. She'd been here before, and I didn't even know. She traveled with consulting scientists now and then. She must have come earlier when I was in the middle of an investigation, too distracted to pay attention."

"We can't know everything about someone else's life," she said, "even the people we love. So she came back, posing as an amateur photographer until she got to Jacob's Mountain. And then what? She entered as a lone-wolf geologist and got in? Even as a geologist, I can't see her just walking in without permission."

"Makes me wonder if the same two goons who're probably expecting me to show up were waiting for her. I really want to punch their lights out. After I get answers from them." Elbows on his thighs, he hung his head. "Let's piece together what we can. We can surmise that she suspected someone knew what she was up to and she was scared she was being followed as Amos Fitzgerald took her island hopping to take photographs. And, for some reason, more samples. We don't know what that was about yet. He flew them over Essack Island and Jacob's Mountain, but we don't know if they landed or if she took more samples then. She came back to Shadow Gap and put those pictures in the safe deposit box. It's only a hunch, but I'm leaning toward Amos Fitzgerald being the man who used a false ID and did a great job forging my signature. Then Jennifer left Monica the key and message."

"But Monica disappeared."

"In June, Jennifer chartered the *Sea Mist*, and sounds like she didn't learn about Monica's disappearance. We don't know what she was doing between the time she opened the safe deposit box and last saw Monica and the time she chartered the *Sea Mist*. As far as I know, she remained in Alaska." Trevor drew in a heavy breath. "We need to check the timeline on Amos's death."

"I can answer that," Chad said. "It was early June."

"Amos referred her to you, Chad, before he died," Trevor said. "Probably was the pilot who dropped her off at Shady Cove. Then you delivered her to Jacob's Mountain, and that's the last anyone has seen of her, that we know of."

"You definitely need to get more answers from EchoGlobal," Carrie said.

"Maybe they wanted her to take those additional samples while she was on leave. Someone definitely knows something," he said. "Chief Long has someone on it."

A few moments of silence passed between them.

"Look, I feel bad for what happened to your sister," Chad said. "I would do the same thing if it were Daphne." He suddenly tensed, tightening his grip on the wheel. "I have an idea."

Without saying more, he focused on steering the *Sea Mist* around the southern portion of the island.

"Well?" Trevor asked.

"In this business, I have connections. I know an old guy who knows the island really well. I'll see if I can arrange a meeting, and maybe he can tell you how to find out what you need to know. It's something. It's all I've got."

"I think it's a good idea, don't you?" Carrie asked. "We need to know more. You need to find another way in."

"Let's meet with your friend, then," Trevor said. "Let's hope this doesn't take too long."

Carrie sensed that even though Jennifer disappeared over a year ago, they were running out of time. If any evidence was left, it was now well on its way to being hidden.

They know we're coming.

Carrie and Trevor were a threat to their plans.

"If someone wants to take the wheel," Chad said, "just keep hugging the island. We're going all the way to the south end until you see the next town. I need to grab my satellite phone and find his number."

Trevor stepped forward and took the wheel. "How about we just show up?"

"I don't know where he lives, okay? He likes his privacy." Chad started down the steps belowdecks.

"What can you tell me about him?"

Trevor's question drew him back. "I don't know much. Rip is just a guy who's lived on the island for decades. He knows this whole region. I'd guess he knows every nook and cranny on the island. He hunts, fishes, and caves."

Not unusual here. "Seems like a lot of people would know the island," she said. "Why'd you think of *him* if you don't know him that well?"

Chad huffed. "Do you want to ask him your questions or not?"

"Yes, please contact him," Trevor said. Chad went down the steps this time, and Trevor gave her a look.

"What? You started the million questions. I was just adding to them." Carrie joined him at the helm and leaned in. "Do you trust him? I want to, but I don't. Not really."

"You can't trust anyone after what happened to you."

He glanced at her, and his eyes had turned dark, and it scared her—for him. He was so close to finding those who had brought harm to his sister, he could taste it. And there was no question someone had hurt her. Likely killed her, but Trevor never said those words.

Chad returned to the wheel. "I called him. We're all set to meet him in about an hour. Can you handle this a few more minutes for me?"

"Sure," Trevor said.

"I'll be back." Chad disappeared down the steps again.

"That's good news. We might find a way inside this mining operation. And if we get inside, then what?" she asked. *Because I really don't want to get irradiated if I don't have to.*

"One thing at a time."

"That's another way of saying you're making this up as you go." *Which I already knew.*

He shrugged, then angled toward her. Lifted a few strands of her hair. "You got me this far, Carrie. I couldn't have done it without you."

She didn't know if that was entirely true, but she would take the compliment, along with the warm feelings swirling inside. His tenderness nearly undid her. Earlier he'd been calloused, pretending to toss her aside, when she could see in his eyes that it hurt him the same as it hurt her. And yet he'd only wanted to protect her. Get her somewhere safe and distance himself from her emotionally.

I totally respect that. Unfortunately, now I'm that much more into you.

And that was behind them. She was all in, and Trevor knew that.

A lump grew in her throat, and she swallowed, hoping to push the emotion back down. Carrie didn't even recognize herself. She blinked back ridiculous tears. She'd seen too much. Been through too much, and the river had run dry. At least she thought so. But Trevor sparked a tenderness in her she believed was long gone.

"And no matter what happens, Carrie, if Chief Long hasn't already found Isaac's killer, I promise I'll track him until I find him."

"I don't care about our deal. It's more important to me that you find your sister and we make it out of the Mountain of Death with our lives."

TWENTY-TWO

The forest was thick and nearly swallowed the town of Yakutan. Trevor would have missed it, but Chad had taken over at the helm again just in time. They took the dinghy in after Chad anchored the *Sea Mist*, claiming the dock was old and couldn't accommodate the trawler.

Once they stepped off the dinghy and onto the rickety dock with wobbly planks, Trevor agreed with his assessment.

Trevor remained cautious and wary as they made their way to meet Rip Franklin. Yakutan was a village so small, he half expected it wouldn't have electricity. One thing he'd learned on this trip was that not all communities in Alaska had power, and most villages weren't connected to a major power grid. The mountains and distance, waterways and lack of roads made a statewide electric system impossible.

In Alaska, rural literally meant you were on your own.

He noticed a neon sign hanging in the window of a shop. Ah. Maybe they'd secured hydropower somehow. The "operation" north of here had to have power to function.

Essack Island was thirty-two miles wide, thousands of square miles, and hosted two other communities. Chad told them all about it as they cautiously entered the village. Since Chad captained a charter boat, he had to serve as a guide as well. Trevor didn't need him to explain that the island was a massive, tangled mess of Tongass National Forest and mountains.

"We're not stopping anywhere in town. Instead, we're meeting Rip down the road. That means we need to hike up the trail." Chad pointed to a totem pole near a trailhead.

"Why doesn't he just meet us in town?" Trevor asked.

"He doesn't want anyone to see you talking to him. What do you think?"

Fair point.

"But you'll be seen with us." Carrie frowned at him.

"You chartered my boat, so I have an excuse, but Daphne and I are leaving the area for a while until this—whatever it is—blows over. And I'll make sure Carrie gets home safely. You have my word on that."

Carrie didn't offer up an objection, but he wouldn't put it past her to argue later. Still, she was no fool and would do what was best. They continued to hike the trail up a hill and then down a bit. No getting off the path because the underbrush was too thick. Finally, through the trees, he spotted a one-lane gravel road below the hill. They waited behind a mossy boulder and watched two junker trucks pass, then an old Army-green Jeep CJ came into view and slowed at the curve in the road before parking off to the side.

"That's him," Chad said. "Hurry."

They rushed down the hill, fighting the thick underbrush as they went, then hurried across the gravel to scramble into the vehicle. Rip had a gray beard and wore a camo ballcap that shadowed his eyes. No introductions were made as Chad's friend expertly turned around on the narrow road, then sped deep into the forest. The gravel road grew increasingly rough. Trevor didn't know the forest could be so dark in the middle of the day. He couldn't help but have a bad feeling about this entire affair he'd agreed to.

What if this was a trap? What if Chad, for his and Daphne's safety, had agreed to turn Trevor and Carrie over to the people after them? Trevor could be sure of nothing, but he hoped and prayed his conspiracy theory was just that—a theory and nothing more.

While Carrie and Trevor crammed together on the small bench back seat, Chad sat up front and engaged in small talk about the local fishing and lumber on the island. Given the strangeness of their meeting, Trevor thought it best to wait for a signal from Chad before he questioned the mysterious Rip. No sense in coming this far, wasting all this time, only to ruin their chance at help by saying the wrong thing at the wrong time.

In all his days, even as a Deputy US Marshal, he had never been involved in so much cloak-and-dagger. To think that his own sister created this troubled situation rife with danger. Why hadn't she trusted him enough to tell him? he repeatedly asked himself, even though he knew the answer. She couldn't very well tell her law enforcement brother she was involved in a covert whistleblowing operation. He seethed at the thought. Fisted his hands again.

Carrie drew his left hand into hers and squeezed. She'd figured him out quickly, and he smiled inside at the thought. Her green eyes knocked on the door to his heart at that first moment, so it didn't take long for her to find her way inside—despite his resolve after Lisa's infidelity to never get involved with anyone again. Why go through that pain?

Then he suddenly had a reason to expose himself, to take a risk, when his path crossed with Carrie James's. But this was in no way the time or the place. And he didn't know her. Not really. But that didn't stop his heart from waking up to what could be.

Finally, the Jeep rolled into a less-than-stable-looking structure attached to a large cabin well hidden behind a thick grove of spruce trees, as if the guy wasn't already keeping his privacy out here.

After Chad hopped from the Jeep, he assisted Carrie out of the tight space. Trevor exited on the other side, and they all joined their host at the door to Rip's rudimentary cabin. A veritable castle on this remote island in Alaska. Rip led them inside, where a savory aroma wafted over Trevor.

"Welcome to my humble abode." Finally, the guy addressed them, acknowledging their existence. "I have some pollock chowder ready. I hope you're hungry."

"Thanks for having us in your home. I'm—"

"No names, please." Rip cut Trevor off.

"What?" Trevor had already been told his name was Rip, or was that false information? He looked between Chad and "Rip."

"Not until we get to know each other a little better."

He eyed the man. Was he for real? *You already brought us to your home, man.*

Rip held up his hands as if to calm Trevor. "You have a lot of questions, and so do I."

Trevor took a breath to ask more, and Rip cut him off again. "Eat first, then talk."

He glanced at Carrie to gauge her reaction. She shrugged. He hoped they weren't going to be drugged and then buried on this island. He remained wary even as he sat at the table and watched Rip ladle chowder into bowls for Carrie and Trevor as well as for himself and Chad. Trevor's anxiety eased a little.

Then Rip sat at the table, bowed his head, and said grace. Even better. The tightness in Trevor's chest lessened. Regardless, he waited until the man had eaten from his bowl before he decided it was okay to dive in, and after Rip shared a few stories that had them all in stitches, Trevor believed he could trust the man, but he would remain on guard.

He finished his soup and was growing impatient. "Thanks for agreeing to meet us."

Rip shoved his bowl forward. "I didn't want to. I don't need any trouble or to open the gate for it to flood this community, but"—he hesitated and glanced at Chad, then back to Trevor and Carrie—"I don't like what's happening to my island. I've been hoping and praying someone would shine a light on what's going on."

My sister tried to do just that. Trevor clasped his hands and leaned forward. "What *is* going on?"

"The rivers and lakes are polluted. Fish are dying. The ones that live have abnormalities. We sent a letter to the powers that be, and they *assured* us they're cleaning it up." He leaned back and scowled. "The company hired to do the job isn't. Something else is going on. I don't know what. Now, I want to hear *your* story."

"My sister was trying to find out. Or maybe she already knew. And now *I'm* trying to find out what happened to her. But I can't just walk through the front door and ask."

Rip chuckled. "Well, you can, but you might not get very far."

"Chad told us that you might know a way for me to get in."

"I can't guarantee your safety. I can't even guarantee it's a way. It's a far cry from walking through the front door. And once you get in, I don't know what you think you're going to do."

He was formulating a plan, and maybe it was completely idiotic. But he couldn't sit around and wait for law enforcement to act. He intended to get solid evidence. Working for the Marshals, even though he tracked fugitives, he still understood that whistleblowers often needed to change their identities. While gathering the intel, they were on their own.

He was here to finish what Jennifer started and bring her justice.

And with that thought, he knew what he had to do. "Let me worry about that."

Rip dipped his chin. "Fair enough. I spent time up on and around that mountain. Four decades ago, before the mine for uranium, I explored and mapped a cave system, and then eventually, as the mine became operational, I discovered the man-made tunnels connected with a natural cave."

"Is that common?"

"Have you ever stopped to think about what's beneath your feet? Thousands of spaces in the earth that have no entrance to the surface. Those spaces become caves when an opening large enough to enter is created. That can occur naturally or not. To answer your question, yes. It happens. Caves are often discovered through mining operations." He leaned back and scraped his jaw, then blew out a heavy breath. "I was wrong to offer this as a viable plan. This is nothing. I don't know why I even considered it."

"Why don't you show me what you can and let me decide?"

The older man's lips flattened into a straight line. He got up and moved over to a massive bookshelf where he pulled out a folded map. Placing it on the table between them, he unfolded it. "These are the caves I've charted. This entire region is mostly karst."

"Meaning?"

"The land is mostly limestone. It becomes eroded. Basically, the island is like swiss cheese. Deep fissures—think as deep as the Empire State Building is tall. Underground rivers. Pits and caves are everywhere, but that doesn't mean you can see them. The Tongass hides them. Cedars and devil's club shrubs. Moss. And even if you do know about them, they aren't easy to get to. Most are impossible."

"What are you saying? We can't get to where we need to go?"

"If it's still there. Mining operations, or whatever they're doing or not doing on Jacob's Mountain, could have changed everything. I haven't been back in years."

"If you can just help me get there, I'll take the supplies I need and go as far as I can."

"Ever been caving?"

"No. I don't need to explore. All I want is to gain access to the facilities." Was his desperation clouding his judgment? He stared at the map of caves. *It's a way in.*

Once inside he could pretend to be one of the crew.

Or not.

"Maybe we're thinking about this all wrong," Carrie said. "Jennifer went in as a geologist. I know I said you can't just walk in, but maybe you can. After all, you're law enforcement, and as such you also have a background that could get you in. Lead with that and walk through the front door. Say you're investigating a missing woman, only when you do this, Trevor, bring backup with you."

Trevor was so desperate to get inside, he couldn't see straight. Think clearly.

"You walk into that place, and you're not coming out," Chad said.

"If I have other law enforcement with me, it could work. Chief Long or her AST brother. They'd support my questions. I'd ask the local police, but I have the feeling they're letting suspicious activities go on under their noses."

Chad shifted toward the map. "Let's say you get in. Nothing happens to you. They don't kill or hide you. But they also don't tell you anything that will help. They aren't going to say anything about Jennifer. They aren't going to tell you anything useful. We didn't see her go in, so we can't even claim that."

True enough. *Lord, what should I do? I've come this far.*

"What if you go in as an investigator and ask questions first," Rip said. "Then, depending on what you learn, if anything, you can move to your next idea—go through the back-door cave. You're law enforcement, and they're not going to keep you or make you disappear. They don't need anyone looking for you and asking questions."

"If I don't come out, that's the evidence we need. Troopers will descend on the place. I'll contact Chief Long and let her know what's going on. Though this is out of her jurisdiction, her brother can help."

"Nolan can't help you if you die in there," Carrie said. "They could simply say it was an accident."

He considered Jennifer's reasons for not sharing what she was up to with her own brother. If only she'd confided in him. Maybe he could have helped her. He wasn't going to make the same mistake going into a situation without help. The thing was, for all he knew, Jennifer *had* confided in someone.

In fact, Chad knew more than Trevor.

And her guide, Amos Fitzgerald, might have been killed for what she confided in *him*. Trevor hadn't been on her list of those she would confide in.

He shoved back the anger and hurt. "I'll call Chief Long today."

Rip moved to the counter and poured coffee. "You're welcome to make yourself at home while you're here. Anyone want coffee?"

"I'll take some," Carrie said, and grabbed herself a mug too.

After taking a sip of coffee, Rip said, "I don't trust our local police chief. He's in their pockets."

Trevor's thinking too. "Carrie, can I have a word?"

Her eyes widened, and she looked between Rip and Chad, then back to Trevor. "Sure. Of course." She set the cup on the table.

Trevor took her hand, then led her outside onto the porch. They'd become familiar with each other. Grabbing hands, holding and hugging and relying on each other. He faced her and took in her worried expression. He admired her courage and the anchor she'd become for him, even after the recent tragedy she'd experienced. "Thank you for your help getting me this far."

"You're welcome." She angled her head.

He easily read the question in her eyes—*You didn't bring me out here to thank me, so what?*

"You know I have to do the rest of this alone."

She nodded. "I want to help if I can."

He sighed. "You're a distraction."

"You need all the help you can get. Haven't we had each other's backs through this? I want to see it through with you. I won't be a distraction. I won't get in your way."

His heart pounded. Concern for him filled her eyes, and it shifted a wall inside. He could admit to himself the real reason he didn't want her along, well, in addition to wanting to keep her safe.

"I don't mean it like that." He tipped her chin up. He might not get another chance to tell her. "Before Jennifer left for Alaska, we argued. I don't even remember what it was over. We were fine—siblings fight. But I would give anything to have those last few moments with her again so I could make things right. I'm not going to leave anything unsaid with you."

"Trevor, you're scaring me. You're acting like we'll never see each other again. That's not how this is going to end."

"I love your positivity, even after everything you've lived through."

"And died through."

"I wish we'd met under different circumstances." He found her intriguing and resilient, all of it, beneath a beautiful face. Her pristine features belied the experiences of her soul and the wisdom behind her eyes.

God, I want to know her.

Before he knew what he was doing and stopped himself, he leaned in and pressed his lips against hers. Supple, and suddenly eager. She slid her hand up his neck and pulled him closer. He wrapped his arms fully around her, savoring this unexpected tender moment between them.

A throat cleared—Chad opened the cabin door, then closed it—and Trevor reluctantly ended the kiss. He looked into her eyes and saw she was equally dumbfounded by his actions, but she'd kissed him back. "I mean it like that." His words came out breathless.

She wiped her mouth and turned away. "I'm sorry. I shouldn't have done that."

What? He kissed *her*, and he wasn't sorry.

She whirled around. "We're helping each other, Trevor, nothing more. I should warn you that I'll never trust another soul with that kind of love. Never. Not even you who is bent on finding out what happened to your sister, no matter the cost." Unshed tears shimmered in her eyes.

Carrie hopped off the porch and disappeared around the corner of the cabin.

Trevor started to follow, then stopped himself.

He sighed. She wasn't ready, but he might never see her again. Still, he knew that when it came to trusting her heart to someone, she was as fragile as they came.

He grabbed his satellite phone and called Chief Long. She answered on the first buzz. "Detective West, I'm glad you finally called. I have some more information for you."

It hadn't been *that* long. "What have you learned?"

"Cameras across the street from the bank at the Rabid Raccoon caught an image of your sister with Amos Fitzgerald entering the bank. We showed his picture to the bank employees, and they agreed he was the one who assisted her in opening the safe deposit box."

"So he must have known what she was trying to do."

"That's a strong possibility considering his cooperation. We'll be investigating his death to see if there's a possible connection."

"Thanks for letting me know. I suspected as much, and now we have proof he was with her. Let me know if you can confirm anything on his murder."

"Will do. On EchoGlobal, Grier is actively working to track down Jennifer's supervisor who left the company shortly after

Jennifer disappeared last year. He's also trying to talk to her co-worker, Amy Welsh. I'll let you know when he makes contact."

"I appreciate all you're doing on that front. I have a feeling we might actually get answers soon. In fact, I wanted to update you on what I've learned. And what I'm planning." He squeezed the bridge of his nose. Trevor relayed everything he'd learned from Chad, and that he intended to walk in and simply ask questions about a missing woman. Find out what he could, but he'd appreciate it if he didn't have to go in alone.

Silence met him over the phone. He glanced at the screen to see if the call had been dropped.

Finally, Chief Long spoke. "I'm not in the position to send in the cavalry. I don't think I could get movement from the ABI yet. There's nothing to go on. No real evidence. I'd say we could go in under probable cause or exigent circumstances, but the information you've shared is convoluted, at best, so that's probably not the way to go."

"I have a feeling that whatever evidence exists will be destroyed—and soon. So I want to go in quickly and try to get it."

"Like your sister tried?"

"I'm *not* my sister. I'll go in with my badge."

"You're out of your jurisdiction."

"Doesn't matter. They'd be foolish to try anything with me. But as I mentioned, I'm hoping you can help me."

"I understand you need answers. If your sister was murdered because she was trying to find information she could use to 'whistleblow,' as you said, then you're not going to get a welcoming party. On the contrary, Jacob's Mountain is a hostile environment."

"And I'm not expecting a welcoming party. Since the Tlingit call it Mountain of Death, we should plan for trouble." He drew in a breath. He needed her support. "Listen, as far as going in to find out what happened to my sister, you'd do the same, and you know it."

"Hold on." Chief Long spoke with someone. "Good news. Nolan is in my office."

"You had me on speaker."

"Yes. He'll come down as your backup. Just wait. He can be there tomorrow."

Trevor paced, aggravating the creaking planks. He had to think about it.

"Look," Nolan said. "It's been months. Another day isn't going to hurt anything."

"That's where you're wrong. Another day could be all it takes. Someone knows we're coming. They could already be hiding evidence."

"Trevor." Chief Long this time. "Detective West. You're a smart man and a good investigator. Don't be an idiot. Wait for Nolan. You know I'm right."

I do. "Okay. I'll meet him at Yakutan. Just give me a heads-up when he'll arrive. Give him my number. You've got Carrie's too, though she won't be coming with me on this expedition. And thanks for the help, for the backup, even though this isn't my jurisdiction. I don't want to step on anyone's toes."

"You know that we often travel to investigate out of our regions of authority. In this case, you're not on an official investigation, but no one is going to stand in your way. I'm sorry that we didn't discover this information early on. But now that you have, I want you to have the resources you need, and at the right moment we'll take it from there."

"Detective West," Nolan said. "We work together around here. Make do with what we have. We don't want to lose you too, so wait for my arrival tomorrow. We'll finish this together. In the meantime, I'm going to learn what I can through the state about the operation at Jacob's Mountain."

Relief rushed through him. This was really happening. He was going to get answers, and he wasn't alone in this. Maybe he'd been disappointed about the lack of information regarding Jennifer's disappearance before, but he wouldn't hold that against the AST or law enforcement. They were stepping up to the task.

"I'll see if I can recon the area before you get here. Get a handle on the mining crew, equipment, activities, and structures."

"That's a good idea. Just be careful."

"Will do." Trevor hopped off the porch to give himself room to pace with this new adrenaline rush. "Chief Long, what do you have for me on Isaac's death?"

"Isaac was wanted for questioning regarding a murder in Zhugandia—that's a country in Africa, in case you didn't know—ten years ago."

"Meaning, he was never questioned and instead fled to the US?"

"Something like that."

And now *Isaac* was dead.

"Whose murder?"

TWENTY-THREE

After fighting his way through the thick undergrowth in the temperate rainforest, sweat drenched Trevor's back as he topped the incline. He couldn't even see the sky. Above him lichen hung from the trees, and moss carpeted boulders and downed trees, while huge ferns and bushes covered the ground between the Sitka spruce and cedars.

Because of the effort he was making, the rainforest didn't feel so temperate or cool, but warm, as if he were in the Amazon. He stopped to catch his breath and look at his GPS location on the satellite smartphone. But the image didn't tell him what he really wanted to know.

"How much farther?"

"Depends," Rip said.

"What kind of answer is that?"

"The only appropriate reply. There's a ridge up ahead. The map doesn't do it justice, so we're going to hang north for a quarter of a mile."

Great. A quarter of a mile in a forest like this could take hours. But Trevor refused to complain. "Lead on."

Rip shoved past and paved the way for Trevor.

"Believe it or not, this is a game trail."

"Yeah. I don't believe it." Every inch of the forest looked the same.

After a half an hour more, Rip stopped and pointed west. "Through those trees you'll have a view. Make sure they don't spot you."

"I know how to do this. But where are you going?"

The man offered a tenuous grin. "I have another viewpoint up a ways. We'll use the radios if we need to communicate. I figure we should watch from different angles for an hour or two, at least, unless we see something that needs longer monitoring."

Trevor's recon mission had turned into surveillance, but either way, he would gather intelligence. As a former Deputy US Marshal and as a county detective, he always surveilled before making a move, especially when it came to complex investigations. He wanted to have an idea about what he was walking into.

The older man dipped his chin in his characteristic way, then turned and disappeared through the emerald forest. Trevor hoped they saw something that would give them answers, but he knew it would feel like an eternity sitting in one spot and observing in what was sure to be an uncomfortable stakeout. It wouldn't be the first time, only in the past he'd at least had the comfort of his vehicle.

Trevor peered through the foliage at the mining operation below, a good two hundred yards from him. Located on the northwest side of Jacob's Mountain, an area had been stripped of trees for an open-pit mine, but he also noted a large entrance tunnel into the earth, through which huge dump trucks entered and exited. Beyond that, numerous portable buildings of various sizes created a mining camp. He couldn't see beyond the buildings. Maybe Rip would get a better view.

Dropping his pack on the ground, he tried to make himself an acceptable stakeout spot. Once he was in position, he pulled out the binoculars Rip had loaned him to get a closer look.

The thing was, he didn't know what he was looking for or even *at*. Jennifer had searched for something, but Trevor couldn't look at a mining operation and recognize illegal activity when he saw it. He tried to envision what Jennifer went through. She left him those pictures, hoping he would make his way to this point.

She escaped an abuser, a life-threatening situation, only to jump headfirst into another one.

He shook off the morbid thoughts. He was here to find out what happened to her and to bring justice. Admittedly, his hope of finding her alive had decreased, and now it barely registered on his internal radar. And really, the hope remained only because he refused to let it die.

God, please kindle that hope, if it needs to burn bright.

He dragged on a bottle of water, but not too much so he could conserve what he had. If he was lucky, he would see the men who had followed him and Carrie somewhere at the operation on Jacob's Mountain. That would confirm what he already suspected.

In the meantime, Trevor lowered the binoculars. His eyes burned with sweat—of course a heat advisory had been issued today. He leaned against the tree trunk and bark scratched his back as he rested his eyes before looking through the binoculars again. He allowed himself to think about Carrie. He would see her at least one more time—tonight—before he headed to the mountain. And chances were, with Nolan along, he would return. He'd let his fears get the best of him when he kissed her. Or maybe it was much more. He'd let his feelings for her get the best of him. Everything about her pulled him in. She was almost irresistible, and he knew after she kissed him back that she wanted more with someone. She wanted to offer her heart. To trust. But wanting and being able to do it were two separate things.

Besides, Trevor probably wasn't the best man for her since he couldn't let go of his search for the truth. He had to know, and the search had fallen to him. So he had to finish and couldn't stop. Even for Carrie—a living, breathing, desirable woman whom he'd grown to care about.

He knew deep inside that given time, there could be much more between them.

Something good.

But Carrie had nailed him with her words.

"Not even you who is bent on finding out what happened to your sister, no matter the cost."

The cost. He was willing to pay a high price for justice. She'd spoken the truth, but was there some other meaning in her words?

Trevor peered through the binoculars again and realized the activity had a new rhythm to it. An upbeat, get-out-of-Dodge rhythm. Some equipment was being off-loaded onto a huge barge. What did it mean?

His satellite phone rang. Chief Long again? Trevor answered. "What's up?"

"Can you talk?"

"Believe it or not, I can watch the mine and talk at the same time."

"Good. Because I have news. Grier talked to Amy, Jennifer's coworker. Turns out she was supposed to go with her to Alaska but claimed she was sick. But the truth is she was scared. She's still scared. When investigators talked to EchoGlobal about Jennifer, no one ever talked to Amy. EchoGlobal made sure of it. She said Jennifer had suspicions about GenCorp Mining, but GenCorp is an EchoGlobal client and she was ignored. Her boss, Emily, was willing to listen, and the three of them made a plan to get evidence, including samples from several mining claims recently purchased by GenCorp. Emily let Jennifer use the company credit card, but EchoGlobal found out and fired her. She disappeared or, rather, is keeping a low profile."

Anger boiled in Trevor's gut. "Find out more about EchoGlobal's connection to the mining operation. Maybe GenCorp is more than simply a client."

"Grier is already on it. Sounds like there's a bigger connection and someone is involved in a big coverup. We still don't know what Jennifer was looking for. Amy continues to work for EchoGlobal because she's hoping to get another opportunity to find out what was going on."

"So she didn't come forward sooner because she was scared."

"That she would disappear like Jennifer. This is bigger than we imagined."

Trevor blew out a heavy breath.

"Are you all right?"

No. "Yeah. Thanks, Autumn. Thank Grier for me for what he's doing. I look forward to seeing Nolan tomorrow."

"He's trying to get there sooner."

"Sounds good." He ended the call. A twig snapped and foliage rustled. Rip was coming back too early. Something must have happened. Why hadn't he radioed? Unless Rip wasn't the one approaching. An animal could have made the sound.

Trevor readied his gun and crouched behind a tree. Waiting. Listening. Hoping to see a small animal at worst and Rip returning early at best.

A sound came from behind and he whirled, but Moosehead and his sidekick had the drop on Trevor. He ground his teeth.

They obviously knew their way around the forest surrounding the mountain and worked to keep it secure from intruders. But they weren't dressed for a trek in these woods. They didn't look like security guards either. Both wore blue coveralls and bright orange helmets. His gut coiled. He'd wanted a chance to face off with these guys and ask questions, but not at the business end of a pistol.

"How did you know I was here?"

Moosehead angled his head and looked up into the trees.

Trevor followed his gaze, then spotted a small camera. They'd found Rip's lookout spot and set up a camera. Of course. Trevor wouldn't mention Rip—maybe they hadn't found his other spot.

"What can I do for you?"

"You can drop the gun, the radio, and the phone, and then come with us, that's what."

Trevor didn't have a choice, and he did as they asked. But he could still try to talk some sense into them. "Look, fellas, you don't want to do this. I'm a police officer, and you're asking for more trouble than you can handle."

To Trevor's surprise, the two glanced at each other. One licked his lips. Nervous?

"How about you drop the weapons and ask me nicely," Trevor said.

Moosehead didn't lower the gun. "Come with us, *please*."

At least he got that much. Looked like he was going in today instead of tomorrow, after all. "Come with you please where? Where are you asking me to go?"

"Someone wants to meet you." The guy gestured toward the mining operation below them. The hike down was going to take some time.

"Well, why didn't you say so?"

After everything he and Carrie had been through, he had no doubt the men would use the guns if Trevor showed signs he wasn't going to comply. And he really wanted to land a few punches to Moosehead's face. He'd been counting the hours until he would be able to do just that, but now wasn't the moment—he was getting in, though not exactly the way he'd planned. But often that was how it worked.

You just started walking and then doors opened.

He marched down the mountain with them, glad someone else was cutting a path for him, but more than that, he was relieved Rip hadn't gotten caught up in this mess along with him and been carted off too. If anything, Rip could report back to Carrie and Nolan that Trevor had disappeared. Or if Trevor was lucky, Rip was watching from the woods and could report that he had been taken into the dragon's lair.

Right where he'd wanted to go.

Only he'd wanted to go in asking questions and not under duress.

Two different scenarios.

Whatever the circumstances, Trevor intended to ask questions, but it remained to be seen if he would come out with answers. It could be like Chad said—"*you walk into that place, and you're not coming out.*" He'd make sure to let them know they would be raided should he not exit safely. Maybe he'd keep to himself that law enforcement was already on the way to knock on the door.

Or maybe he should fight his way out of this now, while he still had the chance, and go in with Nolan tomorrow as planned. He stumbled through the rainforest with the bullies and along the way calculated his ability to take both men out or escape into the trees—and get lost.

"I'm looking for my sister. Her name was Jennifer Warner, or you might have known her as Lori Fisher." He stopped and lifted his hands. "I'd show you a picture, but you have my phone."

"We don't know anything about your sister."

"Then what *do* you know?"

"That you shouldn't be in these woods looking at the mine, a private operation, with binoculars."

"Why not? This isn't your land."

"It's a private claim. The boss wants it to stay private."

"Who is the boss?"

"You'll meet him soon enough."

Trevor plodded down the hill and then the scarred earth—the open pit where trees had been removed. Soon they passed the portable buildings that facilitated a mining camp. He stumbled.

"Keep going." One man led him forward. The other prodded him with the gun along a path around the pit and toward the opening in the mountain.

The heavy equipment rumbled, making it impossible to talk. Workers in blue coveralls and helmets operated the equipment and rushed in and out of the buildings and the tunnel. No one gave his abduction a passing glance, but Moosehead and Sidekick were regulars around here, so why would they? They kept their guns out of sight.

He knew if he tried anything, he would be shot. Besides, he was close to getting answers. They entered the long, wide tunnel and walked down concrete steps edged with log handrails on either side. Overhead, rebar reinforced the tunnel and protected against falling rocks. Cables ran the length of the tunnel to power the lights.

He was literally being forced into a dungeon.

At the bottom of the steps the tunnel opened up to a few portable buildings erected *inside* the mine. The miners entered and exited the mine with a purpose he didn't know, but he definitely sensed urgency in their movements. Still, no one paid attention to Trevor and his captors as they urged him deeper into the tunnel.

"Where are you taking me?"

He hadn't expected an answer, and he didn't get one. Iron bars were secured over a man-made cubby in the rock wall. A couple of empty barrels sat in what appeared to be storage space that had already been cleaned up, except for the barrels. He was forced into the cage.

Moosehead waved him back away from the entrance. "You need to wait here." Then he closed the barred door and locked it from the outside.

Trevor banged on the bars. "Wait. I need some water. Come back. I thought I was supposed to meet someone."

This is just great. He scraped both hands through his sweat-soaked hair. *Some investigator I am. I landed myself in an underground prison.*

If he'd known he would be locked alone in a cage and not given a chance to question anyone or speak his mind, he wouldn't have let them so easily capture him. He would have taken his chances in the woods. Escaped and waited for Nolan.

He kicked the bars hard enough to ignite pain in his toes.

What did they want with him?

Should he shout out that he was a cop and someone was going to come looking for him? Nah. They already knew that, and if they didn't, that would only get him killed and buried faster.

You wanted in. Now deal with it.

TWENTY-FOUR

This is wrong, all wrong.

Carrie boarded the *Sea Mist*. Trevor was in the woods with Rip somewhere, observing the mine. She should have insisted she go too, except he'd utterly disarmed her with that kiss, convincing her that she was a distraction to him. And with his confession that he wanted to say what was on his mind, in case something happened to him—like the message Jennifer left with Monica—Carrie had almost been undone.

She thought back to his words, which had slipped right under the walls of her heart and settled in to stay.

A thrill raced through her.

"I'm not going to leave anything unsaid . . . I wish we'd met under different circumstances."

Carrie had soaked up the emotion in his eyes, the tenderness in his voice, and she certainly more than responded to his kiss. Could she be more pathetic? Maybe she would feel less connected to him if she didn't fear that he was in over his head.

God, please protect him.

At least he'd agreed to wait for Nolan. Carrie had done her part in this, and she needed to let go of this almost-romance she never should have gotten sucked into.

She understood his need to see this through to the end. To be the one to get those answers. To bring justice for his sister. He'd failed Jennifer, and he was desperately trying to right what was wrong in his life as if it all fell on his shoulders.

But Jennifer could still be alive.

Now Carrie was taking up Trevor's mantle—hoping, believing for an unlikely outcome. Never mind that Jennifer hadn't contacted him in months.

Carrie sighed. Hung her head.

She wanted to wait in Yakutan, but with the danger ramping up, she and Chad would be safer if they headed away from the island. Plus, Chad needed to meet Daphne at an agreed-upon location and then go from there, and they would stay off-grid and off-radar until this was over.

But more than that, she didn't want to hang around and watch Trevor get hurt. Or witness his pain when he found the answers he sought. Biting back tears of fury, she stared out over the water. She didn't want to see someone else dead. And it gutted her to think about how much this guy meant to her.

I barely know him.

She couldn't care that much.

Because she knew, from experience, that even someone she loved and trusted would kill her for money. Would choose wealth over love. Over her.

Or, in Trevor's case, he would choose finding justice over her.

Oh, come on, that's not fair. She couldn't blame him for that, and there wasn't anything brutal or illegal in it. Trevor was one of the good guys. Still, she'd believed that before of someone else, and she couldn't have been more wrong.

"You ready?" Chad's question pulled her thoughts to the moment and out of the dark agony in her heart.

"No, I'm not. I shouldn't leave him." Her own words surprised her. She was ignoring her better judgment and following her heart.

"That's the plan, though." Chad arched a brow. "We already decided."

"It's a bad idea. I never should have agreed to it."

"Well, it's your decision. I can't force you. But I need to get out of here and pick up my sister. Stick with the plan. I think you should stick with it too." Chad moved into the pilothouse and stood at the helm.

Carrie followed. She didn't know what to do. Sticking to the plan was probably best. It wasn't like she was going to hike into that jungle of a rainforest and find Trevor and Rip on her own.

"He likes you, ya know?" Chad's words caught her off guard.

"What?" She whipped her head around in surprise and wished she hadn't. It made her look too eager to know more. She shouldn't care if he liked her. Carrie couldn't find the words to express her thoughts or even ask Chad to explain.

"The detective. He's into you."

Really? Chad had seen them kiss, after all. So why was he saying this? Still, her heart skipped a few beats. Yep. She was pathetic.

"I can see you're into him too."

Oh, please. She waved him off and shook her head. Bit back a ridiculous traitorous smile. "I only just met him."

And that's why I kissed him back?

She couldn't really be "into" Trevor. And if she was, then how could Chad know what she didn't even know? Oh, right. Chad had a sister, and maybe he was just good at reading women. But Carrie wasn't into Trevor, was she? Not in a way that anyone on this planet, especially someone who didn't even know her, could tell, even after witnessing one quick, impulsive mistake of a kiss.

Chad sent her a knowing, teasing grin. He was loving it. Or maybe he was trying to distract her. Well, it was working.

Chad shrugged. "Doesn't always take long to know."

To know what? "Oh yeah? I don't see your wife or girlfriend hanging around somewhere. Huh?"

"That's because my wife died."

A wave of regret hit her. She'd opened her mouth without knowing anything about Chad. "I'm so sorry."

"It was a couple years ago. We'd only been married a year. We met when I took her and her parents on a fishing trip. Two months later we got married. But she got sick a year into our marriage."

"Chad, I didn't mean—"

"It's okay. I'm just saying, everyone's different. You can know someone for a long time and still not truly know them. Or you can know them briefly and know them *deeply*, better than anyone else. You know what I mean?"

Wow. The guy was surprisingly profound. Wise beyond his years.

"I wish I could say I didn't understand, but I do." She worked with Darius for a couple of years and thought she knew him well.

And see what happened? She was certainly no good judge of character. Or maybe it was more that people couldn't even count on themselves in the end.

He started up the boat. "Before I take her out, I need to know—are you in or are you out? I hope you're in, because I promised the guy I'd look out for you, though it's not like you really need the help. You're a bush pilot, right? So you're accustomed to being on your own in Alaska."

"Yep. And I've got a lot of experience."

"But there's the other side of things. Men after you. Sabotaging your plane. There's safety in numbers. So your man, your guy. Trust him."

"He's not my man or my guy, but I'll let the detective do his job." *And hope he comes back so he can help me find Isaac's killer.*

Oh, man. She wanted him to come back for so many more reasons.

"Okay, let's go already."

Her gut soured at the thought of leaving. This wasn't *her* search, but she'd brought Trevor this far and it felt right to stay. But he didn't need her help now, and state law enforcement would be here tomorrow to hopefully end the search.

"Let's go."

She hugged herself and stared ahead as he steered the boat away from the village and deeper into the inlet. Isaac's message that someone was after her had been cryptic at best. Those men from Angoon were all about Jennifer, and wanted to stop her from helping Trevor. Vandyke was probably one of them too. But really, with or without her help, Trevor eventually would have ended up on this island. He was determined and had all he needed.

At least they connected with Chad and his charter boat. He shared a lot of information about Jennifer, including the box she left with him.

Carrie gasped. "Wait. Stop the boat. We should leave the box for Trevor."

Chad gave an uncharacteristic scowl. "He didn't ask for it. Rip isn't around either. I can't take it up to the cabin. What will we do with it?"

"We'll figure it out."

"I think you're stalling. Trevor would have said something if he'd wanted it." Chad continued steering away from the island.

Am I just looking for an excuse to stay? Carrie bounded down the short steps to the galley below and found the box.

She opened it and picked up the hazmat suit.

Just seeing the Geiger counter stirred up nausea. She dropped the suit back into the box and turned her back on it. Trevor was waiting on Nolan. He wasn't going in and didn't need it. She was stalling, all right.

A flash of blue caught her attention. Cobalt blue. She stopped and stared at the cubby over the kitchen counter. A small gem rested inside. Fear knotting in her gut, she approached the counter. Then she reached inside the cubby, grabbed the rough uncut gem, and brought it out to examine.

Her heart beat erratically.

Breathe, Carrie, breathe! Why does Chad have this?

Carrie closed her fingers around the uncut gem—merazite. The same gem Darius smuggled out of Zhugandia. The whole reason he pushed her out of the plane.

This gem being here could only mean that Darius was also here, or somehow connected. They had to go back now. She suspected she knew who was behind Jennifer's disappearance, and if she was right, and Darius Aster was here, then he would kill Trevor.

He could have killed Isaac.

Oh, God, please, no.

Her knees shook as she closed her eyes and remembered falling.

It can't be. This can't be real. Why?

The wind rushed at her back, roared in her ears.

Her arms and legs flailed. Her heart was in a thousand pieces, tumbling along with her body.

But Chad—what was his role in all this?

Trevor and Rip were walking into a trap. Were already in the trap.

Chad seemed kind and thoughtful, and he brought them to Rip. It didn't make sense.

But the rock didn't make sense either—it was worth a small fortune. It couldn't be a coincidence. Had he been paid off? Everyone had their price, and she knew that better than most.

Suddenly an arm gripped her wrist. "What are you doing with that?"

Lungs burning and heart pounding, she opened her eyes and sucked in a breath. Chad's grip tightened.

She threw a punch at his throat, but he blocked it.

And grabbed her other wrist.

TWENTY-FIVE

I need answers.

But at what cost?

Trevor paced the small space he was locked in. Activity in this part of the tunnel was nil. The mine was chilly—probably forty or fifty degrees. He didn't have his jacket because it had been hot up in the forest. Scraping both hands through his hair, he released a slow growl.

How could I let this happen?

He would be the first to admit that he'd made a colossal mistake. But he couldn't wait here and twiddle his thumbs. He should have expected something like this. They hadn't brought him to meet someone, after all.

God, it was a mistake to think I should keep pushing to get answers, no matter the cost.

He was willing to pay, or so he thought. He had no idea if he was getting out of this alive, even though he had reassured Carrie that he would come back and help her. He'd been overconfident on that point, believing he would escape when Jennifer hadn't.

And now that he saw things from inside this small space,

with no obvious escape, he realized he'd been selfish. While he intended to follow through in helping Carrie, he couldn't help her if he was stuck in here. Or dead and buried in this mountain when this was all over. He wouldn't be such a fool to think they would let him go.

I'm a dead man walking. Did whoever was behind his being taken against his will know that law enforcement was on their way? Well, the law other than him. *Please, Nolan, bring reinforcements with you.*

But his thoughts were not enough to warn the Alaska State Trooper.

He paced and growled. Pounded the rock wall a time or two. Jennifer wasn't here. She was gone. While he still wanted answers, he also wanted to live. He wanted answers and justice for both Jennifer and Isaac.

And he wanted to see Carrie again for reasons that had nothing to do with finding Isaac's killer. In the short but eventful time he'd spent with her, she'd ignited something in his heart that he'd buried deep for good reasons. But now those reasons no longer seemed to matter. A spunky bush pilot with bright green eyes and a determined spirit had pulled him out of a long, deep sleep. He needed to survive for a million reasons, but one had everything to do with wanting to get to know Carrie James better and seeing where life took them.

After what he learned from Chief Long, and the fact that Isaac believed Carrie was in danger, Trevor knew the past Carrie shared with Isaac was coming back to get her. He just didn't understand who was behind the threat. Regardless, he realized much too late that he needed to give up this search and protect Carrie from those demons of her past.

And he'd sent her away, believing she would be safer.

He pressed his back against the wall and slid to the ground. Hung his head.

God, I'm an empty shell, aren't I? I've got nothing to offer.

Nothing to give here. I'm completely and utterly destitute and have nothing except you.

Please, God, just give me another chance. I need to make this right.

Nothing left to give, except himself. All he could do was rest and pray and wait for the moment he could make his move.

If he got the chance.

The next time someone opened that door, he was taking action, and he would live or die with that action. It might be his last chance, and he wouldn't wait for a better opportunity.

Because he might not get one.

TWENTY-SIX

Carrie kicked Chad in the groin.

Growling, he released her. She whipped around and raced up the steps and back to the stern where she could get on the dinghy and escape.

Heart pounding, she tried to figure out how to lower it to the water, but it would take too long. She'd have to jump for it and swim, but then he could just turn around and steer right over her. Kill her.

Did Chad want to kill her? She couldn't fathom it. Couldn't stomach it. She'd grown to trust him for reasons unknown, even after her personal experience with trusting the wrong person.

Darius. He'd turned dark and cold and evil in a flash.

This was what Carrie got for trusting even one person.

"Carrie!"

"Don't come any closer." Or what was she going to do? She'd lost her Ruger in the plane crash. But still, he had his hands up in surrender as if she was going to somehow hurt him. She would at least try.

"I shouldn't have grabbed you like that. I thought you were stealing the gem. I shouldn't have reacted that way. And you still have it, but it's not worth my life. I thought I could trust you. Thought I was protecting you. But clearly you have your own plans."

What are you saying? "What? You're the one who betrayed us. He bought you off, didn't he?"

"Who bought me off? What are you talking about?" Chad frowned. "Jennifer gave that to me."

"You're lying."

"No, I'm not. Why would I lie?"

"Why would Jennifer give this to you? And how and why would she have it?"

"I think there's been a big misunderstanding here. She gave it to me as payment for helping her, though, really, my help might have gotten her killed." He sagged and averted his gaze.

"Why didn't you tell us?"

"That she paid me with a rock?"

"A rock worth a lot of money." She wouldn't tell him possibly millions, if he didn't already know. "Why didn't you say anything?"

"Look, she said it was worth a lot but to be careful. I have dreamed of upgrading the *Sea Mist* one day. If it really was worth that much, it was like a dream come true. I didn't tell you or Trevor because Jennifer gave it to *me*, and I was afraid you might take it away." He lifted his regret-filled eyes.

He was telling the truth.

"I'm sorry I suspected you. That you were working for him."

"Working for him? Who are you talking about?"

She held the gem in her hand as if weighing it. Were her suspicions correct? She couldn't believe this could be a coincidence. "I'm pretty sure I know who's behind everything."

"How do you know? What's going on? Just because of that rock?"

She gulped. Where did she even start?

"Just relax," he said. "Tell me what you know."

Her legs shook. She wasn't sure she *could* speak. She didn't want to feel utter terror or relive the pain on multiple levels.

"Darius Aster is a dangerous man. Last time I saw this gemstone, it was in a box on a cargo plane I was flying out of East Africa. Darius tried to kill me over it, thought he had killed me. I don't know the circumstances under which Jennifer got her hands on it, but it ties this situation to my past. If I'm here and this rock is here, then it's all related. It must be."

She approached him. Pulled his hand up and stuck the gem in his palm. "It's yours. Jennifer gave it to you. But like she said, be careful. People have died over it. Honestly, I'm not sure it was hers to give you, but then again, someone could have legally given it to her. I just don't know."

He looked at it and huffed. "If it has caused all this trouble, I don't want it." He offered it back to her. "It's yours. You take it, if you want it. You have a history with it."

Did she want it? She took it from him. "I'm going to hold on to it only because I don't want it to cost you your life. But I promise I'll try to make sure you're reimbursed so you can make your dreams come true."

He smiled and shook his head. "That's not necessary. You owe me nothing."

She nodded. "I'm sorry I kicked you and thought you were a bad guy. But we have to go back. Trevor and Nolan are not walking out of there."

"Apology accepted. I shouldn't have grabbed you either." Chad scraped a hand through his hair and paced. "That's not the plan. I don't think this should change what we're doing."

"Just drop me off and you can go."

"That would make me a total jerk."

"No. It won't. You agreed to take me with you, and you're helping Trevor, taking that burden off his mind. Helping me too. But this is my choice. You would only be a jerk if you didn't turn the boat back."

He sighed heavily and steered the *Sea Mist* back to the village.

After docking, Chad helped Carrie off the boat with her duffel bag and the satchel she'd transferred Jennifer's hazmat suit and Geiger counter into.

"I'll wait with you until Trevor and Rip get back, then we can decide what to do. I have to call Daphne and let her know I'll be delayed."

Carrie hiked along the boardwalk with Chad, who carried the satchel. She kept the gem in her pocket, where it felt like it was burning a hole through the material. Maybe even her hand. Her heart hadn't stopped pounding since she found it.

But she put one foot in front of the other. *Please, God, let me see Trevor again. Let me find him and warn him.*

Rip rushed toward them—alone—his expression grim.

"What happened?" Chad asked. "Where's Trevor? Shouldn't he be with you?"

Rip pulled them into the alley between some buildings. "Keep your voice down, will ya? Two men took Trevor at gunpoint."

"What?" Carrie couldn't catch her breath. "You let them take him?"

"I couldn't do anything. I'd taken up a different position to watch the operation. He didn't respond on the radio, so I went to check, and he wasn't where I left him, but his pack was still on the ground along with the binoculars. I knew something was wrong. I looked through them and saw two armed men escorting him into the mine."

"Then we have to get the locals involved," she said.

Rip frowned. "There's no one here who can help."

"But the nearest AST can," she said. "They're closer than Nolan coming from Shadow Gap, and now we have evidence. You saw them take him."

His face grew dark. "They won't believe me. I can't get involved. You can call them and do what you can, but leave me out of it."

"What? No, Rip. Please, he trusted you. Help him."

"I had a run-in with the law before. They're not going to listen to me. They'll just think I'm making it up to disturb the operation, because it wouldn't be the first time."

Her throat grew thick and tight.

What should I do, Lord? What would Isaac do?

Isaac would do whatever it took to save Trevor, but Isaac wasn't here.

Breathe. She could do this. She could fix this. Find him. Save him.

She slowed her heart. Calmed her breaths. Stopped pacing and stared at Rip. Made sure he was looking in her eyes and taking her seriously. "That back entryway you were telling Trevor about. Take me there."

He shook his head. "He wouldn't approve of that. Call the AST. The guy he was waiting on. Get him here sooner."

"I'll call him, all right. But I'm not waiting. There's no time. Listen, I know who's behind this, and I know it can't end well. I'll pay you to take me there. Name your price."

"If it was about money, I would be somewhere else doing something else."

"Then let it be about Trevor's life."

Those words were the password. Rip gave a nod of approval. "Ever been caving?"

He'd asked Trevor the same thing. She slowly shook her head. "I prefer the wide-open spaces of the sky."

"I'll take you all the way in. But it'll take a couple of hours of hiking in rough terrain to get to the cave entrance." He leveled his gaze. "Tell me now if you're no good for that. I can't carry you back."

I'll have to be good for it. "You won't have to carry me. I can make it."

God, please let me make it.

"It's not too late to change your mind and wait for help to arrive."

Was she making an impulsive decision? Would Trevor die if she waited? Would they both die if she didn't wait? She'd never been a coward, and on the surface it seemed like a big mistake, but she couldn't waste any more time.

"I have to try. You know it takes too long for help to arrive."

"That, I do."

"What about me?" Chad asked. "What can I do?"

"You'll hold down the fort," Rip said.

"Whatever that means."

"What about Daphne?" she asked. "You need to get her and make sure she's safe."

"If you get Trevor out," Chad said, "then you'll need off the island. I might be your only ride."

"But you've already helped us so much, and I don't want Daphne to be in danger. Go, Chad. Get her and stay safe. I'll be in touch. And there's the matter of making sure you get paid. I'll make it right."

"Call me if you need me for any reason." Although appearing reluctant, Chad left her with Rip.

Trevor was going to be either grateful or angry and disappointed at what Carrie was doing. She hoped she found him and he was angry with her. That would at least mean she'd found him alive.

While Rip gathered supplies at the Yakutan General Store, Carrie found a few items to take along as well. Then she called Chief Long and was disappointed to have to leave a message, but she made it clear that Trevor's life was in danger and to send help as soon as possible. The chief knew the stakes, but she also knew help never arrived fast enough. Carrie wouldn't waste a single minute.

In fact, she'd already wasted too much time.

Supplies in tow, Carrie and Rip went to his cabin and reviewed the cave map. He had planned to take her all the way, but she needed to know the lay of the land too, in case contingencies had to be made.

"The first time you showed this, you said you created it."

"Cave mapping was a hobby of mine. But I gave it up. After a while it seemed pointless. I haven't done it in years. Now I see a purpose in it—you need it to get inside the cave and save your man."

He's not my man. But she didn't bother correcting him. Her actions might say otherwise.

Rip helped her stuff supplies into their packs. They both needed to know what they had and where to find it.

"Here's a handgun for you," he said. "A Smith and Wesson 9mm, along with the ammo."

"Are you sure?" She took the gun, holster, and ammo from him.

"I wouldn't want you to be without protection. We hope for the best but prepare for the worst. Understand?"

She nodded.

"You know how to shoot?"

"Yes. Thanks." She stuck the pistol in the holster.

Rip secured several knives on his person to go with the handgun—dangerous creatures lurked in the woods.

Maybe inside the cave too.

She packed something special for the cave, just in case. She would also bring the satchel with Jennifer's suit along as well. What if the reason Jennifer had brought it was that she planned to use it as part of a disguise?

"Rip? Did you see anyone there wearing hazmat suits?"

"Not on the surface." He looked at the suit. "What are you thinking?"

"I thought if Jennifer had planned to use it as a disguise, maybe I could go in the front, like Trevor."

"If she used it even once, for real, and encountered radiation, it would still be radioactive."

Her eyes widened. She hadn't thought of that. She grabbed the Geiger counter and switched it on. "It's showing there's some radiation."

Rip peered at the instrument.

"That's normal. It's in the environment around us. The suit itself isn't showing more than normal radiation."

"Right. And if Jennifer had encountered dangerous levels, she wouldn't have left it with Chad." She looked up at Rip. "Listen, I know how to fly a plane through the mountains, in and out of rough terrain and tights spots, through the worst weather. I have no experience with this. Maybe I've got no business going in, but if there's a chance I can help him, I have to try."

Rip scratched his head. "You're right." He eyed her. "But you're smarter and braver than most. You'll figure it out as you go. I'm here to help you."

A frown slipped onto his face. *What is he thinking?*

He looked around his cozy home, then back at her. "Ready?" His voice sounded apprehensive.

"As I'll ever be." She wasn't sure if he was eager to go caving again or if the tension in his voice had to do with the danger they could face.

She'd never been one to sit back and wait.

"The hike to the cave entrance is going to be a long haul through the rainforest to the far side of Jacob's Mountain. The cave entrance is practically on the other side of the mountain from the mine entrance. Then once we get to the cave, we have to travel underground through that system before we connect with the mine. Expect it's going to take hours."

Hours Trevor might not have.

TWENTY-SEVEN

Rip stopped about ten yards ahead of her and turned back, waiting. He waved her forward. She told him she could do this, but two hours into it, she had second thoughts—times ten. But it was too late now.

They'd spotted Vandyke, of all people, up on a ridge, looking into this part of the forest with binoculars. Did he know about the caves too? Trevor had been taken, and thinking about what could be happening to him, or had already happened, was pure torture.

Even if Vandyke wasn't out in the woods searching for her, she couldn't give up. She couldn't wait and hope Trevor made it out. Or Nolan got here in time with a friend or two or three.

"How much farther?"

He chuckled quietly. "We're here."

"We are?" Too much excitement came out in those two words. She hurried forward to stand next to him.

Going into a deep, dark cave was at the top of her I-never-want-to-do-this bucket list. Still, Carrie never thought she'd be glad to say goodbye to the forest, except maybe just this once.

Sidling up next to him, she swiped the sweat from her eyes and dropped the satchel and the pack. "I don't see a cave entrance."

He shoved a bush around with his foot to reveal a small opening.

Huh? "I thought it was a cave. That's just a small hole in the ground." Could Rip even get through it?

"We'll lower our packs separately. Got any experience with climbing?"

"No. You didn't say anything about that."

"You won't have to rappel. I'll lower you and then follow."

He was going to drop her off inside a hole?

I'm not a coward. I'm not a coward.

But she didn't want to be too stupid to live. Maybe that was a long-foregone conclusion.

She shook her head. "I don't know about that. How about you go first?"

He stared at her. Didn't like her answer?

"I'll tie the rope off," he said. "Means we'll lose rope we might need later. Can you climb a rope?"

"That I can do."

He cocked a brow.

"I was in the Army, okay?" Over ten years ago, but still . . .

After securing the rope to a tree, Rip turned to her. "I'll climb down, then you pull the rope up and tie off one bag at a time."

"Why don't we drop the bags? I don't have anything that can break."

"The Geiger counter can break. I have a few things I don't want landing in the wrong place."

"Okay, then. Let's lower the bags after we get our helmets and headlamps on. Gloves too—for the rope. We can put on the rest once we're down there. I don't want to wait too long with someone tracking us."

Rip disappeared into the hole, his headlamp visible until it wasn't.

Oh, great. She glanced up at the island forest that was suddenly closing in around her.

"Okay," Rip shouted from below, his voice echoing. "Pull up the rope and start lowering the bags."

Carrie went through the motions for their packs and the hazmat suit satchel, along with a pack of essentials containing a first aid kit, other tools, and a bag of craft beads she'd bought at the Yakutan General Store.

The beads were bread crumbs. Rip might not agree, but in a worst-case scenario, she would not die lost in a cave.

After the bags were in the hole, Carrie gripped the rope with her gloved hands.

I can do this. God, please help me do this.

And if she couldn't? She was going to be the broken bag at the bottom of the cave. Muscle memory kicked in, and she slowly climbed down the rope, focusing on the task at hand. She didn't worry about the bottom of the cave or getting there.

"That's it. Nice and easy," Rip said.

Finally, she let go of the rope and landed on her feet. Rip patted her on the back.

She smiled at him. "You act like that surprised you."

"You said it."

"Honestly, I surprised myself."

"Honestly, I knew you could do it."

"What about the rope?" she asked. "If Vandyke finds that, he can just follow us down."

"Finding it won't be easy. Now, let's get geared up and get going." Rip put his pack on.

"Give me a second to catch my breath." Carrie put her hand against the cold, slick limestone. Overheated from the hike and climb down, she wanted to press her whole body against the cave wall.

As if reading her mind, he said, "You'll cool off soon enough. It's forty degrees in this cave."

Then the formations caught her attention, and she stood back to look at the incredible sight. "It's beautiful."

Rip chuckled. "We call the formations speleothems. That's a bit of drapery and a few stalactites and flowstone. Water runs down into the ground and washes away the soft limestone." He shined his headlamp next to her. "There's a vein of marble. It runs through this entire system, and then deeper and on the far side of the mountain is the granite where they were mining deep underground."

"And how deep are *we* going?"

"You won't be able to tell too much. Just focus on pacing yourself and figuring out what you're going to do when we get there."

"To the uranium mine? The Superfund site?"

"We're not going there. I wouldn't take you there."

"What? But you told Trevor."

"I didn't want him to do it. I wasn't completely honest. I came back through when the new mining operations started. Since it didn't seem like the previous mine had been cleaned up, I wanted to know what was going on."

Her throat tightened. "Where are we going, then?'

"The new mine. This cave has so many branching passages—crawlways —mostly horizontal, but some of them are vertical, so be careful. I suspected I could find a back way into the new operation, and I did. But I never figured out what they're doing. And I didn't have any hazard suit either, but that doesn't mean it's not hazardous now. It takes time to stir up toxic materials like radon gas."

She started to open the satchel with the counter. "Maybe I should keep this out. Jennifer had it for a reason."

"She didn't come through the cave, and we don't know the reason. All I know is that the cave connects to portions of the old and new mines, and we will stay away from the uranium mining portion. If that thing registers, we're stopping. Agreed?"

She pursed her lips. "Agreed."

"Lead on." She followed Rip, more grateful to him than she could ever convey.

He probably wouldn't have brought her here if he wasn't sure she could make it. But *she* wasn't even sure, so how could *he* have known, especially since he understood the rough terrain in a way she wasn't able to comprehend?

It was one thing to fly over Southeast Alaska and quite another to trek through an island wilderness area on foot or creep through miles of twisted tunnels beneath the surface.

"Duck your head up here. We'll end up crawling part of the way too."

Lovely.

God, does that verse about walking through fire and water count for small, dark spaces like caves too?

"Watch it." Rip ducked, his words breathless.

She ducked too.

He wasn't the younger man who'd explored these caves decades ago. Was she making a mistake? Was this a ridiculous attempt to rescue Trevor, a man she barely knew? But she *knew* enough.

This was no time to change her mind. They were going all the way in.

Rip got down on his knees and started to crawl.

"Will our packs fit?"

"Yeah. Just be careful you don't snag anything, or you'll get stuck."

"Well, forget that. Can I push my packs through?"

"Now that I think about it, that's a better idea." He backed out and gave her a sheepish look. "I'm out of practice. What can I say?"

"It's okay. You're risking a lot to bring me here. I appreciate it." She couldn't exactly scold him for bringing her on this fool's errand.

"We can push the bags through or tie them off and pull them."

She shrugged. "Up to you."

"I'll push my pack and your satchel. You'll just have the one to push."

"It's okay," she snapped. "I can do it."

"Suit yourself."

He was only trying to help. "I'm sorry. I didn't mean to bite your head off."

"It probably won't be the last time." With that, he pushed his bag through the opening.

And Carrie followed.

The space tightened around her so that her quickening breaths echoed off the walls back at her.

Focus, focus, focus.

A knot lodged in her throat, constricting her air. She couldn't swallow for a few tries.

Come on, Carrie. You've been through worse. Focus on something else besides this small space.

God, please let the cave not be radioactive.

She suddenly realized she couldn't see Rip ahead of her because the tunnel had taken a turn.

"How much farther?" she called. "Don't leave me, Rip. Wait for me."

Rip didn't answer.

Carrie tried to push her bags faster. The pack snagged on something.

Oh no. "My bag."

The only thing that could make this worse was if the cave were underwater and she were in a scuba suit pushing her tank through.

What in the world?

She found the issue. A small speleothem had hooked the shoulder strap. After she freed her pack, she continued pushing forward. Crawling through a small cave, pushing through panic with barely enough oxygen was not going to kill her.

Finally, she exited the tight space and spotted Rip sitting in a cathedral-sized chamber, drinking from his bottle. She crawled all the way out and sucked in air. She wouldn't tell him she feared he'd left her.

I am not losing it.

She sat next to him and joined him in hydrating. "How much farther?"

"We get there when we get there."

They climbed up, slid down, and crawled through holes until she thought claustrophobia would be her death. To think, the idea of entering the mining operation through a back way, without anyone being the wiser, had seemed like a great idea. Now she knew she'd made a big mistake.

Maybe it would have been better to waltz in through the front door and ask them to take her.

Rip suddenly stopped and pressed his finger to his lips. They listened.

Water trickled.

Did that mean something to him? He drank more from his bottle and gestured that she should do the same. When her mouth was moist again, she asked, "How much longer?"

Maybe she should have said, "Are we there yet?"

He averted his gaze in a way that sent a chill through her.

"How much longer?" she asked again.

"I haven't been here in years."

Okay. She didn't like his answer. "Do you even remember the way?"

"I have a map." He pulled it out and shook it in her face.

But something had changed. What was it? Or had he made a mistake in his map?

"You wanted a plan B. You were desperate. The detective was desperate." He huffed, his breathing heavy. "You want to go back? Let's do it."

"Look. I didn't say that. Besides, people are still out there looking for us. We might as well go forward until we find what we're looking for." *If it's even possible.*

Carrie could maneuver a plane into and out of precarious situations, but all that training didn't help her in these caves. She was completely dependent on Rip.

And God.

Isaac's voice rose in her mind. *"Focus on what you've always done, Carrie—caring for others—and you'll heal on the inside, just like you have on the outside."*

On the inside she wanted to throw a tantrum. Shoot, she wanted to throw a tantrum on the outside. Rail and scream and pound the limestone walls, marble walls. Whatever they were. Knock down stalactites.

They continued making their way deeper. "Okay. We're getting there. Not much farther."

Am I dreaming? She'd never heard more beautiful words.

"You know, if this was the rainy season, we wouldn't have gotten this far or gone this deep," he said.

"Let's just make sure we get out of here before the rainy season starts."

Rip stopped and leaned against the wall and grimaced.

"Are you okay?" she asked.

"Just my angina acting up."

Angina? That didn't sound good. She'd heard that term. But . . . "What's angina?"

"Nothing." He dug around in his shirt pocket and pulled out a prescription bottle. He struggled to open the child-safe cap, then finally popped a pill, sticking it under his tongue.

"What is that?"

"Nitroglycerin. Helps to open up my vessels."

Oh boy. He was leading her into this cave with a serious medical condition that required explosives? She should laugh at the insanity. Instead, she stared. She wasn't sure what to think. What to do next.

He stood taller and released a breath. "That's better."

Guilt filled her. *What have I done?* Trying to save one man only to lose another?

Carrie touched his arm. "Please, Rip, we don't need to continue. It's not right for you to come with me if you . . . you know . . . shouldn't."

"I'm not an invalid. I'm in the best shape of my life. It's all good now. While this is more danger than I've seen in decades, I feel more alive than I've felt in ages. You don't worry about me. You wouldn't make it without my help. That boyfriend of yours might not make it without yours."

Boyfriend. That couldn't be further from the truth, but she wouldn't argue that point.

Because right now, both she and Rip needed to conserve their strength for what they might face later.

"Okay. Lead on."

A few more yards and a ticking sound drew them to a stop. She glanced at Rip.

"That what I think it is?" he asked. "Because if it is, you agreed to stop."

She glanced at the Geiger counter and what she saw sent spikes of terror through her.

Another sound warned them—someone else was in the cave. Someone was coming for them.

Now we're trapped.

TWENTY-EIGHT

Clomping boots echoed in the tunnel.

Relief rushed through him. He hadn't been forgotten, left down here while everyone else cleared out. He wouldn't waste this chance.

Trevor scrambled to his feet. No matter who opened the door, he was pushing his way through and out. That someone had come for him and would actually open the door was presumptuous. He'd been expecting his old friend Moosehead, but instead, a thirtysomething man wearing blue coveralls and a helmet like the rest of the mine workers stood there holding a gun with an unsteady hand.

Keys jangled when he inserted them. "Get back from the door."

Trevor's best opportunity for escape was here and now as the man herded him out of this cell. He couldn't afford to wait and hope for a better scenario.

The door swung out and Trevor waited. The man waved him out of the cell. Trevor had hoped he would step inside first, but he could roll with the proverbial punches as they came. He stepped out, and as the man reached to shut the cage, Trevor disarmed him.

Now *he* had the gun and aimed it at the man's chest.

"What's your name?" Trevor might get more information if he used a different tactic.

"Eddy." His eyes narrowed. "Why?"

"Well, Eddy, I want to know the name of the guy who's trading places with me. Now, inside and over by the wall."

"You're not going to get out of here."

Still aiming the gun, Trevor stepped forward to urge the man farther into the cell. "A second ago, I might have agreed with you. Hand over your communication devices—radio, cell, satellite phone."

The guy's eyes widened. He tugged out his phone and radio.

"Put them on the floor and slide them over."

Flattening his lips, Eddy complied and kicked the radio and phone over to Trevor.

Without taking his eyes off the gun or Eddy, he reached down and grabbed the items. "Where'd they put my gun and my phone?"

He shook his head. "I'm just a delivery guy. I don't know anything."

"Is that right? Well, delivery guy, where were you supposed to deliver me?"

"To a room up front. That's all I know. Someone is going to talk to you there."

Perfect timing. "Thanks for giving me the information. One more thing, do you know what happened to Jennifer Warner? She was with a group of scientists who came here last year."

The man shook his head again, and Trevor suspected he really had no clue. He swung the door of bars closed.

"Wait. You can't leave me."

"Why not?"

"Because." Fear rippled over his face. "They'll forget about me, and I'll die here."

Once Trevor was out of there and had his evidence, he intended to bring in the Alaska State Troopers and other agencies to search every inch of the facility for his sister. "You're not going to die here. But I get the feeling something is going down. What haven't you told me?"

"We're clearing out for now. The whole place is gonna blow."

Trevor stared him down. "What do you mean blow?"

"Use your imagination, man." Eddy approached the bars and gripped them.

"They're covering up evidence, then. Making it look like an accident. What evidence is here that's worth losing millions of dollars in profits?"

Eddy shrugged. "Look. I'm not supposed to know about the explosives, okay? But I saw them being planted. I heard rumors. I was told you're a security threat and to bring you up to the main building. That's it. You know what I know."

"Except how to get out of here."

"I'll have to show you. You're not getting out on your own."

"I'll take my chances," Trevor said. "If you make a noise, I'll have to silence you."

"You can't do this."

"I won't leave you here indefinitely. Don't worry. But I can't trust you." Trevor locked the door, hating this precarious situation, then pocketed the keys. "How much time before the place blows?"

"I don't know. We've been told to evacuate due to contamination. I don't know if that's true, but I do know about the explosives."

"So who's the boss?"

Voices drew Trevor around. No time to find out. He moved deeper into the tunnel, then hid in the shadows. Eddy shouted, "Hey, let me out of here!"

What had he expected? Maybe he should have brought Eddy with him. Toward the entrance to the tunnel, heavy equipment started up, drowning out Eddy's shouts. Or so he thought. Three men hurried toward the caged man. Great.

Trevor moved deeper into the narrowing tunnel and crouched into a shadowed fissure. This was the wrong direction, but if he was lucky, those men would leave and he could follow them out. If he didn't get out of here, he'd become part of the mountain.

Even if he did make it out, if the mine was under rubble, all the evidence would be destroyed and he might not ever learn the truth about what happened to Jennifer.

Rip had mentioned access to the mine via caves. If Trevor searched for an exit that way, he would probably get lost in there and die when the explosives took out portions of the mine.

Lord, what do I do?

What he needed was to talk to someone in the know—the man in charge. He thought about all the possible ways he could have gone about learning the truth. Ways that wouldn't have landed him in a mine that was about to be obliterated—but that was hindsight, and he couldn't have known then what he knew now.

As soon as Eddy was out of the cell, he pointed toward the deeper part of the mine, and the four men headed in Trevor's direction. This was getting better and better.

He had a gun, but he didn't want to start a gunfight.

Maybe he could lure them into this narrow gap he'd found and take them out. Switch out clothing. But it was four against one. Whatever he did to get out of here, he couldn't leave people behind to die. Maybe he was better off letting the men take him to see the man in charge. But he'd wanted that conversation to be on his own terms, and not while he was held at gunpoint.

A noise from deeper in the tunnel drew not only his attention but that of the four men who rushed right past where he was hidden. He could take this opportunity to head in the opposite direction, but he spotted a flashlight shining through old boards hanging loose over an opening.

Trevor sucked in a breath.

Was this the cave that Rip had told him about? Someone was in that cave, trying to get through.

The four men kicked at the boards and loosened them, pulling them away, and yanked out a body in a hazmat suit.

He couldn't breathe as he watched.

When the helmet was removed, long blond hair fell out over her shoulders.

Carrie.

She was here to help him. Rip had obviously shared what'd happened to him, and *this* was his answer? To take Carrie all the way through the caves to this entrance? And where was Rip? Had he left her to do the rest alone?

Trevor didn't have time to process his frustration and tried to concentrate on the exchange.

He couldn't understand the words, but the tone told him she was acting as though she was officially inspecting the mine. But the men weren't buying it. They took items from her, including a handgun, then yanked her forward. Demanded she get out of the suit.

He hoped she hadn't passed through a radioactive area, because the men would now be exposed too. She needed to somehow decontaminate.

How was he going to get her out of this?

Forced to go with the men, Carrie walked forward, holding her head high as they passed where he remained undetected in the shadows.

Think. Think. Think.

Eddy turned to look back—he hadn't forgotten Trevor, but his associates waved him forward, now clearly more interested in Carrie's arrival. They stopped at the cell where Trevor had been kept and pushed her inside, then locked the door. One of the workers radioed, and Trevor couldn't make out the exchange with the squawking and static. The men left Carrie in the cell, then headed back into the deeper tunnels to search for him.

Now was his chance. He moved out of the shadows, then hurried toward her.

Her eyes widened at the sight of him. She gripped the bars. "Trevor! You're alive."

His heart jumped. He tried to keep the keys from jangling as he opened the door. "What are *you* doing here?"

"I came to rescue you, what do you think?"

"Looks like we're rescuing each other." He swung the door open and it squeaked, making far too much noise. "Let's get out of here."

A racket sounded from deeper in the tunnel. They were coming back.

"Let's go!" They walked briskly in the direction of the main tunnel entrance. "Stick close. I'll do my best to get us out of here. I've got a gun, a radio, and a phone. I'll call for help as soon as I can."

Equipment started up again, this time sounding like it was moving out of the mine. Up ahead they could see workers carrying crates. "Keep your head down. Maybe we can blend in."

"Right. We're not dressed in the coveralls."

"Not everyone is. We can act the part. Everyone is trying to get out of here." He kept his voice low as he continued walking toward a big stack of crates. "Why the hazmat suit?"

"A precaution. We ran into increased radiation, but Rip took us down another path."

"Rip? Where is he?"

"Vandyke was in the cave. Rip got me as far as he could, then sent me on my way. He planned to lead Vandyke away. I left bread crumbs in case I needed to find my way back, but Vandyke might have followed those right to us. I don't know what happened with him and Vandyke. But I couldn't have gotten here without Rip."

I don't know if that's a good thing.

He wanted to tug her close and kiss her. *Wrong place, wrong time, man.*

"You've put yourself into a whole lot more danger by coming here."

"I needed to warn you. And I want to see him, face him in person. He's behind the mine."

"What are you talking about? Face who?"

"Darius Aster."

"Who?"

"He's the man who tried to kill me. I think he killed Isaac."

What? She wasn't making any sense. He gripped her shoulders. "While I'd love to hear how you know this, we're running out of time. They've rigged the mine to blow, so we need to get out of here."

"That doesn't make sense. Whatever he found here must be worth billions."

They approached the crates as two men each lifted a crate and carried it forward. He gestured for her to follow, then stopped at what was left of the stacked crates. Standing on each side, they worked together and lifted a crate like the others were doing.

Her features were strained as they carried it forward. "What's in this thing?"

"Keep your head down. Workers are moving so fast to clean this place out, no one is going to notice us."

Another series of portable buildings sat to the right inside the cave. A man rushed out of one of the buildings, and Trevor braced himself, but he paid them no attention. Crates were loaded in a semitrailer. They needed to stack theirs and find another disguise. But Carrie suddenly directed their movement toward the portable building.

"What are you doing?" he asked, his whisper practically a shout.

She continued forward until they were next to the building the man had exited.

"We can set this down here." She lowered the box, and he followed her lead.

She had her own plans, and Trevor had no choice but to go along with them unless he wanted to draw more attention. Head held high, she opened the door and rushed inside as if she belonged. He followed quickly behind.

For the moment they were alone in the office.

"What are you doing? This isn't the plan! We have to get out of here."

She closed the blinds and locked the doors, then glanced around the space that included a few desks, boxes, and a computer. "Looks like the computers are all boxed up except for this one. Let's see what we can learn."

She tugged out a USB drive. "Compliments of Rip. He was an activist before. While I'm in here, I might as well get all the goods." She gestured at the door. "You're my muscle, so you get to guard the door."

"This isn't about Jennifer anymore, is it? How do you think Aster fits into this?"

Carrie tugged the gem from her pocket and set it on the desk while she woke up the computer. She stared at the screen.

"Don't you need a password or something?"

"The guy who left didn't log off. He's probably coming back. We have to hurry." She stuck the thumb drive in.

"Now, you were telling me about how Aster is involved because of this rock?"

"Gem. Jennifer gave it to Chad as payment. It's still uncut. This is the gem Darius smuggled out of Africa ten years ago. For all I know, he went back for more. Or maybe he found a deposit here and that's what they're mining for."

"How does that connect Aster to this operation?"

"What more proof do you want?"

He squeezed the bridge of his nose. "This isn't proof at all."

"It can't be coincidence, Trevor. First, it's uncut. Whatever he took from Africa would have been sold and refined into a fine gemstone. I don't know how she got an uncut gem, but Jennifer took it."

"That would make her a thief."

"Or she was collecting evidence and got out with that gem and needed a way to keep Chad silent. Or buy his help. She was alone and had no choice. So, moving on. I'm sure Darius killed Isaac. He must be behind his murder."

Trevor stared at her. He would have to tell her now in the middle of this. "You're making a lot of assumptions."

"Remember when you told me that you could track someone by looking at their past to predict where they might go?" she asked.

"Go on."

She continued searching the computer as she spoke. "Isaac's murderer has to be someone who held a big grudge against him. The gem could have been found by anyone who works here. It was a newly discovered gem ten years ago, and it's still as valuable now. But with Isaac's death, and men after me . . ."

"This isn't hard evidence there's a connection, but I'm tracking with you. You'd make a good detective."

"I don't want to be a detective. I want to take *Darius* down this time."

He didn't miss the surge of unshed tears before she inhaled deeply and downloaded entire files. "We can figure out what's on them later."

Voices grew louder. Closer. Trevor moved to the door and positioned himself to protect Carrie as she scooped up the gem and put it back in her pocket. He held his gun at the ready. "If we're discovered, I'm not going to be able to hold them off. We're trapped in here. I'm not sure stopping here to get data was the best idea. It was foolhardy."

"Foolhardy? Who uses that word anymore?"

"This is serious." He gripped his gun. "I don't know what's going to happen, Carrie, but I'll do my best to give you a chance to live, and you'd better take it. One of us has to make it out alive to tell the world what happened." And maybe, just maybe, Jennifer would get what she wanted in the end.

Someone tried to open the door. Then pounded. "Open up in there."

Trevor seethed at this turn of events. He was furious at Rip for leading Carrie to him through their plan B caves. Now they were caught and could both die on this mountain.

Someone then tried unlocking the door. Keys jangled amid a heated discussion about which key would work. Then there was cursing from one of the men. How many were out there?

"They're going to take us, Trevor," she said. "But I have something on Darius, and I've already sent that to Chief Long and Nolan. Nolan arranged for the nearest AST field office to come to the mine and hopefully get you out safely. We have to survive until help arrives."

"I told you about the explosives. The mine could be gone before they get here." *And us with it*. What he had to say next, he hadn't wanted to tell her now. Not like this. "And you don't have anything on Darius, Carrie. Darius is dead. Ten years ago, Isaac was wanted for questioning regarding his murder, so he left the country—with you, of course. I think that was to protect you both."

"That can't be true. I can't believe that Isaac killed him. And I can't believe Darius is dead."

Trevor wasn't sure which detail shocked her more. That Isaac would kill someone or that Aster had met his justice.

A gunshot rang out from the other side of the door.

We're out of time.

Again.

TWENTY-NINE

With her heart pounding, she could hardly move. In case she lived through this—*God, please let us live through this*—she forced her fingers to tug the USB away from the computer and place it in her pocket, then she returned the screen to the home page.

Men would be through the door in seconds.

These could be my last seconds.

"Trevor," she said with a gasp.

A vein pulsed at his temple as he gripped his pistol, aiming at the door.

I did this to him.

He'd wanted to escape, to get out of the mine and save them both. But no, she pulled him into this room to get evidence.

Another gunshot ricocheted off the walls and vibrated her bones.

Trevor would be killed instantly. He was holding a gun. He might be a great shot, but he was outnumbered. He would stand his ground to protect her and, at the very least, be wounded, and she couldn't risk even that. This was all on her.

God, there's nowhere to hide. What do we do? What do I do?

Hands shaking, she tried to pull him back. "Get behind me," she said.

"No."

Of course he'd say that. Before he could protest more or shove her out of the way, the door burst open. She held her hands high and jumped in front of Trevor.

Three men rushed in loaded for bear and aimed pistols at Trevor and Carrie.

They didn't shoot, but fear shot through her all the same.

She'd hoped they wouldn't kill her—that she was valuable to whoever was behind this. Time to take charge—as much as she could and with a confidence she didn't feel. The news that Darius was dead was hard to swallow. But he was still connected somehow.

"You brought all those guns for little old me? Take me to Darius."

"Who?"

She shook her head. "Take us to your boss. I have information he wants."

The security guy scowled. "You're trespassing. Who are you and what are you doing here?"

"I'll inform the man in charge," she said.

"I'm in charge of security. You can inform me."

What if I have this all wrong? "I'm only talking to the man in charge."

"You'll talk to the police, then."

Carrie glanced at Trevor. "Fine by me."

The security guard relieved Trevor of the radio, satellite phone, and gun. "If you'll please come with us."

Carrie and Trevor were escorted down the long, man-made granite corridor. No more beautiful, nature-made limestone caves carved from water and time. Despite her serious issues with caves, seeing the difference made her appreciate what Rip showed her earlier. Not all the caves were small, dark spaces.

They climbed a lengthy concrete staircase with wooden rails on each side, then stepped out of the tunnel and into the bright sunshine.

Carrie squinted and shaded her eyes as she took in the ugly sight of an open-pit mine. They were digging on the surface as well as underground. "What are you mining here?"

"Terbium, dysprosium, erbium, and yttrium."

"Oh, is that all?"

"No, not all. They're heavy REE—rare earth elements," the security guard said. "We mine some light elements too. But don't ask me what. I'm in security, and that's the extent of my knowledge on rocks."

Carrie and Trevor were herded to a group of portable buildings—a mining camp for the workers since no roads came to the mine. The equipment was transported via the water and air, making the operation that much more expensive.

The security guards stopped at one of the buildings and opened the door. "Wait here."

"For how long?" Trevor asked.

"Until we can arrange for you to be handed over to the authorities."

Trevor stepped inside without a fight. If she weren't with him, would he resist? Did these guys know the plan to blow up the mine? Or was that misinformation to begin with?

The small room was empty. No table. No chairs. No bed. Nothing on the walls.

The man started to close the door, but she stepped into the doorjamb. "What are we waiting here for? How long are you going to keep us? Remember, I have information to share with your boss."

"I don't have an answer for you just yet." He closed and locked the door, and that's when Carrie saw the woman gagged and bound on the floor in the corner.

Daphne?

A pang shot through her.

She rushed forward and removed the gag. "Daphne? What are you doing here?"

"Untie me. Get me out of this. What does it look like I'm doing? They grabbed me after you left."

Daphne was taken because she talked to Trevor. Did Chad discover his sister missing? Or had he been taken too?

Carrie's hands shook as she tried to open the plastic ties. "I can't get this to unlatch."

Trevor knelt next to her and worked the plastic straps until Daphne was free. She rubbed her wrists. Once her ankles were also free, she stood but was wobbly, so Carrie steadied her while Trevor paced the small empty room.

"When did they take you?" Trevor asked. "Your brother was on the way to get you."

"They took me before Chad got there. I hope they didn't get him too. If they did, I haven't seen him. They haven't put us together."

"Let's hope he hasn't been captured."

At least two people—Rip and Chad—knew what was going on and could serve as witnesses when law enforcement finally arrived.

"Something's wrong here," Carrie said. "The security guards who dropped us off here—they seemed to actually be security guards. Legitimate. And I hope they do call the police. I was starting to think I was wrong about everything until I saw Daphne here."

"Don't forget, Carrie, the men who've been following us took me captive. While the real security guards who put us here don't act like they intend to harm us, I learned something from Chief Long. Jennifer was investigating suspicious activity in the mine, and now her coworker is scared and her boss was fired and is keeping a low profile. We can't trust anyone here. I admit, it's possible these men might not be involved in the underhanded activity going on, and that's why they think *we're* criminals and are holding us for the police."

"What about me, huh?" Daphne huffed.

"Who brought you here?" Trevor asked. "Were they wearing security guard suits with an emblem?"

"I don't know. Just two jerks."

"One of them wears a moose cap?"

Her eyes widened. "Yeah, one of them. The other one had a cockeyed stare."

Carrie paced the small space. "This doesn't feel right."

"No kidding. We have to get out of here," Daphne said.

"How do we do that? Do you have any ideas?"

The locks clicked. Carrie pushed Daphne behind her, and Trevor stepped forward to protect them both. She appreciated him trying to be the hero, and wouldn't expect any less of him, but she didn't want anyone else dying while trying to protect her. And that's what happened to Isaac—he died because he had protected her. Saved her. She knew it. Now she just had to prove it.

A man in a wheelchair, flanked by the security guards, entered their portable prison room. Carrie, Trevor, and Daphne backed against the wall to give him a wide berth.

She'd wanted to speak to the man in charge—and she assumed this was him—but now the words wouldn't come. Darius was dead, but this man had to be connected.

Darius is dead. Darius is dead.

"You're trespassing, and I'd like to know why—although I already have my suspicions." His voice was thick and gravelly. "You're activists, and you've sabotaged this operation by contaminating it with radioactive materials. We found the leaking barrels. You want to shut me down for harming the environment, yet you've intentionally brought harm."

Anger and loathing seethed from him.

Trevor stepped forward. "Whoa, you've got this all wrong.

We're not activists. I'm a police officer investigating a missing person, Jennifer Warner. You also might know her by the name Lori Fisher. Your men abducted me and brought me to this mine, and now they've manhandled us and locked us in here. If you let us go, no harm no foul. But I'd still like to get answers about Jennifer."

Seconds ticked by. Then, finally, he responded. "I've never heard of her, so I can't help you. My apologies for your treatment. My men are instructed to protect the property. I'll send someone to assist you in getting back to where you came from, but if you're responsible for the contamination, I'll be filing charges against you."

He tapped his hands on the wheelchair arms.

The head of security spoke. "Sir, my men haven't abducted anyone. That's ludicrous. In fact, we only brought these trespassers, one man and one woman, here for their safety. Not—"

"Daphne Bateman," she said. "As if you don't know. I was abducted from Shady Cove."

Frown lines increased on the guard's face. "Not by me or my men. No matter how you got here, it would be best for your safety if you waited here until we can arrange transport. Heavy equipment is being off-loaded, and the entire mining crew is evacuating. Other agencies are arriving to monitor the mine. Someone will come for you in short order, after which we can sort out with the authorities what's going on."

Carrie stepped forward and locked eyes with the man in the wheelchair. "You haven't told us your name." *Or your connection to Darius Aster.*

Like the security guards, the man seemed to be running a legitimate operation. But that didn't explain being followed, the burning lodge, the attacks on Carrie, their abductions, and the news Trevor had learned from Autumn.

"I'm Joseph Schroeder, head of GenCorp Mining."

He started exiting the room.

"Wait." Daphne sprung forward. "You're lying. You know Jennifer Warner. You left her to die in that cave without protection. You're going to pay."

Daphne's words surprised Carrie, and she assumed Trevor too. How did she know? She didn't miss the sting of grief, the blaze of anger, in Trevor's eyes.

Joseph angled his head as if hurt by her words. "I'm sorry for your loss, Miss Bateman."

"Your men abducted me and brought me here. They wouldn't do that without your instructions."

Carrie wished Daphne would stop. If Schroeder kept his word and let them go, they might have a way out of this for now—but Daphne was stirring things up. She squeezed the woman's shoulder, hoping to calm her down.

"Please send someone to help us home," Carrie said. "We'll leave your property. If you don't know Jennifer, then you don't know her."

"Make the arrangements," Schroeder said to his men. "Know that we'll be transporting you to meet with a trooper to answer questions about your reasons for being here. Maybe they can determine the truth."

The way he said *truth* let her know he didn't necessarily believe their story and might still be leaning toward them being the activists who planted barrels of leaking radiation.

Then Schroeder backed his wheelchair out, followed by his security guards, who shut and locked the door. For their safety? They were, in fact, captives.

Carrie turned to Daphne. "What were you doing?"

"Don't be fooled for a second. He's lying, and we're going to die just like the whistleblower."

"The whistleblower," Trevor said. "You mean Jennifer when you say that?"

"I think. I guess. They talked about her and used that word."

"You obviously know what's going on." Trevor's tone was

low and steady as he ground out the words. "Why didn't you tell us this before?"

Daphne's eyes widened, and she took a step back. "I didn't know it before. The two men who took me, I heard them talking. They were idiots to have said so much in front of me, but I had a bag over my head, and I guess they thought that meant I couldn't hear. Or that I was going to die so it didn't matter what they said. In that case, why put a bag over my head? Idiots!"

"What else did you learn?" he asked. "Think. Tell me everything."

Tears welled in her eyes. "Nothing more. I've been moved around to a few places since arriving and ended up here. I've been so afraid they'll stick me somewhere to die of radiation poisoning. Alone. Now at least I won't be alone."

"The Alaska State Troopers are on the way," Carrie said. "Someone will be here soon."

"What? They've been here already. Nothing happened." Daphne stalked around the small space.

Carrie looked at Trevor again. "It wasn't Nolan. He wouldn't have left. He requested help, remember? The nearest detachment is in Ketchikan. There's a post in Prince of Wales too."

"When were they here, and how do you know?" Trevor asked. "You've been tied up."

"They had to move me to hide me. I caught sight of two troopers through the window before the bag was put over my head again. I got dropped into this room a couple of hours ago. They've been here and nothing happened!" Daphne slid to the corner and pressed her face against the wall.

I don't like this.

"What do you think that means?" Carrie directed the question to Trevor.

"Maybe Nolan or Chief Long contacted the local detachment, and they arrived and asked questions and were given satisfying answers."

"I told Chief Long you had been abducted."

He shrugged. "They could have been shown around but avoided the more dangerous sections. It doesn't matter. We have to act like we're on our own, even though this Schroeder guy and his security guards sounded like they were going to get us out of here. Something's bothering me about this. They could be good liars, but I don't think they're in on what happened to us."

She leaned against the wall and slid to the floor to sit. "I hope Nolan is still coming. I hope the answers didn't satisfy him."

"Even if someone else is coming, we can't count on Schroeder. He could be lying." Trevor rubbed his chin. "We can't wait on a rescue."

"I agree. But there's no way to even pick a lock. The door has no handle from this side. Seems to me it was created to hold people captive."

"Listen, you guys, I don't understand why they would abduct me. How am I a threat?" Daphne hugged herself. "I didn't know anything before I came here."

She'd lasted this long, but now since Carrie and Trevor had joined her, she was struggling to hold it together. Carrie thought about it. "They don't know that. They know you sent us in this direction. You talked to Trevor. It seems like they're trying to tie off any loose ends."

And to do that, it would be best to leave them here to be buried with the "accidental" blast.

Before Carrie could voice her thoughts, Daphne stood taller, wiped her nose and eyes, and dragged in a breath. "I'm okay. I'm ready to help us get out of here. I understand that your sister was a whistleblower, but what did she learn? Chad never told me."

"Probably to protect you."

"For all the good that did. Look at us now!"

"I don't know all of it," Trevor said. "I've been able to piece together a small part, and you've confirmed the whistleblower part. She was a geologist, and it sounds like she found an anomaly, something she wanted to check out, so she collected more data here. I have every intention of finishing what she started." His voice cracked on the last words.

The pain in his tone cut through her.

"Trevor? You okay?" Carrie asked.

A deep frown carved in his features as he shook his head. "I can't reconcile the fact that she never said one word to me."

He scraped both hands through his hair.

Carrie understood Trevor's frustration. Jennifer didn't think she could trust him? That news hurt Carrie too.

How could Jennifer miss that her brother was the greatest guy in the world? She totally should have trusted him.

Oh.

I get it.

"I think I understand. She just wanted to protect *you*, Trevor. If you'd had a clue what she was up to, she knew you'd come charging in, guns blazing. But when things got dicey, she left you the clues before it was too late, in case the worst happened. Subtle clues, so no one else would steal them or hide them from you. No one else would look at those photographs and determine to follow her path except for you, the brother who loves her."

Loves. Because Trevor still loves her—dead or alive.

"So you have all the answers now." His voice was gruff.

And wow, that hurt. But she knew he didn't mean it that way, and she wouldn't respond. He needed space to process everything.

Time to focus on more urgent matters. "Even if they plan to come back for us, if this place is rigged to blow like you said, Trevor, then we can't wait for them."

"What?" Daphne screeched. "Why didn't you say something? We'll be buried alive!"

She rushed to the door without a handle and started pounding on it. After a few moments, she moved to the back wall and dropped to sit again. "I guess it's better than dying of radiation poisoning. No one is going to dig this up to look for us because they would risk exposing more radiation."

We can't just give up.

The door suddenly opened. The head security guard looked at Carrie. Carrie held her breath, and she suspected Trevor and Daphne did as well.

"You said you had information for our boss, and he'd like to speak with you." He glanced at Trevor and Daphne. "Alone."

THIRTY

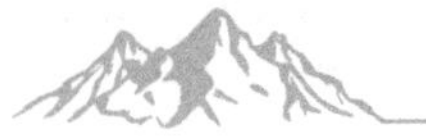

Trevor pushed Carrie behind her. "She isn't going anywhere with you."

He calculated diving into the man, disarming him. But it came with significant risk. Still, he couldn't let Carrie go with them. Not alone. He expected her to state that he had to come with them. They were *together*.

She stepped forward. "I'll go."

She sent him an apologetic look.

Wait! "What are you doing?" Trevor blocked her path forward. "You can't do this. All of us should go. We should stick together."

And maybe we can even overpower this guy and take his gun and get out of here. But Carrie couldn't read his mind, even though they'd worked well together throughout this entire experience.

She sighed. "It's okay, Trevor." Her tone was soft and gentle, like she was talking to a child, and that only made him angry. "I think I know what's going on here." She stared at him as if willing him to understand. To read *her* mind.

While he couldn't read her mind, he saw the deep concern she had for him.

She stepped out of the space without him.

"What, are you keeping us here like prisoners? Do you understand I'm a detective?"

The man only stared at him. "Then you'll understand this is part of our security protocol in case of armed trespassers. We'll turn you over to the Alaska State Troopers."

"They were already—"

The guard shut the door in Trevor's face, and he growled.

"Here. Well, this is just great."

"You tried," Daphne said. "There's nothing else you could have done."

"I could have disarmed him, but I didn't want to risk either of you getting shot. Instead, I let him take her. I should have done something."

"What do they want with her? Why did he take her?"

"She said she had information."

"So does she? Or is she just buying us time?"

"If she has information, she didn't tell me what it was." And he realized he never even asked. "The longer we can stay alive, the better the chances are we can survive this."

He'd been so determined to find out what happened to Jennifer. He wanted—beyond hope—to find her alive. Though he hadn't found her body, with everything he'd learned so far, he was pretty certain she was murdered. All because of her own determination to right the wrongs she witnessed.

But at what cost? Her life?

He could ask himself the same question. The cost of this mission to find out what happened to her was rising. Carrie and Daphne both could end up paying the price for Jennifer's determination and his pursuit of answers.

Grief slammed into him. Now wasn't the time. He had to focus on helping Daphne and Carrie make it out alive. Squeezing his eyes shut, he did the only thing he could and prayed.

God, I made a mistake. I don't know what to do now. Please,

please save Carrie. Save Daphne. Keep them safe. Help us out of this, if it's your will.

"Are you *praying*?" The question sounded incredulous.

He turned around and leaned against the door. Blew out a breath. "Yes. We're going to need help getting out of this."

Machinery started up outside nearby, and Trevor held Daphne's wide-eyed gaze. The sound grew louder like it was coming right at them. He'd spotted a crane truck earlier but hadn't paid much attention, given their circumstances and the fact that the mine was supposedly being evacuated. But he had a gut feeling that crane was coming for them now.

The aluminum building jolted. Twisted and shifted. One end of it rose up. He and Daphne fell against the far wall as the building tilted onto its side.

"What's happening? What's going on?" Her voice was high-pitched.

"They're moving the building."

"What? Why? Where? Oh . . . no, no, no, this can't be good."

"I would agree, except this could be our chance to get out! These buildings are supposed to be disassembled before the crane moves them." The building might not be able to withstand the move without at least some bending or cracking. Anything at all to give them a chance.

Then again, maybe whoever was behind the move didn't care if they were crushed inside—in fact, that could be the whole purpose.

The corner on the opposite side cracked open.

"I think they want to kill us!" Daphne said. "They're just dumping us into an early grave."

An explosion was no guarantee they would be buried under the rubble—deep enough. This would ensure the evidence was gone.

That was it, then. He pictured a big hole, and they were going to be dropped into it, then buried.

Daphne cried again. "I don't want to die."

"You're not going to die."

Carrie remained at the forefront of his mind. If Daphne and Trevor were so easily disposed of, what was happening to Carrie? He couldn't help her if they didn't get free.

"Stay close, Daphne. I'm going to try to open up enough room for us to get out before it's too late."

Trevor scrambled up to the upward side of the building and grabbed onto a strut. He couldn't grip it very well, but he used it to support himself while he kicked on the loosened wall.

Again and again.

Harder and harder.

With each kick, the aluminum gave a little and the space grew wider. And with each kick, the building shook, the metal sounding like it would twist and crush them as the crane moved.

Losing his grip, he dropped against the wall and slid down to the opposite wall next to Daphne. She couldn't have looked more terrified. He regretted meeting and talking to her, but he couldn't have known that would lead them both here to face certain death.

The building suddenly tilted, and he grabbed Daphne's hand. "Hang on."

The floor separated from the side wall. He wanted to dive through the opening, but not before seeing where it would drop them. He had a feeling it didn't matter. The entire building was going to be dropped into a gaping hole in the earth.

"Do you trust me?"

"No?" Daphne's fear-filled eyes looked doubtful. "But what choice do I have?"

"We're getting out of this while we still can. Hold on to me. Whatever happens. Hold on."

He took her other hand.

Then the bottom opened up to a deep pit below them.

THIRTY-ONE

Carrie sat in an office with windows that allowed her to view the mine, the destruction of this side of the mountain with the open pit, and the tunnel. She stared out the window, trying to come up with an escape plan while also wanting more than anything for a chance to face off with Joseph. She intended to find out what his relationship to Darius is. Was.

Whatever.

She'd been left here alone.

I'm not a prisoner.

Honestly, she didn't care what Joseph would say. She had to get out of here. When law enforcement finally arrived and an investigation was conducted into this operation and what had happened to Jennifer, her, Trevor, and Daphne, she could get her answers then.

At this moment, she couldn't fathom why she thought she could get answers from that computer and then escape.

Because I'm invincible, that's why.

After surviving an "unsurvivable" fall, she'd only *imagined* that she was invincible and could somehow serve her own brand of justice. But not if Darius was dead. That changed everything.

Oh, Isaac . . .

Did Isaac kill Darius?

She wasn't really coherent after the fall. Her memories were fuzzy. Squeezing her eyes shut, she tortured herself with the cold darkness she'd seen in the eyes of the man she'd given her heart to, fully. Wholly. She wasn't sure even the fall was as painful as that heartbreak.

Air whipped around her. Roared in her ears.

Carrie had taken a few dives with a parachute. She knew how to jump. This wasn't the first time she'd spread her arms and flown. But this time she tumbled toward the earth without a parachute—to her death.

Resistance was everything. She spread her arms and legs wide and created resistance. But really, she had no idea what purpose this would truly serve. In less than two seconds, she'd hit the ground.

God, help me.

God, I love you.

The earth came at her.

Then darkness.

Breathing hard, Carrie jerked in the chair, her eyes open. She hadn't wanted to think about those last moments. To relive them. But now she remembered—she'd been overcome with peace. God had wrapped his arms around her even as she fell and hit a thicket.

Carrie remembered waking up in a hospital. Isaac talking to a doctor about transporting her to a major hospital. "Save her." She broke so many bones. After rehab, Isaac moved them to the other side of the world, to another hemisphere.

"I let him think you were dead," Isaac had told her. "I paid the hospital to keep your privacy. In Africa, such things are possible."

Carrie sucked in a breath or two. She couldn't dwell on the past now. Would she be murdered after she met with Joseph? While waiting, she perused a few images on the wall of his portable office. One image drew her out of the chair and over to view a map of the entire mining operation. Her heart rate kicked up at the sight of a helipad. She'd bet that facilitated Joseph's transportation to and from his mine.

A noise outside the door signaled it was time to get back in her chair.

The door behind her opened, and she recognized the sound of the wheelchair. It rolled around to park behind the big desk. Joseph Schroeder, head of GenCorp Mining.

After positioning himself just right under the desk, he removed his sunglasses to study her.

"Do I know you?" she asked.

"We've never met until today," he said again in that thick, gravelly voice. "You said you had information for me." He clasped his hands on the desk.

"I thought you were someone I knew. I had information for *him*."

"Who did you think I was?"

"It doesn't matter."

"If it has to do with my operation, then it matters. Do you have information for me regarding the sabotage of my mine? Are you responsible?"

Heart pounding, she shook her head. "I thought you were Darius Aster. But he's dead." She pulled the uncut gem from her pocket and set it on the desk. "Have you ever seen this before?"

He picked it up and examined it. "It's a gemstone. Miss—"

"James. Carrie James."

"Miss James. I don't know what it is you think we do here, but we aren't digging up diamonds and gems. We dig out the REE—rare earth elements. The nearby mine was for uranium, but here, uranium is a by-product of the minerals we unearth.

We send rocks and dirt off to a processing plant that extracts the minerals."

Is he lying?

She didn't think so. "Whatever's going on is happening right under your nose."

He sat back at those words. "What do you think's happening?"

Carrie didn't know where to start with this guy or how to unravel things. *Could I have it all wrong?* "Listen, I have some ideas, but I need to confirm them."

He smirked. "I'll let you talk to the troopers about it, then."

He didn't believe her, and she didn't blame him. She couldn't wrap her mind around the idea forming in her head.

I must be losing my mind.

"While I'm waiting on law enforcement, could I look at pictures of your mining crew? I think I could identify the troublemakers. But you should also know there are rumors that someone has rigged enough explosives to blow the mine." It was a long shot, but if Joseph was on the up and up, that didn't mean everyone on his crew was.

His eyes narrowed. "I'll talk to my security head and let him take it from here. If there's something more that I need to know, he'll inform me."

"But what about the explosives? Aren't you concerned?" Unless he was involved.

"It would take a significant amount to destroy a mining operation, but the right amount placed in the exact right position could cripple it. I'll let security know."

In other words, he was done with her. "I understand."

She couldn't be sure he wasn't involved somehow, but she didn't take him for someone who used low-level thugs to follow and abduct people.

Joseph backed from the desk and wheeled out of the room.

"Okay, then," she said to herself.

What am I supposed to do now? Wait for the security guy? Would he let her look at photographs of the crew? Or she could just walk out of here and free Trevor and Daphne. She could identify the men later.

That was it—she was getting out of here. Carrie moved to the door and, to her relief, found it unlocked. But she peeked out first.

The security guard was heading her way. She was too late to escape. Then a man stepped from behind another building and shot the guard in the back. Shock rolled through her. The man slowly looked at her. She bit back a scream as he headed her way.

I have to get out of here! She slammed the door and locked it, then raced to the window. But it wouldn't open. She'd have to break it. Carrie grabbed a chair and moved back to the window to throw it through, but paused to watch the semi-truck on which they'd loaded crates head down the dirt road, kicking up dust and crunching gravel. When it passed, a man wearing a hard hat and mining crew coveralls stood with a wide stance, hands on hips, watching it go.

The side of his face was burned. He looked familiar and yet not. He lifted his face toward the window as if aware he was being watched, then his eyes snagged hers. Even from this distance, she would recognize those cold eyes. Darius tipped his helmet to her, then jogged after the truck and disappeared.

So he wasn't dead after all.

THIRTY-TWO

A window shattered, and Trevor shoved Daphne between the buildings and shielded her.

They had successfully hidden their escape after dropping into the side of the pit and scrambling out before the building plunged, crashing into the deep hole in the earth. Trevor and Daphne had spent the last several minutes sneaking around big equipment, edging close to buildings trying to avoid being seen by the crane operator, but Trevor came face-to-face with Moosehead as he rounded the corner of a building. Trevor quickly disarmed him and knocked his lights out. Then he retrieved his own gun and smartphone from Moosehead's pockets as the guy lay facedown in the dirt.

Daphne had wanted to make a run for it into the woods, but Trevor wouldn't leave Carrie, and Daphne wouldn't go it alone.

He hadn't heard gunfire, so no one was chasing them—yet. Still, even though he'd tried to remain quiet and keep them hidden, that shattered window might draw unwanted attention.

He needed to check it out.

Peering around the corner, he spotted the window and below it on the ground, a chair and a body.

Carrie!

"Stay here." He left Daphne and weaved in and out of buildings until he got to Carrie.

Had someone thrown her out of the building? The chair was bent and she lay on her side, groaning. He would drop to his knees but for the glass.

"Are you okay? What happened?"

"I'm escaping."

He looked up at the window. The drop wasn't that far. She must have thrown the chair through after she couldn't get the window to open.

"What were you thinking?"

She squinted up at him. "I'm just trying to survive. I saw you through the window. Stop asking questions and let's get out of here."

Shouts resounded from the window above them, but Trevor couldn't see anything as he assisted her to her feet.

"Are you sure you're okay?"

"No." She looked up at the window. A chunk of glass had cut a gash in her forehead. He'd deal with it later.

"Let's get out of here," she said.

When her first step was a limp, he lifted her in his arms, ignoring her protests, and ran forward, joining up with Daphne who waited behind the portable buildings used for mining camp housing.

Behind the building he set her down and looked her over. "You could have killed yourself. You know that? How's your leg?"

"I gave myself a chance. As for my leg, it picks the worst times to give me trouble. I'll be fine. Now, please follow me. We're getting out of here. Someone shot the security guard and was headed for me next. They're after me. They're after us. I have a plan."

"Wait!" He positioned her against the wall. "This will hurt."

"What are you doing?"

"Pulling the shard of glass from your head." He carefully removed the glass as she cringed.

"Here." Daphne handed him the shirt she'd worn over her T-shirt.

He took it, ripped off the sleeve, and handed the rest of the shirt back. "Does it hurt?" he asked as he pressed the torn fabric piece against her cut.

"I don't really feel it. Must be the adrenaline."

The cut bled a lot, and Carrie's limp would slow them down. "Press that against your head. I don't think you can lead us anywhere like this. I'll carry you, and you direct me."

"Darius is alive, Trevor."

He hadn't expected those words. "What?" He stared at her.

"Listen, Joseph Schroeder isn't the bad guy here," Carrie said. "I don't think so, anyway. I saw someone shoot his head of security. I think I know what's going on. I saw him."

"Who did you see?"

"I was looking out the window to watch that semi go by. You know the one that had all the crates? And that's when I saw Darius."

Oh, Carrie. "Listen, we've been over this already. Darius is dead."

"And I'm telling you I saw him through the window. He recognized me. He was looking right at me and tipped his helmet. He's here. I think I know what he's doing. He has his own mining operation and is stealing right from under Joseph's nose."

Gunfire rang out somewhere near the buildings, but Trevor couldn't see the shooters. "I want to hear those details, Carrie, but I think it's best if we get out of here while we still can."

"Okay. I'll explain everything later."

"Agreed." He finally lifted her. "You said you had a plan?"

"There's a helicopter pad on the other side of this group

of buildings, closer to the mine entrance. There should be at least one helicopter, because that must be how Joseph travels to the mine. I haven't heard one power up and leave. It must still be here."

He carried her to the end of the row of temporary housing and stopped to set her down.

She pulled the cloth back from her forehead and looked at the blood.

While Trevor peered around the building, Daphne eyed the cut. "It's mostly stopped bleeding."

He spotted a black helicopter on the pad. "You're right. There's a helicopter. But—"

Carrie started forward as if to step out from the cover of the building, and he pulled her back. "We can't make it. The helicopter is another fifty yards. We would be too exposed. Why don't we go down to the water? The tree line isn't that far. We can use the trees for cover and take a boat, or just run deeper into the woods and get as far away from this doomed mining project as we can."

Trevor stared at Carrie, waiting on her decision. He should just lead them into the woods and count on them to follow, but Carrie was strongheaded and determined. She was still eyeing the helicopter.

He could tell the moment hope for that ride ran out of her. Her shoulders slumped and she frowned.

"You're right," she said. "It could be too risky. Besides, that has to be Joseph's ride, and I don't want to take it from him. I honestly believe that he and his security guards intended to help us get out of here even if it was into the hands of law enforcement."

"Oh yeah? Then why did Daphne and I end up fighting for our lives when the building we were in was picked up and dropped into a hole?"

"Because that wasn't him. Don't you see?"

"No, I don't see. You can explain that to me later as well."

"Okay, what's your plan?" she asked.

"You and Daphne head for the woods. I'll follow and cover you. I ran into Moosehead and got my gun and satellite phone back, after I left him eating dirt. No matter what happens, keep running and take cover. Find a boat. Get out of here, even if you have to swim."

She glanced at the weapon. "We go together, Trevor. Or we don't go."

"We go together." He said the words and hoped they would happen. But plans made often didn't happen how one hoped. Trevor peered around the building, looking both directions. "Crouch and run for the trees. I'll watch your backs. It's now or never."

He peered around the building first, then waved them forward. Carrie limped, and Daphne raced ahead of her.

Trevor pulled up the rear.

Someone rushed toward them through the woods.

"It's Vandyke!" Carrie shouted.

Trevor ran forward—passing Carrie, then Daphne—and met the man with an elbow to his nose.

"Go! Go!" He urged them onward.

Through the woods he spotted the water and a substantial dock meant to support the heavy equipment loaded onto the barges. A big cargo plane sat in the water near the dock.

"To the cargo plane!" Carrie said. "We can make it."

They raced between the trees toward the water and the hefty plane.

"You can fly that?" Daphne asked.

"Oh yeah. I used to live to fly these."

Trevor pulled up the rear and turned to give them cover if needed while the women continued putting distance between them and the mine. He monitored their progress as he watched for danger. They headed down the incline—though, again, Carrie was taking too long. He wanted to rush over and carry her, but she wouldn't make it if he didn't stay behind.

Three armed men rushed through the trees toward them.

Behind him, Carrie shouted, "Trevor, come on! We can make it."

"Go," he called over his shoulder. "I'll lay down cover."

He ducked behind a tree as a bullet whizzed by.

"Not without you."

She was coming back.

He turned. "If you don't get Daphne to safety, she could die. Go! Start that plane up. You're our ticket out of here. I'll make it, or I'll find another way."

Fear erupted in her eyes. She acted as if she would run toward him, but then more gunfire cracked the air. She nodded, fierce emotion spilling from her eyes.

"It's the only way." He turned and fired the Beretta, trusting that Carrie would make her way onto that plane and get away. Get free.

He hadn't saved his sister, but he could get the bush pilot—the woman he was falling for—a fighting chance.

THIRTY-THREE

Pain sliced through Carrie's crippled leg. Even though she ignored the pain, she couldn't force her leg to cooperate as she rushed forward. Daphne waited for her behind a tree, then when Carrie got there, they both crouched in some bushes.

Gunshots rang out behind them—Trevor exchanging gunfire with the men after them. Fear that Trevor wouldn't make it strangled her. Squeezing her eyes closed, she tried to shut out the sound of the gunfire.

When I pass through the waters, you will be with me; and when I pass through the rivers, they will not sweep over me. When I walk through the fire, I will not be burned; the flames will not set me ablaze.

"Come on." Daphne stood.

"Not yet." Carrie tugged on her arm. "That equipment transport barge is too close."

"It's moving away from the island. I don't think they're looking at us or care."

Daphne was right. Carrie was looking for one more reason to wait for Trevor.

"That plane could be the last ride out of here," Daphne said. "And you're sure you can fly it?"

How many times would she ask? "Yes. This's right up my alley." Even after ten years of flying her smaller one-engine plane, she had no doubt she could handle this bigger baby. "Only thing is I don't have time for a preflight check."

The propellers started up.

Daphne's eyes widened. "I think someone has done that for you. We need to get inside before he takes off."

"Run!" Trevor shouted.

Carrie and Daphne sprang from their hiding place and raced across the boardwalk. Daphne assisted Carrie. They cautiously rushed into the open back of the plane, which was filled with crates—the same ones she and Trevor had carried and seen loaded onto the truck inside the mine.

Carrie took a peek into one of the crates. Dirt and rocks. Not surprising. She thrust her hand in and dug around until her fingers closed around something that felt familiar. She tugged it out and dusted it off.

Though rough and uncut, it was a gemstone.

As she'd suspected, Darius was running an operation under Joseph Schroeder's nose—just like he'd done with the humanitarian organization, using the cargo planes to transport contraband. But he wasn't doing this alone.

"Carrie," Daphne whispered. "What are you waiting on? Let's go."

Was Darius in the cockpit? If not, then it was someone on his payroll.

Either way, they couldn't hitch a ride. They had to commandeer the plane.

Unwanted memories of the contraband Darius smuggled out of the country that nearly cost her life a decade ago accosted her mind. *Not now!* She shoved the past where it should go. She'd held the memories too close for too long.

Time to get over it.

She weaved carefully between the boxes. She wanted to wait for Trevor, so she'd have to take the pilot out before he took off. Or was he waiting for someone too? Against the wall she found a secured toolbox and grabbed a tire iron from inside.

Pressing a finger against her lips, she telegraphed her plan to Daphne, though she had probably already figured it out. She approached slowly, relieved Darius wasn't sitting in the cockpit.

The single pilot had a gun in his shoulder holster—he was the one who shot the head of security!

She didn't want to kill anyone, but she had to hit him hard enough to knock him out so he wouldn't shoot *them*. She could take his gun and Daphne could tie him up.

Heart pounding, she slammed the tire iron against his head, and he slumped forward. He didn't even see what hit him.

"Quick. Get rope or duct tape. Anything you can find to bind him before he wakes up." Carrie relieved him of the gun, then unstrapped him and pulled him out of the chair.

Man, he was heavy, and her leg almost gave out. With Daphne's help, she pulled him out of the cockpit, then they laid him on the floor.

"We can just tie him up in the seat using these loose cargo straps. I couldn't find anything else." Daphne helped Carrie get him up into the seat and hold him in place, then Daphne buckled him using the seat belt and tied the cargo straps around his arms in a way that both secured him for the flight and restrained him from hurting them.

This is taking too much time.

"Now, sit down and strap in. But please try to keep an eye on this guy. I'm giving you the gun. You know how to use it?"

Daphne nodded. She took it with confidence. Good enough.

"If anyone besides Trevor comes in that back door, shoot them."

"But what if it's the security guys? The regular guys."

"I don't think it will be. Just use your judgment."

Pulse racing, Carrie got in the cockpit and strapped in. She pulled in deep breaths, but it was no use. Her hands still shook.

Glancing out the window, she had a limited view of what was going on in the vicinity where the cargo plane she was taking—a flying boat, really—had been docked on the water. She couldn't see Trevor.

Nor did she hear the gunfire.

Is that a good thing? Or a bad thing?

Once again the image of Isaac in a pool of blood rushed through her, but she saw Trevor in that pool of blood instead.

No!

She couldn't let herself think about the worst-case scenario now. He must have run out of ammunition, that was all. And he was now racing toward the plane.

Get on the plane. Get on the plane. Get on the plane.

Before it's too late.

Carrie looked at the dash and got familiar. All she had to do now was rely on her knowledge and experience, and taxi out over the water until she could gain enough speed to lift.

And fly away.

"You see anything, Daphne?"

"What?"

"Is Trevor on board?"

"No."

His words rushed back through her. *"I'll make it, or I'll find another way."*

Pain shot through her heart as she hit the switch to close the cargo door. For a brief moment, she closed her eyes. Breathed slowly to calm her racing heart.

I don't want to leave you, Trevor!

What should she do? If she waited and the men got to them, this would all have been for nothing. If Trevor didn't make it, and they were taken anyway, he would have given himself up for nothing.

"Uh, Carrie! Someone is on the plane."

"Is it Trevor?"

"I don't know. I don't think so."

A gunshot rang out.

Daphne screamed. Then she said, "I'll shoot you. Don't come any farther."

"What's this, Carrie?" a familiar voice shouted. "You stealing from *me* now? You self-righteous hypocrite."

Darius. Her heart jackhammered. She needed to take off now. Could she trust Daphne to handle him?

No. Definitely no. She flipped the switch to lower the cargo door, because no way was she taking off with Darius on board. Unstrapping, she crouched as she maneuvered out of the cockpit. Daphne hid behind a crate.

They were stacked high so she couldn't see the back, but she heard the hydraulics of the door opening.

"Get off this plane, Darius!" she shouted.

"I don't think I like that idea."

"See that button right there?" she whispered to Daphne.

Daphne nodded.

"Hit it when I tell you. I'm going to flush him out. The cargo door needs to close, and then I can take off."

"But what about Trevor?"

"We'll pray he gets out alive."

Taking the pilot's 9mm pistol from Daphne, Carrie crept around the crates. She wouldn't have this battle in the air. "I'm not letting you take the plane, Darius. These gemstones don't belong to you. You stole them right from under Joseph's nose, which knowing what I know about you now, doesn't surprise me."

"This is my plane, Carrie. Mine. And you're not taking it."

Her gut tensed as she crept quietly between the crates. He

was hiding in here somewhere. She just needed to sneak up behind him.

And there he was, crouching, peering around another crate with his back to her. She had the drop on him.

Despite what he'd done to her, she could never shoot someone in the back.

"Move, and I'll shoot you."

Darius moved, and she shot a crate near him to make him understand. He stopped moving.

"Toss the gun."

He tossed it.

"Now, step off this plane or I will shoot you."

He turned around and smiled—that same disarming smile she'd fallen for. Dimples in his cheeks, dark eyes that no longer held appeal, and half his face burned. She wouldn't bother asking him how that happened.

"You have five seconds to get off, or believe me, I will shoot you."

Instead of getting off, he stepped forward. "You can't shoot me, Carrie. It's not in your blood to harm others. Or else you would have stuck with me years ago. You couldn't even bother to stand by while I smuggled out gemstones."

Another step. "So no, Carrie James, you're not going to shoot me."

Her hand shook. *No, I'm not going to shoot you.*

A growl came from behind and Daphne rushed forward, aiming for Darius. Carrie joined her in shoving him back and out of the cargo plane and down the ramp. Caught off guard, he fell, then rolled the rest of the way until he landed on his backside on the dock.

Carrie hit the button, and the hydraulics kicked in, slowly closing the ramp.

Daphne reached down and picked up Darius's gun, then

pointed it at him. "You get us out of here. I have no problem shooting this guy if he tries to get back on."

Carrie took one last look at Darius, the moment surreal. She might be leaving him behind at this moment, but she doubted she was rid of him.

With a quick glance around, she hoped to see Trevor on his way. But he was nowhere.

Her shoulders sagged. Back in the cockpit, she looked at all the switches, levers, and buttons on the dash, and the indicator light informing her the cargo door had closed and was secure.

Time to go.

She taxied until the plane was directly in the wind. With that barge taking up so much space in the water, she hoped she had enough room to lift out of here. She lowered the flaps. She didn't have a kneeboard with checklists for this aircraft, so she couldn't be sure of the flap setting.

Do not panic. You can do this.

After raising the water rudders, she held the yoke all the way back to keep the propeller out of the water and applied full takeoff power. A few more maneuvers and the loaded cargo plane lifted completely.

Airborne!

"What about Trevor?" Daphne shouted. "You're just going to leave him?"

Carrie didn't respond.

A fist squeezed her heart. *Please be okay. Please make it.*

The plane gained altitude, and she glanced out her window, searching for Trevor.

She spotted him looking up at the plane, watching her go. He'd *wanted* her to go without him. Then he sprinted toward Jacob's Mountain, their old buddies in pursuit.

He was leading them away.

Pursing her lips, she shook her head as tears welled, blurring her vision. Detective Trevor West—*her man*, as he'd been labeled—was trying to save them.

And she couldn't waste his efforts.

She increased speed and flew back over the mine to get one last look. Joseph's helicopter was gone, but another had taken its place on the pad. She noted the N-Number in case that information was needed later, then directed the cargo plane loaded with valuable gemstones away from Essack Island.

"You are. You're leaving him. I can't believe it," Daphne shouted, but Carrie could barely make out her words over the roar of the plane.

She finally donned the headset to dampen the noise and replied under her breath because Daphne wouldn't be able to hear her anyway. "Trevor is capable of protecting himself. He's giving us a chance to get away, and we have to take it." But the words were more for herself than for Daphne.

Even as the plane lifted and the island grew distant, guilt rose in waves. She kept the tears at bay. She had to make sure she hid her regret, her second-guessing, from Daphne. Maybe even from herself, though she was dying inside.

She was forced to leave with Daphne. If she'd been on her own, she would have stayed. Trevor had put himself in a dangerous position to give them a chance to escape. She hoped—*God, please*—that he didn't have to give his life. But his staying meant he was *risking* his life.

For them.

She wasn't sure when it had happened, but at some point she'd begun to believe that at least one man in this world, besides Isaac, could be trusted. She'd hoped but was too afraid to admit that Trevor was that man. He was a man she could trust with her life.

And with my heart?

In the air, flying steadily for the moment, Carrie exhaled.

They were off the island. But she couldn't get past the grief of leaving Trevor behind.

Daphne appeared in the doorway. "Where are we going?" Daphne sniffled. Crying because she was happy to escape? Or because they'd had to leave Trevor behind?

Maybe both.

"Away from the Mountain of Death, and then we'll get help. Thanks for assisting me back there."

"Oh, with that guy? Who was he anyway? You seemed to know each other."

"Long story."

"I'd love to hear it when you're ready. Do you think you'll see him again?"

"I hope not."

But yes, definitely yes. Darius was coming for her.

The note she found at Isaac's cabin was meant for her, not Isaac.

THIRTY-FOUR

From behind an excavator, Trevor watched the plane grow smaller as it flew away. Carrie and Daphne were safe. That was all that mattered. It had to be all that mattered. Learning what happened to Jennifer—the whole reason for this misadventure—didn't even matter at this juncture. Not really.

Life, the living, that was what mattered.

At least he'd glimpsed the plane and the amazing Carrie James in the cockpit.

Now to find a way out of the mining camp. The mining crew had evacuated, leaving behind some of the bigger equipment and the portable buildings.

And . . . the men after him.

Three men had been pursuing him—Moosehead and his cockeyed sidekick, and then the man Carrie had called Vandyke. Trevor was surprised he hadn't already been gunned down.

A beefy man tackled him from behind, shoving him into the dirt. Trevor twisted around but caught a fist in his face. Blinding pain ignited in his nose.

Moosehead stood over him, aiming his automatic rifle at Trevor's face point-blank. That was seriously overkill.

Trevor was out of ammunition, and they knew it, so they took the pistol from him. "Where are the others?"

Trevor couldn't help the laugh that escaped. Like he would tell them. But oddly, the fact that his ploy had worked filled him with joy. They'd completely ignored the plane and run after him.

Moosehead yanked Trevor to his feet. His sidekick stood on the other side of him. They gripped each arm and half walked, half dragged him. Time to shake off the daze and his smile.

"Where are we going?" He should have expected his words would sound garbled. His lip was swelling.

"To your grave."

"Thanks for such encouraging words."

They dragged him toward a waiting helicopter that was already powered up—not the black mining company one Carrie had thought to take. That one was gone, so Schroeder had presumably already left Jacob's Mountain.

This was a smaller bird.

With each step he took, Trevor felt his adrenaline surge, increasing his strength and resolve. He'd wanted to get the best of the men who'd chased them through Southeast Alaska and whom he blamed for sabotaging the plane, but they were working for Darius Aster, and now Trevor wanted a piece of that man too.

They neared the helicopter.

Where were the police when you needed them? He chuckled to himself.

I'm the only law enforcement on the premises at the moment.

He was losing it, really losing it. And not thinking this through with clarity.

Come on. Think. Get a grip, Trevor.

"Nothing funny about this," Moosehead said.

Wait. He couldn't let them take him—nobody would know where to look for his body. Trevor slowed his steps, forcing the men to have to work to drag him. Trevor was desperate for answers, and Jennifer wouldn't get justice if he died.

And what about Carrie?

As they stepped up to the open door of the helicopter, the pilot looked out the window. Trevor caught the cold eyes of a man whose face was burned on one side. What did they want with Trevor? Maybe they had preferred Carrie but got him. Or maybe Trevor would be a way to bring Carrie to them.

Didn't matter. He wasn't going with them.

Vandyke and Sidekick rushed around to the other side of the helicopter while Moosehead tried to force him inside. He probably wasn't expecting Trevor to resist, considering his profusely bleeding nose and how he had acted injured and compliant.

But no more. Time to use that to his advantage.

He shifted away and landed a punch to Moosehead's throat, snatched the automatic rifle away, then rolled under the helicopter and fired the gun. Sidekick took a bullet to his leg, and Vandyke dragged him into the helicopter.

Shouts rang out from inside the bird, and it started lifting away. Someone tossed Moosehead a weapon from the bird.

Time to go. Trevor made a run for it, but the helicopter was between him and the woods.

Still on the ground, Moosehead looked like a seriously angry bull, and Trevor could imagine the horns sticking out of his head. Trevor turned and raced away, swiping the blood out of his face. The only thing in front of him was the yawning opening to the underground mine where the explosives had been set—*if* they'd been set.

Great. The exact place from which he was trying to escape. But the more immediate danger was the man behind him. Trevor angled and walked backward to fire on him, then had to take cover in the mine. The open pit offered no protection.

Now his pursuer couldn't see him, and Trevor had the advantage. "You know he's going to blow this place!"

"I don't care. It's my job to make sure you're dead. That there's no chance you survive the explosion."

Seriously? "We're both going to die if we're still here."

But it didn't seem like the guy was going to listen to reason, and maybe that's because taking Trevor down had become personal. Trevor had gotten the best of Moosehead. He and Carrie had escaped his every attempt to take them down. Harm them or abduct them.

Moosehead spoke into his radio. Communicating with the pilot, who had the detonator? So maybe this place wouldn't blow until Trevor was dead.

Moosehead started toward the cave. Trevor tried to fire, but the rifle misfired.

Keeping to the shadows, Trevor moved deeper into the mine. The radio squawked in the distance, sounding as if the man was moving away from the opening. Was he going to leave Trevor in the mine to die, after all? The pilot could set off the detonations, and the whole thing would come down on him.

He wasn't staying for that. He raced toward the entrance, then peered out and spotted the helicopter hovering, waiting to take him out should he leave.

Gunfire pelted the entrance.

No. Not waiting. Pushing him deeper. He couldn't survive that barrage of bullets.

He was trapped, and he'd done this to himself.

Carrie came through the cave system from the far side of the mountain to get here. That would have to be his way out. She'd mentioned bread crumbs. He would have to take his chances. While he wasn't sure he could make it out before Aster detonated the explosives, he couldn't exit the front of the mine either without being shot to death.

Trevor raced straight to the back of the mining tunnel where he'd been held captive. He wound his way through, trying to remember where Carrie had exited the cave in the hazmat suit and entered the mine. That was his way out. Finally, just past where he'd been held captive, he found the hole.

But . . . the radiation. What had she said about it? She'd worn the suit as a precaution?

Then he wouldn't waste time putting it on, only to die in the explosion. But he needed the helmet. He found it next to the suit and turned on the headlamp. She left her pack here, so he grabbed it too.

He could die if this took too long.

Though he wasn't wearing a suit, he picked up the Geiger counter and dashed through the opening. The counter ticked away, but only edged to the danger zone. He didn't have much choice, so he kept going. He could either get killed running out of the mine or take his chances through the cave.

Then he spotted a flash of color. He stopped to glance at it, then picked it up. A blue bead.

The bread crumbs.

Trevor continued on, keeping an eye out for beads until he came to a space he would have to crawl through. Could he even fit?

He could do this, had to do it.

He thought of Carrie's bright green eyes filled with determination and passion and wanted the chance to kiss her lips again. To move forward and focus on the living, as well as get justice for Jennifer. He took off the pack and pushed it through the hole.

How did Rip and Carrie make it through this? Or was he going the wrong way? Suddenly he couldn't move at all. He couldn't go forward. No way he could fit through the narrowing walls ahead.

Trevor was stuck.

THIRTY-FIVE

Carrie paced the Ketchikan Alaska State Trooper Detachment A offices, trying to ignore the throbbing cut on her forehead. Chief Long, Grier, and Nolan arrived a half an hour ago.

Two hours ago, a good portion of the mine was obliterated. The entrance was blown, and they couldn't be sure about the rest of the tunnels.

On their way from Shadow Gap, Autumn, Grier, and Nolan had done a cursory flyover to look at the devastation and search for Trevor, and then headed down to Ketchikan to talk to her, while others were focused on the search and rescue efforts. After contacting Joseph Schroeder, the AST believed that most of the crew had been evacuated due to the possible toxic leak, and Schroeder claimed no responsibility for the explosion.

Carrie had flown the cargo plane to the closest safe place, though it still took forty-five minutes to get there. She handed over the plane filled with what she believed was contraband and evidence against Darius Aster and his gang of mining misfits. The pilot was being held for questioning as well.

Would the ABI be able to unravel what happened? She wasn't so sure. But she would share her theories.

She paced back and forth and chewed her nails.

I never chew my nails.

She needed a new way to fight her nerves and push past the guilt of leaving Trevor behind. The *pain* of leaving him behind. Her heart ached, though it wasn't shattered. There'd been no good options. At least Daphne and Chad sat in the corner together. She'd contacted him to let him know where they landed.

She and Daphne had given their statements and been grilled repeatedly. But Carrie kept the USB drive to herself. Her trust issues had started rising as she conversed with law enforcement here. She preferred to share the data she'd collected with Chief Long and her brother—people she knew. She hadn't forgotten what Rip said about the local police on Essack Island. Besides, Carrie wanted to see what was on that drive before anyone else, and then make copies before she handed it off to strangers who could lose it accidentally or deliberately or be bought off. Seemed like a lot of that kind of thing went on anymore. She wouldn't be a fool.

Money changes people. No one knows that better than I do.

She'd been through the worst kind of betrayal, so caution was her friend.

Chief Long approached, and Carrie stopped pacing. She wouldn't bother trying to hide her fear that Trevor was gone.

"They'll find him, Carrie. Don't worry."

She stared at the floor, anguish coursing through her. How? How could they find him?

Alaska Search and Rescue Emergency Response arrived at the site twenty minutes ago.

Twenty. Minutes.

That was a couple of hours or more after the explosion.

Emergency response took entirely too long in this part of

the world. The day couldn't get any longer as she held on to hope—impossible hope—that Trevor had survived. She finally understood his deep need to believe that Jennifer was still alive after disappearing over a year ago.

"They haven't been at it long. You have to trust the process. If he's still there, they'll find him."

"But so far nothing?"

"I've heard nothing yet."

"What about Darius Aster?" Carrie asked. Did he die in the explosion? She left him behind. Kicked him out of his own plane.

"They're looking for him as well as the other men. I know you gave your statement before Nolan and I arrived." She gestured toward a corner in the busy room. "I'd like to hear your story, especially since you believe this Darius Aster is responsible for Isaac's murder."

Carrie nodded, relieved that Autumn wanted to listen to her story as well. She'd kept the information she shared with the lieutenant to the facts of today. But there was so much more to tell. Carrie sat at the desk and Autumn joined her, sitting close so they could keep their conversation private.

Autumn placed her cell on the desk. "Do you mind if I record this conversation?"

"No, of course not."

"Tell me everything."

"Everything?"

"Start at the beginning, whatever that means to you. I read the statement you gave." Autumn leveled her gaze. "I want to hear the *whole* story."

Carrie huffed a laugh and rubbed her eyes and face. "With Trevor still out there—" She shook her head.

"Come on, Carrie. If you want us to catch this guy, then we need to know everything. Talking about it will take your mind off other things."

Frowning, Carrie nodded. Stared at her hands and shared with Autumn that Darius smuggled for years under her nose while they were in Africa. She didn't have to tell Autumn *everything*. Like how she'd fallen in love with him.

"So when I saw the uncut gem on Chad's boat, and he shared that Jennifer had given it to him, I knew it couldn't be a coincidence."

Autumn's brows were furrowed as she nodded and listened intently.

"Darius majored in getting in and out of hard-to-reach places. In Africa, humanitarian NGOs—non-governmental organizations—always provided a way for him to stay connected. He worked for Action Against Hunger before moving to Global Relief Services, where I met him."

Waves of nausea rippled through her.

"It's all right. Just take your time. You need some water?"

"Yes, please." *And I fell in love with him.* The fact that she'd loved someone who committed such atrocities was hard to forget. To let go and move on.

Autumn returned with a small cup of water from the cooler, and Carrie drank it all.

"Fast-forward to today. Trevor and I were 'caught' by security guards at the mine and held in a room. We then met Joseph Schroeder, and everything coming from them was so different from the men who had followed us."

"Like Vandyke?"

"Yes. Unless he's a great liar, Joseph didn't know anything about gems being mined."

"It just didn't add up for you, did it?"

Carrie shook her head.

"Go on. Piece it together for me."

"I started to think that maybe Darius hadn't died after all. Maybe he faked his death. Something. But he had to get out of Africa and find another way to confiscate gemstones. What if someone found them inside Jacob's Mountain? I don't know the connection, but somehow Darius could have learned about it and gotten on with the crew and started his own private mining operation to dig up the gems right under Joseph's nose. Maybe a supervisor or two was in on it. After all, the miners don't share in the profits.

"I saw a dump truck of dirt being loaded to haul off to process for REE, just like Joseph said, but the crates filled with rocks—those were the gemstones, and Joseph didn't know about those. Then I saw the semi pulling those crates away. And Darius. I saw him, Autumn. He was there, and he tipped his hard hat at me. So I was right. He was stealing gems from the mining operation."

Autumn said nothing and remained thoughtful for a few moments, then asked, "How do you think this pertains to Isaac's death? Or even Jennifer Warner?"

"Jennifer was with the group of consulting geologists hired by Joseph. I don't know what she saw that sent her back to the mine, but she was trying to get evidence. She was going to blow the whistle. It's possible she discovered Darius's operation, and he killed her for it. I think his gunmen for hire were instructed to make sure Trevor didn't come looking for her, or find her, and that's why we were followed."

"Schroeder claims someone sabotaged the mine."

"I think that's possible. Rumors of radiation or someone deliberately causing the contamination meant the mine would be evacuated. Trevor said someone had informed him the place was rigged to blow."

"So they planned to blow it up and cover the evidence."

"And Jennifer's body."

"Right. Daphne said she overheard them saying Jennifer had been left to die." Autumn shook her head. "And Isaac?"

"I believe that note left on Isaac's desk was from Darius. I think somehow he found us. He's the only person I can think of who would want to kill Isaac. But it was left after Isaac was gone. I believe it was left for me." A chill raced up her back.

"And did you know Isaac was wanted for questioning in Darius Aster's murder? As in, he was a suspect?"

"No, I didn't." Tears streamed down her cheeks. "I don't believe he could have murdered anyone."

"I'm having a hard time believing it too. But people do unexpected things sometimes."

"Since Darius isn't dead, then Isaac didn't murder him."

"I'll have to look into the details—a murder means there was a body. So someone's body was found." Autumn shut off the recording. "Thank you, Carrie. You've shared plenty with me, and this is a lot to untangle. I'll share this with the board of investigation when we get to that point. In the meantime, we need to confirm that Darius died on that mountain today." Autumn stared at Carrie.

"If he did, it's because Daphne and I pushed him off his own plane to escape."

"His plane with stolen cargo. If he's still alive, he might intend to come for you."

Like he did for Isaac.

"I need to check on a few things. Will you be all right?" Autumn stood.

"No, I won't. I want to be there and search for Trevor too."

"You know that's not possible. The entire site is extremely dangerous, not to mention a crime scene."

"How are they searching it?"

"They know what they're doing and how to handle these kinds of situations. But you're not going back there until it's deemed safe and confirmed to be radiation-free. Besides, Nolan wants to talk to you too. I'll tell him to give you a few minutes, though."

I can't take this anymore! "I need a computer. Can I use a computer?"

Nolan was on his cell and appeared to have heard her question. He eyed another trooper, who nodded. "Take the one on that desk. You can log in as a guest."

Chief Long followed her. "What are you doing, Carrie?"

"Nothing. I just need to check emails." Carrie sat at the desk and turned the computer away from everyone else.

Autumn narrowed her eyes.

Carrie pursed her lips and after logging onto the computer as a guest, she signed into her email. But what she really wanted to do was peer long and hard at the data she'd collected on the USB drive, as if she could actually understand any of it. She made a show of staring at her emails—like she had more than two. What if Joseph knew about the gemstones and was in on it? And what were the stones exactly? There was so much destruction over them.

While her insides remained twisted over Isaac's death, Trevor was now at the forefront of her thoughts. *God, please, please let him be okay. Let him survive.*

He'd wanted to get out of there, but no. She had insisted she gather intelligence. *He* was the detective, and who was she? Nothing but a bush pilot. He'd protected her every step of the way.

To the very end.

This can't be the end. It just can't be.

She focused on the screen but watched the room in her peripheral vision, trying to make a move only when no one was paying attention to her. Chief Long had gotten on her cell phone and now stood in the far corner. Once in a while she glanced up and looked at Carrie.

The woman was suspicious. No doubt about it. Fortunately this computer required a mouse. She had the USB in her hand, along with the mouse, and moved the mouse up just so. Without looking at her hand, she stuck the drive into the computer. Then clicked so it would open up the data.

She had no idea what she was looking at, or for. Information to confirm Jennifer's findings, whatever those were? Had Darius and Joseph been in this illegal business for years? Had they taken advantage of people in third-world countries, stealing their resources from them, and now found a way to take advantage of a remote location in Alaska?

Then she spotted one oddly named file.

Chief Long pushed from the far wall and started walking toward her.

Carrie emailed the file to herself, closed out of her email, snagged the USB drive from the computer, then logged out of guest browsing. Carrie stood as Autumn approached.

"Find what you were looking for?"

She shook her head. "I don't know what I'm looking at. But I trust you to make sure this gets into the right hands."

She lifted Autumn's palm and set the drive inside, then closed her fingers around it. The chief seemed to understand Carrie was asking her to use discretion. Not here. Not now. But later, with someone she trusted to look at the information. Autumn nodded subtly, then turned to face the lieutenant in charge of the Ketchikan field office.

Autumn slipped the drive into her pants pocket, or at least Carrie thought she did.

Lieutenant Parker looked between Autumn and Carrie. "We've located the helicopter you identified. It landed in Juneau. All the passengers escaped except for one—the helicopter's owner. Dwayne Kincaid." He showed Carrie the picture on his cell.

"Vandyke," she whispered. "That's the man who tried to abduct me in Mountain Cove. He was on the island and followed me into the cave."

"He's talking, so we'll get as much information as we can from him. The pilot you hit in the head is still recovering in the hospital, and we'll question him as soon as we can."

"And Darius Aster?"

"Kincaid claims he didn't make it onto their escape helicopter. He knew you'd taken the plane. Aster, whom Kincaid called Teller, radioed that he would be riding out with Kincaid, but Kincaid said one of the remaining security guards shot and killed him."

"Do you believe him? I mean, do you think Darius is dead?"

"It's too soon to confirm anything, but it's likely he didn't survive."

He'd survived after supposedly being murdered in Africa, so Carrie wouldn't count on that.

"Kincaid stopped talking when his lawyer arrived, but we were able to gather a few details about the deliberate radiation leak deeper in the cave. Contaminated toxic waste barrels were brought over from the old uranium mine that hadn't been completely cleaned up. News of a radiation leak was the catalyst to start the evacuation of the mine, and then explosives were set. Kincaid seemed to resent Teller for those actions. And we also gathered that Schroeder and his organization could share some responsibility in what happened."

The USB drive could contain that information, though Carrie knew she hadn't obtained the information in a legal manner. But she wasn't law enforcement, so maybe it could help them learn more.

Lieutenant Parker slightly narrowed his eyes. "How'd you know about that cave intersecting with the mine?"

"A local showed me."

"That local wouldn't by any chance be Rip Franklin, would it? He's an activist we've run into in the past. He hates what's been done on the mountain. I could see him helping you."

What do I say? I can't lie. Rip doesn't want to be involved. "Look—"

"Parker." A trooper interrupted and drew him away to speak to him.

Carrie slowly released a breath. That was a close call.

Nolan approached. "We'll be talking to the mining crew as well. I've contacted an expert to look at the contents of the crates on that plane. In the meantime, we've taken the plane as evidence and are off-loading the crates to a highly secured location."

Good, though she doubted any of them fully understood the value of those crates.

But Darius did. There was something inside that he wanted, or else he wouldn't have been at the mine.

And she'd taken his prize.

Lieutenant Parker returned and glanced at the floor, his lips in a grim line. His eyes darted up between them again. "I'm sorry, but there's still no sign of Detective West. Specialists will arrive in the morning to measure the safety of the site for a ground crew and a recovery operation."

A recovery operation? Instead of search and rescue?

"You're not giving up on finding him already, are you?"

"Of course we're continuing to search, but . . ."

She wanted to argue with him, but emotion grew thick in her throat and she couldn't speak.

She didn't hear his response. An exhale punched from her. Carrie tried to keep a straight face and simply nod and act unemotional. She hadn't wanted to care so much ever again.

Carrie tried to hide the deep hole that opened up in her heart. But she couldn't contain the eruption.

And turned into Autumn to sob on her shoulder.

THIRTY-SIX

A soft purple dawn lightened up the morning skies the next day. The winds were five miles per hour out of the northwest, and skies were clear.

Nolan had helped her secure a small plane from a local bush pilot—Tim Albert. He was sorry to hear about Isaac's death and offered Carrie the use of his Cessna 172 floatplane for the foreseeable future. She would return it as soon as possible. Holding the yoke, she had to concentrate on what she was doing. She didn't need another plane crash to add to the one she'd finally reported to the NTSB.

Nolan had instructed her that "under no uncertain terms" was she to land anywhere near Jacob's Mountain, but he wouldn't prevent her from flying over. She had to look for Trevor herself, see the area around Jacob's Mountain, and until she did, she thought she might just lose her mind.

Just like Trevor never gave up on finding his sister alive, Carrie wouldn't give up on finding Trevor *alive*.

Nor would she think about the fact that he hadn't found his sister.

The sun wasn't spilling gold on the horizon yet, but the

thought reminded her of the last time she and Trevor flew, and she believed he might have fallen in love—just a little—with flying. Of course, that was the same day they crashed and came close to dying.

She released a heavy sigh.

Her entire life had changed in the course of a few days.

Again.

The moment she discovered the contraband on the cargo plane over Zhugandia, her life was upended. With the loss of Isaac—her mentor, her friend—the last few days felt much the same.

As she neared the island, her thoughts returned to Trevor. She didn't know how she could exist in a world without both Isaac and Trevor.

Approaching the island, she shifted the yoke and skirted the edges.

Maybe I should just land at Yakutan and find Rip to see if he made it. He might be able to help me locate Trevor.

She'd left him out of her statement, well, because she felt she owed that much to him. He had reasons for keeping to himself, and he risked a lot to help her. She wouldn't cause him trouble.

She hoped that he had made it out of the caves alive. And if he had, after everything that happened, he could have decided to disappear for a while and go on the lam. He might not want to talk to her. Or maybe his perspective would be a positive one. Rip could hold to the fact that she and Trevor brought light to the serious issues going on at Jacob's Mountain.

In the distance, she saw the mountain—still tall and lofty. But the open-pit mine was all but demolished. Rubble spilled into it on one side of the mountain where the tunnel had collapsed. The underground mining operation had been obliterated, and the crushed remains of the portable buildings left no doubt that no one inside could have survived. She tried to fly in close, but two helicopters were approaching to land—likely the group who would confirm whether it was safe to do a more thorough ground search.

If only she could be on the ground with them now. She hoped Trevor had been able to get far away from the mine before the explosion, but if he had, why hadn't he contacted her?

Carrie swiped at errant tears. *What am I even doing here?*

She had to see for herself. That was what. She had to make sure someone was searching for Trevor in other places. Maybe he *did* escape but was injured.

Her heart said he was alive out there somewhere.

Carrie circled the island twice, and soon the sun spilled gold again. Her heart would have been full . . . but . . . *Trevor.*

The blue-eyed detective.

God, I long to see those eyes looking at me again. And, yeah, maybe I wouldn't mind him kissing me too.

After another time around the island, then across it, she finally admitted what she'd already known—she wouldn't be able to observe anything from the air. She couldn't see past the thick canopy of the lush Tongass National Forest—great for hiding people and the things they did.

She hugged the coast and disturbed a flock of birds that fortunately took off toward the trees instead of into her path. She had nothing left in this world except the one thing.

Flying.

And that would be okay with her. Just her and God and the sky.

But Trevor had changed that for her.

She flew in closer to the edges of the island, looking at the few pebbled and rocky beaches.

Something—a boat or a shape in the wrong place—drew her attention. But she flew by it. She circled around, then flew straight for the coast, where she thought she'd spotted something floating. No. Not floating.

Okay. Yes. Floating and partially lying in the sand between the rocks.

A body.

Her heart jumped to her throat. Relief twisted with grief. Trevor's body? Living? Breathing? She couldn't tell from the sky.

All the nerve endings in her body sparked with anguish. *Please, let him be alive.* She landed the seaplane and taxied all the way up to the smooth section of the beach, then shut off the engine. Carrie jumped out onto the pontoon, then hopped over pebbles and sand, splashing in the cold water until she reached Trevor.

His face wasn't in the water but turned to the side. Her body shaking, she hovered her hand over his face. Where should she touch?

I know this. I know how to take a pulse.

But she was scared to learn the truth. If Trevor was alive, he could die of hypothermia. She grabbed him under the shoulders and struggled to drag him carefully onto the gray sand covered with too many pebbles. Then she sat down and hugged him to her, like she was cradling a child.

He was cold, definitely cold.

It wasn't lost on her that she'd held Isaac's body, too, when he was already gone.

Squeezing her eyes shut, she rocked back and forth as if that could stop the wail that built in her chest. Was this how Isaac felt when he found her barely alive in that thicket that saved her? Cushioned her fall?

Was she such a coward that she couldn't search for a pulse and get Trevor help?

But no.

Wait.

She felt his heartbeat against her chest.

"You're alive!" she cried with joy. "You're alive. But you won't be alive for long if we don't get you warmed up."

Carrie didn't think she could get him in the plane on her own. She slid out from under him and touched his bruised, swollen face. Gently slapped his cheeks. "Trevor, wake up. We need to get you somewhere safe. Somewhere you can get medical attention."

A groan escaped him.

"Trevor? Wake up. Please, I need you to walk. Can you walk?"

He groaned again. "I'll walk already. Just stop slapping me."

Then he opened his eyes. His gaze wasn't focused, and that worried her. She held her breath, then laughed. "I promise I won't slap you again, but please, we have to warm you up or you'll die."

He closed his eyes again. "I thought I'd never see you again."

"You and me both. Can you sit up?"

"No."

"What? Why not? Are you hurt?"

"Stop with the questions. I'm hurt, but not too hurt for this." Trevor gripped her arms and pulled her down to him so they were face-to-face. Then he pressed his lips against hers. Kissed her thoroughly.

Kissed her breathless.

Then he fell back and dropped his arms as if the effort had zapped the last of his energy.

No!

"Trevor!"

"I told myself if I survived this, I would try to change your mind."

"Change my mind?"

"You said you'd never trust anyone again."

With her heart. With that kind of love. *He remembered.*

"Did it work?" he asked.

THIRTY-SEVEN

Was he dreaming? Or had he lost his mind?

Maybe he'd read the situation wrong—like he was in any condition to read a situation.

Maybe she would give him a pass, for making a pass at her, since he might be hypothermic. And with the thought, he shivered. He shouldn't think about kissing her or a future with her, but he couldn't forget that she'd responded. Oh yeah, she'd responded.

Finally, her features softened, and her voice was husky as she said, "I'm going to need more than one kiss to make up my mind." Then a brilliant smile flashed. "Come on. Let's get you out of here."

Her words ignited hope in his heart.

"We have to get you to the plane." She crouched next to him to assist him up. "Can you get up? Can you walk? Because I know you can kiss."

"I guess we'll find out." He was glad to have her help sitting up as vertigo slammed him.

She tried to help him stand, but they both ended up on the ground.

"Come on." Carrie tried to shoulder him to his feet.

Not happening.

"Wait. Just give me a minute."

"Let me know when you're ready. I want to get you in the plane and turn the heat on."

He took a few breaths. Getting the oxygen going could power up his strength. Maybe.

"Okay. Let's do this."

Finally, he was standing but leaning on Carrie. He tried not to put too much weight on her as he stumbled on a rock or two, and she helped him right himself.

At the plane, he refused her help and steadied himself. Stepped onto the pontoon near the door, then into the seat. She closed the door and scrambled into the back two rows, searching for something.

"Ah. A blanket." The space was small and confined, but Carrie didn't seem to notice her proximity to him as she wrapped him in a blanket. Her concern was endearing.

"Thanks. I got it." He smiled.

She looked up and was close, so close when she smiled back. Then she maneuvered into her seat. Started up the plane. "The heat will kick in once the plane is going since the exhaust pipes warm up the air."

Carrie taxied the plane on the water, then increased speed. The next thing he knew, they were in the air. For the first time, flying didn't make him nervous.

Trevor rested in the seat. "How did you find me?"

"I was flying around and over the island looking for you. I knew—I hoped—you'd somehow survived. That you were somewhere out there. Trevor, I'm so sorry for leaving you."

"You saved me, Carrie. You found me. If you hadn't, I probably would have died." He wasn't entirely sure he was going to live. "You did the right thing. I wanted to leave with you, but those men weren't going to let us take the plane. And Daphne is safe?"

"Yes."

"Can you give me an update?"

"The authorities are making sure the site is safe. They're looking for you and anyone else, but they're calling it a recovery effort, they said, because of the massive explosion."

He took that in. "They thought I was dead."

A few breaths passed before she responded. "Yes. But I had to search myself."

"I'm glad you did."

"Daphne and I got out. I flew straight to the Alaska State Troopers offices in Ketchikan, and we gave our statements. Autumn and Nolan met us there. But I got a plane and came back to look for you."

"And Schroeder?"

"They're talking to him as well as the mining crew, but that plane we escaped in? It was filled with those crates we saw. They contained gemstones, Trevor. And then Darius tried to keep us from taking the plane."

He hadn't totally believed Carrie when she first said she'd seen the man.

"They caught Vandyke and are questioning him. He claims Darius is dead."

"Do you think he's telling the truth?"

"It's hard to know."

"You could still be in danger. And I promised I would find Isaac's killer and protect you."

"You found Isaac's killer by bringing me on this journey with you to this mine."

"You can't know that Darius killed him."

"Yes, I can know it, but I can't prove it. Not yet. Autumn's working on it, though."

"And those men with him, the ones who followed us, I think

they were tasked with making sure Jennifer's only surviving relative—me—didn't come looking for her. But I'm law enforcement, so they targeted you. Maybe that's what happened to Fitzgerald and my other bush pilot. It's just a theory, but I'll share it with Autumn."

"They have a lot to unravel," Carrie said.

"If Aster was responsible for her death . . ." He couldn't wait to get his hands on that jerk for what he did to Jennifer and Carrie. If the guy was dead, then maybe poetic justice had been served.

The plane banked and swooped low. He took in the glorious morning sky and the pristine waterways below, the snowcapped mountains that went on forever.

"How am I ever going to thank you for coming after me? For finding me?"

"You being alive is thank you enough. I held on to hope that you were still alive."

Like he had with Jennifer.

"So what happened after we left the island?" she asked. "How did you end up beaten and floating?"

"That's a long story."

"I'm here with you all day, Trevor. I'm not leaving your side."

He liked the sound of that. "I ended up trapped inside the mine, so my only way out was through the cave system. Good thing you left the bread crumbs—those beads came in handy. I got stuck once but pushed through. Then I heard the rumble through the mountain and thought I was done for. I'm not sure if the cave system collapsed near the mine, but I was almost out when the explosives blew. I climbed the rope left behind."

"But that doesn't explain the condition I found you in."

"Moosehead had it out for me because I bested him. I thought everyone would think I was dead. After all, they herded me into the mine so I could die under the rubble. I made my way through the woods as long as I could until it was too dark. Then I set up camp out in the open because I knew there would be a rescue crew, or at least I'd hoped. I made a fire. Then early this morning, I heard a sound and woke in time to miss a punch to the face."

"It was Moosehead?"

"He obviously knew about the cave system, but he told me it was his job to make sure I died before the explosion. Since he hadn't been able to do that, I guess he needed to make sure I hadn't somehow survived. I gave myself away with that fire."

"I can't believe he didn't just shoot you in the head while you slept."

"Come on. That would've been too easy. He wanted to best me in combat, and I have to admit, it felt good to go hand-to-hand with him after what he put us through."

"Looks like you got the bad end of that."

"We fought and both ended up falling off a ridge. I woke up to you slapping me. I thought I was dreaming."

"So he could have survived too."

"Possibly, but I'm pretty sure he hit a rock on the way down." He cringed at the thought. "Sorry if that's too gruesome."

"It's okay."

"But you know it isn't over yet if the man after you, the man who killed Isaac, is still out there."

"The authorities believe he's dead. But they also thought you were dead. I'm glad they were wrong on that count."

Me too. "Where are we going?"

"First stop, Ketchikan. They have a hospital, and you can talk to the troopers there who are informed about what's going on. Then I'll take us home. A friend loaned me this plane. There's also the matter of my crashed plane. The NTSB is looking into the cause. I believe they'll confirm the sabotage."

Home? Thinking about his home in Montana so far away from Carrie James pained him.

Trevor was due back at his job next week, but he'd told Carrie that he would track Isaac's killer, and he felt like that mission was only now beginning. At the very least, he needed to confirm that Darius Aster was the killer, even if he had died on that mountain.

THIRTY-EIGHT

Two weeks later.

Carrie sat at the desk where Isaac used to sit and stared at the collage of notes, lists, and pictures he'd pinned to the corkboard on the wall. She didn't have the heart to remove anything that belonged to him. Everything remained the same in his cabin. They had been partners and purchased the land and business together, but he left his portion to her.

The ME had finally released his body and determined he died from a blow to the head. The funeral was two days from now. And after that?

Did she want to stay here and keep working as a bush pilot?

How do I get over the horror of what happened here at the hangar?

At least David was willing to keep working with her clients, delivering supplies, as he built up his own business, adding pilots. She was in no state of mind to function. David assured her that she could have them back when she was ready—she had a feeling he was interested in her, personally.

But she was interested in only one man. Mr. Blue Eyes. He had gone back to his detective job in Montana but had also been working to track Isaac's killer—Darius. Two bodies were found in the debris from the mining explosion, including a woman, but their identities had not been confirmed yet.

Today Trevor was on his way here to Shadow Gap. He'd been able to piece together more of the puzzle regarding Jennifer's travels. She convinced her superior at EchoGlobal of the possible indiscretions by Schroeder's mine, but they needed proof. She took the leave of absence so her company wouldn't officially be involved, however, she was allowed to use a company credit card to pay for the guide and her travel. Another geologist had intended to go with her but claimed to be ill, and Jennifer continued with her plans, using the photography cover. Trevor had decided she must have taken samples at various locations to make sure atrocities weren't being committed.

In the end, her activities caught up to her. Still, her determination shone light on the illegal operations. Carrie just wished it hadn't cost Jennifer her life.

And she hoped that her next move, which was very risky, would not cost her her own life. Trevor had warned her to be careful and watch out for Darius, who was still out there.

He'd also asked her on a date.

A real date.

Once this was over. Would it ever be over? Even if Darius was caught and the investigation closed, Trevor lived in Montana. And she lived here. This couldn't go anywhere.

But a date with Mr. Blue Eyes would be nice.

Still. First things first.

She knew she had to find her way again after Darius. After Isaac. And after Trevor went back to his own life. Her eyes focused on the desk, and she stiffened when someone approached from behind. She smiled to herself. Just the man she'd been waiting for.

He reached past her to set a purple polished stone about the size of her palm on the desk in front of her.

Her breath hitched.

She closed her eyes.

Darius.

He pulled up a chair and sat entirely too close. She slowly lifted her gaze to meet the stone cold of his soulless eyes again.

He smirked, and his shoulder bobbed with an internal laugh. "Do you know what that is?"

She shrugged, trying to act nonchalant. Like she wasn't scared. She wouldn't let him get the best of her this time. "Why would I?"

"You haven't learned anything in a decade?"

"Why are you here?"

"I think you know."

To finally kill me? But she couldn't say the words out loud. She wouldn't play his games.

"So, what is it?" She looked at the glistening, deep-purple gem.

"It's been called an emerald by day and a ruby by night." His eyes grew bright as he spoke. "It's a chameleon."

Like you.

"In the sunlight it's emerald green, and by candle flame or low artificial lighting it's a deep purple like you see here."

Carrie didn't want to admit the gem mesmerized her as well. She whispered, "What's it called?"

"Alexandrite," he whispered in response. "It's extremely rare and was first discovered in 1833 in Russia near an emerald mine."

"So named after one of the czars?"

"Alexander II."

"And of course, it's valuable."

"One of the most expensive gems on the market. There were no more deposits found in Russia, and then it was discovered in Jacob's Mountain. And this is the highest quality yet to be unearthed." He sounded giddy, overly excited. "It's the discovery of a lifetime, Carrie."

Carrie narrowed her eyes. "How do you know this?"

"I'm a geologist, and I work with a mineralogist, what do you think?"

They never discussed his background when she worked with him at the NGO, probably because he wanted to keep it hidden.

"Why not do all this aboveboard? Why go to all these lengths?" In Africa and now here in Alaska—and who knew where else.

"Come on, Carrie. You can't be that dense. This isn't my mine. Rather than get my own claim and hope it produces, it's faster and much more profitable to take what's already there."

"This new alexandrite needs a source. You can't just sell it without revealing where it was discovered."

He shook his head. "And here I thought you knew me. I have a source already in place. Buyers lined up and waiting. But there's one catch, and the irony isn't lost on me that here you are again, standing in my way."

So he would try again to kill her. *Not if I can help it.*

"The troopers in Ketchikan, they don't have a clue what they have, and I doubt their experts will know either. It took me two years to set up this operation, Carrie. Two. Years. You destroyed two years of my life in one day."

"So you were stealing right under Joseph Schroeder's nose."

He scrunched his face. "No. He knew about it, but he couldn't say anything because I knew what he was doing and held that over him. He was illegally mining from the old uranium mine he was supposed to clean up. He had no permits and incorrectly disposed of pollutants, which leached into the local streams. But I had him, so he looked the other way and let me mine the tunnel where I found what I needed."

"And Jennifer Warner? She found out about you?"

"No. She found out about Schroeder. She wanted to collect the necessary evidence, but shining the light on his illegal activities would mean exposing me." He sighed. "I tried to pay her off."

"With merazite."

He shrugged. "She took it, so I thought I'd bought her off. But turned out she only meant to use it against me. My mistake. So she had to go. Let's just say the operation had some collateral damage."

Like me. "Is that what I was to you? Simply collateral damage when you pushed me out of that plane? Is that why you're here? To exact some sort of revenge? Have you been looking for me for ten years?"

"Honestly, I never gave you another thought. I sent men to make sure Detective West didn't make it to the mountain. He had to be deterred rather than murdered. Murdering the cop who was searching for his missing sister would make things worse. Just target the pilot and make it look like an accident. He got a pilot, all right. Apparently the wrong one, initially. When Kincaid sent me your picture after running into you in Mountain Cove, I was stunned, honestly. I couldn't believe you actually survived that fall. But there you were, bright emerald eyes, long blond hair. Determined and apparently resilient. After researching your operation, I went to the hangar looking for you but found Isaac."

"And left the note."

"The note was for you. I had already killed Isaac by then. I went back to leave the note after the locals searched for evidence. I wanted you to know."

"In that case, you should have left it in my apartment. Leaving it on his desk only confused the matter. I didn't even think of you when I saw that note."

His eye twitched. "The hangar was locked up tight, okay? Isaac's cabin was easy to get into. You found the note, so that's what matters."

Whatever. "Why kill him?" Tears twisted with fury. "It was me you were after. Isaac only helped me. He never hurt anyone."

"He never told you? He took my plane down with a rocket

launcher. It crashed and burned." He gestured to his face. "The authorities thought I was dead. I was coherent enough to switch out my watch and a few items with my burning copilot and crawled to safety, where they found me and misidentified me. Good time to reinvent myself. I had connections throughout the world, but no one ever knew my real name. I needed to get out of Africa, and I landed a nice operation in Russia, and by extension, Alaska became a new prospecting region. Did you know Jacob's Mountain started out as a diamond mine, then the mining was shifted to uranium? I came here first as a consulting geologist and hit the jackpot with my discovery."

"So that's how you do it."

"Eh. It's only one way."

A twisted grin dimpled in his cheeks. She used to love that grin.

"I'll have to change my name and reinvent myself again. Start over. Because of you, but no matter." He leaned in close.

She shut her eyes. She couldn't bear to look at him. Heart pounding, she remembered when she used to love his nearness—and kissing him. Pressing her quivering lips together, she tried not to show her repulsion.

She couldn't fathom now how she had ever loved him.

He gently took her hand. She tried to snatch it back, but he gripped it hard. She wouldn't cry out in pain.

She opened her eyes to stare into his black, dead ones. "What do you want from me?"

He ran his thumb down her cheek. "Hmm. Let me think. I know. Since I've lost most of my crew, thanks to you, you're going to help me get those crates and fly them out of the country."

"And what makes you think I would do that?"

"If you don't, I'll do to your detective friend what I did to his sister and to Isaac."

Think, Carrie, think. You wanted to face him, so now what?

Her cell buzzed with a text. She tried to grab it, but Darius was faster. He smiled when he read the text. "He says, 'Get out of there, Carrie. Darius is in Shadow Gap.'" Darius looked at her. "He's too late to save you, but I'll make that deal with you now. Help me this once, and we'll call it even. I promise you'll never see me again. I won't haunt your dreams or come back to kill your man."

Your man. Carrie slipped her free hand holding her new Ruger from under her leg.

"You're right. You won't," Trevor said.

THIRTY-NINE

Because I'm here now." Trevor aimed his handgun at Aster. "So step away from Carrie and lift your hands over your head where I can see them."

Aster would try to take Carrie as a hostage. He had no other choice. Trevor had warned her hours ago to leave, and he couldn't believe she was still here. He'd also contacted Autumn, and she sent an officer out here, but Trevor found him unconscious next to the hangar outside.

Trevor aimed his 9mm at the man responsible for his sister's death. He'd heard enough of the conversation as he approached. Trevor did what he said he would do. He tracked Isaac's killer all the way back to Shadow Gap. Back to the hangar with Carrie.

God, please let this end well, because I don't have a good feeling right now.

He couldn't fail someone he cared about again.

Darius stood and slowly lifted his hands, but Trevor braced himself. The guy would try something, no doubt.

"Detective West. You have no jurisdiction here, and you can't arrest me, but you *could* shoot me."

The man turned around to face Trevor. "But I don't think you will. You're not a murderer, even when faced with the man responsible for your sister's death."

"I'll shoot if you give me a reason to do it. I don't have to arrest you. Shadow Gap PD is on the way."

"Am I supposed to be intimidated?" Darius stepped toward Trevor. This guy was something. So arrogant. He'd been running around the globe committing crimes, and who knew how many murders, to serve his own purposes for years. Now he thought he was invincible.

Trevor would like nothing more than to end him, but there were better ways to serve justice.

Carrie suddenly stood, holding her pistol point-blank at Darius, then stepped around to the side of him so he could see her fury-filled eyes.

Oh, Carrie, don't. Though Trevor understood she had multiple reasons to want Darius dead.

"Carrie, what are you doing? I got this. Step away from him, and let the police handle it."

He understood her then. She had gotten his warning and stayed, hoping to see Darius. Hoping to face off with him. At least she'd been forewarned and had her gun ready.

"Thank you for discovering an alexandrite deposit in Alaska. The state is going to be grateful. I'm not letting you take this find out of here."

She started stepping back toward Trevor when Darius reached out and disarmed her.

He pointed the gun at her at the same instant Carrie grabbed the large gemstone and slammed it into his temple.

He dropped the gun, stumbled back, and crumpled.

Carrie and Trevor rushed forward.

Trevor felt for a pulse. "He's alive. An ambulance will be here soon. I called for one for the Shadow Gap police officer when I contacted Autumn."

Guns drawn, Chief Autumn Long rushed in, along with Grier and Angie.

Trevor breathed a sigh of relief, and he took Carrie's hand and pulled her away from Darius Aster. She appeared shocked—numb even—and he pulled her into his arms. She didn't resist and pressed her face into his chest.

Trevor explained what happened to the Shadow Gap PD while paramedics hurried to Aster's side. Autumn cuffed him as he was loaded onto the gurney.

"Be careful with that one," Trevor said. "He has a long trail of destruction around the globe."

"I'm aware, Detective West. I'll need your statements, but I'm going to give you two a few moments."

Trevor held Carrie until she was ready to step away. "It's over. You're safe now."

"How did you know, Trevor? How did you know where he was? That he was here?"

"I've been searching for him, tracking him this whole time."

"I thought you were back in Montana."

"I went back, yes, to take a leave of absence. A deal's a deal. I told you I would track Isaac's killer. And I found him in Ketchikan, surveying the secured storage where the crates of alexandrite were being kept, but he got away."

"And he came here."

"I figured he had two choices—ditch the valuables he believed belonged to him and leave the state or secure assistance to get them out. Either way, he wasn't going to leave without tying up all the loose ends."

"And I was a loose end. Collateral damage. But he wanted me to work for him one last time."

"I heard. That's when I cut him off. What would you have said to that, Carrie? What was your plan?"

"Honestly, at that moment, I was thinking about how he

threatened to take you out. How he called you my 'man.' Everyone refers to you that way, and I don't know why."

He looked at her, searching her eyes. "You don't?"

"I admit, I kind of like that people think you're my man. Let's be real here. I don't even know you. But I'd like to get to know you better."

"Good. I'm glad you feel that way." *I think there's something here I want to explore.*

She gave him a half smile. "I know you said we would go on an actual date when this is over, but I hope you weren't thinking tonight."

"I understand. It's too soon. It's going to take you some time. This has all been a shock." Trevor stepped close and kissed her on the forehead. Carrie had to be the strongest person he'd ever met. She'd been crushed multiple times, and he had no doubt she would get back up again.

He wouldn't even ask what came next for her, because even though she mentioned that date, he feared her plans would take her far from him.

FORTY

One month later

Carrie flew the Cessna—turned out Isaac had finished it for her before he died. Elias and Koda sat in the back seat, eager to finally get back home. And next to her was her surprise passenger.

Kaya Omondi had made the trip to see Carrie in Alaska after singing with her a cappella group in Texas. She'd also come for Isaac's funeral and then rejoined her group but was back in Alaska again to see Carrie. Then she would head back to Zhugandia. Kaya had known Darius was still alive because she had a connection with him through a distant cousin and had kept loose tabs on him for Isaac. She learned only a few months ago that he was, in fact, in Southeast Alaska.

Kaya and Isaac had arranged for Carrie to come see her when Kaya was in Texas partly to give Isaac space to deal with Darius. They had tried to protect her.

Carrie landed the plane on the river near Elias's home, and his neighbor, Red, waited for them at the small pier near where he'd also parked his boat. Together they assisted Elias up the hill, though he continued to insist he was fine. He would have to be to survive here alone.

Koda barked and ran around like he was glad to be back.

"Remember, next week I'm bringing up Hank, Sandford, and Otis to hang out here with you for a few days. I still think you should have let them come this week so they could help you get things back in working order."

He waved her off. "Nah. I can do that on my own. I look forward to seeing you next week too, Carrie. I'm glad you found me when you did, or I'd be pushing up fireweed."

"You take care, and I'll see you soon."

Isaac's words came back to her again, echoing through her heart, her soul. She fiercely missed him. *"Focus on what you've always done, Carrie—caring for others—and you'll heal on the inside."*

Isaac had been right, and maybe, finally, Carrie had let go of the past. She was finally able to trust. And . . . love.

Red walked with her and Kaya to the edge of the incline. "Don't you worry about him, Carrie. I intend to stay until I know he's good for it alone."

"Thanks for being such a good neighbor, Red," Carrie said, then she and Kaya hiked down the incline, where she once again spotted the moose and her calf, only they were down by the river. "Let's get in the plane."

Before I have to face that moose again.

On the flight back to Shadow Gap, she and Kaya reminisced about the good ole days and avoided discussing the day Darius changed all their lives.

As Carrie taxied toward the dock of the SEA Skies hangar, she sighed. "I wish you didn't have to leave tomorrow, Kaya. I'm so glad you came all this way, because you helped me to feel more settled after everything that's happened."

"You know it'll take time. If ever you want to come back to Africa, you have a place to stay."

"That's just it, I don't know where I belong anymore."

At the dock she hopped out to secure the plane but was surprised when Trevor emerged from the hangar to work the lift. Kaya stepped onto the dock with her, and then the plane was raised out of the water.

Carrie smiled, unsure what to say, but she found it hard to pull her gaze away from him.

I missed you.

Kaya smiled and started heading inside the hangar. "I'll just give you two some privacy."

"No, Kaya. Hey, that's not nece—" But Kaya was already out of sight.

Kaya had seen that need before Carrie had. Her heart kicked around inside her rib cage, but Carrie kept it cool.

"I'm surprised to see you, Mr. Blue Eyes."

"Mr. Blue Eyes?"

"Yeah. That's what I've called you in my head . . . well"—heat rushed to her cheeks—"from that first moment I saw you."

What's the matter with me? She was sharing entirely too much.

Sometimes the only way out of the fire was to walk through it—and she was definitely facing a one-of-a-kind fire.

He came closer and tugged her forward. Maybe she'd been gone the first time she'd seen him.

"That makes me think you might have actually missed me." His voice was husky, and the warmth from his smile curled around her heart.

"I thought you were working in Montana." *Just don't get your hopes up. Don't even go there.* "So why are you here?"

"I missed you, Carrie." He shifted away from her.

Maybe she was sending him the wrong vibes. She was trying too hard to be off-putting. To protect herself.

But do I need to protect myself anymore?

"I don't want to lose the connection I found with you, and

I'd like to see where this takes us. Plus, I'm responding to an ad you placed for a general manager and mechanic for SEA Skies Transport Services, Inc."

Carrie's heart pounded. "What about your job in Montana?"

"I resigned. I have nothing to keep me there. I moved there for Jennifer."

"So you aren't kidding, then. You're really interested in the job?"

He nodded and smiled.

"You're not an airplane mechanic."

"But I could manage your business."

"You don't even like to fly."

"That's where you're wrong. I love to fly. You made me see the error of my ways." His gaze pinned her with such emotion, such conviction.

Carrie rushed to him and pulled him to her, then stood on her toes and planted her lips on his. She was rewarded for her efforts when he wrapped his arms around her and deepened the kiss. She could so love this man if she didn't already.

When he finally loosened his arms and freed her lips, he said, "Does this mean I got the job?"

"For as long as you want it, Mr. Blue Eyes."

ACKNOWLEDGMENTS

In my early childhood, my mother planted the seed of writing deep in my heart. She watered and nurtured it through the years, and God sent others along the way to encourage and inspire me. Writing novels for a living is the most amazing job I could ever hope to do, while at the same time, it can be the most crushing and brutal of activities. Writing a novel is hard, and it takes a village to bring it to life. Only other novelists truly understand the complexities and that there can be no real balance between writing a novel and life. Writers need other writers to encourage them, family to believe in them, and an exceptional publishing team to bring their books to the world.

To Lisa, Shannon, Sharon, Susan, Chawna, Michele, Lynette, Lynn, Pat and so many more friends—thank you for your endless encouragement and support.

To Brice Jones—thank you for answering all my questions about flying a floatplane in Alaska, and adding the kind of details that make Carrie James come to life.

To my four precious and beautiful children—I couldn't be more proud of you, and I couldn't have continued writing without your wholehearted support.

To Gabriel—you're so adorable and a real character. I'm definitely going to put you in a book or two or three.

To the love of my life, my husband, Dan—this has been quite the journey, and I can't wait to see what God has in store for us next.

To Rachel and Amy—I'm beyond blessed to have you as my editors. You're amazing.

To the Revell marketing and publicity team—Brianne, Michele, and Karen—you guys are the absolute best and I love working with you. I still have to pinch myself sometimes to know that I really am writing for Revell and not just dreaming.

Steve—I'm so grateful for your encouragement and support through the years. It seems like yesterday I was sitting across from you at the ACFW writing conference pitching my ideas.

Turn the Page for a Sneak Peek at the Next Heart-Racing Installment in the

MISSING IN ALASKA SERIES

COMING SOON

Glacier Bay, Southeast Alaska

Get in, get out . . . a blizzard's coming.

A path had been plowed through deep winter snow, guiding Ivy Elliott toward the cabin half buried in the white stuff and surrounded by heavily frosted spruce trees. It was a photo opportunity, if there ever was one, but she wasn't here to take pictures.

And she was running out of time.

Her boots clomped onto the sturdy wood porch. Instinct kicked in, and she ducked out of the way when a large clump of snow slid off the roof—a mini-avalanche that could have buried her where she stood. She calmed her pounding heart and stepped up to the door. Drawing in a deep breath, she knocked. The door creaked open. It wasn't latched.

"Hello? Anyone home?"

No one answered.

Prickles crawled up her back. She sensed something wasn't right, but even so, she was uncomfortable entering the man's cabin, so she knocked again.

A muted stillness, silence that only a beautiful snow-covered landscape could create, closed in on her. She glanced at the eerie setting, expecting serenity to flood her. Instead, she was pinged with the intense sensation of being watched.

After removing her gloves, Ivy reached under her coat, freed her handgun from its holster, and gripped it at her side. She drew in a breath of arctic cold and puffed out white clouds.

She knocked again.

No one was home, and they left the door open.

Common sense, reason, told her this was a fool's errand. That she should turn around and go. But she wasn't leaving without what she came for. She eased the door open. "Hello? Anyone home? Sorry for the intrusion, but I'm only checking to make sure you're all right."

Deep shadows obscured the interior of the cabin. Not even a fire burned in the fireplace to provide warmth and light. She opened the door wider, and the gray light of day illuminated the dim space inside, revealing an overturned table and toppled chairs. A familiar coppery scent met her nose. Her breath caught. She pushed the door all the way open and stepped inside.

She gasped. A man lay on the floor, his body in a pool of blood. Stunned at the sight, her heart seized.

He moved his hand.

He's still alive!

She rushed forward and dropped to her knees. "Just hold on. You're going to be okay," she lied. A knife was buried in his chest. "If I pull it out . . ." He could bleed out. Considering the amount of blood on the floor, it might already be too late.

She put her gun away and yanked a blanket from the nearby worn-out couch, then pressed it against the wound as best she could with the knife in the way. "I'm going to call for help. You must have a radio or a satellite phone. Something." But she already knew from experience that not everyone in remote Alaska wanted to be connected or bothered or found.

With her hand pressed against the wound, she glanced around the cabin and spotted a radio on the kitchen counter. Taking his shaky, weak hands, she placed them on the blanket covering the gash. "Here. Press here. Can you keep the pressure on? I don't want you to lose more blood."

Even in the shadowy room she could see his pale gray skin, and that he was almost gone.

"Stay with me. Stay with me." *God, what do I do? Please don't let this man die.*

When his hands slid away, she pushed harder against the blanket, willing the blood to stop.

"I need to get to that radio." Though she hated to leave him, she had to call for help and started to get up.

His mumbled words drew her back to him, and she leaned down until her ear was near his lips.

"Find . . . her." He released a long, slow breath as if it was his last.

She looked into his eyes and watched the life fade away. Grief constricted her chest.

Find her . . .

Heavy footfalls bounded across the porch and into the cabin, startling Ivy. She looked up to stare point blank at the muzzle of a gun and lifted her bloody hands in surrender.

I didn't kill him.

Elizabeth Goddard is the *USA Today* bestselling and award-winning author of more than fifty novels, including *Cold Light of Day*, the Rocky Mountain Courage series and the Uncommon Justice series. Her books have sold nearly 1.5 million copies. She is a Carol Award winner, a Readers' Choice Award winner, and a Daphne du Maurier Award finalist. When she's not writing, she loves spending time with her family, traveling to find inspiration for her next book, and serving with her husband in ministry. For more information about her books, visit her website at www.elizabethgoddard.com.

Missed the First Novel in the Missing in Alaska Series?

Pick Up *Cold Light of Day*

"Elizabeth Goddard has created a novel that immerses the reader in small-town Alaska. From the first page, it's a race to stay alive and solve a number of ever-spiraling mysteries."

—CARA PUTMAN,
award-winning author of *Flight Risk*

a division of Baker Publishing Group
www.RevellBooks.com

Available wherever books and ebooks are sold.

Discover More from Elizabeth Goddard with the Rocky Mountain Courage Series

"Goddard increases the stakes and highlights the power of hope, faith, and trusting God in the darkest times in this rush of a series."

—*Publishers Weekly*

Revell
a division of Baker Publishing Group
www.RevellBooks.com

Available wherever books and ebooks are sold.

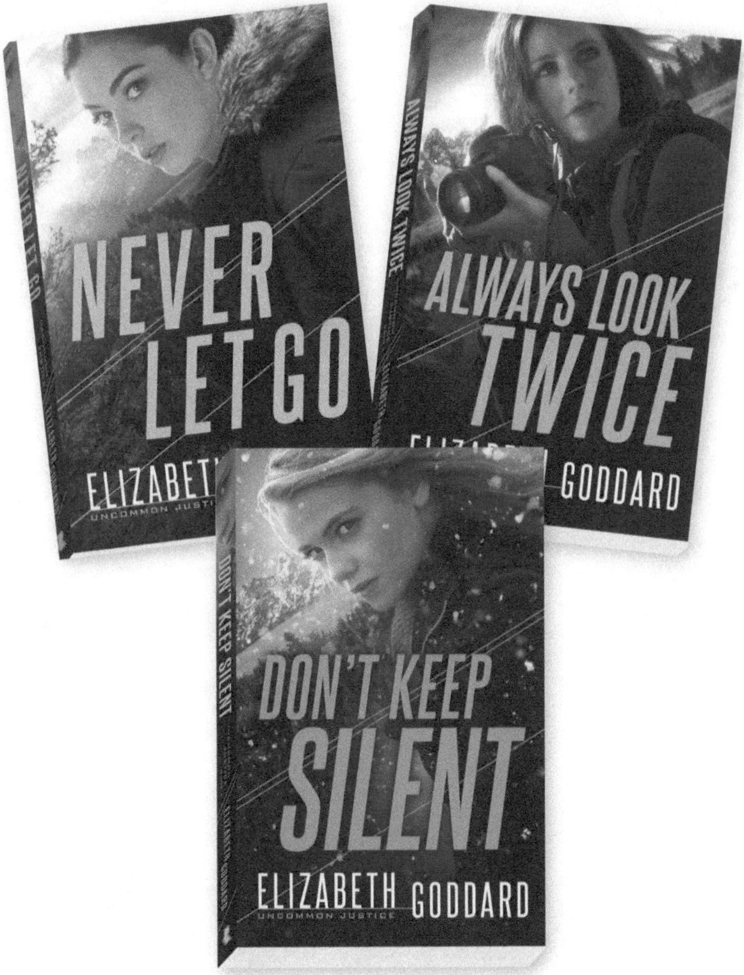